She was an unusual girl, he mused, focusing on her naked thighs. She seemed intelligent enough and she was extremely attractive, so what was she doing working in a run-down village pub? Glimpsing the tight material of her white panties clinging to the firm cheeks of her rounded buttocks as she leaned over the table and wiped the surface, he felt a stirring between his legs. Not only was she intelligent and attractive, but eminently beddable. Unable to drag his gaze away from her long legs as she returned to the bar, Jim wished that he was younger than his forty years. There again, if his luck was in, she might be attracted to older men.

GW00361777

Also by Ray Gordon

Undying Lust
Sexual Revenge
Dark Desires
Dangerous Desires
School of Corruption
Sex Crazed

RAY GORDON

Sex Dungeon

NEW ENGLISH LIBRARY
Hodder & Stoughton

copyright © 2003 by Ray Gordon

First published in Great Britain in 2003 by Hodder and Stoughton
A division of Hodder Headline

The right of Ray Gordon to be identified as the Author of
the Work has been asserted by him in accordance with the
Copyright, Designs and Patents Act 1988.

A New English Library paperback

1 3 5 7 9 10 8 6 4 2

All rights reserved. No part of this publication may be reproduced,
stored in a retrieval system, or transmitted, in any form or by any
means without the prior written permission of the publisher, nor
be otherwise circulated in any form of binding or cover other
than that in which it is published and without a similar
condition being imposed on the subsequent purchaser.

All characters in this publication are fictitious
and any resemblance to real persons, living or dead,
is purely coincidental.

A CIP catalogue record for this title
is available from the British Library

ISBN 0 340 82166 3

Typeset in Plantin by Hewer Text Ltd, Edinburgh
Printed and bound by
Mackays of Chatham Ltd, Chatham, Kent

Hodder and Stoughton
A division of Hodder Headline
338 Euston Road
London NW1 3BH

Sex Dungeon

I

Jim Foster scrutinized the young girl behind the bar as she pulled him a pint of best bitter. She was about eighteen, with long black hair and full breasts ballooning her low-cut top. Her deep mammary cleavage reminding him of a pair of firm buttocks, Jim imagined sliding his cock back and forth between her young tits, his throbbing knob shooting his spunk over her pretty neck. Raising his eyes and focusing on her delicious mouth, he realized that his thoughts were becoming lewder by the second. But he was a desperate man.

After a disastrous five-year marriage, Jim was alone in the world. His wife had walked out on him, and he was now consumed with longing for physical comfort, desperate for the feel of a hugging pussy around the rock-hard shaft of his rampant cock. He'd eyed delectable young girls in the street, glimpsed schoolgirls' knickers as they'd cycled past, hung around seedy bars until the early hours in the hope of pulling a teenage beauty . . . But all his efforts had so far proved fruitless and he'd been forced to resort to masturbating over girlie magazines. Life was far from sweet for Jim Foster.

The barmaid's succulent red lips furling into a smile as she placed his drink on the counter, Jim wondered whether she had a boyfriend. Did she fuck rotten? he wondered. Did she take it up her arse? As she caught his

eye, he speculated whether she'd been mouth-fucked. Had a purple knob ever slipped between her glossed lips and pumped spunk over her pink tongue? Lost in his erotic daydream, he pondered on the colour of her panties. Red, pink, blue, white cotton . . . Were they moist with the lubricious juices of her tight vagina? When had she last been pleasured by a length of solid cock? Perhaps spunk was oozing from her sex hole and filling the tight crotch of her panties at this very moment.

Sipping his drink as he looked around the pub, Jim shook his head despondently. No music, no atmosphere, no colour, no girlies . . . The place was bland and boring. It was no wonder that he was the only punter, he thought, eyeing the tatty velvet curtains hanging either side of the sash windows. The nicotine-brown net curtains looked as if they'd been used for the blowing of noses and the wiping of grubby hands. Not to mention the wiping of . . . No, surely not. It was a great shame, he reflected. The Tartan Vicar was the only pub in the idyllic country village. Business should have been thriving, the till constantly ringing. Turning his attention again to the pretty barmaid, he reckoned that she was the only attraction the pub had to offer.

'You just passing through?' the girl asked him as he downed his pint and placed the glass back in front of her.

'Not exactly,' Jim replied mysteriously, watching her pulling another pint. 'I'm sort of passing, but not through. Are you the only member of staff?'

'I am now,' she said, her dark-eyed gaze catching his. 'Why do you ask?'

'Just wondered,' he sighed nonchalantly. 'From your remark, do I gather that until recently there was someone else working with you?'

'Yes, the manager. He walked out amid a hail of abuse and expletives last week,' she informed him. 'Silly sod.'

'Oh? What was the problem?'

'This and that,' she breathed. 'There was some trouble over . . .' Her words tailing off, she obviously didn't want to say too much.

'So, you run the place alone?'

'I do at the moment. But not for long. The brewery is sending someone down to take over.' She gazed at his suit, his crisp white shirt and tie. 'You're not from weights and measures, are you?' she asked him concernedly.

'No, no,' Jim laughed. 'I'm from London. It's very quiet in here. Does the place liven up later?' He checked his watch. 'It's just gone six. I expect there'll be a few regulars in before long?'

'A few,' she said, frowning at him, her suspicion obviously rising.

'You must be looking forward to having someone take charge. Running the place by yourself must be quite a feat. Quite a leg, even.'

'A leg?' she echoed, cocking her head to one side. 'Oh, I see. Yes, very funny.'

'The manager walked out, you're the only member of staff, the place is devoid of customers . . . Do the regulars help you out with the beer barrels and . . . More to the point, *are* there any regulars? By the look of the place, I doubt that—'

'If you don't mind my saying so,' she interrupted him. 'You seem overly interested in the pub. Why is that?'

'I'm thinking of moving into the village,' Jim announced proudly. 'My wife walked out on me last month so I'm planning to leave the marital town and make a fresh start in a virginal village.'

'Your wife walked out? I'm sorry to hear that.'

'So was she. To be honest, it was the best thing that could have happened. We never did get on. My mother did warn me that marrying my sister wouldn't work, but I didn't listen.'

'You married your *sister*?'

'My brother's sister, twice removed. My wife, er . . . She went off with another woman.'

'Another . . .' Her dark eyes reflecting amazement, she forced a smile and changed the subject. 'As you're thinking of moving here, I'll tell you about the village. This is the only pub. There's a local shop, which sells just about everything from toothbrushes to pine-apples—'

'Tell me about yourself,' Jim interrupted her. 'I'm sure that you're far more interesting than the wares for sale in the local shop. Tell me about *your* wares.'

'Oh, er . . . I don't know what to say,' she murmured sheepishly. 'There's nothing to tell, really.'

'Oh, come on. A pretty young girlie like you . . . Boyfriend?'

'No, not at the moment.'

'Girlfriend?'

'Certainly not. I was seeing a local lad but, what with running the pub, I didn't have a great deal of time for . . . for things like that.'

'Things sexual?' Jim ventured, again pondering on the colour of her panties. Perhaps she wasn't wearing any. Perhaps the lips of her vulva were naked beneath her short skirt.

Whenever Jim met a teenage girl, he thought about sex. His musings centred on lickable pussy lips, gaping vaginal valleys, solid clitorises pulsating in orgasm, to the

extent that he was unable to hold a sensible conversation with the young woman concerned. The barmaid must have been into masturbation, he decided, focusing on the ripe teats of her nipples pressing through her flimsy top. Did she bring her breast up to her wet mouth and suck on her nipple bud as she frigged her clitty to orgasm? Hoping that she was a nymphomaniacal whore, he wondered whether she finger-fucked her tight bottom-hole.

'So, what do you do with yourself?' he asked her, picturing her fingertip encircling the sensitive brown ring of her anus.

'All I do is work,' she sighed. 'When this man arrives from the brewery, I'm hoping to get a little more time to myself.'

'To do what?' he chuckled. 'With all undue respect to Willycombe Village, there doesn't seem to be a great deal of excitement here for an enchanting teenage girlie such as yourself.'

'Oh, you'd be surprised,' she giggled. 'There's plenty here to keep me . . . Er . . . Have you found a place to live yet? There's a house for sale on the other side of the green. Or were you thinking of renting?'

'No, no,' Jim murmured pensively, eyeing her miniskirt as she left the bar and collected a couple of empty glasses from a table. 'I'm not sure what I'm looking for. I mean, I know *exactly* what I'm looking for. But not when it comes to accommodation'

She was an unusual girl, he mused, focusing on her naked thighs. She seemed intelligent enough and she was extremely attractive, so what was she doing working in a run-down village pub? Glimpsing the tight material of her white panties clinging to the firm cheeks of her rounded buttocks as she leaned over the table and wiped

the surface, he felt a stirring between his legs. Not only
was she intelligent and attractive, but eminently beddable. Unable to drag his gaze away from her long legs as
she returned to the bar, Jim wished that he was younger
than his forty years. There again, if his luck was in, she
might be attracted to older men.

'Hi, Jack,' she trilled as a middle-aged man wandered
into the pub. 'Usual?'

'Please, Cleo,' he sighed, plonking himself on a bar
stool. 'Has the new governor turned up yet?'

'No, not yet. He was supposed to have been here at
lunchtime. Perhaps he was held up.'

'We're going to have to put him straight, Cleo. We
don't want any changes, right?'

'Don't you worry yourself, Jack,' Cleo giggled. 'We've
been through all this before. Once he realizes that I'm the
boss . . .'

'But you're not, are you?' he whined. 'What if he's the
type who wants to change everything? What if he decides
to—'

'Listen to me,' she whispered, glancing at Jim before
leaning over the bar. 'One flash of my fanny, and I'll have
him eating out of my knickers.'

'I hope so, Cleo. We have a hell of a lot at stake.'

'Do you think I don't know that? Don't worry, Jack. I
know exactly what I'm doing.'

Trying to listen to the murmured conversation, Jim
grabbed the local paper from the bar. Making out that he
was reading the news, he knew that the girl was suspicious of him as she continued to whisper to her customer.
Weights and measures? he chuckled inwardly. *Hardly*.
The only things Jim wanted to weigh were the barmaid's
tits and he'd certainly have liked to give her a damned

good measure of cock. Did she take it up her tight little arse?

Cleo and Jack's voices becoming softer, Jim was unable to hear exactly what they were saying. They were worried about the new governor, that was for sure. The customer seemed far more concerned than the barmaid, which Jim thought odd. But people didn't like change, he reflected. Especially village people. Set in their ways, the tight-knit community probably had good reason to worry about their local pub. Glancing at the middle-aged man as he finished his drink and announced that he'd be back later, Jim looked up from the newspaper as Cleo moved along the bar towards him.

'He didn't stay long,' he said as Jack left the pub. 'In fact, the length of his stay was surprisingly short.'

'He'll be back later,' she said. 'He always calls in for a pint on his way home from work.'

'You have *one* regular customer, then?' Jim quipped. 'One is better than none.'

'We have *several*, actually,' she retorted defensively.

'I'm sorry. I didn't mean . . .'

'You won't be having another drink, will you?' Cleo sighed. 'I expect you'll want to be going now, won't you? You don't like the pub, so why stay?'

'I didn't say that. In fact, I quite like the pub. I'll have another pint, please. Oh, and one for yourself.'

'No, thank you,' she responded coldly.

'My name's Jim, by the way.'

'Really?' She shrugged dismissively.

'Jim by name, stud by nature. And you're Cleo? I overheard that man mention your name.'

'Will you be staying long?' she sighed, obviously wanting to get rid of him.

'Why do you ask?'

'The locals don't like strangers. Especially strangers who ask questions.'

'There's nothing strange about me. Well, that's not strictly true. I'll let you into a little secret,' Jim murmured, looking over his shoulder as if making sure that they were alone. 'I've come here to brighten up my life. I'm looking for some excitement, and after my wife walked out on me . . .'

'You won't find any excitement here,' Cleo stated firmly.

'Oh, I don't know about that.'

'What *do* you mean?'

'A colleague of mine put me onto this place. He knew that my marriage had fallen apart and I was feeling down. He reckoned that I'd find everything I wanted in this pub. He said that I needed satisfaction and—'

'It's all right, I understand,' she interrupted him, her full red lips smiling, her dark eyes sparkling. 'But you should have said so earlier. I really thought that you were from weights and measures. We've had one or two little problems recently.'

'Really?'

'Nothing to worry about. So, you've come here for some excitement and satisfaction?'

'That's right. After my wife left me, I sort of lost my direction in life. As I said, it was a friend from work who put me onto this place. When he told me about it, I knew that I'd find just I wanted in the Tartan Vicar.'

'You've been told what to do?'

'Oh, yes,' Jim replied confidently. 'I know *exactly* what to do.'

'Your friend . . . Did he tell you about the bar?'

'Of course. Now it's my turn to ask you something. Why all these questions?'

'Obviously, I have to be sure that you're all right. As you'll understand, I have to be very careful.'

'Er . . . yes, of course,' he breathed, wondering what the hell Cleo was talking about. 'You needn't worry about me. I know far more about this pub . . .'

'Then shouldn't you be standing at the end of the bar?'

Watching as the girl walked to the end of the bar and knelt down, disappearing from sight, Jim frowned. Confused, he peered over the counter but could only see her feet. Perhaps she was looking for something, he mused, hearing a tapping sound. Moving to the far end of the counter, he looked down and noticed a hole in the wooden fascia of the bar. This was most odd, he thought, squatting and spying through the hole. Gazing at the girl's eye as she looked through the hole, he stood bolt upright. What the hell was she doing? he wondered, scratching his head. The hole was level with the zip of his trousers, and he could only think that she got some kind of kick out of eyeing her customers' crotches. This was most peculiar, he thought, watching her wiggling finger appear through the hole.

'Come on, then,' Cleo whispered urgently. 'We have to be quick in case someone comes in.'

'Er . . . yes, right . . .' he stammered, wondering what on earth she was talking about.

'Do you want a blow job or not?'

'A blow— Of course I do,' he chuckled, catching on at long last as she withdrew her finger.

Unzipping his trousers, Jim slipped his semi-erect penis through the hole and leaned on the counter. This was an incredible situation, he reflected as the girl fully

retracted his foreskin. The barmaid might have been the only attraction the pub had to offer. But *what* an attraction. Her wet tongue snaking over the silky-smooth surface of his inflating glans, teasing his sperm-slit, she sucked his penile globe deep into her hot mouth. Trembling uncontrollably as she expertly gobbled and mouthed on his purple helmet, he couldn't believe that this was happening. This was a fantasy come true, he thought happily.

This must have been what the middle-aged man was talking about, he reckoned as the barmaid took his solid knob to the back of her throat and sank her teeth gently into his veined shaft. His concern was obviously that the new governor was going to put a stop to the in-house blow jobs. Gasping as Cleo bobbed her head back and forth, repeatedly taking his bulbous glans deep into her hot mouth, Jim pondered on the swell of her pussy lips. Did she shave her pubes? he wondered as he neared his mouth-induced climax. She was a dirty little whore, that was definite. *One flash of my fanny, and I'll have him eating out of my knickers.* Recalling the girl's words, Jim realized that everything made sense. The barmaid not only served drinks, but supplied another service. It was no wonder that the locals didn't want any changes.

His sperm finally jetting from his knob-slit, gushing into the barmaid's gobbling mouth, Jim leaned on the bar and breathed heavily as his cock twitched and his balls drained. This was sheer sexual bliss, he thought, rocking his hips and gently mouth-fucking the pretty teenager. He could feel her tongue sweeping over his throbbing glans, her mouth tightening around his orgasming sex globe each time she swallowed his creamy

spunk. This was not only sheer sexual bliss, but a damned good scheme. Anyone walking into the pub would have no idea that he was flooding the barmaid's mouth with his salty sperm. And no one would think anything of the hole in the bar. The pub was tatty, and the hole in the well-worn planking of the bar certainly didn't look out of place.

Finally withdrawing his spent penis from the hole and zipping his trousers, Jim grinned at the girl as she stood up and licked her spunk-glossed lips. Noticing his orgasmic cream dribbling down her chin, he watched her pink tongue snaking down and capturing the escaping sex milk. She really was amazing, he mused, wondering how many *regulars* she had. Sipping his beer as Cleo poured herself a large vodka and tonic, he plonked himself on a bar stool and relaxed in the aftermath of his unexpected orgasm.

'Well?' she giggled. 'Was that to your liking?'

'Most definitely,' he replied, sheer satisfaction plainly apparent in his expression. 'Now, that's what I call customer service.'

'Your colleague was right. You *have* found satisfaction here. That'll be twenty, then.'

'Twenty?'

'Pounds. Twenty pounds for the blow job.'

'Oh, er . . . yes, of course,' Jim stammered, taking a note from his wallet and passing it to her. 'You must do pretty well out of this?'

'I get by,' Cleo said, slipping the money down into the deep ravine of her young breasts. 'What did you say your name was?'

'Jim, Jim Foster.'

'Well, Jim, I'm sure that if you move into the village . . .'

Her words tailing off, her face turned pale. 'Oh, er . . . Jim Foster? *The* Jim Foster?'

'The one and only.'

'You're the new—'

'Indeed I am.'

'Why the hell didn't you say so?' she snapped, glaring at him. 'For fuck's sake, you should have . . .'

' "For fuck's sake"? That's no way for a lady to talk. Good grief. There I was thinking that your oral skills were—'

'God, I should never have opened my big mouth.'

'I'm rather glad you did,' Jim chuckled. 'You live in, don't you?'

'Er, yes, yes, I do,' Cleo stammered, obviously highly embarrassed. 'I live in the annexe. Your flat is upstairs. You really should have told me . . .'

'I did try to tell you. I said that I'd come here to brighten up my life and find some excitement and satisfaction. What I meant was that I'm taking over the pub.'

'But I thought that a friend of yours . . .'

'That's right. A colleague at the brewery put me on to this place. The boss was all for it when I suggested that I—'

'God, I've made a complete cock-up of this,' she sighed.

'Not at all,' he consoled her. 'I rather like a good cock-up. In fact, I think we got off to a pretty good start.'

'I've never been so embarrassed in all my life.'

'I have. I remember the time I was arrested behind the local girls' school. The judge reckoned that . . . I'd better not go into the sordid details.'

'Yes, well . . . Look, I don't normally do that sort of thing. It's just that I thought . . .'

'Say no more, Cleo. Your oral secret is safe with me. My lips are sealed. I'm glad yours aren't,' he quipped. 'Right, well . . . I suppose you'd better show me the ropes.'

'There *are* no ropes,' she laughed, obviously feeling a little easier. 'Basically, the pub runs itself.'

'That's not what I was told. I'm here to make a success of this place, Cleo. The pub runs at a loss. I suppose you're aware of that?'

'Well, not a loss, exactly. It's quiet, but . . .'

'Quiet? It's dead,' Jim chuckled. 'It's like a graveyard in here. In fact, there's probably more life in the grave-yard. Necrophilia isn't a fetish of yours, I hope?'

'Of course not.'

'Good, good. Those curtains will have to go. They look more like rags than curtains. And we need some music.'

'There's no music system.'

'Don't you have a radio? That would be better than this deafening silence. It's giving me a bloody head-ache.'

'I suppose so,' she sighed. 'I'll go and get it.'

'I like young teenage girls who go and get it.'

'I don't think the regulars will like it.'

'I suppose you give it to all the regulars?'

'I meant, they won't like a radio playing in the bar.'

Walking behind the bar as Cleo went out to a back room, Jim looked around. The place was a mess, he mused, eyeing a pile of newspapers on a shelf beneath the counter. The vinyl flooring was sticky with beer, the mirrors behind the optics were grimy and smeared, the

till was open . . . But he was looking forward to the
challenge of transforming the country pub into a thriving
business. He was also looking forward to fucking Cleo's
pretty mouth again, *and* getting his hands inside the
cunny-wet crotch of her tight panties. With the girl
living in, he reckoned that he'd have plenty of opportunities to have his wicked way with her.

'There,' she said, dumping a radio on the counter and
switching it on. 'Happy now?'

'Well done,' Jim congratulated her, tuning in to a
light-music programme. 'That's much better. Er . . .
what are all these pieces of paper stuffed by the side
of the till?' Grabbing the papers, he frowned as he flicked
through them. 'Fred, thirteen pounds fifty. Ian, sixty-
seven pounds . . . Are these bar tabs?'

'Er . . . well, sort of,' Cleo, confessed softly.

'Sort of? Jesus, there's one here for two hundred and
eighty pounds. And it goes back six months.'

'Ah, er . . . that's Barry's. He . . . he works on the local
farm. The trouble is that he only gets paid monthly.'

'Cleo, apart from anything else, this is illegal. Things
illegal are—'

'No, it's not.'

'You're giving people credit, and that's illegal.'

'Yes, well . . . Most things here are illegal. Especially
the blow jobs.'

'Are you saying that this is a den of illegality?'

'We stay open later than we should, we serve under-
age customers, we . . .'

'Good grief. I'm aghast.' Frowning, Jim gazed into the
dark pools of Cleo's sparkling eyes. 'Under-age customers?' he breathed. 'Giving blow jobs through the hole
in the bar is one thing, but serving under-age customers?

They're not, er . . . they're not young schoolgirlies, are they?'

'We do have one or two girls in from the local convent. They *are* sixth-formers, so . . .'

'Sixth-formers? Things are definitely going to have to change, Cleo. Not the schoolgirlies from the convent, of course. They can come and go as and when they wish. Come rather than go, I mean.'

'What *are* you talking about?'

'I really have no idea. If the law come in . . .'

'The law *do* come in. The local copper is a regular. He knows what goes on here and he doesn't have a problem with it.'

'*He* might not have a problem with it, but *I* do. Does he know about the hole in the bar?'

'Of course not. There *are* limits.'

'Thank God for small mercies. Now, this business of the blow jobs. I realize that you've been earning extra cash on the side, but it will have to stop.'

'Stop? But . . .'

'Cleo, this is a pub, not a sordid backstreet brothel.'

'If you say so,' she sighed despondently.

'I do say so. OK, I want you to clear up behind the bar. All this rubbish has to go, the floor needs cleaning, the till . . . Why is it open?'

'It won't close. It's been like that for years.'

'In that case, I'll get a new till. To leave it open like that is asking for trouble. It's like you sitting around with your legs apart. Someone's bound to get their hands into your knickers. Right, I'm going to move my things into the flat. I'll leave you to get on.'

'Yes, boss,' Cleo giggled. 'Right away, sir.'

As Jim took his cases from his car and lugged them

up to the flat, Cleo grabbed a damp cloth and began cleaning the mirrors behind the optics. He wasn't too bad, she mused, hearing him singing and banging about upstairs. He was somewhat peculiar, but she reckoned that she'd have no trouble with him. She'd go along with his ideas for a while just to keep him happy, she decided. Once he'd settled in and come to accept the pub the way it was, he'd soon forget about changes. As for her lucrative little sideline, she reckoned that she could still earn extra cash by servicing the punters through the hole in the bar.

'The Tartan Vicar,' she said, answering the phone.

'Cleo, it's Dave. Has he turned up yet?'

'Yes, he's upstairs,' she whispered.

'What's he like?'

'Strange, weird, peculiar . . . But he won't be a problem.'

'"Strange, weird, peculiar"? What do you mean?'

'I don't think he's quite all there. He's perfectly harmless, but lacking in brain cells.'

'That sounds ideal. If he's a bit dopey . . .'

'He's not totally stupid, Dave. I'll have to humour him for a while, go along with his daft ideas. But nothing will change here.'

'Thank God for that. So, you can't see any problems with you-know-what?'

'Er, well . . .'

'If he sees the hole in the bar . . .'

'No, no, it's all right. He . . . he knows nothing about the hole. Although I'm going to have to do something about the bar tabs.'

'Rip them up or something.'

'I can't. He's already seen them.'

'Fuck. You don't reckon that he'll discover our other little business?'

'I hope not.'

'Hoping isn't good enough, Cleo, We need to be certain. Look, I have to go. I'll be in touch.'

Hanging up, Cleo threw the cloth into the sink and poured herself another large vodka. Cleaning wasn't her forte, she thought, looking down at the beer-sticky floor. Besides, it was Friday. The little cleaning she forced herself to do was always on a Wednesday morning. Sipping her drink, she gazed at the velvet curtains. They *were* rather tatty, she thought. But they'd been there for ever and no one had complained. The punters liked a traditional pub, she reflected. The nicotine-brown ceiling, well-worn furniture, the smell of beer and state tobacco smoke, the hole in the bar . . . That was what the punters wanted in a village pub.

'I heard the phone ring,' Jim said as he walked into the bar.

'Did you?' Cleo asked him.

'Who was it?'

'No one.'

'It must have been *someone*.'

'No one phoned.'

'But I heard it ringing. Oh, not to worry. Right, I've settled in upstairs. It's a nice flat. I only wish that the bar was as clean and tidy. Pour me a pint and we'll have a chat about the pub.'

'There's nothing to chat about,' Cleo sighed, pulling a pint of bitter.

'There's *every*thing to chat about. Take Sunday lunchtime.'

'Take it where?'

'I mean, look at Sunday lunchtime.'

'I can't look at Sunday lunchtime. It's Friday.'

'No, I meant . . . The traditional British pub opens at midday on Sundays. There are bar snacks, lumps of cheese, peanuts and bits and pieces . . . And no cock-holes in the bar.'

'We don't do bar snacks. The punters don't come here for lumps of mouldy cheese and urine-tainted peanuts.'

'I know *exactly* what they come here for, Cleo,' Jim quipped. 'And they won't be coming again. Not in that sense, anyway. Good grief, I've never known—'

'*You* were quite happy to use the hole,' she cut in angrily.

'That's different. I'm the boss, remember? It's the boss's right to fuck the barmaid's mouth. OK, that's the first thing we'll change.'

'What? Fucking my mouth?'

'No, no. Sunday lunchtime snacks and nibbles on the bar. *Not* nibbles *below* the bar. Ah, we have a customer,' he chuckled, grinning as the door opened. 'You carry on with the cleaning and I'll—'

Staring in disbelief as two teenage girls wandered up to the bar, Jim felt a stirring in his loins. They certainly weren't old enough to drink alcohol, he suspected as the giggling pair perched their firm bottoms on bar stools, their wide eyes gazing up at him. One was blonde with small breasts, her ripe nipples pressing through the tight material of her very low-cut top. Far too young to . . . The other girl, with her black hair cut in a bob framing her angelic face, appeared to be even younger. This was fucking illegal, Jim reflected, imagining the girls kissing each other with his purple knob sandwiched between their succulent lips.

Jim stared aghast at Cleo as she poured the nymphettes two large vodkas and topped them up with tonic. This was blatantly against the law, he thought, his gaze returning to the pretty wenches. He should throw them out, he knew. He should assert his authority and . . . But they were extremely attractive and their pretty little mouths with succulent red lips were perfect for . . . Holding his head and grimacing as Cleo scribbled something on one of the bar tabs, Jim knew that he had to make a stand.

'Where's your money?' he asked the girls. 'I see no money belts around your squeezable waists.'

'Money?' they breathed in unison, obviously perplexed by his question. 'We don't have any money.'

'Then you can't . . . Besides, you're far too young to be drinking in a pub.'

'We're old enough to fuck,' the blonde giggled, shocking Jim. 'If we can fuck, then we can drink.'

'She has a point,' Cleo joined in, winking at Jim.

'She has lovely points . . . I mean . . . Firstly, bar tabs are illegal, secondly, under-age drinking is illegal, thirdly . . .'

'What's thirdly?' the dark-haired girl asked him impishly.

'Thirdly, you shouldn't be swearing.'

'They're both eighteen years old,' Cleo said. 'So that deals with secondly, doesn't it?'

'Eighteen? More like fourteen, if you ask me.'

'We've both got two tits,' the blonde chuckled.

'So I see,' Jim breathed. 'Look, I don't care how many tits you have between you. You can't come in here and—'

'We did have pubic hairs,' the other girl trilled.

'*Did* have?' Jim gasped, holding his head again as he imagined standing in court in front of a judge.

'We shaved them off.'

'You . . . Good grief.'

'Jim,' Cleo whispered, taking him to one side. 'Leave them alone. They never cause trouble so leave them in peace. Besides, I thought that you wanted to make a success of the place?'

'Yes, but not by allowing fourteen-year-old schoolgirls in.'

'They're both eighteen, Jim, as I've already told you. They're sixth-formers from the local convent school. And they pay their tabs off regularly. They receive their allowances from their parents each week and pay their tabs on Monday evenings without fail. That covers firstly and secondly. Right?'

'I suppose so,' Jim conceded. 'But they still shouldn't thirdly, I mean, they shouldn't swear. What would the Reverend Mother say?'

'You'll have to ask her. She'll be in later.'

'The Reverend Mother comes in?' he gasped. 'Good grief.'

'Only for a nightcap.'

'You'll be telling me that the vicar—'

'Ah, the vicar,' Cleo breathed. 'No, he doesn't come in. In fact, he's anti-pubs, anti-drinking, anti-smoking, anti-sex . . .'

'What a boring life. OK, so I'll allow the girls to stay,' Jim said, pleased that he'd made a managerial decision.

Sipping his drink as Cleo chatted to the girls, Jim couldn't help imagining squeezing the little blonde girl's petite breasts. Her newly developed mammary spheres would be as hard as rock, he mused. Her fresh milk-teats would be ripe for the sucking. His balls rolling as he wondered how to glimpse her shaved pussy, he won-

dered whether he was dreaming. Had they really shaved their pussies? Or were they lying to conceal the fact that they were too young to have pubes? If that was the case . . . It didn't bear thinking about, he decided, watching Cleo refill their glasses with vodka as he again imagined standing in the dock while a judge pronounced sentence.

Fuck the judge, he mused But if the brewery boss himself came in and saw the under-age drinkers, Jim knew that there'd be big trouble. Still, the girls were so fresh and young and firm, with beautifully formed little . . . They *were* under-age, he reminded himself, gazing at the triangular patch of tight white panties fabric hugging the blonde girl's full sex lips as she parted her shapely thighs. Unable to drag his gaze away from the alluring sight, he knew that he had to get a grip on himself. Business before pleasure. Perhaps he'd enjoy a quick wank later. That would certainly be one way of getting a grip on himself.

Leaving his drink on the bar, he rubbed his chin as he walked around the pub. *His* pub. The place had great potential. The brewery had made a wise move to put him in charge, he reflected. He'd never run a pub before, but the brewery bosses had obviously realized that he had great business and managerial qualities and was the only man who could save the failing pub. This was his chance to prove himself, Jim knew as he gazed out of the window at the village green. As the evening sun began to set behind the abattoir, he reckoned that he wouldn't only fit into the local community, but he'd also be very happy in his new role as landlord of the Tartan Vicar.

2

As the pub began to fill up, Jim felt quite at home working behind the bar with Cleo. So far, the customers had appeared to accept him. Apart from one or two complaints concerning the dreadful music on the radio, everyone seemed happy enough. The schoolgirls had left earlier, which had pleased Jim. As much as he'd loved their company, lusting after their youthful bodies, dreaming about sucking the girl-cream from their fresh vaginas, he knew that it was pretty dangerous ground. The firm mounds of their breasts were like a minefield, he reflected. One false move and—

'Evening,' the local copper murmured as he approached the bar. 'A pint of best, please.'

'Certainly,' Jim said, smiling as he grabbed a glass. 'You must be the neighbourhood bobby?'

'How astute of you. Did my uniform give the game away?'

'Yes, no, I mean . . .' Jim stammered, pouring a pint of bitter.

'You should have been a detective. The name's Brown, PC Brown.'

'Foster, Jim Foster. It's nice to meet you.'

'I'm the law,' Brown stated firmly. 'I uphold the law around here.'

'That's what policemen do,' Jim laughed, placing the man's drink on the bar.

'Is that your car outside? The blue Ford . . .'

'Yes, that's right.'

'I'll be keeping an eye on it,' the constable breathed, his beady eyes staring hard at Jim as he sipped his drink. 'A close eye.'

'Oh, thanks. Although I doubt that anyone would steal it. I can't imagine a local stealing—'

'I meant that I'll be keeping an eye on the road tax, the state of the tyres, the general condition of the vehicle.'

'Oh, I see.'

'You have an MOT certificate, I hope?'

'Of course. You'll have no worries as far as my car is concerned. I keep it in tip-top condition.'

'I'm glad to hear it. Er . . . you're not a drug dealer, are you?'

'Of course not,' Jim returned indignantly. 'Good grief . . .'

'You're a London boy, aren't you?'

'I worked in London for several years, yes.'

'Take my advice and don't bring any of your underground contacts to the village. One step out of line, and I'll nick you.' Raising his glass, the man grinned. 'Cheers.'

'Oh, er . . . Cheers,' Jim said. 'That'll be two pounds—'

'Lesson number one. I don't pay for anything in this village.'

'Er . . . Right you are.'

Shaking his head as the policeman walked to a table and sat down, Jim reckoned that he'd soon get on all right with him. Before long, they'd be chatting, laughing and

joking. But it might be an idea to get an MOT certificate
before getting to know the local copper. It was going to
take a while before the villagers accepted their new
publican fully, he knew as he poured himself half a pint
of bitter. Once he'd met everyone, got to know their
names, their quirks, he'd be well in with them. After all,
this was his first evening. He couldn't expect miracles.
There again, Cleo was a fucking miracle.

'The lager's gone,' Cleo said, turning to Jim.

'Gone where?' he chuckled.

'Gone, as in run out.'

'Right, I'll go and change it.'

Making his way down to the cellar, Jim turned the
light on and looked at the row of barrels. This was a
doddle, he thought, slipping the connection off the
empty lager barrel. There was nothing to running a
pub. Changing barrels and ordering stock was no problem. But there was more to it than that, he reflected
pensively. A landlord needed charm and charisma. People wanted to be greeted with a warm and friendly smile.
And who better to greet the customers than Jim Foster?

Connecting the new barrel and making his way back
up the cellar steps, he rubbed his hands together gleefully. This was his new life, he thought happily. Far away
from his lesbian wife and the house of marital grief, he
was sure that things were going to turn out very well.
He'd already enjoyed Cleo's oral skills, he mused as he
returned to the bar. What better way to start his new life
than by fucking a pretty teenage girl's mouth?

Gazing in disbelief at a young girl wearing a microskirt
hardly concealing the tight crotch of her panties, Jim
couldn't believe his eyes. Dreading to think how old she
was – how *young* she was – he glanced at PC Brown

sitting in the corner. The man seemed oblivious to the girl as he sipped his pint, which was just as well. The pub enjoyed quite a following of young girls, Jim ruminated. Wondering whether this latest beauty was from the local convent school, Jim asked Cleo about her.

'She's the vicar's daughter,' Cleo enlightened him.

'The vicar's daughter?' Jim gasped, watching the young beauty sit at a corner table. 'Jesus fucking Christ, she's absolutely . . . Is she a regular?'

'She's in most nights.'

'And her father allows that? What sort of man—'

'Her father believes that she goes to a youth club in the next village. She's safe in here because he never sets foot in the place.'

'Just as well,' Jim murmured. 'We don't want the wrath of God set upon us. What with under-age school-girls and now the vicar's daughter . . . I won't ask you how old she is. I think I'm better off not knowing. Where the hell does she get the money from to spend on drink? Don't tell me that she, too, has a bar tab?'

'No, no. She pays cash. She nicks it from the collection box in the church.'

'Is there no end to . . . No, I suppose not. When I came here, I was expecting the customers to consist solely of retired villagers. Old boys in their seventies accompanied by their ageing, wrinkle-faced, haggard wives. Not illegally young teenage girls wearing skirts so short that—'

'Are you complaining?' Cleo giggled.

'No, no, not at all. But I must say that, of all the country pubs I've been to, none were anything like this place.'

'We're unique, Jim.'

'You can say that again. Who's the girl with? The

vicar's daughter, I mean. Am I the luckiest man alive? Jesus, I could be arrested for what I have in mind. I could be thrown to the fucking lions.'

'She's not with anyone. She always comes in on her own. Would you like to meet her?'

'I'd like to get my hands up her . . . I mean . . . Yes, yes, very much.'

'I'll warn you now. She swears a lot.'

'The vicar's daughter swears a lot? God save us from vicars' daughters.'

'You'd better believe it.'

'Satan, deliver us unto vicars' daughters.'

Leading Jim to the girl's table, Cleo introduced her as Mary. Wearing a tight-fitting white blouse, her long blonde hair framing her fresh face, Mary really was a rare little beauty. But Jim had to remind himself that not only was she the vicar's daughter but she was extremely young. Too young to fuck, he reckoned, sitting opposite her and gazing at the tight material of her blouse faithfully following the contours of her petite breasts. She was the essence of feminine beauty, he thought, losing himself again in his erotic dreams.

Her underwear was undoubtedly white, he mused. A silky-white bra cupping the petite mounds of her youthful breasts, white cotton panties hugging her vulval flesh, bulging to contain the swell of her virginal lips of love . . . She was heaven-sent, he decided. The epitome of youth, of femininity. Radiating an air of angelic innocence and yet acute sexual awareness, Mary was a goddess of love and lust. Venus reincarnated, Jim mused, picturing the hairless lips of her vagina swelling in their hairless glory. Naked, impeccably symmetrical as they rose either side of her creamy-wet valley of carnal desire.

Displaying a perfect row of white teeth as she smiled at him, Mary asked Jim whether he intended to make any changes to the pub. The only changes he intended to make at that moment were changes in his thinking. Married to a woman in her forties for five years, he was now free to enjoy life. Sagging tits, floppy lips, unshapely hips . . . Divorce was heaven. Now, free from the restraints of marriage, he recognized the sheer beauty of youth in the girl sitting opposite him. Why had he punished himself with nightly images of the saggings of middle age when the likes of Mary were inhabiting the world? Marriage was a fucking sin.

'So, are you going to change the pub?' she asked him again.

'Everyone seems to be worrying about that,' he replied as Cleo returned to the bar.

'No one likes change,' she said. 'Things are great the way they are.'

My God, you're beautiful.

'Why fuck something up when it doesn't need fucking up?' Mary went on.

'Er . . . yes, quite. And things will stay the way they are,' Jim reassured her, a desperate longing to lick the smooth lips of her pussy driving him wild. 'Your father—'

'My father's a fucking prick,' Mary cut in. 'Fucking toss-pot.'

'Oh, er . . .'

'A first-class fucking wanker.'

'Doesn't he wonder where you get to every evening?'

'Yes, he does. I tell him that I go to a youth club but he knows I'm fucking lying. He's always asking me where I'm going and what I get up to. Since my mother left him

for a choirboy, he's been really protective towards me. I have to slip into the fucking garden fucking shed to change into my decent fucking clothes.'

'If he saw you dressed like a . . . dressed like that . . .'

'He'd go fucking mad. There again, he's always going fucking mad. He wanted me to become a fucking vicar. Can you believe that? *Me*? A fucking vicar? I don't know what Lucifer would say.'

'Neither do I. You have a lovely turn of phrase,' Jim chuckled. 'Do you go to the local school or . . .'

'I don't go to school. Of course, prick-head doesn't know that. The prat believes that I go off to school every morning.'

'But you *do* wear navy-blue knickers? Sorry, I got carried away by the sheer beauty of your oh-so-young and beauti-fully alluring . . . So, where *do* you go every day?'

'Here and there. I usually go into town and hang around the filthy, dirty, seedy bars. I often stay out all night, walking the streets. What do *you* do all day?'

'Filthy, dirty, seedy . . . How pleasantly unpleasant. What better way to while away your time? As far as my days are concerned, I have quite a challenge ahead of me with this place. No major changes, you understand. But I do want to get this pub up and running. It's Friday evening, and there are no more than half a dozen people here. I mean, what's the fucking point in having an empty fucking pub . . . Sorry, I got carried away again. It's a family trait. The truth of the matter is, I want to see this venue heaving with punters every night of the week.'

'Venue? Ha!'

'What's so funny about that?'

'Nothing. Er . . . How are you going to do that?'

'That's a good question. A decent music system would

be a start. Mary, if you don't mind my asking, why do you come here every evening? What's the attraction?'

'I come here because . . . I mean . . . There's nothing else to do, nowhere else to go.'

'I see. It seems odd that this place attracts young girls from the convent school. I suppose, like you, they have nothing else to do. I might bear that in mind,' he murmured meditatively. 'The more the pub attracts young people, the better. Look at the place. It's as dead as . . . Wait a minute,' he breathed, turning and staring at the bar. 'There were two men there just now.'

'Two men where?' Mary asked, glancing at the bar.

'Standing at the bar.'

'Perhaps they've gone to the bog for a fucking piss.'

'The toilet door is only a few feet away from this table. I'd have seen them if they'd gone for a fucking . . . They were talking to Cleo at the bar, and now they've disappeared into thin air. No one's come in or gone out since I've been here with you.'

'Does it matter?'

'Yes, it does. There's no other way out of the pub.'

Jim was about to go to the bar and ask Cleo where the men had gone when he happened to glance down at Mary's naked thighs. Her legs apart, the triangular patch of her white cotton panties displayed to his wide eyes, he wasn't sure whether or not she was deliberately exposing herself. Parting her slender legs further, her microskirt stretched across the tops of her young thighs, the outer lips of her vagina swelled at each side of the thin strip of material running over the gentle rise of her vulva. The exposing of her most intimate place *was* deliberate, Jim decided. After all, no one inadvertently sat like that. What sort of girl was she? he wondered. A slut-whore?

There was nothing he liked better than a young and not-so-innocent slut-whore, he reflected. A little nymph with straggly golden locks cascading over her pretty face, a slag who swore like a fucking trooper, drank too much, showed off the wet crotch of her white panties . . . The sort of girl one could take home to meet mother, he mused, gazing longingly at the wet patch that was visibly darkening the crotch of her tight panties. Again picturing the fleshy lips of her vulva, her creamy-wet wet crack of desire, he imagined licking her there. To taste her cream of youth, to lap up her liquid desire . . .

Tearing his gaze away from Mary's blatant exhibition-ism, Jim looked up as the door opened. This was in-credible, he thought, gazing in disbelief as another young girl wandered into the pub. Dressed in her school uni-form, her short gymslip doing nothing to veil the tight crotch of her navy-blue knickers, she could have been no older than . . . He didn't dare to think how old she was as Cleo poured her a large vodka. Again thinking how odd it was that young girls were attracted to a dull and incred-ibly boring village pub, Jim reckoned that something was going on. The male customers seemed oblivious to the young girlies, which was also extremely odd. Unless they were all gay perverts who preferred to suck spunk from cocks rather than girl-cum from pussies.

'Do you know that girl?' Jim asked Mary.

'I don't think so,' she replied, barely glancing at the schoolgirl. 'Why?'

'Oh, I don't know,' he sighed, again focusing on Mary's outer lips ballooning either side of the tight crotch of her white panties. 'Something's going on here, but I don't know what.'

'Going on? What the fuck do you mean?'

'Those men disappearing, young girls flocking to this place as if it was a nightclub . . . and *you*, Mary.'

'What about me?'

'Why are you sitting like that?'

'I always sit like this,' she giggled.

'With your legs wide apart and your panties . . .'

'Are you complaining?'

'Not at all. It's just that . . . When I lived in London, I went everywhere in search of fresh young girlies – without much luck, I have to say. Now I'm in a small village pub, I'm surrounded by little beauties. It doesn't make sense.'

'Does it have to?' she asked him, pulling the crotch of her panties to one side and exposing the hairless crack of her young pussy.

'Mary . . . For goodness' sake . . .'

'Don't you like my cunt?'

'Bloody hell. Of course I do, but . . .'

'My uncle taught me to sit like this.'

'Your *uncle*?' Jim gasped.

'My dad's brother. He's a Catholic fucking priest. And a fucking pervert. He likes me to sit with my cunt on show.'

'This is unbelievable,' Jim breathed, shaking his head in astonishment. 'Your father is a vicar, his brother is a Catholic priest, and you . . .'

'My dad's brother loves my pretty little cunt. Do *you* like it?' Mary asked him impishly, pulling the swollen lips of her vulva wide apart. 'I'll bet you'd like to shove your cock in there,' she giggled, looking down at the open hole of her cream-drenched vagina.

'Jesus Christ,' Jim gasped. 'I don't know what to say.'

'You don't have to fucking say anything. Just push your finger into my cunt.'

'Mary, is this the way you usually behave?'

'Usually behave?' she echoed, frowning at him. 'You mean, opening my cunt to men? Yes, of course it is. Men like cunts, don't they?'

'Yes, but . . .'

'But what? You're not fucking bent, are you?'

'Of course I'm not fucking bent. God, you've got me fucking swearing now.'

'If you're straight, why don't you finger my cunt?'

Straight? he mused. Of course he was straight. But he wasn't used to such blatant offers from young schoolgirls. *Why don't you finger my cunt?* The girl's words rattling around his confused mind, he knew that this was very wrong. And bloody dangerous. If the vicar came in . . . If the brewery boss turned up . . . The country pub wasn't at all what he'd envisaged. Where were all the old boys wearing their Harris Tweed jackets and cravats? Jim wondered, eyeing the gaping entrance to Mary's youthful vaginal sheath. He'd expected the pub to attract the Major Higging-bottoms of this world. Captain Dunging-Brown, Sir Henry Cumforth-Smythe, Lord and Lady Smegcock-Poole . . . Rather than retired old farts, the village was overflowing with fresh schoolgirlie cunt.

Finally reaching between Mary's parted thighs, Jim slipped his finger between the girl-wet inner lips of her young vulva. She felt so hot and creamy-wet, he mused, running his fingertip around the pink funnel of flesh surrounding the gaping entrance to her young cunt. It was best not to miss such an opportunity, he decided. Such openings didn't appear every day. A dirty little teenage slag begging to have her cunt fingered? This was, indeed, a rare opportunity.

Massaging Mary's sex cream into the sensitive flesh of her open love-hole, Jim drove his finger deep into the tight sheath of her teenage cunt as she gasped and writhed with pleasure. Looking around the pub, he didn't reckon that his illicit act could be seen as he pushed a second finger into the girl's tight vaginal duct. This really was incredible, he reflected as she grabbed his hand and pistoned her young sex hole with his cream-drenched fingers. Cleo had sucked the spunk out of his cock, and now he was fingering a schoolgirlie's wet cunt. *Incredible?* he asked himself. It was fucking marvellous.

'More fingers,' the sex-crazed girl-slut breathed.

'Hang on,' Jim said, looking around the pub. 'If we're seen . . . Where's that schoolgirl gone? She was there just now.'

'Please, give me more fingers,' Mary begged him, parting her legs to the extreme. 'Finger-fuck my hot cunt.'

'Wait a minute,' Jim murmured, slipping his wet fingers out of the girl's tight sex duct. 'She was at the bar talking to Cleo, and now she's disappeared.'

'Fuck her.'

'I'll fuck *you* in a minute.'

'Ooh, yes, please.'

Leaving the girl desperate for more fingers – and a huge cock – Jim walked to the bar and asked Cleo where the schoolgirl had gone. Accusing her of lying as she said that the girl had gone into the toilet, Jim walked into the back room. Finding no trace of the girl, he licked his cunny-slimed fingers and went down to the cellar but there was still no sign of the schoolgirl slut. Looking around, he scratched his head. This was insane, he mused, rubbing his chin pensively. Two men and a girl

disappearing into thin air? Something was definitely going on.

'Jim, what are you doing?' Cleo asked, descending the cellar steps. 'Mary's asking for you.'

'Where are they?' Jim snapped. 'Two men and a girl have disappeared. Where the hell are they?'

'Disappeared? I don't know what you're talking about. The girl went to the loo. She said that she wanted to pee before leaving the pub.'

'No one went into the toilets and no one left the pub. OK, you'd better tell me what this is all about. The place has been crawling with fucking schoolgirls and—'

'I haven't seen any schoolgirls fucking,' Cleo giggled. 'Why don't you relax?'

'Relax? Christ, I've got customers disappearing into thin air. I might be arrested for doing away with people.'

'This is ridiculous,' Cleo sighed. 'A couple of people leave the pub without you noticing, and you start—'

'Cleo, they did *not* leave the pub.'

'OK, anything you say. I'm going back to the bar. I'll keep my eyes open for missing persons, if it'll make you feel better. Perhaps we should put up a notice in the bar. Missing persons: the following individuals . . .'

'All right, all right.'

Sighing as the girl climbed the cellar steps, Jim reckoned that she was right. It was pointless getting wound up. But he couldn't stop wondering about the mysterious disappearance of three customers. Returning to the bar, he pushed a glass up to the vodka optic. It was time for some serious drinking, he decided. Schoolgirls flashing their panties, a young girl asking him to finger her cunt, people disappearing . . . This was more than enough to drive a man to drink. Looking around the pub, he sighed.

The only customer was Mary and, judging by her glazed eyes, she was the worse for wear for booze.

'You all right for a few minutes?' Cleo asked him. 'I'm just nipping out.'

'I think I'll manage,' he muttered despondently. 'There's hardly a rush on.'

'It'll pick up later, so don't worry,' she said, walking towards the door.

'I certainly hope so,' he sighed.

Watching Mary gulping down her vodka, the spirit dribbling down her chin and splattering her tight blouse, Jim lowered his eyes to her parted thighs. Her panties pulled to one side, the swollen lips of her vagina fully exposed, she was obviously out of her head with alcohol. Imagining sucking on the elongated teats of her petite breasts, he felt his cock twitch, his balls roll within their hairy sac. He was going to have to fuck her, he decided. Whatever her age, whatever the consequences, the whore-slut was going to be shafted rotten.

Seemingly oblivious to her blatant exhibitionism, Mary climbed to her feet and staggered across the room to the bar. Her long blonde hair was tousled, the buttons of her tight blouse almost at bursting point. The girl looked as though she'd already been fucked rotten, Jim thought, gazing at her flushed face. Unable to believe that she was the vicar's daughter, he wondered whether he'd get to meet her father. Hopefully not, he thought.

'I'll have a large fucking vodka,' she slurred. 'And a length of hard cock.'

'You'll have neither,' Jim returned. 'Look at the state of you. Good grief. It's positively disgusting, carrying on the way you are.'

'I *like* being disgusting,' Mary giggled, joining Jim

behind the bar. 'Go on,' she breathed, pulling her wet panties down to her knees and leaning over the bar. 'Give me one from behind.'

Unzipping his trousers, Jim hauled out his stiffening cock and slipped his purple knob between the slut's dripping inner cunt lips. His shaft swelling, his knob inflating, he drove his flesh rod deep into the hugging sheath of her drenched vagina with such force that he almost winded her. Again realizing that it was best to grab such opportunities while he could, he lifted her skirt up over her back and parted the firm cheeks of her rounded buttocks. Focusing on the tightly closed eye of her anus, he withdrew his penile shaft and again rammed his glans deep into the wet heat of her young vagina. The puckered star of her bottom-hole was tightly closed, lickable, fingerable, fuckable . . . She'd endure an anal shafting before sunrise, that was for sure.

'Fuck me, you're big,' Mary gasped, her arms stretched across the bar, her hands clinging to the edge of the polished wooden surface. 'Spunk my fucking cunt. I want to feel your spunk drowning my hot cunt.'

'Good grief,' he breathed. 'Never have I heard such foul language from a girl so young and outwardly virginal.'

'Never have you fucked a girl so young,' she giggled.

'How do you know?'

'If you had, you'd be in fucking prison.'

'Jesus Christ.'

The vicar's daughter certainly had a way with words, Jim mused, repeatedly ramming his cunny-slimed cock-shaft deep into her tightening sheath of illicit ecstasy. *In prison? Fuck me.* It would be interesting to meet the vicar, he thought, the squelching sounds of indecent sex re-

sounding through the pub. Though preferably not while he was fucking the man's daughter over the bar. But it would be most enlightening to encounter the man of God. It was just as well that the bar couldn't be seen from the street, he thought, watching the pub door as Mary screamed out in the beginnings of her cock-induced orgasm.

The pub was appropriately named, Jim mused. The Tartan Vicar? The tart was enjoying a good fucking and the vicar . . . God only knew where he was. Hoping that Cleo was right about the cleric never setting foot in the pub, he grabbed Mary's shapely hips and increased his pistoning fucking rhythm. Again screaming out as her orgasm exploded within the solid nub of her clitoris, she clung to the bar for dear life as Jim reached his earth-shuddering climax.

'I can feel your spunk,' the girl cried, as if desiring to inform half the village about the forbidden vaginal spunking. 'I can feel your fucking spunk.'

'Keep your voice down,' Jim breathed, his swinging balls battering her hairless mons.

'Yes, yes! Fuck my cunt harder. Fill me with your fucking spunk!'

'Fucking hell, girl. Hush your mouth or you'll wake the dead.'

'Fuck the dead.'

'God save us. If your father—'

'Fuck my father.'

Mary was well worth knowing, Jim thought as his sperm jetted from his throbbing knob and bathed the doughnut-like ring of her young cervix. A filthy, dirty, foul-mouthed whore of a slag-slut, she was exactly the sort of girl he liked. She obviously used her cunt solely to

satisfy man's appetite for crude and forbidden sex. She
probably pleasured any man who happened to come her
way. She seemed to think that her young body was purely
for offering to men in the name of obscene lust. And that
suited Jim admirably. The filthier the young slut, the
better, as far as he was concerned.

Wondering, as his balls finally drained, whether
Mary would enjoy a damned good anal rogering, he
imagined forcing the swollen globe of his penis past her
tight brown ring and sinking his veined shaft deep into
the dank heat of her rectum. Her vagina was snug in
her tender years, he mused. The sheath of her hot
rectum would be incredibly tight, hugging his solid
cock like a velvet-jawed vice. Wondering how many
cocks she'd had up her cunt as she shuddered her last
orgasmic shudder, Jim moved back slowly and withdrew his spent penis from the burning heat of her well-
spermed pussy.

Eyeing the brown ring of Mary's anus, he licked his
lips. His wife had often begged him to commit anilingus,
he recalled. But he'd always dreaded the thought of
licking her arsehole. Mary was different, he mused, again
picturing the meaty shaft of his cock penetrating her
tight little bottom-hole and stretching her rectal sheath
wide open. Watching his creamy sperm oozing between
the hairless lips of her pussy, he reckoned that the slag
would allow him to commit any and every act of gross
sexual indecency. Including an anal tongue-fucking.

'I needed that,' Jim breathed shakily, zipping his
trousers as the girl hauled herself upright and swayed
on her trembling legs. 'You're a good fuck, Mary. A
bloody good fuck.'

'You're not so bad, either,' she giggled, pulling her

panties up and tugging her skirt down. 'You remind me of my candle.'

'Your candle?'

'The one I keep beneath my pillow. It's fucking huge, just like you.'

'Oh, er . . . well, I *am* rather well endowed,' he chuckled proudly.

'Well endowed? You're fucking enormous.'

'Yes, yes, I am. Careful,' he said, clutching her arm as she swayed in her alcoholic haze.

'I think I need another fucking drink,' she breathed, making her way back to the table and plonking her rounded buttocks on the chair. 'A fucking large vodka should do the trick.'

'Fucking coming up . . . I mean . . . I really must stop swearing.'

Pressing a glass to the vodka optic, Jim couldn't stop grinning. This was only his first day at the Tartan Vicar pub and he'd already fucked Cleo's pretty mouth and spunked Mary's tight little cunt. If this was what the future held, then he'd be more than happy in his new job. A sluttish barmaid, the whorish vicar's daughter, and a never-ending supply of fresh convent schoolgirlies . . . His luck had definitely changed for the better. Mary would endure an anal fucking before the night was over, he thought again as he placed her drink on the table. The slut would be so pissed before long that she'd—Spinning round on his heels as the door opened, he donned a huge smile.

'Good evening,' he said, gazing at a middle-aged woman. 'How can I help you?'

'You the new landlord?' she snapped.

'Indeed I am. Jim Foster, Lord of the Land.'

'I want a word with you.'

'Certainly, madam,' he said, moving behind the bar. 'I'm at your service.'

'You allow young girls into this den of iniquity, don't you?'

'Young girls?' he breathed, grimacing as he glanced at Mary. 'Er . . . I have no idea what you mean.'

'Sluts, harlots, Jezebels . . .'

'Good grief. What an appalling accusation.'

'Take that slag over there,' the woman said, nodding in Mary's direction.

'I already have,' he chuckled. 'I mean . . .'

'Filth, that's what it is.'

'That slag over there, as you put it, happens to be my daughter.'

'Your daughter? Don't talk rot. Her name's Mary. She's the *vicar*'s daughter.'

'Ah, er . . . she's a twin. They're both twins, you see.'

'Twins? What are you talking about, man?'

'That's Mary, my daughter. Her sister, also Mary, is the vicar's daughter. They have different fathers but they're twins.'

'Oh, I see. In that case, I apologize. Having said that, do you think it wise to allow your daughter to sit in a pub? Look at the state of her. She's fast asleep, slumped across the table. Has she been drinking?'

'No, no, no. She's . . . she's ill. A duodenal wart, that's what it is.'

'Don't you mean ulcer?'

'Probably. Would you like a drink?'

'A pint of best bitter, please.'

Frowning as he poured the woman's drink, Jim knew that she was going to be trouble. Having no idea who she

was, he thought that he'd better play things by ear. For all he knew, she might be the local copper's wife. Placing her drink on the counter, he scrutinized the woman. Wearing a high-neck blouse, her tousled black hair cascading over her sagging breasts, she was far from attractive. Some poor sod probably had to fuck her, he reflected, thanking God that his wife had left him. Tits like shrivelled leather bags, sweaty armpits, greying pubic hairs . . .

'You're new here, aren't you?' she asked him.

'Yes, I came today. Twice, actually.'

'You came twice?'

'Once in Cleo's . . . I mean, I *arrived* today.'

'I'd better introduce myself,' she breathed, sipping her drink. 'My name's Rottweiler, Ruby Rottweiler.'

'What a lovely name. It suits you.'

'What do you mean by that?'

'Nothing.'

'I'm chairperson of the WVLA. The Willycombe Village Lesbian Association.'

'You're a lesbian?' Jim chuckled.

'And proud of it. As far as I'm concerned, you can keep your cock.'

'Why, thank you. I have to admit that I've grown rather fond of it over the years.'

'That girl over there. Your daughter. You don't allow men near her, do you?'

'Certainly not.'

'I'm glad to hear it. All the filthy bastards want to do is get their hands up her skirt. It's disgusting.'

'I couldn't agree less. Er . . . More or less.'

'Now, you listen to me. I've come here to warn you.'

'About men getting their hands up—'

'To warn you about allowing young girls into this filthy, seedy den of iniquity. I'll be keeping an eye on this place. If I so much as see a young girl hovering outside, I'll come down on you like a ton of bricks.'

'You don't have to worry, Ruby,' Jim said as she downed her pint and slammed the glass on the counter. 'This is a girl-free zone, I can assure you.'

'I'm glad to hear it. Right, I have to be getting home. I suggest you take that girl of yours to bed.'

'Oh, I intend to,' Jim chuckled.

'Get her beneath the quilt and keep her warm.'

'I'll warm her up, don't you worry.'

'Long live lesbians,' Ruby cried, leaving the pub.

Shaking his head, Jim couldn't believe the characters he'd met. Willycombe Village was quite a place, he mused. Far from what he'd expected. Helping Mary up, he walked her through the back room and up the stairs to his flat. He could hardly send her home in that state, he knew as he laid her down on his double bed. The girl had said that she often stayed out all night, so he didn't think her father would worry too much. Leaving her on the bed and returning to the bar, he was about to lock up when Cleo walked in.

'You were a long time,' he said, closing and bolting the door.

'I was waylaid,' she replied. 'You weren't too busy, were you?'

'No, no. I was about to go to bed. So, where's your flat?'

'Through the back room. There's a door beneath the stairs that opens into the annexe. Right, I'll see you in the morning. Unless you'd like to come in for a coffee?'

'Er . . . some other time,' Jim said, desperate to get his

hands on Mary's petite breasts. 'I'm pretty tired, to be honest.'

'Oh, well . . . In that case, I'll see you in the morning.'

'Yes, yes, of course. Tomorrow, after we close . . . I'd like to have a coffee with you, Cleo.'

'Yes, all right. Good night.'

'Good night.'

Switching the lights off, Jim climbed the stairs to his flat and slipped into the bedroom. It had been an interesting day, he reflected. And most rewarding. He'd have loved to have had a coffee with Cleo – coffee and rampant sex. But Mary was so young, fresh, alluring, sexually obscene, dirty, filthy . . . There'd be plenty of opportunities to shaft Cleo's tight little pussy, he mused, unbuttoning Mary's blouse. The village girls were just going to have to be patient and wait their turn, he thought, lifting Mary's bra away from her young breasts bumps. Eyeing her ripening nipples, he could hardly believe that this was happening. Life at the Tartan Vicar was going to be most rewarding. In more ways than one.

3

Waking to find the naked girl sleeping next to him, Jim propped himself up on one elbow and ran his fingertip around the ripe teat of her sensitive nipple. Squeezing her mammary spheres, he was amazed by the firmness of her young breasts. Newly formed, rock-hard, petite, they were delightful. Closely examining her milk teats, the brown protrusions standing proud from the dark discs of her areolae, he leaned over and sucked each nipplette into his mouth in turn. The girl stirred, breathing heavily through her nose as he sank his teeth gently into the sensitive protuberance of her nipples.

Pushing the quilt back, Jim eyed Mary's almost boyish figure. Her skin was smooth and unblemished in youth, the fleshy swellings of her vulval lips were smooth, firm, warm, hairless . . . Her outer labia perfectly formed, beautifully symmetrical, the creamy valley of her pussy invited his tongue. Moving down to her vulval flesh, he ran his wet tongue up and down the tightly closed crack of her vagina, tasting her sex-cream, breathing in her girl-scent as his penis stiffened fully and his full balls heaved.

In her alcoholic haze the previous evening, the girl had been in no fit state for sex when Jim had gone to bed. He had fiddled with her, fondled her and fingered the tight sheath of her vagina, but had finally given up. Now she

was stirring, stretching her limbs and beginning to wake. Settling between her parted thighs, he continued his vulval licking, savouring the aphrodisiacal taste of her teenage juices of desire as she let out low murmurs of sexual satisfaction. Parting the fleshy hillocks of her firm outer labia, exposing the intricate folds nestling within her sex valley, he repeatedly swept his tongue over the sensitive nub of her erect clitoris. Mary stretched her limbs again, opening her slender legs to the extreme as Jim worked on her solid clitoris.

Parting her love lips with his thumbs, fully exposing the pinken bud of her solid clitoris, he sucked her pleasure nub into his hot mouth and snaked his tongue over the ultra-sensitive tip. Murmuring words of sex in her dreamy state, the girl began to tremble, her juices flowing from the gaping entrance to her sheath of lust as Jim mouthed and sucked on her pulsating clitoris. She was exquisite, he mused, breathing in her girl-scent again. Young, fresh, angelic . . .

'I'm coming,' Mary gasped, her head tossing from side to side as her naked body shook uncontrollably. Driving two fingers into the tight duct of her hot vagina, Jim massaged her G-spot, taking her closer to her sexual heaven as she writhed on the bed. Her love muscles tightening around his thrusting fingers, her lubricious juices flowing over his hand, her young body became rigid as her pulsating clitoris exploded in orgasm.

Her cumbud pulsating beneath his sweeping tongue, Jim sucked out her pleasure, sustaining her climax as she clutched his head and ground her cuntal flesh against his gobbling mouth. The squelching sound of her orgasmic juices reverberating around the room as he finger-fucked her young cunt, Jim felt his cock twitching, his expectant

knob swelling. His balls fully laden, he wondered whether to pump his sperm deep into her young vagina or flood her bowels with his orgasmic cream. The succulent lips of her gasping mouth looked inviting, he thought, imagining filling her cheeks with his spunk.

Finally coming down from her massive orgasm, Mary lay quivering on the bed as Jim teased the last ripples of sex from her deflating clitoris and slowed his pistoning rhythm. Unable to speak, the girl murmured incoherent words of sex as Jim slipped his cunny-dripping fingers out of her young pussy and pressed his lips hard against the pink funnel of flesh surrounding her yawning hole. Sucking out her vaginal cream, draining her sex cavern, he drank from the sexual centre of her teenage body until she'd recovered from her earth-shattering climax.

Now was the time to drive the huge shaft of his solid cock deep into the tight sheath of Mary's young pussy, Jim decided. Slipping his tongue out of her hot vagina, he positioned his purple knob between the pinken wings of her inner lips. Stabbing at her tight vaginal entrance, his knob slipping past the wet petals of her inner labia, he drove his veined rod deep into the heat of her velvety cunt and impaled her fully on his solid penis. She gasped, lifting her head off the pillow and gazing down at the alluring sight of her outer lips stretched tautly around the base of his huge member as he withdrew his sex-slimed cock and rammed into her again.

'Fucking hell,' she breathed, her head flopping onto the pillow as her naked body rocked with the illicit fucking. 'Your cock's so fucking big, you're going to rip my cunt wide open.'

'You can take it,' he chuckled, proud of his magnificent organ as he repeatedly withdrew his sex shaft and

rammed it back into her young body. 'Just out of interest, how many cocks have you had?'

'I've lost count,' Mary gasped. 'God, that feels good. Fuck me as hard as you can. Ram your knob up me until my womb splits.'

Increasing his pistoning rhythm, his swinging balls battering the rounded cheeks of her pert buttocks, Jim imagined having the girl as a live-in sex toy. Looking down at the ultra-tight lips of her vagina rolling back and forth along his veined shaft, he was again reminded of her tender years. A slut she might have been, he mused. But a very young slut. To move her into the flat and use and abuse her for vulgar sex probably wasn't a good idea. Apart from her age, there was her father, he reflected. The last thing he needed was the local vicar storming into the pub with his accusations of drunkenness and illicit girl-shagging. Trying to push the dreadful thought to the back of his mind, he felt his sperm pump burst into action.

'Here it comes,' he gasped, battering the girl's ripe cervix with his throbbing knob. His spunk gushing into her contracting vaginal duct, he imagined forcing the swollen knob of his cock past her anal ring and driving his penile shaft deep into the very core of her young body. Her rectal duct would be fiery-hot and extremely tight, he mused, picturing the tight ring of her anus stretched tautly around the thick root of his huge member. Whether she wanted it or not, she was going to endure a crude rectal shagging, he decided.

Again and again, Jim propelled his throbbing glans deep into the heat of her contracting cunt, his spunk filling her vaginal cavern, overflowing and splattering the pale flesh of her splayed inner thighs. Writhing,

gasping, Mary screamed out as her clitoris erupted in orgasm, sending shock waves of pure sexual bliss rolling throughout her trembling body. She was a right little slut, Jim mused, watching his cream-dripping penile shaft repeatedly emerge and drive back into the girl. A dirty, filthy whore-tart.

'God, my fucking cunt,' she gasped as he finally stilled his spent shaft, his swollen glans absorbing the inner heat of her young body. 'You're a fucking good shag.'

'I'm the best,' Jim chuckled, pondering again on fucking her tight rectum.

'Jim, are you coming down this morning?' Cleo asked, tapping on the flat door.

'Er . . . Be right with you,' he called, slipping his flaccid cock out of the teenager's sperm-bubbling cunt. 'Shit, look at the time,' he breathed.

'Fuck the time,' Mary giggled. 'And fuck *me*. Again.'

'Later, my horny little slut. I have work to do.'

After a shower, Jim dressed in an open-neck white shirt and dark trousers. It was another warm day, he observed, gazing out of the bedroom window as Mary pulled the quilt over her naked body and went back to sleep. His second day at the pub, and he was looking forward to meeting the lunchtime customers. If there were any, that was. Finally leaving Mary to sleep, he bounded down the stairs to the bar and grinned at Cleo.

'Late on parade,' he said. 'Sorry about that.'

'I trust you slept well?' she asked, suspicion mirrored in her dark eyes.

'I fucked well,' he chuckled. 'I mean, I slept fucking well.'

'I know *exactly* what you mean,' Cleo retorted, obviously jealous. 'I've cleaned the floor behind the bar.

Apart from spilled beer, there was a whitish starchy substance splattered—'

'Ah, er . . . coffee liqueur,' he murmured. 'I spilled some last night.'

'Really? That's odd, seeing as we ran out the other day. Talking of which, while you were upstairs, *sleeping*, I put the order in to the brewery.'

'Ah, good, good. So, I wonder what today will bring? More disappearing customers?'

'Don't start that again, Jim. It's Saturday, so lunchtime should be pretty busy.'

'Ah, Saturday. You know what that means, don't you?'

'No, but I'm sure you're going to tell me.'

'Freshly cut sandwiches.'

'What?'

'Freshly cut . . . We're now doing lunchtime bar food.'

'Are you?'

'Yes, *we* are. Only at weekends, initially. Just to test the water, so to speak. OK, nip out to the local baker and buy—'

'Who, exactly, is going to make these sandwiches?'

'You, Cleo. Who else?'

'I thought as much. Look, the bar is busy enough at weekends without adding to the workload.'

'We're adding to the takings,' Jim said, rubbing his hands together. 'Take a ham sandwich.'

'No, thanks.'

'Two pieces of ham and a couple of slices of bread will cost us, say, twenty pence. If we sell them for one pound seventy . . . Hey, that's one pound fifty profit. Not bad, huh?'

'No, no, no. You've got it wrong, Jim.'

'I haven't. One pound seventy minus twenty . . .'

'Is one pound fifty.'

'That's what I said.'

'Minus my cut, fifty pence, and you make one pound per sandwich.'

'What?' he gasped. 'You want fifty fucking pence for each sandwich you make? That's fucking extortion.'

'It's fucking wages. Take it or leave it.'

'I'll have to take it, won't I?'

'You can hardly complain, Jim. You make a quid per sandwich, and you don't have to buy the bread and the filling *or* make the bloody things.'

'Yes, I see your point,' he sighed.

'Seeing as I've lost my income from the hole in the bar, the sandwiches will help to make it up.'

'We could always . . . No, I suppose we'd better not.'

'What?'

'I was going to suggest that you carry on with your other job. Job, blow job . . . Get it?'

'Very funny. I suppose you're going to suggest that I suck off the punters and you take half the cash?'

'Something like that. There again, I'm trying to steer the pub away from illegal activities. Just out of interest, how much were you making each week?'

'Two to three hundred a week.'

'At least two blows a day?'

'Usually, yes.'

'Very interesting. But no. We can't allow what would be deemed as brothel activities to take place in the Tartan Vicar. It wouldn't be right.'

'You'd be a pimp.'

'Disgusting. I can't abide making money by exploiting teenage girls. There again, it might be worthwhile. I'll give it some deep throat . . . ah, deep thought.'

'Yes, Jim, you do that. Perhaps you'd be good enough let me know whether you intend to sell my mouth for fucking?'

'Of course, I . . . I'd consult you first, Cleo. Anyway, enough about blow jobs. It's ten o'clock. Shouldn't we be open?'

'We've been open since eight.'

'Oh, right. *Eight*? That's illegal. Er . . . yes, well. OK, you go and buy the bread and stuff and prepare for a busy, and most profitable, lunchtime session.'

'I *am* giving head, then?'

'No, no. I meant the sandwiches.'

'I could suck the punters while they eat,' she giggled. 'Eat, suck, eat, suck, slurp, gobble, eat, suck, swallow . . .'

'The bread, Cleo.'

Watching the girl grab some cash from the till as she left the pub, Jim reckoned that he was going to do very well from selling food. This was what people expected from a country pub, he mused. Freshly cut sandwiches, pies . . . Cornish pasties and pork pies were a must, he decided. Jumbo sausages . . . Not a good idea. Cleo couldn't cope with the sight of a big, juicy length of pork. She'd be creaming her knickers and . . . There again, she could cope only too well with several lengths of meat. But there'd be no sausages left for the customers. Fanny-hot sausages? No, maybe not. Was she wearing any knickers?

Grabbing a blackboard he'd noticed in the back room, Jim found some chalk and began scrawling the lunchtime menu. Wondering whether Cleo could cook, he pondered on such delicacies as shepherd's pie. Quiche would go down well with the lunchtime punters, he mused. But he couldn't spell the word. It was best to start off with

sandwiches, he decided. He'd add jacket potatoes and quiche to the menu once word had got round that the Tartan Vicar was the 'in' place to eat. Propping the blackboard up in a prominent position close to the bar, he grinned as Mary appeared. She really was a stunning little slut, he mused, eyeing her tousled blonde hair cascading over her angelic face. A beautiful bit of rough, looking as though she'd been dragged backwards through a hedge. Au naturel?

'I'd better get fucking home and face the prat,' she sighed, rubbing her bleary eyes.

'The prat? Oh, your father. Will you be in this evening?'

'Yes, if you're going to fuck me senseless again,' she breathed, her succulent red lips furling into a salacious grin.

'In that case, you'll be in,' he chuckled. 'And so will I.'

'It's coleslaw,' she said, gazing at the blackboard. 'Not fucking *coal* as in the fucking stuff you burn.'

'Oh, er . . . right,' Jim stammered as she left the pub.

Correcting his mistake, he stood back and admired his handiwork. Cheese-and-pickle sandwiches, smoked ham, egg-and-tomato . . . This was going to be a winner, he was sure as he went behind the bar and started polishing the pumps with a duster. A well-run country pub with lunchtime food was a profitable pub, he concluded. Eyeing the hole in the bar as he polished the brass pumps, he pondered again on Cleo's little sideline. Two to three hundred pounds each week was a considerable sum, he mused.

'It's *cole*slaw,' Cleo sighed as she lugged several carrier bags into the pub. 'Not *cold*, as in freezing.'

'Coal, cold, cole . . . Fucking hell, does it matter?'

'Of course it matters, Jim. You don't want people to think that you're illiterate as well as stupid.'

'I'm neither, I'll have you know.'

'And what's that?' she giggled, dumping the bags on the bar and pointing at the board. 'What the hell is tuner? It's a knob on a radio, isn't it?'

'It's that dreadful fish stuff that stinks like a prostitute's fanny,' Jim returned.

'You mean tuna. T U N A.'

'If you're so fucking clever, why don't *you* do the blackboard?'

'I'll have to, by the look of it. Anyway, I didn't buy any tuna.'

'Just as well, really. This place already stinks like a prostitute's—'

'Coffee?'

'A prostitute's coffee? What are you talking about?'

'Would you like a cup of coffee?'

'Oh, er . . . yes, that would be nice. I reckon we should sell coffee. One pound per cup . . .'

'One thing at a time, Jim,' Cleo sighed, lugging her bags into the annexe. 'I suppose my flat is now the catering department?' she asked him, turning in the doorway.

'Well, there's nowhere else. May I come and see your flat? I'd love to take a look at your bed.'

'No, you may not. Besides, you have the bar to run.'

'Do you masturbate in your bed?'

'I'll bring your coffee through and then get down to the sandwiches.'

Picturing Cleo naked on her bed, her thighs spread, her fingers massaging her ripe clitoris to orgasm, Jim knew that she was still disgruntled over Mary staying the

night. He should have gone to Cleo's flat and had coffee with her the night before, he reflected. She was obviously up for a screw, but he'd set his eyes on Mary's young body. Maybe he'd have coffee with Cleo that night, he thought. If she invited him to her flat, that was. This was far removed from his boring life married to an old hag, he reflected. Running his own pub, surrounded by exquisitely attractive young girlies . . . This was sheer bliss. Far better than constant nagging, a slack fanny, saggy tits, the stench of armpit juice . . .

'Hi,' a tall, slender blonde trilled as her long legs carried her into the pub. Wearing her school uniform, she was the epitome of fuckability.

'Oh, er . . . Hi,' Jim murmured, his eyes locked to her naked thighs emerging from her incredibly short skirt. 'You must be from the convent?'

'That's right. I'm a boarder, so you'll be seeing a lot of me. Especially at weekends.'

'I'll look forward to seeing a *lot* more of you,' he breathed, gazing at the tight material of her white blouse ballooned by her young breasts. 'Jim, Jim Foster. Landlord of the—'

'Yes, I've heard all about you.'

'Really?'

'It's all round the convent.'

'What is?'

'The news about you taking over the pub. I'll have a gin and tonic with ice and lemon, please. I was relieved to hear that you serve under-age customers.'

'Under-age . . . God forbid,' he gasped as she sat on a bar stool and grinned at him. 'Yes, well . . . You'd better keep it to yourself. I don't want to get into trouble.'

'Oh, *I* do,' she giggled. 'That's what the weekends are

for. Getting into trouble. We have to endure boring lessons all week, act ladylike and—'

'Hi, Crystal,' Cleo said, placing Jim's coffee on the bar. 'How are you?'

'Not too bad. The Reverend Mother's been up to her tricks again.'

'Oh?'

'She's discovered that I've been making money from the sanitary-towel machine. I fixed the mechanism so that the machine needed two pounds to dispense a pack of towels instead of one pound. One pound for me, and one for the convent. I was doing pretty well until she realized that one of the keys was missing. That's my weekend drinking money down the drain.'

'That's illegal,' Jim breathed.

'I know that,' Crystal giggled. 'Anyway, I have another scam in mind.'

'What's that?' Cleo asked her.

'Selling dirty knickers.'

'Good grief,' Jim gasped. 'You can't—'

'I can and I will. I was looking through a dirty mag the other day. Soiled panties are selling for a small fortune. And I have access to a laundry room that caters for six hundred girls. Cool, huh?'

'Very cool,' Cleo laughed.

'It's beautifully obscene,' Jim murmured, wondering whether to put in an order for a pair of cunny-stained navy-blue knickers. 'I must say, you're quite resourceful.'

'I'm simply trying to survive,' the girl giggled.

'Right, I'd better get back to my own money-making scam,' Cleo said. 'I mean, making the sandwiches.'

'We're now doing food at lunchtime,' Jim announced proudly. 'Freshly made sandwiches and—'

'I can help you out there,' Crystal offered.

'It's all right. Cleo is going to make the sandwiches and . . .'

'Bread, butter, ham, cheese, eggs, pickles, mayonnaise, salad stuff . . . I'll charge you half the shop prices, OK?'

'Half the . . .'

'Ring your order through to me, and I'll have the stuff delivered. Cleo has my mobile phone number.'

'I take it that you have access to the kitchens at the convent as well as the laundry room?' Jim asked her.

'You name it, I have access to it.'

'Well . . . let's see how it goes. If I find that the food is popular among the punters . . .'

'Then we're in business. It'll certainly make up for the loss of profit on the sanitary towels. I don't suppose you have a market for that sort of thing?'

'Not really,' Jim laughed. 'I really do find Willycombe Village amazing. Scams, rip-offs, backhanders, prostitution . . .'

'Prostitution?' Crystal echoed, frowning at Jim. 'What do you know about that? Who's been blabbing?'

'Well, no one. I was joking.'

'Oh, right. So, here's to our new business venture,' she said, raising her glass.

Eyeing the girl's succulent lips, Jim wondered what other money-making schemes she was running. Did she offer blow jobs? he mused, imagining the purple globe of his cock encompassed by her pretty lips, his spunk bathing her pink tongue. The idea of fucking a convent schoolgirl's hot mouth stiffening his penis, he imagined the swollen lips of her young pussy rising alluringly either side of her lickable crack of desire. Was she wet with arousal? he wondered, adjusting his solid cock

through his trousers. Did she masturbate? Better still, was she having lesbian sex with her schoolfriends? Reckoning that the dormitories resounded with the whimpers of young girls shuddering in orgasm every night, he could hardly believe his luck. There was far more to Willycombe Village than the local shop and an ordinary pub.

Watching Crystal sipping her gin and tonic, Jim left the bar and began arranging the tables and chairs in an effort to spy her tight panties. Sitting on the bar stool with her young thighs parted, the girl must have known of Jim's male thoughts. Thinking that, if he were a schoolgirl, he'd always be flashing his knickers at men, he concealed a grin as her thighs parted further. Gazing at the triangular patch of white cotton clinging to her puffy love lips, he felt his stomach somersault. Crystal was going to endure a damned good arse-fucking before the day was over, that was for sure.

'You don't want to make too many changes,' the girl said, parting her thighs further as she followed Jim's gaze to the crotch of her panties. 'People don't like change.'

'You're telling me,' he sighed, leaning on the bar next to her. 'Just about everyone has asked me what changes I'm going to make to the pub. Apart from food at weekends, and perhaps some music, I don't intend to change anything. I'll have to change my underpants, of course.'

'Shame there's no market for *men*'s soiled pants,' Crystal giggled.

'What other business ventures are you into?' he asked her, becoming desperate for the feel of her succulent lips wrapped around his solid knob, her wet tongue sweeping over his sperm-slit.

'A few of the girls . . . er . . . This and that,' she replied nonchalantly, obviously not wanting to reveal too much.

'A few of the girls? What were you about to say?'

'Er . . . nothing. Just that they'll be in later.'

'I'd be very pleased to meet your friends, Crystal. If they're anything like you . . .'

'In what way?'

'I'll let you into a secret,' he murmured mysteriously, looking around the pub. 'I'm somewhat of a schoolgirl connoisseur. I appreciate the . . . er . . . certain aspects of schoolgirlies.'

'Tell me more,' Crystal breathed, cocking her head to one side. 'You intrigue me.'

'Most men enjoy ogling young girls in their school uniforms. But they don't appreciate the concept of . . . What I mean is . . .'

'I think you're trying to say that most men chase after schoolgirls with a view to fucking them.'

'Good grief.'

'Whereas you appreciate the bewitching angelic qualities of young teenage girls, the enchantment of their feminine beauty.'

'Yes, that's right.'

'Your initial thoughts aren't about fucking.'

'Damned right they are . . . aren't.'

'You appreciate the firmness of their breast bumps, their ripening nipples, the allure of their sweet pussy lips, their exquisite sex-slits.'

'Yes, yes, yes,' Jim breathed eagerly.

'A flash of a young girl's knickers as she cycles past excites you. A glimpse of her firm breasts as she leans forward and her school blouse falls away from her young body sends quivers through your—'

'Good grief,' Jim gasped. 'You seem to know more about the way I feel than I do. How do you know these things?'

'Experience,' she giggled, placing her empty glass on the bar. 'I think I'd better have another G and T.'

'Coming right up,' Jim said excitedly.

'You'd enjoy our village-green cycling competition.'

'Oh? What's that?'

'Ostensibly, the idea is to test the girls' cycling proficiency. The truth of the matter is that the girls flash their panties as they ride their bikes to excite the male onlookers. The girls wear their very short gymslips and cycle around obstacles on the green. They put on quite a show.'

'I can well imagine,' Jim laughed. 'But surely it's pretty obvious that—'

'No, no. They're schoolgirls, Jim. Who would dare to suggest that they deliberately expose their panties? Would you?'

'No, no, of course not. So, what do the girls get out of it?'

'Offers of . . . er . . . Fun, that's all. You'd love our parents' evening at the convent.'

'But I'm not a parent.'

'None of our visitors are parents. What happens is—'

'Crystal,' Cleo cut in as she emerged from the back room carrying two plates of sandwiches. 'I think you've said more than enough.'

'No, she hasn't,' Jim snapped. 'I want to know about—'

'I was only joking,' Crystal said. 'We . . . we don't really have parents' evenings without parents.'

'Oh, right. So, Cleo, how are the sandwiches going? They look pretty good to me.'

'All done,' the girl replied, glaring at Crystal. 'Where are we going to put them? We need one of those display cabinets.'

'Put them on the bar,' Jim suggested.

'Health and hygiene, Jim. We can't have uncovered food on the bar.'

'Ten quid,' Crystal said, unclipping her mobile phone from the waistband of her skirt.

'What is?' Jim asked her.

'A display cabinet. I'll have one here within fifteen minutes, OK?'

'Er . . . OK,' Jim agreed.

Pouring himself half a pint of bitter as Crystal made a phone call, Jim wondered whether the convent was a front for a brothel. It was wishful thinking, he mused. Convent schoolgirls weren't heavily into debauched sex sessions, were they? Watching Cleo bring out two more plates of sandwiches and plonk them on the bar as he sipped his drink, Jim reckoned that he was going to do well from the lunchtime food. The brewery boss was going to be proud of him, he was sure. Turning a failing business into a highly profitable . . .

His mouth hanging open as he gazed at two convent schoolgirls wandering into the pub, Jim couldn't believe his eyes. Their white school blouses hanging open, the petite mounds of their breasts devoid of bras, they were obviously deliberately showing all they'd got. Or, as he decided on closer scrutiny, all they had *not* got. This was getting out of hand, he mused as Cleo poured two large vodka and tonics for the girlies. OK, so it was the weekend and school was out. But to flagrantly break

moving along to the next viewing window. Gazing up the other girl's short skirt, his eyes almost popped out of his head. Not only was her hairless pussy knickerless, but she had a huge candle emerging from between the pouting lips of her vagina.

'Fuck me,' Jim breathed as the girl slipped her hand up her skirt and pushed the candle fully home. His cock solid within his tight trousers, he wondered again who would have installed the spying windows. Did Cleo know about them? he mused. Looking around the dimly lit corner of the cellar, he realized that anyone looking down through the glass from the bar would see nothing but darkness. This was all very clever, he thought. And most ingenious. As for the schoolgirl with a candle stuffed up her tight little cunt . . . Fiddling with a barrel as he heard someone descending the stone steps, Jim looked up as Cleo appeared.

'Just familiarizing myself with the cellar,' he muttered.

'I wondered where you'd got to,' she said. 'Guess what?'

'What?'

'I've just sold a round of ham sandwiches to the local postman.'

'Ah, you see? I was right, wasn't I? I reckon that you'll be making a hell of a lot more sandwiches before the session is over.'

'I can't There's no more bread.'

'Fuck me, Cleo.'

'Not now, I'm busy.'

'You can buy some more bread, can't you?'

'Maybe.'

'Maybe? I do wish that you'd show a little enthusiasm. After all, you *are* making money from our new business

venture. By the way, I think I'll put some lighting in that corner. It's dark and dingy and, with some decent lighting, we might be able to utilize the space for—'

'Er . . . no, no,' Cleo cut in fretfully. 'Why waste your time with lighting?'

'The space might be useful. What's the point in having a dark corner like that? We could store . . .'

'I'd better get back to the bar.'

'OK. I'll be up in a minute.'

Cleo knew about the viewing windows, Jim was positive as she climbed the steps. But, surely, she didn't stand in the cellar spying up schoolgirlies' short skirts? Or did she? The hole in the bar had been a surprising find. To now discover purpose-made spying windows was incredible. Perhaps Cleo was a bisexual slut? Wondering what other dirty secrets the Tartan Vicar held, Jim made his way back to the bar and poured himself another drink. Did the schoolgirlies know about the viewing windows? he wondered. More to the point, which of the naughty young girls had a huge candle stuffed deep into the tight sheath of her wet cunt?

Nonchalantly wandering around the pub with his drink, Jim eyed the backs of the girls' legs, their short skirts billowed by their pert buttocks. The girl who had a candle stuffed up her tight cunny could be detected by squirming movements, he reckoned, watching closely for the give-away signs. The dark-haired girl was wiggling most of the time, but the blonde . . . Apart from the odd twitch of her cute backside, she remained pretty well motionless. It was the dark-haired girl who was enjoying a candle-fuck, Jim was certain.

'Mornin',' the postman called from a corner table.

'Oh, er . . . Good morning,' Jim replied, walking towards him. 'Are the sandwiches to your liking?'

'They're very good. You must be the new guvnor?'

'Indeed I am. Jim Foster.'

'Pat, Pat Cummings. You ain't going to make no changes to the pub, are you? People round 'ere don't like change, they don't.'

'Yes, I know,' Jim murmured, forcing a chuckle. 'It seems that the people of Willycombe Village—'

'Are very wary of newcomers,' the postman cut in. 'Take the last bloke.'

'The last bloke?'

'The bloke what 'ad this place afore you. Tried to make changes, 'e did. The girlies soon 'ad 'im out.'

'Girlies?' Jim echoed.

'The girlies what come in 'ere from that there covenant. I been in this 'ere village all me life. You take it from me, guvnor. No one 'ere don't like no changes.'

'The girlies . . . What did they do?'

'They 'ad 'im out, they did.'

'Yes, but how?'

'You ask young Cleo there. She knows what goes on round 'ere.'

'Are you gossiping again, Pat?' Cleo asked as she took his empty plate from the table.

'I was just tellin' the new guvnor 'ere that . . .'

'Don't you go telling anyone anything,' Cleo giggled. 'He's an old gossip,' she said, turning to Jim. 'Oh, here's Mr Hops,' she said, returning to the bar as the door opened. 'He comes in every Friday.'

Gazing in horror at his boss, Jim turned and looked at the schoolgirls leaning on the bar. 'Shit,' he breathed as the man stood next to them and asked Cleo for a pint of

best. He'd obviously come to check up on things, Jim thought, ignoring the postman's ramblings and heading for the bar. This was all he needed, he knew as the girls giggled and downed their vodkas. Banging their empty glasses on the bar and ordering Cleo to fill them up, they were going to cause problems, he was sure.

'Mr Hops,' Jim said, grinning as he joined the man at the bar. 'What a pleasant surprise.'

'Ah, Foster,' the man grunted. 'People usually find my unexpected arrival an *un*pleasant surprise.'

'No, no, not at all. It really is good to see you. You may have noticed that we're now doing food . . .'

'Food? Good God, man. People come here to drink, not eat.'

'Well, yes . . . but . . .'

'You'll be telling me that you plan to have bloody music blasting out next.'

'Oh, no, no.'

'People don't like change, Foster. Remember that.'

'How can I forget it?'

'This is a quiet country pub. A quiet village pub where people come to relax.'

'Yes, yes, of course. But to increase the turnover, I was thinking that we should—'

'Do nothing, Foster,' the formidable man bellowed, downing his pint. 'That's what we should do.'

'Oh, right. Forgive me, Mr Hops, but I thought that you'd placed me here to—'

'Run the place. That's what you're here for. Take it from me, Foster. Do as I say, and you'll do well. I didn't get where I am today by making changes. I'm a self-made millionaire. When I took over the brewery from my grandfather, I didn't make one change. I own one of

the oldest breweries in the land, and it's also the most successful. Why?'

'Er . . .'

'Because I don't go changing things every five min-utes. Good God, I've lost count of the name-changes of the other pubs in this county. One week, it's the Hen and Chickens. The next, it's the Cock and Bull. Plastic pubs full of plastic people, Foster. We don't want that, do we?'

'No, no.'

'Good man. How are you getting on with young Cleo here?' he asked Jim, winking at the girl.

'Oh, just fine.'

'She's the best, salt of the earth.'

'Yes, yes, she is.'

'Right, I must be going. Er . . . Cleo, a word outside, if you will?'

'Of course.'

'Be seeing you, Foster. No changes, right?'

'Er . . . right.'

Shaking his head and frowning as his boss led Cleo outside, Jim couldn't understand the man's attitude. It was almost as if he didn't *want* Jim to turn the pub into a thriving business. The place had been running at a loss, and the idea had been to . . . Not even bothering to think about it, Jim refilled his glass and leaned on the bar opposite the young schoolgirlies. *Fuck old man Hops*, he thought. There were more important things to concen-trate on. Namely, heavy drinking and rampant sex with convent schoolgirlies. Now, which little beauty was being fucked by a huge candle? And which little beauty would appreciate a length of hard cock up her arse?

4

The lunchtime session had gone very well. Not only had the sandwiches sold out, but Cleo had had to buy more bread and make several extra rounds. It had been an extremely good result, Jim reflected. Apart from old man Hops and his peculiar attitude, that was. *No one likes change*. Cleo wouldn't say what the boss had wanted to talk to her about, but Jim reckoned that it was nothing to warrant concern. He reckoned that Hops probably just wanted to whinge to Cleo about changes. As he cleared the tables of empty glasses and plates, he decided to forget about his boss and get on with building up the business.

Gazing at the schoolgirlies who were still sitting on bar stools and were pretty much the worse for wear due to drink, he wondered again which one was enjoying the candle. Hairless pussy lips, tight cracks, hot pussies . . . The place was rife with hot young cunt, Jim mused. He could almost smell the perfume of girl-sex hanging in the air. But was this normal? Was this usual for a country pub? No, it wasn't. Glancing down at the glass panels in the floor, he was determined to discover what was going on at the Tartan Vicar. At least no customers had miraculously disappeared this time, he thought, watching Cleo washing up behind the bar.

'No homes to go to?' he asked the horny schoolgirls.

'Yes, but not yet,' the blonde replied. 'Same again, please.'

'We're closing in five minutes,' Jim said, checking his watch. 'It's almost three o'clock.'

'Jim, we don't close,' Cleo enlightened him, refilling the girls' glasses.

'We don't . . . Oh, right.'

'We usually have the convent netball team in on Saturday afternoons.'

'Really?'

'They play other schools in the county and come in for a few drinks on their way back to the convent.'

'In that case, hadn't we better make some more sandwiches? The girls will be ravishing after . . . I mean, ravished, famished . . .'

'Fuck the sandwiches,' the dark-haired girl laughed. 'It's the gin you'd better break out.'

'They do tend to drink rather a lot of gin,' Cleo said. 'Particularly if they've won.'

'Which they always do,' the blonde said. 'They've never lost a game.'

'They must be good,' Jim breathed.

'They fucking cheat,' the dark-haired girl laughed. 'They rough up the other team before the game. A few bruises and breakages, and the opposing team are fucked.'

'Fucked, yes . . . er . . . Cleo, how are we doing for gin?'

'We've more than enough, so don't worry. By the way, Crystal will be back later with the display cabinet for the food. She had a problem with the caretaker.'

'I'm not surprised. Stealing from the convent like that . . .'

'No, no. He was going to deliver the cabinet but he was waylaid. Will you be all right for a while? Only I want to tidy up my flat.'

'Yes, yes, that's fine,' Jim replied, reckoning that this was his chance to get his hands up the dirty girlies' short skirts. And, hopefully, his chance to discover which of the horny little sexpots was secretly candle-fucking.

Wondering how to make his move, Jim poured himself another drink and peered down the blonde's gaping blouse at her beautiful breast bumps. The alluring mounds of her mammary hillocks were divine, he thought, deciding that her sweet nipples were in dire need of sucking. Adjusting his stiffening cock through his trousers as the girls sipped their drinks and giggled, he couldn't help but picture the hairless flesh of their young vulvas. He was going to have to make his move, he knew. But how? He could hardly just thrust his hands up their skirts and suggest that they take his solid cock deep into their virginal pussies. *Virginal*? That was a laugh. They'd probably been fucked rotten time and time again and . . . A thought hitting him, he frowned and rubbed his chin. *There were no young lads in the village*. Willy-combe Village was teeming with young schoolgirlies, but there were no young lads.

'I haven't seen any young men in the pub,' he said, leaning on the bar and again ogling the blonde's spunk-able breast bumps.

'Young men?' she echoed? 'What do you mean?'

'The pub attracts quite a following of young girls. Usually, where there are gatherings of highly delectable girls, there are hordes of young men.'

'Oh, I see,' she murmured. 'Well, we wouldn't know anything about that.'

'They've gone,' the dark-haired girl slurred. 'They've all followed the Pied Piper and gone away to—'

'Shut up, Melanie,' the blonde snapped.

'No, no,' Jim said. 'Let her finish.'

'She doesn't know what the fuck she's talking about. Followed the fucking Pied Piper, for fuck's sake. The stupid fucking cow's fucking pissed. Anyway, you're new to the village so I wouldn't ask too many fucking questions if I were you. Not if you want to stay here, that is.'

'What's going on?' Jim asked her. 'What the hell's going on in this village?'

'Going on? Nothing's fucking going on.'

Downing his drink, Jim poured himself another half and pondered on the recent events. Cleo sucking cock through the hole in the bar, the disappearing customers, Mary, the vicar's dirty little daughter, convent school-girlies . . . And he hadn't seen one young man in the pub. There was a conspiracy, he was sure as he recalled all those who'd warned him against change. *People don't like change. The locals don't like strangers. Especially strangers who ask questions.* Eyeing the young girls as they joked and giggled, Jim decided that, after another couple of drinks, they'd open up and reveal the secrets that the mysterious village harboured.

'I knew a girl who lived in the village,' he said, an idea coming to mind.

'Really?' the blonde murmured dismissively.

'Blimey, did she tell me a few stories about this place!'

'Stories? Er . . . what sort of stories?'

'Nothing I can repeat, I'm afraid.'

'This girl. What was her name?'

'Jane. I'm going back a few years now. You wouldn't

have known her. She reckoned that the convent girls . . . No, I'd better not say anything.'

'Did she tell you about the vicarage?' the dark-haired girl slurred.

'Shut the fuck up, Melanie,' the blonde hissed.

'It's all right, I know all about the vicarage,' Jim chuckled.

'You *know*?'

'Oh, yes. Jane told me everything there is to know about Willycombe Village.'

'So, you know about the dungeon?'

'Er . . . the dungeon . . . Yes, yes, of course. When were you last there?'

'We're always there,' the dark-haired girl blurted out.

'Melanie, unless you shut the fuck up, I'll rip your fucking nipples off.'

'It's all right,' Jim laughed. 'Don't go on at her. As I said, I know all there is to know.'

'Tell me, then,' the girl breathed, her blue eyes staring accusingly at Jim. 'Tell me all there is to know.'

'Oh, no. I'm not saying anything. But I will say that I know about the illicit and beautifully disgusting use of candles.'

'Candles? Er . . . what candles?'

'There's a candle not more than a couple of feet away from where I'm standing. It's hot, creamy-wet . . . Tell me that I'm wrong.'

'I have no idea what you mean,' she returned uneasily. 'I can't see any candles.'

'He's talking about the candle you have shoved up your—'

'Melanie! Right, that's it. One more fucking word from you and I'll shove a candle up your arse.'

'Ooh, please do.'

Looking up as Cleo breezed into the bar, Jim grimaced. Her untimely entrance had blown everything, he reflected. Just as he was getting somewhere . . . At least he now knew which of the horny little girls was enjoying a candle-fucking. Making out that he was going to get something from his flat while Cleo chatted to the girls, he slipped into the back room and listened to the whispered conversation. Unfortunately, he couldn't make out what was being said since Cleo made a hell of a noise by emptying the ice bucket into the sink. Quiet finally settling over the bar, he moved closer to the doorway.

'He knows nothing,' Cleo murmured.

'But he said that he knows all about the vicarage and—'

'He's bluffing,' Cleo laughed. 'He knows that something's going on and he's trying to find out what. The trouble is that you lot can't keep your mouths shut.'

'I haven't said anything,' the blonde retorted. 'Fucking Melanie keeps fucking blabbing. Stupid fucking bitch.'

'Carole, I am *not* a stupid fucking bitch. *You*'re a stupid fucking *cow*. You and your fucking—'

'All right, all right,' Cleo sighed. 'Let's not argue. The thing to do is say nothing to Jim. Try to keep quiet about you-know-what and, if he persists with his questions, just ignore him.'

'He knew about my candle,' Carole said.

'Candle?'

'I have a candle up my cunt. How the hell did he know that?'

'You have a candle up your—The floor tiles,' Cleo breathed pensively. 'He was lurking in the cellar earlier. He must have discovered the glass tiles.'

'He's been looking up your skirt,' Melanie giggled. 'He's been looking up your skirt at your dirty little cunt.'

'He knows too much for my liking.' Cleo said. 'But he doesn't know about the vicarage, I'm sure of that. I'll tell him about the glass tiles and . . . I'll say that they were put there to let some light into the cellar.'

'But he'll wonder why you mentioned it.'

'I'll bring it up in conversation. When he comes back, say nothing, OK?'

Rubbing his chin as he lurked in the back room, Jim was more confused than ever. What the hell went on at the vicarage? he wondered. According to Cleo, the vicar was a strait-laced, anti-drink, anti-sex, anti- . . . She was lying, he was sure as he recalled Mary's blatant exhibitionism. The vicar's daughter was a dirty, filthy little whore-slut, and her father knew it. Getting drunk, staying out all night, fucking rotten . . . Mary was a slag, and her father knew exactly what she got up to. If that was the case, the vicar obviously didn't condone her despicable behaviour. Perhaps the vicarage was a brothel? Jim mused. *Dearly beloved, we are gathered here today to fuck schoolgirlies' tight cunts*. The vicar was probably a drug-dealing pimp.

Making his way down to the cellar, Jim decided to take a good look around. There might be other interesting secrets within the bowels of the pub, he mused, rummaging through a pile of cardboard boxes. The place needed tidying up, that was certain. Boxes, old furniture, piles of rubbish . . . Apart from bringing some organization to the cellar, a good clear-out might unearth something. And some lighting in the dingy corner. Deciding to call in the local electrician, Jim turned as Cleo called him.

'Jim, what *are* you doing?' she asked as she descended the steps.

'Er . . . clearing up,' he replied. 'Look at the state of this place. It's a bloody nightmare.'

'I'll do that,' Cleo sighed. 'You have more important things to do. After all, you're the governor. You should be in the bar, not clearing up down here.'

'Yes, you're right,' he said proudly. 'I'm the governor, not a skivvy. I'm not saying that you're a skivvy. Actually, you *are* a skivvy . . . What I meant was—'

'I know what you meant. Er . . . the girls said that you were talking about the vicarage. Have you been there?'

'No, no. I was just saying that I'd like to take a look around the village when I get time. I'd like to take a look at the church and the vicarage. I'm interested in old buildings, you see. Buildingology. It's a hobby of mine.'

'Ah, right. I think the girls would like to take a look at your flat.'

'The girls want to see my flat?'

'Yes. They were saying how well they got on with you and they'd like to get to know you a little better.'

'Really?'

'You're a very attractive man, Jim. I'm not surprised that they want to get you alone. The blonde girl, Carole, is particularly interested in you.'

'Oh, well . . . I *am* rather an attractive man. Yes, I might show them around the flat later.'

'I'm sure they'd like that. By the way, the glass tiles in the floor . . .'

'Glass tiles?' he echoed, frowning at the girl.

'Haven't you noticed them?'

'No, no, I haven't,' he lied, concealing a grin. 'Where are these tiles?'

'They're . . . You'd better get back to the bar, Jim. The netball team will be here soon.'

Leaving the cellar, Jim smiled as he made his way through the back room to the bar. The schoolgirls were now more than worse the wear for drink, and Jim reckoned that the time had come for a quick mammary grope. Pouring himself a drink, he stood next to the blonde and peered down the front of her blouse. He was determined to squeeze the petite mounds of her breasts, suck her ripe nipples into his wet mouth and tease the sensitive protrusions of her milk teats with his snaking tongue. Looking around the pub, making sure that he was alone with the nymphettes, he slipped his hand into the blonde girl's blouse and ran his fingertips over the dark discs of her areolae.

'Oh,' she gasped, looking up in astonishment. 'What the fuck are you doing?'

'Sorry,' he murmured, squeezing the firm roundness of her breast. 'I couldn't help myself.'

'It looks as if you *are* helping your fucking self.'

'It's a family trait, I'm afraid. My great-grandfather was arrested for schoolgirlie groping. You don't mind me having a quick grope, do you?' he asked her, pinching and pulling on the elongated teat of her nipple. 'I like to keep up the family tradition.'

'Mind? Well, I . . . I must say that I'm not used to being fucking groped like this.'

'Lying fucking cow,' Melanie giggled. 'She's always being fucking—'

'Shut the fuck up, Melanie.'

'Now, now, girls,' Jim laughed, cupping the warm mound of the blonde's breast in his hand. 'Let's not argue. I know that you're both dying for my most intimate attention.'

'My tits are bigger than hers,' Melanie said, yanking her blouse open and exposing the firm bumps of her young breasts, her suckable nipples. 'Why don't you grope *my* tits?'

'I will,' Jim breathed, his cock now fully erect, his full balls rolling. 'To be fair, I'll grope both of you. I'll grope all four tits.'

'Cleo said that you might show us around your flat.'

'Yes, yes, of course I will.'

'Did I hear my name mentioned?' Cleo asked as she entered the bar.

'The girls want to see my flat,' Jim said, yanking his hand out of Carole's blouse.

'OK, I'll look after the bar.'

'Great. Er . . . come on, girls. This way to my den of . . . to my flat.'

'Have you got my bag, Cleo?' Carole asked the grinning barmaid.

'There we are,' Cleo said, passing the girl a carrier bag.

'What's that?' Jim breathed.

'Just something I left here. Shall we go?'

'Right, follow me.'

Leading the schoolgirls through the back room and up the stairs to his flat, Jim knew that his chance to use and abuse the little beauties had come at long last. Reckoning that they were naive and gullible, he decided to teach them the fine art of vulgar and obscene sexual acts. A rampant fanny-shagging followed by an anal rogering would be a good start, he mused, leading them through the front door to the bedroom. The girls had made out that they were extremely sexual and up for anything, but Jim was sure that it was all talk and they were almost as pure as the driven snow.

Apart from the business of using a candle for cunny-fucking, that was.

'Strip off, then.' Carole giggled, placing her bag on the floor by the double bed.

'Oh, er . . . right,' Jim chuckled, hurriedly unbuttoning his shirt. 'I thought you wanted to see the flat, but—'

'Fuck the flat,' she retorted, winking at Melanie.

'It's your cock we want to see,' Melanie slurred, leaning on the door frame to steady her swaying body.

'Mmm, very nice,' Carole trilled, eyeing Jim's erect cock as he finally stood naked in front of her. 'OK, lie on the bed.'

Taking his position on the bed and spreading his limbs, Jim couldn't stop grinning as he watched Melanie slipping her blouse over her shoulders, fully exposing the petite mounds of her young breasts. With small breasts, a hairless pussy, a boyish figure, hair dark hair framing her angelic face . . . she really did look young. Too fucking young to fuck, Jim mused, focusing on the fleshy swell of her vaginal lips. But, at that moment, nothing mattered other than appeasing his rampant cock, draining his sperm-brimming balls. Too young to drink but old enough to fuck?

As the girl stood beside the bed, showing off her naked body, Jim focused on the naked lips of her vulva. Her vaginal hillocks were incredibly puffy, the pale skin tinted pink, he observed as she moved closer, giving him a better view of the most intimate part of her teenage body. Standing proud from her hairless vulval flesh, her outer labia pressed together like a tightly closed mouth, concealing the inner lips of her vagina. She was exquisite in every way, he mused, gazing at the gentle rise of her stomach, the beautiful indent of her navel. Her young

body unblemished in youth, she was a picture of angelic innocence.

As the dark-haired girl moved away, Jim turned his head and gazed at Carole's naked body. Her small breasts topped with delicious milk teats, the lips of her pussy swollen in her desire below the delicate rise of her smooth mons, she was another picture of feminine beauty. Her long blonde hair cascading over her naked shoulders, caressing the petite mounds of her teenage breasts, her feminine form was all a man could want. Her boyish figure somehow accentuating her youthful fem-ininity, she was eminently fuckable. Far *more* than any man could want.

Taking several lengths of rope from her carrier bag, Carole giggled as she pulled Jim's hands behind his head and bound his wrists to the brass bedstead. Parting his feet wide and securing his ankles with rope, she finally stood back and admired her handiwork. Jim said nothing as the girls stood either side of the bed, showing off their petite breasts, their ripening milk teats. Feasting his wide eyes on the sheer beauty of their naked bodies, he didn't care what they planned to do with him. Besides, he was rather partial to a little bondage.

'Now you're at our mercy,' Carole said, slipping the candle out of her tight pussy and sitting beside Jim's naked body. Running her fingertips over the heaving sac of his scrotum, she giggled. 'Completely at our mercy.'

'Indeed you are,' Melanie confirmed, sitting the other side of Jim.

'Then go for it,' Jim chuckled. 'I'm all yours. Do with me as you wish.'

'Oh, we will,' Carole murmured, grabbing his solid cock by its base. 'Believe me, we will.'

Relaxing as the girls ran their hands over his naked body, Jim closed his eyes and relished the intimate attention. This was what life was all about, he thought happily, his cock-shaft twitching beneath the girls' caressing fingertips. Far away from his crazy wife and her lesbian desires, this was a dream come true. The perfume of fresh pussy filling his nostrils as the blonde knelt either side of his head and lowered the pouting lips of her hairless vulva over his mouth, Jim pushed his tongue out and tasted the girl's most intimate crevice.

Savouring the teenager's sex juices, Jim lapped at Carole's open hole as she writhed and gasped above him. She really was a horny little slut, he thought, pushing his tongue deep into the tight sheath of her pussy. Her juices of desire streaming from the pinken entrance to her hot love-hole, running in rivers of milk over his face, she squirmed and whimpered as she ground her cuntal flesh hard against Jim's mouth. Looking up at the schoolgirl's mammary mounds as he tongue-fucked her sweet cunt, he focused on the erect teats of her suckable nipples. The naked beauty was heaven-sent, that was certain, he thought, watching as she pinched and twisted the sensitive brown protrusions of her tits.

Wondering what Melanie was doing, Jim worked on Carole's solid clitoris as she swivelled her hips and aligned her pleasure spot with his open mouth. Licking and sucking on the rock-hard protuberance, the warm lips of the blonde girl's vulva pressing against his face, he realized that he'd had more sex in a day or two here than in his entire five-year marriage. He knew that, at long last, he'd found his sexual heaven. Feeling Melanie's fingertips running up and down the solid shaft of his

cock, he hoped that the dark-haired girl was going to take his purple knob into her mouth. There was nothing better than a mouth-fucking from a schoolgirl, he thought, repeatedly sweeping his tongue over the swollen nub of Carole's sensitive clitoris.

'Coming,' Carole cried, her milky juices of desire streaming from her hot cunt and flooding Jim's face. Rocking her hips, grinding her pulsating clitoris hard against Jim's mouth, she threw her head back and shook uncontrollably as her girl-pleasure erupted within the solid protrusion of her clit. Almost suffocating Jim as she slid her hot vulval flesh back and forth over his cunny-wet face, smothering his mouth and nose, she reached down and yanked her pussy lips wide apart to fully expose her cumbud.

Again and again, the girl cried out as she rode the crest of her climax. Flooding Jim's face with her orgasmic cream, grinding the intricate folds of her young vagina hard against his mouth, she finally stilled her naked body. Quivering as Jim sucked out the last ripples of sex from her deflating clitoris, her blonde hair veiling her flushed face, Carole breathed heavily in the aftermath of her coming. Locking his lips to the pinken funnel of flesh surrounding her vaginal hole, Jim sucked out her lubricious juices of lust, drinking from the sexual centre of her teenage body and draining her hot vagina.

'Argh,' Jim gasped through a mouthful of vaginal flesh as Melanie sank her teeth into the rock-hard shaft of his penis. Biting his cock again, the girl let out a wicked giggle as Carole rolled to one side and collapsed in a heap on the bed. Unable to move, powerless to protect his genitalia as Melanie took the entire length of his cock into her hot mouth and positively *gnawed* at his veined shaft,

Jim pulled desperately at the restraining ropes. The girl was insane, he thought as she bit and nibbled on his organ.

'Christ,' he gasped, lifting his head and watching the girl eating his cock. 'Take it easy.'

'Take it easy?' Carole murmured, propping herself up on her elbows. 'We haven't even started yet. Melanie, get the whip from the bag.'

'Fucking right,' Melanie giggled as she slipped Jim's cock out of her mouth. 'I love whipping cock.'

'Whipping . . .' Jim breathed, his dark eyes widening.

'She has a thing about whipping and eating cocks,' Carole said, again kneeling with her thighs either side of Jim's head. 'While she's whipping your cock, you can lick out my arse.'

Parting her firm buttocks, Carole lowered her young body, aligning the tightly closed brown ring of her anus with Jim's gasping mouth. Breathing in the arousing scent of her anal gully, he followed the dirty girl's instruction and pushed his tongue out. Tasting the slut there, licking the bitter-sweet eye of her bottom-hole, he breathed deeply through his nose as Melanie sucked the purple globe of his cock deep into her wet mouth. Sure that she wasn't going to whip his penis, he pushed his tongue deep into Carole's anal hole and licked the dank walls of her rectum as she quivered and writhed above him.

The schoolgirls were far from innocent, Jim reflected as Melanie almost swallowed his purple globe and Carole yanked her naked buttocks further apart to allow his tongue deep access to her inner core. Dirty, filthy, tartish, sluttish, slaggish, whorish cumsluts . . . They were perfect in every way. Savouring the aphrodisiacal

taste of Carole's sweet bottom-hole as Melanie giggled on his swollen cock-head, Jim thought again how lucky he was to have found such bliss in Willycombe Village. But he had to discover the secrets of this rural haven. There was far more to Willycombe than met the eye.

'I'll have to whip your cock,' Melanie said, slipping Jim's knob out of her hot mouth. 'Sorry, but I just can't fucking help it.' His tethered body convulsing as a leather strap swished through the air and flailed the solid shaft of his penis, Jim again reckoned that the girl was insane. Stifling his moans, his pleas for mercy, Carole forced her bottom-hole harder against Jim's mouth as her young friend continued with the gruelling cock-thrashing. Unable to defend his reddening cock or protest, Jim squirmed on the bed as the leather strap repeatedly swished through the air and cracked across his burning cock-shaft.

'Now fuck yourself,' Carole breathed, eyeing Jim's glowing cock. 'Go on, Melanie. Force his cock up your arse and fuck yourself.'

'You'll have to wet my arsehole for me,' the other girl said, standing with her feet either side of Jim's hips and bending over. 'Lick my arsehole and make it wet.'

'You're such a sweet little thing,' Carole murmured as Melanie yanked the pert cheeks of her bottom wide apart. 'You love my tongue up your arse, don't you?'

'Fucking right,' she replied. 'Tongue-fuck my bottom and then I'll fuck my arse with his cock.'

Leaning forward, Carole licked her young friend's anal eye, wetting her tight hole in readiness for Jim's solid cock. Continuing his own anal licking, Jim could hardly believe the depths the girls were sinking to in their quest for debauched sex. Where the hell had they learned such

depraved acts? he wondered, pushing his tongue deeper
into Carole's tight rectal canal. Was there nothing they
wouldn't do in their search for debased sexual gratification? Wishing that his hands were free, Jim imagined
forcing two fingers deep into Carole's tight anal canal.
But the girls were in charge, he mused. He was their
plaything, their sex toy.

'Now I'm ready for his beautiful cock,' Melanie
gasped as she moved forward, slipping Carole's tongue
out of her well-salivated bottom-hole. 'God, he's fucking
big. I hope I can get it all in.'

'Of course you can,' Carole laughed. 'You took that
fucking great church candle up your arse, so you'll easily
take his cock.'

'I hope so,' the other girl breathed, squatting over the
solid shaft of Jim's penis. 'I really do love a good arse-
fuck.'

Grabbing Jim's cock and pressing his purple glans
hard against her tight anal ring, Melanie eased his penile
bulb past her anal sphincter muscles and let out a rush of
breath as his bulbous knob slipped into her rectum. Jim
could feel the burning heat of her dank anal tube as she
lowered her trembling body. His cock-head journeying
along her rectal sheath towards the inner depths of her
bowels, he pushed his tongue deep into Carole's tight
bottom-hole and licked her inner flesh. This was debauchery beyond belief, he thought, the girl's anal duct
spasming as he woke her sleeping nerve endings with the
tip of his tongue.

'Fucking hell,' Melanie cried, the taut flesh of her
rectal ring gripping the root of Jim's cock as she impaled
herself fully on his love staff. 'I've never had such a
fucking great cock up my fucking arse.' This was more

like it, Jim mused, delighting in the savoury taste of
Carole's rectal canal. Cock-whipping was all very well,
but arse-fucking a young schoolgirl was incredible. Melanie was so tight, he thought as her rectum spasmed,
crushing his veined shaft. But that was her youth, he
knew as she raised her young body.

His cock sliding out of her anal duct until the delicate
tissue of her anus barely hugged the tip of his knob, Jim
let out a gasp as she lowered her body, his knob again
gliding deep into the fiery heat of her bowels. Bouncing
up and down, finding her anal-fucking rhythm, Melanie
let out whimpers with every rectal impalement by his
granite-hard cock. Her rounded buttocks repeatedly
meeting his rolling balls, the bed rocking, Jim tongue-
fucked Carole's contracting bottom-hole as the blonde
girl fervently massaged her solid clitoris.

Forced to breathe in the perfume of Carole's anal
crevice as he tongue-fucked her, this was a first for
Jim. Never had he slipped his tongue into a girl's rectal
hole, never had he savoured the intoxicating fragrance of
a teenage girl's anal valley. Lost in his desire as Melanie
bounced up and down on his penile shaft, fucking her
sweet bottom-hole, he closed his eyes and drowned in the
warm ocean of his lust.

Feeling Carole's vaginal juices streaming down his
chin as he tongued her dank bottom-hole and she frigged
her solid clitoris, he knew that the girl was close to her
self-induced orgasm as she began whimpering in her
soaring arousal. He, too, was close to pumping his fresh
spunk deep into Melanie's bowels as the dark-haired girl
increased her bouncing rhythm, repeatedly ramming his
bulbous knob into the very core of her naked body.
These girls weren't just whorish sluts, Jim mused. They

weren't simply a couple of dirty, filthy little tarts. They were the epitome of female decadence. He'd been very wrong in his surmise that they were naive and gullible, he reflected happily. He should have known better, he thought as his cock swelled deep within Melanie's hot rectum. Any girl who goes to pub without knickers and a massive candle stuffed up her cunt was far from innocent.

His face flooding with Carole's orgasmic juices as she frigged her clitty to a massive orgasm, Jim reached his climax and pumped his spunk deep into Melanie's anal canal as the girl bounced up and down on his solid cockshaft. The room echoing with the sounds of female orgasm as Melanie massaged her clitoris to eruption, the slurping sound of sex filling the air, Jim had never known such sexual debauchery. Again and again his throbbing glans thrust deep into Melanie's contracting rectal sheath, his spunk jetting from his knob-slit, flooding the girl's bowels as she massaged tremors of pleasure from her pulsating clitty.

This was amazing, he thought as he tongue-fucked Carole's tight anal hole. Only his second day at the pub and he'd already fucked Cleo's mouth, shagged the vicar's daughter, and was now enjoying the intimate attention of two horny little schoolgirl slags. But he'd still not discovered the mysteries of Willycombe Village. The vicarage, the dungeon . . . What and where was the dungeon? he wondered as his spent cock slowly deflated within the wet heat of Melanie's tight rectum.

'Fucking brilliant,' Melanie gasped, finally stilling her young body with Jim's knob embedded deep within her young arse. 'I'm fucked, fully spunked and—'

'I want it up *my* arse,' Carole breathed, clambering off

Jim's face and settling by his side. 'Come on,' she giggled, slapping his flaccid cock. 'Stiffen up – and then you can give *me* a good arse-fucking.'

'You'll have to wait a minute,' Jim laughed, the taste of the girl's anus lingering on his tongue. 'Just give me a minute to recover, and I'll arse-fuck you rotten.'

'I like you,' Carole said, smiling at Jim. 'You're all right.'

'Tell me,' he breathed, reckoning that the time had come for a few subtle questions. 'When will you next be going to the dungeon?'

'I don't know,' she replied uneasily. 'I mean, I'm not really interested in history, so . . .'

'History?' Jim murmured, frowning at her.

'Traipsing round a museum isn't much fun.'

'What the fuck are you talking about?' Melanie giggled: 'A fucking museum? It's a fucking dungeon, not a—'

'Shut the fuck up, Melanie,' Carole hissed.

'Why don't we all go there?' Jim asked, determined to discover more about the dungeon.

'I don't want to go to the dungeon,' Carole snapped crossly, leaping off the bed and grabbing her clothes. 'I don't know why you keep on about it.'

'Where are you going?' Melanie asked her friend.

'Down to the bar. It sounds as if the netball-team girls have arrived.'

As the blonde girl dressed and left the room, Jim grinned at Melanie. If anyone was going to blurt out the truth about the dungeon and the village, it was big-mouth Melanie. Watching as she untied the ropes, Jim reckoned that she'd open up now that Carole had gone. She was a rare beauty, he thought, eyeing the roundness

of her pert buttocks as she bent over and grabbed her clothes from the floor. Sperm oozing between her firm arse-cheeks and running in milky rivers down her slender thighs, she was in dire need of a damned good spanking, Jim decided as he clambered off the bed. Taking her arm, he kissed her full mouth and pulled her naked body close to his.

'Why don't you lie on the bed?' he asked her.

'Well, I . . . aren't we going down to the bar?'

'In a minute,' he said, easing her down onto the bed. 'I want to show you how I fuck,' he chuckled, rolling her onto her stomach and spreading her limbs. 'How I *really* fuck.'

'All right,' she giggled, allowing Jim to bind her wrists and ankles to the bed. 'But we mustn't be too long. Carole gets pissed off if I—'

'Don't you worry your pretty little head about Carole,' Jim laughed, focusing on the firm mounds of Melanie's naked bottom.

Settling between her parted legs, he pulled the rounded cheeks of her firm buttocks wide apart and gazed at the creamy sperm oozing from the inflamed eye of her anus. Massaging the swell of her fleshy vaginal cushions bulging between her young thighs, Jim cast his gaze over her slender body. She was young, he mused again. Very young. But she was also very sexual, and very naughty. Naughty little schoolgirlies had to be punished, he thought, ramming two fingers into the tightening sheath of her vagina as she gasped and squirmed on the bed. Her naked body bound with rope, her sex holes bared, completely defenceless, she was ready for a damned good fucking. And a merciless thrashing.

5

'Did you go up to the flat?' Cleo asked Carole.

'Yes, but the door's locked. I hammered and shouted but they ignored me.'

'You should never have left Melanie alone with Jim,' Cleo sighed, pouring another round of drinks for the netball team. 'You know that she can't keep her bloody mouth shut.'

'Isn't there a spare key to the flat?'

'No, there isn't. He's probably getting her to talk about the dungeon.'

'Does it matter if he finds out?' the blonde girl breathed, downing another vodka. 'He seems all right to me. I don't think he'll cause trouble.'

'Yes, it *does* matter. As you say, he seems all right. But we don't really *know* him, do we? All we know is that he worked at the brewery and he lived in London.'

'Yes, but I still don't see that it matters. OK, so he finds out about the dungeon. So what?'

'He might go shouting his mouth off. He might have friends in London and start blabbing to them about the dungeon.'

'We don't know that Melanie has said anything yet, so I don't think we need to worry.'

'Carole, you know Melanie as well as I do. She's a blabbermouth. In fact, I wish we'd never involved her in

this. Anyway, it's not just the dungeon we have to worry about. We also have to consider the convent. Christ, if news of the convent . . . It doesn't bear thinking about.'

'You're leaping too far ahead,' Carole said. 'Even if Melanie does talk, there's no saying that Jim will go shouting his mouth off to everyone.'

'Carole, there are things that even *you* don't know about Willycombe Village.'

'Such as?'

'I'm not saying anything. There are also things that *I* don't know. Take this pub, for example. It's been running at a loss for years.'

'Yes, but this is our base, isn't it? This is where—'

'What's that got to do with it? No one at the brewery knows about the dungeon, so why keep the pub on? If they knew what was going on and they were a part of it, then I could understand why they wouldn't close the pub. This place doesn't only run at a loss. The brewery continually plough money into it to keep it going. Why do they bother?'

'You work for them, so you should know. You get on all right with that Hops bloke. He owns the brewery so why don't you ask him?'

'I . . . I can't ask him.'

'Have you got something going with him?'

'Fuck off,' Cleo snapped. 'Of course I fucking haven't.'

'Sorry, I only asked.'

'No, no . . . I'm sorry, Carole. I shouldn't have flown at you like that. Do you want to give me a hand by collecting the empty glasses from the tables?'

'Yes, of course.'

'Christ only knows what Jim's doing. I was hoping

that he'd be helping me, not fucking about with a young girl for half the afternoon.'

Eyeing the thin weals fanning out across Melanie's naked bottom, Jim chuckled. The whip had come in most useful, he thought, watching the sobbing girl's tethered body trembling on the bed. But she wouldn't tell him what he wanted to know. Even after a few stinging lashes of the leather strap, she was determined not to say anything about the dungeon. Focusing on the creamy fluid seeping between the tightly closed lips of her hairless vulva, Jim decided to give her another severe thrashing and discover all there was to know about the village before spunking her young cervix. Raising the leather strap above his head, he asked her again what and where the dungeon was.

'I don't know,' Melanie sobbed, her tear-streaked face looking up at him. 'I've heard about the place, but I don't know where it is.'

'What have you heard?'

'It's some kind of museum.'

'No, it's not,' he snapped. 'You laughed when Carole said that it was a museum. Come on, Melanie. All you have to do is tell me about the dungeon and you'll save yourself from a most severe and gruelling thrashing.'

'I don't know . . .'

'All right, all right. Have it your way. Perhaps you enjoy the whip? Is that it? You enjoy the feel of the leather strap across your sweet bottom and—'

'No.'

'There's a washing-up-liquid bottle in the kitchen. A huge plastic bottle, Melanie. I wonder whether you'd enjoy having it forced up your tight little arse?' Remain-

ing silent, the girl buried her face in the quilt. 'I have some butter in the fridge,' Jim chortled. 'I could grease your tight little arsehole and then force the bottle deep into your bowels. What do you say?'

Bringing the leather whip down across the shaking girl's rounded buttocks with a deafening crack, Jim was determined to thrash the truth out of the little slut. He knew damned well that Carole wouldn't reveal anything about the dungeon. And there was no way that Cleo would spill the beans. Melanie was his only hope, he knew as he brought the leather strap down again across the glowing flesh of her tensed buttocks with a loud report. Her young body convulsing wildly with every lash of the whip, she could obviously take no more and cried out for mercy. Halting the gruelling naked-buttock thrashing, Jim asked her again about the dungeon. Remaining silent apart from her sobs, it was pretty obvious that despite the torture she was going to tell him nothing. But Jim wasn't bothered. The longer she held out, the more pleasure he'd derive from thrashing the burning cheeks of her pert bottom.

Taking a pillow, Jim managed to stuff it beneath the girl's hips, raising her quivering body from the bed. Her rounded bottom high in the air, perfectly positioned for the next bout of cruel buttock-thrashing, he eyed the full lips of her hairless pussy bulging between her slender thighs. Her vaginal cream flowing freely from her sex crack, pooling on the quilt, he looked down at the shaft of his solid cock and grinned. The girl was defenceless and his cock was up for another crude fucking. But not until the girl had endured another merciless whipping.

'Please, no more,' Melanie cried as Jim brought the

leather whip down again across the fire-red flesh of her stinging bottom. 'Please . . .'

'All you have to do is tell me about the dungeon,' he said, holding the whip above his head.

'I . . . I can't tell you about the fucking dungeon. I don't fucking know anything about it.'

'You lie, Melanie. OK, tell me about the vicarage.'

'I've never been to the fucking vicarage. I've never met the fucking vicar, let alone—'

'All right,' Jim cut in. 'Tell me about the convent.'

'It's a school, my school. That's all there is to tell.'

'You're asking for another severe thrashing, Melanie,' he warned her, running the leather whip along the gully of her buttocks. 'Something's going on in this village, and you're going to tell me all about it.'

'Are you fucking deaf? I've told you, I know nothing about . . . Where are you going?'

'To get the washing-up-liquid bottle from the kitchen. I'll try thrashing the truth out of you with the bottle forced up your tight little arse.'

Returning with the plastic bottle and a tub of butter, Jim settled on the bed beside the trembling girl. Parting the burning cheeks of her tensed bottom, he smeared a handful of butter over her anal inlet. Tensing her muscles, trying desperately to close the valley of her young bottom, she knew that the enforced insertion of the plastic bottle was inevitable as Jim eased the cheeks of her bottom wide apart. Smearing more butter up and down her anal gully, massaging the grease into the brown tissue of her anus, he eased two fingers deep into her tight rectum.

'Your tight arse is already bubbling with my spunk,' he chuckled, massaging her inner rectal flesh. 'With a

good helping of butter mixed with my spunk, the bottle will glide into your bum with ease.'

'All right, I'll tell you about the convent,' she finally conceded.

'Go on.'

'Some of the girls have formed a club. They take vodka back from the pub and have all-night drinking sessions in their dorm.'

'And?'

'That's it.'

'The dungeon?'

'I don't know anything about the dungeon.'

Greasing her anal tube, forcing the butter deep into her bottom-hole, Jim finally slipped his fingers out and grabbed the plastic bottle. All-night drinking sessions, he chuckled inwardly. She was lying, he knew as he focused on the tightly closed eye of her bottom. But he'd force the truth out of her if it was the last thing he did. The girl protested as he pushed the container's flat end hard against the delicate brown tissue of her anal ring. Squirming on the bed, pulling against her bonds, she whimpered as he forced her buttocks apart to the extreme. There was nothing she could do to prevent the cruel abuse of her rectum, she knew as she held her breath and squeezed her eyes shut. Nothing, other than tell Jim what he wanted to know.

'Please . . .' she gasped, her anus dilating painfully as the bottle opened her anal eye. 'Please, no.'

'All you have to do is tell me about the dungeon,' Jim told her again, watching her anal inlet open wide as the bottle began to slide into her well-greased hole. 'Once the bottle is forced deep into your arse, I'll push another one

into your tight cunt and then thrash you again. What's it to be, Melanie?'

'Go to fucking hell,' she gasped.

'I was rather hoping you'd say that,' he chuckled. 'That means that I'll have to carry out my threat and torture your beautiful sex-holes.'

Pushing the plastic bottle fully home, Jim decided that the time had come to drain his balls again. Positioning himself between the girl's splayed thighs, he grabbed his solid cock by the root and pushed his purple knob between the firm, hairless lips of her vagina. Driving his cock-shaft deep into the fiery heat of Melanie's teenage cunt until his lower belly pressed against the exposed end of the bottle, he let out a wicked chuckle as she whimpered and writhed beneath him. He could feel the bottle pressing against his cock through the thin membrane dividing the slut's lust-sheaths, her ripe cervix rubbing against the bulbous glans of his rock-hard cock. This was going to be an excellent fuck, he knew as her vaginal muscles contracted, lovingly hugging his huge organ.

'I'll fucking tear open,' she breathed, her muscles spasming wildly, gripping his huge cock, crushing the bottle. 'For fuck's sake, take the fucking bottle out before I—'

'With your arse stretched by the bottle, your cunt is as tight as a virgin's,' Jim gasped, withdrawing his cock and ramming his swollen glans into her young body. 'Of course, you've long since forgotten what it's like to be a virgin, haven't you?'

'I don't care what you do to me, I won't say anything.'

'Oh yes, you will, Melanie,' he chuckled. 'Before you leave here, you'll have told me all you know about the

dungeon. God, I'm looking forward to shagging your tight schoolgirlie cunt. This is going to be the best fuck ever.'

'It'll be your *last* fuck ever.'

'This is the first of many, my girl. I'll fuck your sweet holes every day, fuck and spunk your bottom, your cunt, your mouth . . .'

'Not if the Reverend Mother has anything to do with it.'

'What do you mean by that?' Jim asked her.

'Nothing.'

Increasing the force and speed of his fucking motion, repeatedly propelling his bulbous knob deep into Melanie's vaginal tube, Jim let out a chuckle. At that moment, he didn't care whether the girl revealed the village's secrets or not. *The Reverend Mother?* he pondered. What on earth could some fat old hag-bag do about it? The girl would hardly go running to the woman with her tales of cruel whipping and orgasmic fucking. The girl's naked body rocking with the enforced pistoning of her vagina, Jim grinned. Melanie thought that she could threaten Jim with the Reverend Mother. But, as far as he was concerned, it was the other way round. He held all the cards, he mused, the squelching sound of the girl's cunny juices resounding around the room. If the old bag knew about Melanie and Carole, the way they went around with no knickers, there'd be big trouble. If the woman discovered the truth about her not-so-innocent young schoolgirlies, the crude abuse of huge candles, there'd be a series of expulsions from the convent. Jim was looking forward to meeting the Reverend Mother.

His sperm pump bursting into action, he repeatedly

rammed his throbbing knob deep into the wailing girl's contracting vagina, bathing her cervix with his orgasmic cream. She was tight, hot, and extremely horny, he thought as she struggled against her bonds. Jim's lower stomach repeatedly pressed against the plastic bottle and rammed the huge phallus deep into Melanie's rectum each time he propelled his spunking knob into her young cunt. She cried out as her orgasm erupted within the swollen nub of her erect clitoris.

'Yes,' she breathed, writhing on the bed as her climax shook her very soul. 'Fuck me senseless.' Jim needed no encouragement as he swung his hips and fucked the teenager with a vengeance. Filling her vaginal cavity with his creamy sperm, draining his heavy balls, he continued to fuck the girl in his sexual frenzy. Melanie breathed incoherent words of lust as she rode the crest of her orgasm. Shaking uncontrollably, her anal sphincter muscles rhythmically contracting, crushing the plastic bottle, she finally shuddered her last shudder and lay quivering uncontrollably in the aftermath of her crudely enforced coming.

'God, I needed that,' Jim breathed, withdrawing his cunny-slimed cock from the heat of the girl's inflamed cunt.

'Let me go now,' Melanie gasped, pulling again at the ropes.

'Oh, no,' Jim chuckled. 'Not until you've told me—'

'Jim,' Carole called, hammering on the flat's door. 'Jim, you're wanted in the bar. There's someone here to see you.'

'I won't be a minute,' he replied, leaping off the bed and dressing hurriedly.

'Let me go,' Melanie asked him again.

'I'll be back very soon to thrash you and fuck you senseless,' he chuckled, leaving the room and closing the door.

Leaving the flat, Jim was about to make his way downstairs to the bar when he noticed Carole lurking in the shadows behind a pile of boxes on the landing. There was no one waiting in the bar, he was sure as he descended the stairs, trying to look as though he hadn't noticed the blonde girl. Turning and creeping back to the flat, he saw Carole slip through the front door. She'd obviously gone to rescue her young friend, he thought, following her and hovering outside the bedroom door. Perhaps she too was in dire need of a good buttock-whipping?

'What did you tell him?' Carole asked Melanie.

'Nothing,' the other girl replied. 'Untie these bloody ropes and . . .'

'Are you *sure* that you didn't tell him anything?' Carole persisted as Jim spied through the crack in the door.

'Of course I fucking didn't.'

'I know you, Melanie. You and your big mouth . . .'

'Will you *please* untie these fucking ropes?'

'No, I won't. What did you tell him?'

'For fuck's sake, Carole . . . He asked me about the dungeon and I said that it was a museum. He asked me about the convent and I said that some of the girls had formed a drinking club. And that's it.'

'I don't believe you,' Carole snapped, grabbing the end of the plastic bottle and ramming it deep into the girl's rectal duct. 'I reckon that you told him about the dungeon.'

'You're fucking mad. And deaf. I didn't tell him *anything*.'

'He whipped you, didn't he?' Carole murmured, running her fingertips over the firm flesh of Melanie's glowing buttocks. 'And now *I*'m going to whip you.'

'*What*? For fuck's sake . . .'

'I'll thrash the truth out of you, Melanie.'

'I've told you the fucking truth. I said that the Reverend Mother . . .'

'I knew it. You blabbed about her, didn't you? You told him that she runs the . . . Right, that's it.'

Grabbing the whip, Carole raised it above her head and brought it down across the other girl's taut buttocks. The plastic bottle shooting out of her inflamed rectal canal like a bullet, Melanie let out a scream as the leather strap bit once more into the glowing flesh of her naked bottom. Watching the delightful lesbian thrashing, Jim pondered on Carole's words. *You blabbed about her, didn't you? You told him that she runs the . . .* Wondering what the Reverend Mother ran, he rubbed his chin. Did she run some kind of drinking club? Hardly, he reflected, the sound of the whip cracking across Melanie's twitching buttocks resounding throughout the flat. What would a hag-bag of an ageing Reverend Mother be up to that was apparently tantamount to a state secret?

Watching Carole discard the whip and settle on the bed between Melanie's parted thighs, Jim hoped that he was in for a lesbian show. On her knees with her bottom high in the air, Carole ran her tongue up and down the gully of Melanie's rounded buttocks. They'd obviously done this before, Jim thought as Melanie let out gasps of lesbian pleasure. Licking her young friend's inflamed bottom-hole, Carole thrust several fingers into the girl's sperm-flooded cunt and vigorously finger-fucked her. Listening to the slurping and squelching sounds of

lesbian sex, Jim felt his cock stiffen, his balls roll and heave, as Carole projected her bottom out. Her skirt rising up over her back and fully exposing the rounded cheeks of her pert bottom, the lips of her vulva bulging between her firm thighs, she was asking for a damned good anal rogering.

Wondering whether to join the girls in their sex games, Jim massaged his solid cock through his trousers. Carole's pussy lips were beautifully formed, he observed, focusing on the creamy liquid coursing down her gaping vaginal valley. Perfectly symmetrical, puffy, hairless, swollen . . . the girl's cunt looked good enough to eat, he thought, licking his lips as he imagined running his tongue up and down the drenched crevice of her vulva. About to walk into the room and ram his solid cock into the girl's inviting pussy, he hesitated as Carole murmured something about the Reverend Mother.

'She'll be here soon,' she said, lapping at Melanie's anal hole. 'So you'd better tell me what you said to Jim.'

'I didn't say anything,' Melanie sighed with exasperation.

'I'll bring her up here, shall I? You can tell her what you said to Jim.'

'For fuck's sake, Carole. How many fucking times do I have to tell you? Besides, you wouldn't dare to bring her up here!'

'Wouldn't I?'

'Of course not. You know what happened when she caught us hanging around the vicarage. If it hadn't been for Mary—'

'There you go again,' Carole cut in. 'Anyone could be listening and you're blabbing your fucking mouth off.'

'Of course no one's fucking listening, you daft bitch. I

wish you'd stop going on about what I said to Jim and get on with tongue-fucking my arse.'

'I'll *whip* your fucking arse in a minute.'

'Promises, promises.'

Slipping down the stairs, Jim checked his watch. It was almost five o'clock, and he decided to take a look at the vicarage before the evening session in the bar got under way. Making his way through the sexy girlies dressed in their netball gear as he headed for the pub's exit, he hoped that the team would still be there when he got back. It was a shame to have to go out when the pub was heaving with netball sluts, he mused as he made his way down the lane. Torn between the impulse to return to the pub and grope the girls' young breasts and the urge to satisfy his curiosity by investigating the vicarage, Jim knew that he had to discover what was going on. Business before pleasure?

Creeping around the side of the old house, hoping that the vicar wasn't in, he slipped into the back garden and spied through the kitchen window. He wasn't going to learn anything by gazing at the cooker, he knew as he tried the back door. Turning the handle, he grinned as the door swung open. Perhaps the man of God trusted the locals, he thought, wondering whether there was anything in the house worth stealing as he crept through the kitchen into the hall. More to the point, was the vicar hoarding a gaggle of dirty girlies? The vicarage harboured secrets, of that he was sure.

'Can I help you?' the vicar asked, emerging from the dining room.

'Oh, er . . .' Jim stammered, gazing at the becassocked man. 'I was just . . . Er . . . I'm Jim Foster. Landlord of the Tartan Vicar.'

'Do you normally creep around people's houses like this?'

'Yes . . . No, no. The back door was open. I called out but . . .'

'Landlord of the public house, eh? I can't abide alcohol. The evils of drink lead to vulgar pleasures of the flesh. Filthy drinking dens where Jezebels lurk and—'

'I couldn't agree more, Father. I can't abide drinking and Jezebelling.'

'But you run a public house.'

'It's a front.'

'A front?' the cleric echoed, his beady eyes staring hard at Jim. 'What do you mean?'

'I've taken over the pub as part of my quest to stop people drinking. I'm head of Tits.'

'Tits? Good grief, man . . .'

'T I T S. The Independent Teetotal Society. Running the pub puts me in the front line. I come into contact with the enemy, talk directly to the drinkers and, hopefully, correct their wicked ways.'

'I see. Well, that's admirable. Most admirable.'

'I intend to win the war over the evils of alcohol and the obscene sexual abuse of schoolgirls . . . Jezebels. This is a lovely house. Have you been here long?'

'Twenty years,' the vicar replied, leading Jim into the dining room. 'My father was vicar of the parish before I took over. And my grandfather before him.'

'I never had a grandfather.'

'How sad.'

'Indeed. So, vicars run in the family?'

'You could say that.'

'Talking of families, I met your beautiful daughter,' Jim blurted out, immediately wishing he hadn't.

'Oh? Where was that?'

'In the pub . . . lic library. I don't mean I licked her in the library. I licked her in the pub . . . I met her in the public—'

'There is no library in Willycombe.'

'I met her on the village green. What a delightful girl she is.'

'She *was* a delightful girl,' the man sighed. 'I'm afraid she's gone off the rails. Since her mother left, she's been nothing but trouble.'

'It was a good job she left, then. If she was nothing but trouble . . .'

'My *daughter* has been nothing but trouble,' the vicar corrected Jim.

'Your wife *and* your daughter? I'm sorry to hear that.'

'So am I. I've tried to teach her the ways of Jesus, bring her up to be a good Christian, a decent young lady. But she won't have it.'

'I wouldn't say that,' Jim chuckled. 'She takes it right up her . . . I mean . . . Persevere, Father. I'm sure that, if you persevere, she'll listen to you and return to the fold.'

'She's a tearaway. She stays out all night, hangs around with boys, drinks and smokes . . .'

'Where is she now?'

'In her room, sulking because I won't allow her out. I just hope and pray that she defends her virginity for a while longer.'

'Huh, she's already lost her . . . er . . . I'd say that she's lost her way, Father. I'm rather good with young girls. I don't know why, but they listen to me. They readily open their . . . their minds.'

'Really?'

'Oh, yes. I used to run a Girl Guide group.'

'Surely you mean a Scout group?'

'No, no. I was called in when the Guides became restless and started taking an unhealthy interest in boys. Hormones, that's what it is. Although I say it myself, I'm exceptionally good with hormonal girls.'

'In that case, perhaps you'd talk to Mary?'

'Well, I . . . I am pretty good on the oral front.'

'It's worth trying. The poor girl's gushing with hormones.'

'Yes, I know.'

'You *know*?'

'Er . . . all girls of that age gush with hormones. It's only natural.'

'I'd appreciate it if you'd at least try talking to her.'

'I'd like to help, Father,' Jim sighed, hoping that the man would beg him to go to his daughter's bedroom.

'Then why don't you? Go up to her room. It's the first door on the right at the top of the stairs. You might be able to make her see sense.'

'Yes, I might be able to make her see something.'

'Guide her, Jim. You don't mind my calling you Jim?'

'Not at all. After all, it's what my mother called me. Among other things.'

'Show her the way, Jim.'

'Show my mother . . . Oh, you mean, Mary.'

'Show Mary the way.'

'She already knows the way,' Jim laughed. 'The way to God, I mean.'

'Mary needs someone like you to talk to her. I'm sure she'll open up for you.'

'I have no doubt about that. I've not yet come over a hormonal girl who hasn't opened up for me.'

'If you could get inside her . . .'

'I already have . . . have a way with girls.'

'Get inside her mind, Jim. Open her up and push into the very depths of her being.'

'Oh, I will,' Jim chuckled. 'I'll open her thighs and—'

'Open her thighs?' the priest gasped.

'Her *eyes*, Father. I'll open her eyes to the ways of God.'

'Oh, I see. I have great faith in you, Jim.'

'Thank you, Father.'

'I mean it. You're anti-drink, anti-debauching, you've led Girl Guides away from the evils of hormones and taken them along the path to righteousness . . . If anyone can get inside my daughter, *you* can. Seeing as you're an upright man, a man against the evils of drink and—'

'All right, I'll try,' Jim finally conceded, trying not to grin.

'Good man. I have some paperwork to be getting on with. I'll be in here if you need me.'

'Right, well . . . I'll go and get Mary to open her thighs . . . her eyes.'

Climbing the stairs, Jim thought for a moment and decided that he didn't reckon that the vicar was involved in anything untoward. He couldn't cope with his daughter, let alone get involved with the sluts from the convent. At least Jim had gained the man's trust and confidence. Now that he was well in with the cleric, he might be able to call at the house and go to Mary's room and have his wicked way with her whenever he felt the urge to fuck her. The vicar would readily agree to Jim going to the girl's room and getting her to open up.

Tapping on Mary's door, Jim was sure that the vicar had nothing to hide. So what was it about the vicarage? The place certainly wasn't a brothel or a drinking den.

Perhaps Mary was entertaining men in her room? he mused. There again, if that had been the case her father would have been bound to realize what the girl was up to. He'd never allow such goings-on in his house. So what secrets *did* the vicarage harbour? Whatever it was, Jim was sure that the vicar and his daughter weren't involved.

Gazing at Mary as she opened the door, Jim looked down at the petite mounds of her breasts partially revealed by her parted dressing gown. Her long blonde hair cascading over the silk gown, her fresh face smiling, her blue eyes sparkling lustfully, she looked stunning. Although somewhat bleary-eyed after her drinking binge and the rampant sex in Jim's flat, she was the epitome of teenage sexuality.

'Come in,' she invited him, opening the door wide. 'How the hell did you get in without my father—'

'He sent me to see you,' Jim said proudly as she closed the door behind him.

'He did *what*?' she gasped. 'He'd never allow a fucking man to come up to my room. What did you do? Punch his fucking lights out?'

'No, no. I told him that I wanted to fuck you. I mean, talk to you.'

'He's never allowed anyone to come up to my fucking room before. I don't understand it. He must trust you, fool that he is.'

'He said that you were sulking, Mary. What's the problem?'

'The cunt won't let me go out.'

'The cunt? Oh, I see. Where did you want to go?'

'To the pub. Not that I told prick-face that. It's Saturday night, for fuck's sake. I'll be stuck here with

fuck-all to do while my friends are getting pissed and fucked.'

'Pissed and fucked?'

'Pissed in the pub and fucked in the . . .'

'In the what?'

'Er . . . in the park or somewhere. It's not fair. Everyone's out having fun while I'm . . .'

'You *shall* go to the ball, Cinderella.'

'What?'

'Allow me to dress you, and I'll take you to the pub. It's a lovely evening. I'll tell your father that we're going out for a walk. I'll say that we're going out for a walk and then for a meal. He trusts me, cunt that he . . . I mean, fool that he is.'

'Fucking great,' she trilled, ripping her gown off.

'Good grief. You're absolutely—'

'Fucking beautiful?' she giggled.

'Yes. Absolutely fucking beautiful.'

Dropping to his knees and focusing on the swollen lips of the young girl's vulva, Jim felt his cock stiffen, his balls heave and roll within their hairy sac. Before taking her anywhere, he was going to have to fuck her senseless, he knew as she parted her feet wide and jutted her hips forward. Running his wet tongue over the warm cushions of her hairless outer labia, breathing in the aphrodisiacal perfume of her sweet pussy, he knew that she was heaven-sent. This was meant to be, he reflected. God must have smiled down on him.

Slipping his tongue into Mary's gaping valley of desire as she yanked her outer lips wide apart, he savoured the bitter-sweet taste of her inner folds as she let out a rush of breath. She tasted heavenly, he thought, sucking on the pink petals of her inner labia. God must have influenced

the vicar and allowed Jim to show the misguided girl to way to complete and utter debauchery. Perhaps it was Satan? Jim reflected. Yes, the chances were that Satan himself had influenced the vicar, he decided.

'That feels good,' Mary breathed, her naked body trembling. 'I've been stuck in here all day with nothing to fucking do except frig my clitty. It's good to have a man's tongue do the work for me.'

'My tongue will always work for you, Mary,' Jim chuckled. 'Tell me how you frig your clitty. Do you often masturbate?'

'All the fucking time. I just can't stop frigging. Candles, hairbrush handles, cucumbers, carrots, bananas . . . I fuck my cunt with anything and everything and frig my clit to massive orgasms.'

'You're quite a girl,' Jim laughed. 'If your father knew what went on here . . .'

'My father knows nothing about the fucking dungeon,' the girl blabbed. 'I mean . . .'

'Tell me about the dungeon, Mary.'

'I . . . I can't. I'm bound to secrecy.'

'Just tell me where it is,' Jim persisted, rising to his feet and kissing the ripe teats of her young breasts. 'Please, Mary. Just tell me where the dungeon is.'

Sitting on her bed, the girl hung her head as Jim waited for her to reveal the whereabouts of the mysterious dungeon. Wondering why she was sworn to secrecy, and by whom, he reckoned that the dungeon might well harbour something illegal. Sighing, Mary finally announced that she wasn't going to say anything about the dungeon. With the girl's father downstairs, Jim knew that he could hardly thrash the truth out of her. Perhaps he should fuck her senseless and get her to talk while she

was dizzy in a sexual daze, he mused. The girl was going to have to talk, he thought, determined not to be kept in the dark any longer. The convent girls seemed to know about the dungeon, and Jim was becoming increasingly disgruntled by the situation.

'Are we going to the fucking pub, then?' Mary asked him.

'Yes, yes, we are,' he murmured, deciding to take the girl to the woods and torture the truth out of her. 'What are you going to wear?'

'I have a summer dress,' she replied, moving to the wardrobe. 'It's very short, but it's a fucking warm evening.'

'Very nice,' he breathed as she grabbed the dress and held it against her naked body. 'No bra or panties, though.'

'Of course fucking not,' she giggled, tugging the dress over her head.

'Is that the dress you wear to the dungeon?'

'Either this or my miniskirt,' she murmured pensively, her mouth gaping as she realized what she'd said. 'I meant—'

'Come on,' Jim broke in. 'Let's go to the pub.'

6

Walking across the village green with Mary, Jim hoped that Cleo wasn't looking out of the pub window. Judging from the giggling coming from the pub, the netball team was still there. If Cleo knew that he was on his way to the woods to sexually abuse the vicar's daughter rather than help out in the bar, she'd probably go mad. But he wouldn't be long, he decided. A gruelling whipping and an enforced anal fucking, and Mary would reveal all she knew about the village and the dungeon.

'I don't know my way around yet,' Jim said as they headed towards the village school. 'Is there a park or woodland nearby?'

'The woods are behind the fucking school,' Mary replied. 'I used to play there when I was young. There's a fucking lovely spot near a stream and . . . I thought we were going to the fucking pub?'

'Yes, we are. But I'd like you to show me the woods first.'

'Do I fucking have to?' she whined.

'It won't take long, Mary. I'd like to take a look round and get to know a little about the village.'

'We could do that any time. I'm dying for a fucking vodka so let's—'

'It'll only take a minute,' Jim said, eyeing the ripe teats of Mary's breasts through her flimsy summer dress. 'The

pub doesn't close till eleven. Midnight, more like, if I know Cleo.'

Following Mary along a path beside the school, Jim reckoned that he'd discover all there was to know about the village within half an hour. The girl obviously knew about the dungeon, he mused as they entered the woods. A damned good naked-buttock-thrashing with a thin stick would make her cough up, he was sure. Wishing that he had several lengths of rope to tie her naked body to a tree, it occurred to him that Mary might have a secret spot where she took teenage lads for sessions of crude fucking. He needed somewhere secluded, he mused. A spot where dog-walkers wouldn't stumble across the sexual torture.

'This is a lovely place,' Jim said, breathing in the fragrance of pine as they trekked deeper into the woods. 'Where does this path lead?'

'To Royston Farm,' she murmured. 'The stream is just around the next fucking corner.'

'Ah, yes,' Jim chuckled as they followed the curve of the path and stood by a small stream. 'This is an ideal place for . . . for relaxing. Shall we sit here for a while?'

'I suppose so,' Mary sighed, plonking her rounded buttocks on the grass. 'I don't want to stay here for long, though. It's Saturday night and the fucking pub will be—'

'You're a beautiful girl Mary,' he interrupted her, eyeing the full lips of her hairless pussy nestling between her slender thighs as she rested her chin on her knees.

'You mean, my pussy is beautiful,' she returned. 'That's all men want. No one's interested in me, they just want my fucking cunt.'

'I'm sure that's not true,' Jim breathed, focusing on a

droplet of creamy liquid running down the tightly closed crack of her vulva. 'I'm sure that men find you not only attractive but good company.'

'All men want is my cunt. That's why you wanted to come here, isn't it? You just want to fuck me.'

'Of course I want to fuck you, Mary. You're a very fuckable young girl. But that's not the *only* reason I wanted to come here.'

'You want to find out about the fucking dungeon?'

'The dungeon doesn't interest me. I know all about the place, except where it is.'

'You *know* about it?'

'Of course I do. Cleo has told me everything, but she won't say where it is.' Deciding to make a wild guess, Jim smiled. 'I know that it has something to do with the vicarage,' he breathed. 'It's not beneath the house, is it?'

'I don't know,' Mary sighed.

'I don't suppose it is because your father—'

'He knows nothing about the fucking dungeon,' she cut in.

'There we are, then. It couldn't be beneath the vicarage. You've been there, haven't you?'

'I did go there once,' she confessed. 'I was taken there by . . . by someone. I was fucking blindfolded, so I have no idea where it is.'

'I'd like to take a look at the place. Just out of interest.'

'Just out of interest?' she giggled. 'If you know what goes on there, you'd hardly want to see the fucking place out of interest. Shall we go to the fucking pub now?'

'In a minute. Why don't you take your dress off and—'

'And let you fuck me? All right. But only a quick fuck. I'm dying for a bloody drink.'

'Just a quick fuck,' Jim agreed.

Grinning as Mary tugged her dress over her head and sat with her thighs wide apart, Jim eyed her naked body. It was a shame to have to cover the petite mounds of her young breasts with thin weals, he thought. But he was becoming increasingly angry at being left in the dark and could think of no other way to make her talk. Settling beside her as she lay on the ground, he ran his fingertips around the erect teats of her breasts. She was an extremely sensual girl, he mused as she responded to his intimate caress. Breathing heavily, her smooth stomach rising and falling, she was obviously revelling in his attention.

'I used to come here with my dance teacher,' she breathed.

'Oh?'

'She liked it here in the woods. She said that she could relax and let go beneath the pine trees.'

'What did you do? I mean, did you just sit here or . . .'

'She used to love me. I didn't mind her playing with me because she fucking paid me.'

'She *paid* you?' Jim asked, sure that he'd misheard the girl. 'Paid you for sex?'

'Yes. Nothing heavy, of course. Just licking and fingering and stuff.'

'This village really is an amazing place,' Jim chuckled. 'The pub, the convent school, the dungeon . . . And now I discover that the vicar's daughter had lesbian sex with her dance teacher.'

'Willycombe has always been the fucking same,' Mary breathed as Jim ran his fingers over the smooth plateau of her stomach to the gentle rise of her hairless mons.

'When did you get involved?'

'My dance teacher . . . She brought me here and then I

got to know about the dungeon . . . I mean, she told me that there was a—'

'I think it's time for sex,' Jim said, slipping his shirt off and unbuckling his belt.

Stripping off, he stood astride the girl with the solid shaft of his penis standing to attention. Mary looked up at his rolling balls, grinning as she licked her lips and parted her legs to the extreme. The crack of her vagina gaping wide open, her inner folds glistening in the sunlight streaming down through the trees, she was ready to be fucked senseless. Eyeing the branch of a bush lying on the ground, Jim sat beside the girl and suggested that she roll over onto her stomach so he could stroke the rounded cheeks of her young bottom. Readily complying, the mounds of her buttocks perfectly positioned for a gruelling thrashing, Jim grabbed the branch and sat on her back to pin her down.

'What the fuck are you doing?' she asked, lifting her head off the soft grass and trying to look at Jim. 'I can't fucking move.'

'That's the idea,' he chuckled, running the rough branch over the globes of her naked bottom. 'Now, are you going to tell me where the dungeon is?'

'God, not that again,' she sighed. 'I don't know where the fucking place is, OK?'

'But you do, Mary. And you're going to tell me.'

Raising the branch above his head, Jim brought it down across the pale moons of Mary's young bottom with a loud crack. The birds fluttering from the trees as the second deafening report resounded throughout the woods, the girl screamed her protests. Ignoring her, Jim continued the cruel thrashing of her tensed buttocks, his solid cock twitching as he thought about driving his

swollen knob between her glowing cheeks and deep into the tight sheath of her rectum. Again and again, he brought the branch down, watching as thin weals fanned out across her burning flesh until her screams were loud enough to wake the dead.

'Where is the dungeon?' he asked her, halting the thrashing.

'Beneath the vicarage,' she sobbed. 'Beneath the fucking house.'

'*Now* we're getting somewhere,' he chuckled. 'So, where's the entrance?'

'I don't fucking know.'

'It's in the house, obviously. In which case, your father must know about it.'

'Of course he doesn't fucking know,' she retorted, struggling to free herself.

'He *must* know. If there's a dungeon beneath his house, a dungeon that half the people in the village know about . . .'

'You can't get to it from the fucking house. I don't know where the entrance is, but it's not in the fucking house.'

'The fucking garden,' Jim murmured pensively. 'It must be in the fucking garden. I do wish you'd stop swearing. You're leading me into bad habits.'

'*Me* leading *you*?' Mary laughed mockingly. 'Fuck off.'

'What happens in the dungeon?'

'I thought you said that you knew all about it?'

'I lied.'

'Nothing happens there. It's just a place where people go to fuck.'

'Is that all?'

'What more do you fucking want? It's a safe place for

fucking. Married men go there and fuck their girlfriends. That's why it's such a big secret.'

'I see,' Jim murmured. 'But what I *don't* see is why no one would tell me about the place.'

'You're new here. You're not going to be told fucking everything about the village the minute you fucking arrive, are you?'

'No, but . . . I'd have thought that Cleo would have told me.'

'You're making a fucking mountain out of a fucking molehill.'

'Am I?'

'You go on about the dungeon as if it's a bank vault and you want to get in there to rob the place. It's a dingy old dungeon used by people who want to fuck in private. And, before you ask again, I don't know where the fucking entrance is.'

Climbing off the girl's back and sitting beside her as she rolled over, Jim wondered whether he was making too much of the dungeon. If married men cheated on their wives there, he could well understand the secrecy. But there was more to the village than the dungeon, he reflected. Or was there? Cleo sucked cocks through the hole in the bar. But wasn't that simply her little sideline? The convent schoolgirls were all rampant nympho-maniacs. But weren't most hormone-bubbling teenage schoolgirls nymphos?

'Tell me about your dance teacher,' Jim said, hoping to discover where the lesbian lived.

'There's nothing to tell. We used to lick and finger each other, that's all.'

'You like licking pussy, then?'

'I like licking my own pussy.'

'What? How the hell can you . . .'

Staring in amazement as Mary raised her legs and placed her feet behind her head, Jim thought that she must have been a contortionist. The bulging lips of her hairless pussy only an inch or so away from her mouth as she clutched the backs of her thighs, she moved her head forward and licked the full length of her vaginal crack. Watching in awe as she pushed her tongue into the creamy-wet hole of her tight pussy, Jim felt his balls heaving within their hairy sac. This was a real turn-on, he thought as she managed to part her succulent vulval lips with her fingertips and tease the erect nub of her clitoris with her wet tongue.

'How the hell do you do that?' he asked her, kneeling in front of the rounded cheeks of her bottom with his erect cock in his hand.

'My dance teacher was into fucking yoga,' she replied, sucking on the pinken wings of her inner lips. 'She taught me how to lick my cunt.'

'You can lick this, too,' he chuckled, slipping the purple knob of his solid cock into her yawning vaginal valley.

His eyes wide as her watched her tongue repeatedly swept over the sensitive tip of her clitoris and glide over the silky-smooth surface of his glans, Jim couldn't believe his luck. A nymphomaniac, a contortionist, a shaved pussy . . . What more could he have asked for? he wondered as Mary's tongue slurped at his glans, then teased the ripe nubble of her clitoris. Moving down her vulval valley and slipping his knob into the wet heat of her cunt, he fully impaled her on his fleshy rod. She gasped, licking and sucking on her clitoris as he withdrew his cock and rammed into her. Never had he seen

such an arousing sight. Never had he known such a sexually talented young slut.

'You're amazing,' he breathed as she parted the glowing cheeks of her thrashed bottom.

'Do my arse,' Mary breathed, her anal hole dilated to the extreme. 'Do my arse and I'll tongue my cunt.'

'Like this?' Jim chuckled, slipping his cunny-slimed cock out of her tight pussy and slipping his knob past her anal ring.

'God, yes. Now fuck my arse rotten.'

She has such a wonderful way with words, Jim thought happily as she drove her pink tongue deep into the tight sheath of her vagina. And a wonderful way with her teenage body. It had been a stroke of luck getting in with the vicar, he knew as he drove the massive shaft of his cock deep into the girl's tight rectal duct. The man not only had trust in Jim, but appeared to like him. If he knew that Jim had thrashed his daughter's naked bottom with a branch and was now fucking her tight little arsehole . . . But he didn't know. And he never would.

Pondering on the dungeon as he repeatedly withdrew his cock from the girl's arse and rammed his knob back deep into the heat of her bowels, Jim could hardly believe that the vicar didn't know about the goings-on beneath his house. If the entrance to the basement dungeon was in the garden, then the priest must have seen people coming and going. Apart from that, he'd have discovered the entrance. Jim was going to have to investigate the garden, he decided as he increased his anal fucking rhythm. He'd try to take a sneaky look round for the entrance to the sex dungeon tomorrow morning while the vicar was in church giving his Sunday sermon.

'I'm coming,' Mary announced, sucking on her pain-

fully swollen clitoris. Releasing his sperm as the girl shook violently in the grip of her orgasm, Jim felt her rectal tube spasming, rhythmically contracting and hugging his pistoning cock. Her vaginal juices gushing from the gaping entrance to her teenage cunt, splattering her face, spraying Jim's lower belly, she mouthed and sucked on her pulsating clitoris and maintained her massive climax. Imagining being able to suck his cock, Jim shuddered as he listened to his sperm squelching within Mary's rectum. Wondering, as his swinging balls drained and Mary sucked her pleasure from her pulsating clitoris, whether to take up yoga, he knew that it would be worthwhile getting to know the lesbian dance teacher.

Finally withdrawing his spent cock, Jim sat back on his heels and gazed in astonishment as Mary locked her full lips to the inflamed brown tissue of her anal ring and sucked out his sperm. More than a contortionist, she appeared to have a rubber spine, he mused as she licked and tongued her dilated bottom-hole. Holding the pert cheeks of her buttocks apart to the extreme and sucking out the last of his spunk, she finally uncurled her naked body and lay outstretched on the grass.

'Mmm,' she breathed, licking her sperm-glossed lips. 'That tastes nice. It's handy being able to lick my cunt and my arse. Apart from bringing myself off, I can clean up after I've been fucked and spunked.'

'Do you have many male friends?' Jim asked her.

'No, not friends. I have several men every week, though. They pay fucking well to watch me lick . . . Shall we go to the fucking pub now?'

'They pay well? Do you mean, you're a prostitute?'

'No, of course not,' she giggled. 'I meant, they *play* well. Play well with me.'

'Oh, right,' Jim murmured.

Mary was lying, he knew as she showed him one of her contortionist tricks by parting her legs until they were at ninety degrees to her naked body. Eyeing her swollen vaginal lips rising either side of her gaping pussy crack, Jim licked his lips. She could certainly do amazing things with her young body, he thought as she lifted her legs high in the air and placed her feet behind her head. Eyeing the inflamed eye of her anus, the pink funnel of flesh surrounding the entrance to her tight pussy, he felt his cock stiffen, his balls heave in expectation of another draining.

Curving her spine until her face was only inches from her juice-glistening vaginal opening, Mary slipped half her hand into the tight cavern of her sex sheath. Grinning as she watched her fleshy outer lips stretch to capacity, she managed to sink her fist into her bloated cunt until the petals of her inner lips hugged her slender wrist. Reckoning that she made money by showing men her incredible contortions, Jim was sure that she was a prostitute. Was the dungeon a brothel? he pondered. An underground brothel full of naughty schoolgirlies?

'Fuck my arse again,' Mary breathed, repeatedly ramming her clenched fist deep into her bloated cunt. 'My hot arse will be tighter than fucking ever now.'

'I wasn't going to mention it,' Jim said, pushing his bulbous knob past her brown ring and sinking his cock-shaft deep into the very core of her young body.

'Mention what?' she asked him, her wet tongue lapping at the sensitive head of her ripe clitoris.

'I think your father knows about the dungeon.'

'Of course he doesn't,' she giggled. 'Fucking hell, have you got a big cock!'

'And you've got a tight bum. It's a wonder you don't split open.'

'I'm used to fisting myself. I can fist both holes at the same time.'

Jim decided to try a bit of combined flattery and trickery to get Mary to tell him more. 'Jesus, you're amazing. Your father . . . I'm sure that he knows about the dungeon because he mentioned devilish deeds going on beneath his house. I didn't know what he meant at the time. But now—'

'God, I'm coming again,' Mary whimpered, her wet tongue sweeping over the glowing tip of her painfully hard clitoris. 'Fuck my arse and spunk . . . Fucking hell, I'm . . . Do it now.'

Repeatedly ramming his huge glans deep into the heat of her bowels as Mary sucked her clitoris into her wet mouth and fist-fucked the burning sheath of her cunt, Jim finally pumped out his second load of sperm. Mary wasn't going to talk about the dungeon, Jim knew as she cried out her enthusiasm for the anal fucking. Her young body shaking violently as he filled her anal cavern with fresh sperm, her only interest was in crude sex, illicit sex. His swinging balls battering her rounded buttocks as she sucked the last ripples of orgasm from her inflamed clitoris, he made his final thrusts before stilling his deflating cock deep within her tight anal canal.

Finally yanking his sperm-dripping penis out of the girl's burning rectum, Jim lay on the grass and relaxed beneath the evening sun. He'd never expected anything like this to happen in a sleepy country village. At the most, he'd thought that he'd be happy running the Tartan Vicar, would enjoy meeting the ageing locals and building up trade. To discover that Willycombe

Village was heaving with sex-starved schoolgirls was miraculous. A trip to the convent was in order, he decided, grabbing his shirt and trousers. The vicarage garden, the convent . . . Tomorrow morning was going to be busy.

'Now can we go to the fucking pub?' Mary asked, locking her lips to her anal ring and sucking Jim's sperm out of her rectal duct.

'Yes, we can,' he replied, standing and tugging his trousers up. 'I hope the netball team are still there.'

'They usually stay for the evening,' Mary said, straightening her naked body and tugging her summer dress over her head. 'They stagger back to the convent when the Reverend fucking Mother decides that it's time to go.'

'The Reverend fucking Mother?' Jim breathed. 'You mean to say that she spends the evening in the pub with the girls?'

'Not always.'

'God, that's all I need. Some old hag-bag of a religious nerd sitting in the bar all evening.'

'I think you'll quite like her. She's all right.'

'If you say so. Right, let's go.'

'I'm desperate for a large vodka.'

'And I'm desperate for a few pints.'

Entering the pub with Mary in tow, Jim was pleased to find the netball girls sitting at the tables, laughing and joking. Pleased that the place was heaving with teenage girls, he made his way to the bar and smiled at Cleo as Mary ordered a vodka and tonic. Cleo didn't appear to be too happy, he thought as she scowled at him. Perhaps she was jealous because Jim had been out with Mary. That was it, he decided. Cleo was jealous

because he'd been fucking Mary and she'd wanted a
length of cock herself.

'You're a bastard,' she finally hissed.

'Oh, thank you,' Jim said. 'Any particular reason?'

'Where the hell have you been? I've been run off my
feet here while you've been—'

'Fucking Mary in the woods,' he chuckled. 'Pour me a
pint, will you?'

'Typical.'

'Listen to me, Cleo. I've been trying to discover where
the dungeon is. You won't tell me anything about it. In
fact, no one will say a bloody thing about the bloody
dungeon.'

'Perhaps they don't want you to know,' she retorted,
passing him a pint of bitter.

'Perhaps not. But I'm becoming increasingly pissed
off with all this fucking secrecy.'

'You'd better not swear,' the girl whispered.

'Why the fuck not? Everyone else swears their fucking
heads off. I don't see why I should fucking . . .'

'Because the Reverend Mother is sitting over there in
the corner.'

'Oh, er . . . yes, well . . . What the hell is she doing
sitting there alone?'

'Watching over the girls.'

'Fucking old hag. I can't abide Reverend fucking
Motherfuckers.'

'Why don't you go and introduce yourself?' Cleo
suggested.

'You must be joking.'

'I'm sure that you'll like her, Jim. In fact, I'll bet you a
fiver that you get on very well with her. Have a quick word
with her and then come and help me behind the bar.'

'OK. Er . . . are you all right now? Have you calmed down? Have you got over your PMS hormonal attack and—'

'Yes, of course I'm all right,' she laughed. 'I was just a bit miffed because you cleared off without saying anything. Oh, by the way. Several people have paid their bar tabs. I'm working through the tabs to get them all paid off. You don't mind if one or two people . . .'

'Bar tabs for a few regulars will be fine. If they pay them off each week, of course. Right, I'll go and introduce myself to the reverend hag-bag.'

Making his way through the throng of giggling girls, Jim scrutinized the Reverend Mother. Her pale face framed by her wimple, her head hung low, he couldn't determine her age. Sipping her orange juice, she didn't notice Jim staring at her. It seemed odd that the woman allowed the convent girls to spend hours drinking alcohol in a pub, he mused. Not the sort of behaviour any ordinary Reverend Mother would condone. Perhaps she wasn't ordinary? he mused, eyeing her black habit and wondering whether she'd ever been fucked up the arse by a huge cock. Taking a deep breath, he walked to her table and introduced himself.

'I'm pleased to meet you, Jim' she said, smiling at him. 'I'm Elizabeth. Won't you sit down?'

'Yes, thank you. So, did the netball team win?'

'They *always* win,' she chuckled. 'I make sure of that.'

'You make sure? How?'

'With God's help, I pour neat vodka into the opposing team's water bottles. They start the match feeling somewhat dizzy, to say the least.'

'Oh, right,' Jim breathed, deciding that she was definitely *not* an ordinary Reverend Mother.

'A little itching powder in their knickers also helps,' she said, much to Jim's amazement.

'Yes, I'm sure it does.'

'So, how are you getting on here? Are you enjoying your new job?'

'Yes, very much,' he replied, trying to determine the woman's age. 'Willycombe Village is quite a place. I think I'm going to like it here. Mind you, there's a lot of secrecy . . .'

'Country villages always harbour secrets,' she interrupted him. 'As do convent schools.'

'Really?'

'You'd be surprised, Jim.'

'Yes, I'm sure I would. In fact, I've had nothing *but* surprises since I arrived here.'

'With many more to come, I'm sure.'

'I hope you don't mind my saying so but . . . you look awfully young to be a Reverend Mother.'

'I *am* awfully young,' she giggled. 'With God's help, I lied about my age.'

'I see. So, how old . . .'

'I'm twenty-five. With God's help, I lied to become a nun and lied to get where I am now.'

'You obviously had the calling at an early age?'

'God called me when I was very young. He introduced me to a monk and, as I grew, the monk and I became close friends. God moves in mysterious ways, Jim.'

'So I've heard.'

'With God's help, the monk led me along the path to complete and utter peace.'

'I wish this monk had met my ex-wife,' Jim laughed. 'She could have done with leading somewhere. Hell, preferably. Oh, I'm sorry.'

'Not at all. Speak your mind, that's what God is always telling me. With God's help, I . . .'

'You get quite a lot of help from God, then?'

'In everything I do, Jim. I noticed that you came in with Mary.'

'Yes, that's right. We'd been for a . . . We went for a walk in the woods.'

'Have you met her father?'

'The vicar, yes.'

'He doesn't like me,' Elizabeth sighed.

'Oh? Why's that?'

'He doesn't like the way I . . . Let's not talk about the vicar. Tell me about yourself.'

'There's nothing to tell, really.'

'I'm sure there is. Give me your hand and I'll tell you a little about yourself.'

'OK,' Jim agreed, holding his hand out. 'Are you a palmist?'

'Yes, I am.'

'But you're the Reverend Mother . . .'

'That's one of the reasons the vicar doesn't like me,' she said, taking his hand and examining his palm. 'Oh, yes. It's all very clear.'

Watching the woman as she scrutinized his palm, Jim decided that Cleo had won the bet. He was going to get on very well with the Reverend Mother. Far from an old hag-bag, from the little that he could see of her face he reckoned that she was extremely attractive. Her methods were certainly unorthodox, he mused. Cheating at netball, taking the schoolgirls into a pub, reading palms . . . It was a great shame that she was celibate, he thought, wondering whether she fucked her sweet pussy with church candles and frigged her clitty to orgasm.

'You've had a troubled life,' she breathed mysteriously.

'Have I?'

'Most definitely. Your wife ran off with another wo-man.'

'That's right,' Jim gasped, then immediately realizing that Cleo could have told her a little about his past.

'You allow sex to rule your life.'

'Yes, well . . . Don't most men?'

'Not the way you do. I can see that you have a craving for schoolgirls.'

'Don't most men?' Jim breathed again, deciding that she was a charlatan.

'Not the way you do. My goodness,' she gasped.

'What is it?'

'God has sent you.'

'Sent me where?'

'Unto me. God has sent you unto me to help with the girls.'

'Really?'

'This is, indeed, a joyous moment,' Elizabeth said, smiling at him. 'I've waited many years for this. I have to admit that I've become disillusioned at times. I have even questioned the word of God, but . . . but now I know that—'

'Wait a minute,' Jim cut in. 'How can I help with the girls? What do you mean?'

'For many years, I have been asking God for help. The girls are unruly at times. They have hormone rushes and I have great difficulty in dealing with them. Now that you're here to help me, I feel a great sense of relief.' Looking around the pub to make sure she could be seen, she lifted her habit. 'Look,' she said, parting her naked thighs and showing off her shaved pussy crack.

'Fucking hell,' Jim gasped. 'What the fuck . . . I mean . . .'

'Shush. This is what God wants you to do, Jim.'

'What? He wants me to do your fanny?'

'No, no. He wants you to look after the girls in a most intimate way. But, to ensure that you really have been sent unto me by the great master, you must come to the convent at nine o'clock tomorrow morning.'

'Er . . . right,' Jim murmured as the Reverend Mother lowered her habit. 'I wouldn't have thought that shaving yourself down there was in keeping with God's will but . . .'

'God told me to shave when my pubic hairs first sprouted. The monk used to help me shave. Until he was arrested, of course. Will you be there tomorrow, Jim?'

'Yes, yes, I will. Elizabeth . . . this is all rather odd.'

'What do you mean?'

'Well, you showing me your shaved pussy and . . . What exactly do you want me to do to the girls?'

'Help me with them.'

'Yes, but how?'

'All my convent girls shave. It's one of the rules.'

'They all shave?'

'There are one or two who won't comply with the rule. That's where you come in.'

'This sounds illegal,' Jim breathed.

'Everything that goes on in the convent is done with God's blessing. Man-made rules don't apply.'

'That's an easy way out of it,' Jim chuckled. 'You'll be telling me next that you want me to forcibly shave the girls who won't comply with your rule.'

'It's not *my* rule, Jim. It is the will of God. Now, if you'll excuse me, I have to round up my girls and take them back to the convent.'

'Yes, yes, of course,' Jim murmured, frowning as Elizabeth finished her drink and stood up.

'Until the morning.'

'I'll be there.'

Downing his pint, Jim reckoned that the 'Reverend Mother' was no more a Reverend Mother than *he* was. This was a set-up, he was sure. The girls had dreamed up the idea to lure him to the convent where the *real* Reverend hag-bag Mother would be waiting. 'With God's help, my arse,' he breathed, imagining tying young girls down to a table with rope and shaving their pussies. And as for the woman lifting her habit and exposing her own fanny . . . Cleo and the others were behind this, he was certain as he noticed the Reverend Mother talking to the barmaid. They were laughing, giggling. At his expense, no doubt. The morning was going to be most interesting, he thought, deciding to go along with the game.

7

Waking at eight with a raging hard-on, Jim clambered out of his bed and stepped into the shower. Running the pub was important, he reflected as he lathered his naked body, massaging soap into the purple globe of his swollen knob. Building up the business was important. But visiting the convent school far outweighed any importance the pub had. He'd been set up by someone he believed to be an impostor, he was sure as he massaged his knob faster. But this was an opportunity to get into the convent and take a look around. He had no doubt that he'd bump into the real Reverend Mother, but he'd devised a plan for the inevitable meeting.

Finally leaving the shower before he shot out his spunk, he dressed and crept downstairs. Hoping that Cleo wasn't around, he grinned as he heard her banging about in the cellar. She wouldn't realize that he was up and dressed, let alone out, he mused as he made his escape. All he needed was half an hour to check out the convent and he'd be back behind the bar where Cleo believed he belonged. She was a good girl, he reflected as he walked along the street. She worked hard, and deserved something by way of a reward for her efforts. Perhaps an anal fucking was in order.

Bounding up the stone steps to the Victorian building, Jim slipped through the main doors and looked around

the large entrance hall. A massive flight of stairs facing him, several oak doors lining the walls to each side, he wasn't sure where to venture first. The distant sound of giggling girls echoing throughout the old building, he breathed in the scent of what he thought to be school-girlie navy-blue knickers. Soiled, stained, minge-moist . . . The convent was quite a place, he thought, wondering how many pairs of pussy-bulged knickers the door-mat had seen. Looking down at the mat, he reckoned that thousands of young girls wearing their short skirts had walked across that very spot. *Oh, to be a doormat.*

'May I help you?' a middle-aged hag asked him as she descended the stairs.

'Ah, er . . . I'm looking for the Reverend Mother,' Jim stammered.

'Do you have an appointment?' the woman asked, standing in front of him in a blue dress that was more suited to the style of the Fifties.

'Yes, I have,' he replied. 'God sent me.'

'What?'

'I mean . . . I have an appointment with the Reverend Mother at nine o'clock,' he said, wondering whether this dragon shaved her fanny too.

'This way, please.'

Following the woman, Jim was sure that he could detect the intoxicating perfume of fresh pussy in the air. The fragrance was medium-bodied with a tinge of stale urine, plus hints of girl-juice, perspiration and fresh deodorant. Rather like a decent red wine, he thought, wondering how many pussies were beneath the convent roof at that time. He also wondered where the laundry room was. As the woman knocked on a huge oak door, he wasn't sure what he was going to say to the genuine

Reverend Mother. It was best to play it by ear, he thought, deciding to begin with his plan of making out that he was from the local water authority.

'Jim,' Elizabeth said, smiling at him from behind her desk as he entered the large study. 'Please, come and sit down. Thank you, Catherine, that will be all.'

'I wasn't expecting you,' Jim breathed as the middle-aged hag left the study and closed the door.

'Of course you weren't expecting me,' she giggled. '*I* was expecting *you*.'

'I mean, I wasn't expecting you to be here.'

'Where were you expecting me to be?'

'Anywhere other than here.'

'Who were you expecting to be here?'

'Someone else, but it doesn't matter. Well, it's nine o'clock and here I am.'

'Indeed you are. The girl is in the side room,' she said, pointing to a small door.

'The girl, yes. Er . . . what was it you wanted me to do?'

'I want you to help me, Jim,' Elizabeth murmured, rising from her desk and pacing the floor. 'God has sent you unto me—'

'Yes, we've been through all that,' Jim cut in. 'What, exactly, am I to do with this girl?'

'I have a cunning plan,' she announced proudly, taking a white lab coat from the back of her swivel chair. 'Put this on.'

'What on earth . . .' he began, donning the coat.

'You're a doctor.'

'Am I?'

'I want you to examine the girl.'

'Is she ill?'

'No, of course she's not ill. The idea is that you examine her and tell her that she has some terrible skin complaint and you'll have to shave her pubic hair off.'

'Why this amazing façade to shave her pussy?'

'It is God's wish, Jim. All the schoolgirls have to shave regularly.'

'That's what God wants?'

'Indeed it is. He told me again only this morning. All the girls are to shave regularly. Right, off you go. And remember: you're a doctor.'

'A doctor, yes.'

Entering the small room, Jim looked around what seemed to be a doctor's surgery. Elizabeth was mad, he thought as he stared at a naked girl standing by an examination table. God's wish to shave schoolgirlies' pussies? *Satan*'s wish, more like. The girl was very young, he observed, eyeing her petite breast bumps, the sparse fleece of blonde pubic curls barely covering her vulval flesh. Her long blonde hair framing her angelic face, cascading over her naked shoulders, she was also eminently fuckable. Her sky-blue eyes sparkling, her full red lips furling into a slight smile, when she saw Jim she clasped her hands to conceal the most intimate part of her young body, adopting the classic pose of threatened female modesty. But her genitalia weren't to be concealed for long. Remembering that he was supposed to be a doctor, and not a sad pervert, he ordered her to lie on the examination table.

'I'm Doctor . . . er . . . Beautiful,' he breathed, standing by her side and casting his gaze over the violin curves of her teenage body. 'Absolutely . . .'

'Doctor Beautiful?' she echoed, frowning at him.

'Dutiful, Doctor Dutiful. The Reverend Mother wants me to examine you.'

'So she informed one earlier,' she returned haughtily. 'But one can't think why, as there's absolutely nothing wrong with one.'

'I'll be the judge of that,' Jim said firmly, running his fingertips over the dark discs of her areolae. 'Do you feel any pain there?'

'None at all,' she sighed.

'How about there?' he asked her, moving his hand down over the smooth plateau of her stomach and pressing his fingers into the warm swelling of her outer labia. 'Does that hurt?'

'Not one little iota.'

'Most interesting.'

'No, it's not.'

'Yes, it is. In fact, it's extremely interesting.'

'Why should one find it interesting?' she asked him. 'There's absolutely nothing wrong with one,' she repeated.

'Sadly, one couldn't be more wrong. One has the beginnings of a terrible vulval flesh-lice infestation.'

'Lice infestation?' she gasped. 'That's ridiculous.'

'Ridiculous, possibly. But true, I'm afraid.' Easing the firm cushions of her outer lips wide apart, Jim gazed at the intricate flesh of the blonde beauty's inner folds. 'Mmm,' he murmured. 'Most interesting. Tell me, do you masturbate?'

'Well, er . . .'

'Remember that I'm a doctor and it's very easy for me to tell whether you masturbate or not by checking your clitoral response.'

'Well, one does masturbate,' the girl confessed softly. 'But not very often. Extremely rarely, in fact.'

'Do you insert your fingers into your vagina?'

'No, no . . .'

'Remember, I can tell by checking the rigidity of your vaginal canal.'

'Fingers, yes. And . . . and candles sometimes.'

'I see. Would you roll over, please? I have to administer a severe retro-vaginal examination.'

'What's that?' she asked him, rolling onto her stomach.

'An anal-vaginal fingering . . . er . . . an examination of the anal and vaginal canals using my fingers.'

Parting the young girl's rounded buttocks, Jim focused on the tightly closed iris of her lickable anus. She was a stuck-up little bitch, he reflected. And she was about to have several fingers stuck up her. There was obviously far more to the convent than met the eye, he thought, opening the girl's brown ring with his thumbs and peering into her tight rectal duct. Perhaps it wasn't a convent school? he thought. Perhaps it was a brothel? Wondering about the extremely young and sexual Reverend Mother as he stretched his so-called patient's anus open wider, Jim reckoned that she knew about the dungeon. The convent, the dungeon, the pub . . . They were all connected. But how?

Releasing the girl's firm buttocks and parting her slender legs wide, he ran his fingertip up and down the creamy-warm valley of her teenage vagina. This doctor lark was a great scam, Jim thought, slipping his finger between the puffy swell of her outer labia and opening the fleshy, butterfly wings of her inner lips. But what was it all about? Locating the wet entrance to her tight sex-hole, he pushed his finger into her vagina and massaged her hot inner flesh. The girl squirmed as he parted her naked buttocks with his free hand and pushed his fingertip past the tight ring of her brown anal eye.

She obviously didn't mind the examination, he thought as she let out a gasp of what he reckoned to be pure sexual pleasure. Was she in on the scam?

'Mmm, nice and tight,' he breathed pensively, his solid cock straining against his zip.

'One begs your pardon?' she gasped.

'Er . . . you're nice and slight. Of slender build. Just about right for your age.'

'One is exactly the right weight for one's height. Have you finished examining one?'

'Not yet, my dear,' Jim replied, easing a second finger into the tight sheath of the blonde girl's bottom.

'Ouch, that hurts.'

'Sorry, but I have to get right inside your bottom to—'

'To what? This examination seems rather unorthodox.'

'Not at all. That's it, now I can feel you properly,' he said, managing to drive two fingers into the lubricious duct of her virgin pussy.

'Now that really *does* hurt,' she complained.

'There's only one thing for it, I'm afraid,' he breathed, massaging the hot inner flesh of her sex ducts. 'I'll have to shave your pubic hair.'

'You will do no such thing.'

'Then you will suffer terribly . . .'

'You're not a doctor, are you?'

'Of course I am. I have a degree in psychology, a degree in analology, a degree in vaginalology . . .'

'There's no such thing as vaginalology.'

'Look, do you want me to help you in your plight or not?'

'One does not—'

'Cut the *one* crap, for God's sake,' Jim sighed. 'One this, one that . . . It's confusing. Speak English.'

'My name's Heather,' the girl said, lifting her head off the table and gazing up at him. 'This is a trick. You're not a doctor and there's nothing wrong with me.'

'Of course it's not a trick. It would be deemed highly illegal if I posed as a doctor.'

'I know what's going on. The Reverend Mother wants me to shave, and I won't do it.'

'The Reverend Mother wants you to shave? I've never heard such rot.'

'I'll cut the *one* crap if you cut the *doctor* crap. Now, there are about a dozen of us in the gang.'

'Gang?' he echoed, slipping his fingers out of Heather's hot sex-sheaths.

'We've formed a gang. We're rebels, rebelling against the so-called Reverend Mother. She earns a fortune by selling the girls for sex and—'

'Selling the girls for sex?' Jim gasped, wondering what she charged. 'Good grief.'

'The girls aren't allowed to wear knickers, they have to shave, they're forced to attend the dancing classes naked . . . all for the benefit of the customers.'

'What customers?'

'Businessmen, solicitors . . . She has a nice little business going.'

'What the hell is it about Willycombe Village?' Jim sighed, licking his anal-slimed fingers. 'The place—'

'The place reeks of sex. It all started many years ago. Convent schools attract perverts, you should know that.'

'Well, I . . . There must be hundreds of convent schools in the country. They're not all . . .'

'Certain people connected with the convent saw a

moneymaking opportunity. The sixth-form girls were all for it when they were asked whether they'd put on sex shows for dirty old men. Things got out of hand and . . .'

'Why are you telling me all this?'

'Because I've heard that you've been asking questions. Although you're new to the village, we reckon that we can trust you.'

'Do you know about the dungeon?' Jim asked hopefully.

'No one ever speaks about the dungeon.'

'So I've gathered.'

'We'll have to meet somewhere,' Heather whispered as the door handle turned. 'I can't talk . . .'

'Ah, doctor,' Elizabeth said breezily as she entered the room. 'How are you getting on?'

'Very well,' Jim replied. 'Almost finished, in fact.'

'I see that Heather hasn't—'

'She's going to her room to remove her pubic hairs,' Jim cut in. 'I've explained the situation.'

'I'll go now, Reverend Mother,' Heather said softly, grabbing her clothes and dressing.

Following Elizabeth into the study, Jim wondered whether she was suspicious. If she'd been listening at the door and . . . *He* was suspicious, that was for sure. Why call on him to examine the girl? Was it that he'd been asking too many questions and Elizabeth was trying to discover more about him? By inviting him to the convent, she'd certainly have the opportunity to get to know him. But getting him to pretend to be a doctor and examine a naked schoolgirl? Something was going on.

'Did she mention her gang?' Elizabeth asked Jim as the girl left and closed the study door behind her.

'Gang? No, no, she didn't,' he lied.

'What did she say? Did she tell you anything?'

'She said that she doesn't feel ill and—'

'Yes, but did she say anything about me or the convent?'

'No, she didn't. Elizabeth, what's all this about?'

'The girls must shave and—'

'No, no, no. You didn't ask me to come here simply to get the girls to shave their pubes. You've only just met me. Why ask the landlord of the local pub to make out that he's a doctor and examine a naked girl? What's going on?'

'I told you, Jim. God sent you unto me.'

'That's crap. You were so desperate to get me to come here this morning that you flashed your pussy in the pub. That was obviously designed to entice me here. Why?'

'God . . .'

'OK, have it your way. Look, I have to go. The brewery bosses are coming down to see me,' he lied. 'I'll see you around.'

'I'll call in at the pub this evening.'

Leaving the study, Jim decided to take a sneaky look around the convent before returning to the pub and Cleo's inevitable complaining. Following his nose, he hoped to discover the laundry room and 'borrow' a few pairs of girlie-soiled panties. Solely for his own personal use, of course. Although selling vacuum-packed soiled schoolgirl panties and making huge profits *had* crossed his mind. Hearing giggling coming from behind an oak door, he wondered whether to slip into the room and ask for directions to the laundry room. Pressing his ear to the door as a girl screamed, he listened intently.

'She'll go mad,' a girl gasped.

'She's not due back until this afternoon, so there's no need to worry.'

'If she finds out that Elizabeth has been impersonating her, she'll definitely go mad. What the hell did she do it for? I'm surprised that Catherine went along with it.'

'It was to fool that new bloke from the pub. He's been asking everyone about the dungeon and she wanted to put him off the scent. She also wants to find out about Heather's gang. She thought that Heather might tell Jim something about it and—'

'Heather wouldn't tell anyone about the gang. Anyway, we'd better go to the chapel. If we don't turn up, we'll be in real trouble.'

Creeping along the corridor and slipping into a small room, Jim wondered what the hell was going on. At least he knew now that Elizabeth wasn't the real Reverend Mother. This was becoming increasingly confusing, he mused, looking at stacks of old desks and chairs lining the walls. Deciding to return to the pub, he left the room and sneaked along the corridor to the main entrance hall. Bounding down the convent steps and heading for the Tartan Vicar, he was determined to learn the secrets of Willycombe Village. And who better to torture the truth out of than Cleo?

'Where have you been?' the girl asked Jim as he entered the pub. 'I've cleaned the pipes and prepared the bar snacks for Sunday lunch and—'

'Urgent business. I was called away at five o'clock this morning.'

'Five o'clock? But I heard you leave at ten to nine.'

'I can't explain your mistake, Cleo. Now, tell me about the dungeon.'

'Fucking hell, not that again?'

'Either you tell me, or I'll sexually torture your clitoris.'

'All right,' Cleo sighed, pouring herself a large vodka and tonic. 'There's a basement below the vicarage. It's private, away from prying eyes, and some people go there to have sex.'

'Is that it?'

'Yes, that's it. There's also an old air-raid shelter in the woods. Kids go there and—'

'Where's the entrance to the dungeon?'

'Somewhere in the vicarage garden. I've never been there, Jim. It's used by cheating couples. Married men use it to fuck their tarts. Married women take their lovers there and fuck them. That's all there is to say about the place.'

'So why the secrecy?'

'Because you're new around here. The last thing cheating couples want is you sticking your nose in and shooting your mouth off about the dungeon. Now, shall we get ready for the Sunday lunch session?'

'Er . . . yes, yes,' Jim murmured meditatively.

Cleo's explanation sounded reasonable, he reflected. But he was sure that she was lying. If the dungeon had been nothing more than a safe place for illicit fucking, she'd have said so when he'd first asked her about it. Recalling the disappearing customers, Jim went into the toilets to take a look around. Discovering a fire exit, he grinned. That's how they'd left the pub, he thought. Although he hadn't seen anyone entering the toilets, that was obviously how they'd left without him noticing.

'Cleo, you didn't tell me that there was a fire exit in the toilets,' he said, returning to the bar.

'You didn't ask,' she riposted.

'That's how those customers left the pub without—'

'Some people don't want to be seen walking out of the pub, Jim. So they use the fire exit.'

'That explains everything,' he chuckled.

'I really don't know why you have to have an explanation for every little thing that happens. Instead of wasting time with your detective games, why don't you concentrate on the pub? I thought that you were going to work on the pub and turn it into a thriving business?'

'I am, Cleo,' he stated firmly, moving behind the bar and pulling himself a pint of bitter. 'Starting from now, I'm going to forget about dungeons and disappearing customers. Of course, that still leaves the question of the convent.'

'The convent? What about it?'

'That Elizabeth girl is posing as the Reverend Mother.'

'Elizabeth is the Reverend Mother's secretary, Jim. She assumes the role of Reverend Mother when the real Reverend Mother is away.'

'Oh, I see. But . . .'

'There are no buts, for fuck's sake. Now, shall we get ready for opening time?'

'Yes, yes, of course.'

Watching Cleo place several bowls of peanuts and crisps on the bar, Jim reckoned that she was worth her weight in gold. She'd cleaned the pipes, polished the counter, prepared the snacks . . . It was a wonder that the brewery hadn't put *her* in charge, he reflected, sipping his pint. She knew the locals well and she was damned good at her job. Perhaps they'd thought that she was too young? She certainly made Jim's life easy, but he didn't want to take her for granted. Deciding to put all his efforts into the pub, he checked his watch.

Eleven-thirty. Half an hour until the traditional Sunday opening at midday. Pouring himself another pint of bitter as Cleo went to make the sandwiches, Jim grabbed a handful of peanuts from a bowl. This was going to be a good session, he was sure as he munched on the peanuts and checked his watch again. Looking up as he heard a knock on the door, his face turned pale.

'Fucking hell,' he gasped. 'It's the Rottweiler.'

'She's harmless,' Cleo giggled. 'I wouldn't worry about her. Her bark's worse than her bite.'

'Harmless? She's a fucking evil lesbian.'

'Let her in, Jim. She won't stay for long.'

'Ruby,' he said, smiling at the woman as he opened the door. 'How delightful to see you.'

'There's no need to lie to me,' she snapped, walking up to the bar as Cleo slipped into the back room. 'You were in the woods with a young girl.'

'Was I?' he breathed, rubbing his chin and raising his eyes to the ceiling. 'I have no recollection of a visitation to the woods with a girl.'

'Yesterday evening, it was. You went into the woods with a very young girl.'

'I was here yesterday evening,' Jim said, frowning at her.

'I saw you,' Ruby snapped. 'I saw you go into the woods with a young girl. There's no point in denying it.'

'Ah, yes,' he chuckled. 'I went for a walk with Mary, my daughter.'

'Incest.'

'Where?'

'In the woods.'

'Good grief,' he gasped. 'Incest in the woods? That's illegal.'

'Exactly. What do you have to say about it?'

'Well, I think it should be stopped. I can't abide incest.'

'I'm talking about the incestuous relationship with your daughter . . .'

'My God. Where is the swine? I'll kill the filthy pervert.'

'I talking about *your* incestuous relationship, man.'

'*My* incestuous . . . I'm sorry, but I'm not with you.'

'I followed you into the woods. You were . . . My God. What you did to that poor innocent young girl was vile in the extreme.'

'I do believe that this is a case of mistaken identity, Ruby.'

'Of course it's not. I saw you, with my own eyes.'

'You'd have a job to see me with someone else's eyes,' Jim quipped.

'This is *not* a laughing matter.'

'The girl you saw me with was my daughter's sister.'

'What? You mean that you were behaving in that despicable manner with the vicar's daughter?'

'No, no. My daughter, Mary, has two sisters. There's Mary, the vicar's daughter, and her other sister, Mary.'

'Three Marys?'

'Three Hail Marys. The third Mary is my friend's wife.'

'*Wife*? The girl can't be old enough to . . . Wait a minute, you were having sexual relations with your friend's wife?'

'No, no, no. The girl's husband, that's my friend . . .'

'This is all so confusing,' the woman sighed. 'I think I need a drink. Pull me a pint of best.'

'Certainly, Ruby,' Jim said, moving behind the bar. 'It

is confusing, I agree. In fact, there are times when I get completely mixed up with all these Marys.'

'I'm not surprised,' she breathed, grabbing her drink as Jim placed it on the bar.

'Only last week, I confused my brother's distant sister with my mother.'

'Er . . . yes. But the fact remains that you were in the woods with a naked teenage girl.'

'Yes, that's right.'

'Ah, now we're getting somewhere.'

'You see, I'm a doctor. Mary has this complaint that, for obvious reasons, she'd rather keep secret.'

'You're a doctor?'

'That's right. She asked me to examine her, which I did. You might think it odd that the examination took place in the woods.'

'Most odd.'

'She's terrified that her distant brother will find out. I would tell you more, but I'm bound by medical ethics.'

'Yes, yes, I quite understand,' Ruby replied.

Shaking his head as the woman sat at a table and gazed into her drink, Jim reckoned that he'd confused the old hag enough to put her off the scent. The first time he'd met her, he'd known that she was going to be trouble. Sneaking around the woods, spying on his illicit sex sessions with young teenage girlies . . . She was going to have to be watched, and carefully. Deciding that the woods were now out of bounds as far as shagging was concerned, Jim pondered again on the dungeon. If that was where married men took their tarts, then why couldn't Jim use the place for his illicit fucking?

'I've been thinking,' Ruby said as she left her table and wandered up to the bar.

'Oh?'

'If Mary is your daughter and she has two sisters also named Mary . . . Hang on, I can't quite get my head around this.'

'I wouldn't even bother to try,' Cleo said as she emerged from the back room. 'Jim's family is somewhat complicated.'

'You're telling me,' the woman sighed, finishing her pint. 'Well, I'll be seeing you. And remember – I'll be watching the woods.'

'Of course,' Jim chuckled. 'Take care, Ruby. We'll see you soon, I hope.'

Waiting until she'd left the pub, Jim opened the door wide ready for the influx of Sunday lunchtime drinkers. It was a beautiful day, he thought, gazing at the village green. The sun shining, the birds singing, what better weather to take a young girl to the woods and fuck her sweet bottom-hole? No, Jim reflected. No matter how beautiful a young girl might be, if she tried to entice him to the woods for a session of rampant sex he would not go. There was always his flat, he mused. He'd be far safer enjoying illicit sex in his flat than risking being caught by a hag-bag lesbian in the woods.

Helping Cleo behind the bar as several punters entered the pub, Jim was surprised by the amount of people asking for sandwiches. Wondering what had happened to Crystal and her food-display cabinet, he didn't reckon that anyone from the health and safety department would bother him. Besides, judging by the way the sandwiches were selling, they wouldn't be on the bar for long. Pouring himself half a pint of bitter, Jim scrutinized his customers. Again, there were no young men in the pub, which he found extremely odd. And, unusually,

right now there wasn't one teenage girl in sight. Wondering whether the girls weren't allowed out of the convent on Sundays as he sipped his drink, he frowned as a middle-aged man walked up to the bar and handed Cleo a padded envelope.

'Morning,' Jim said, smiling at the man. 'What would you like?'

'Er . . . bitter, please,' he replied, his dark eyes darting nervously between Cleo and Jim. 'A pint, if you would.'

'One pint of best bitter coming up, sir.'

'Jim, this is Jack,' Cleo said, introducing the customer.

'Pleased to meet you, Jack,' Jim said, passing the man his drink. 'That's two pounds thirty, please.'

'I see you're doing food,' the man remarked, passing Jim a five-pound note.

'Yes, that's right. We have cheese and pickle, ham—'

'Not for me, thank you,' Jack cut in. 'I hope you're not going to make too many changes?'

'No changes at all,' Jim replied, ringing up the till. 'People don't like change.'

'That's very true. So, you're not planning to . . .'

'I'm not planning to do anything,' Jim said with some exasperation, passing the man his change. 'The Tartan Vicar will stay as it is. Apart from the sandwiches, of course.'

'With that attitude, I reckon that you'll do well.' Glancing over his shoulder, the man leaned over the bar and stared hard at Jim. 'People also dislike questions,' he said softly.

'Er . . . I'm well aware of that,' Jim chuckled nervously. 'I never ask questions. As far as I'm concerned . . .'

'That's not what I've heard,' Jack said accusingly.

'According to several locals, all you've been doing is asking questions.'

'I did ask a lady whether there were any nice country walks around here. And this morning I asked someone where the local garage was.'

'I'm not talking about that sort of question. I'm talking about the convent, the vicarage, and the like.'

'I *did* ask an elderly man where the vicarage was,' Jim confessed. 'In fact, I went there and met the vicar. What a nice chap he is, don't you agree?'

'I hear that you've also been up to the convent.'

'That's right. I went to the convent and met . . . Er . . . don't get me wrong, but it's not against the law to visit people, is it?'

'No, no,' the man said, sipping his pint. 'It's just that people like privacy.'

'Jim, would you mind collecting those glasses?' Cleo asked, nodding in the direction of a corner table.

'Oh, er . . . yes, of course.'

Leaving the bar and moving to the table, Jim knew that something was going on between the man and Cleo. Watching out of the corner of his eye, he noticed the girl slipping the envelope behind the till. There were far too many secrets in the village, he reflected. Feeling as though he was the enemy and wasn't to be trusted, he decided to take a closer look at the envelope. He wouldn't usually pry into other people's business, but he was determined to get to the bottom of the secrecy.

Returning to the bar as Jack headed for a table and Cleo served another customer, Jim grabbed the envelope and slipped into the back room. This was very wrong, he knew as he prised the envelope open and peered inside. Frowning as he pulled out several photographs, he stared

wide-eyed at a shot of his wife leaving what had been their marital home. Another photograph was of Jim talking to his brother outside the house. More than odd, this was extremely worrying, he mused, flicking through the remaining photographs. His brother, his wife and her lesbian lover . . . Someone was obviously spying on him and his family. But who? he wondered. More to the point, why? Slipping the pictures back into the envelope, Jim returned them discreetly to their hiding place behind the till.

Oblivious to Jim's surreptitious activities, Cleo washed several glasses as he refilled his own and sipped his beer. What was the interest in his lesbionic wife? he mused. What did Cleo intend to do with the photographs? Deciding to take a walk around the village, Jim finished his drink and slipped out of the pub without Cleo noticing. Looking over his shoulder every few seconds as he walked down the street, he felt like a fugitive. He could cope with the locals and their peculiar ways, he thought, again making sure that he wasn't being followed. But not with people spying and taking photographs: Now he was more determined than ever to unearth the secrets of Willycombe Village.

8

Skulking around the garden of the vicarage, Jim could find no sign of the entrance to the basement dungeon. Wondering whether the whole thing was a hoax and there was nothing beneath the house, he thought that the idea might have been to keep his attention away from something else. Searching a clump of bushes, he decided that there was nothing of interest in the garden and he might as well go back to the pub. If there was a basement, he reckoned that the entrance would be in the house itself. If the entrance *was* in the house, then the vicar knew about the basement. If the vicar knew, then . . . Jim was going round in circles, he knew as he was about to leave the garden.

'What on earth . . .' the vicar breathed, frowning at Jim. 'What are *you* doing here?'

'Oh, I . . . er . . . I was coming to see you,' Jim stammered, forcing a smile.

'You wouldn't have found me beneath the bushes. What were you looking for?'

'I was just admiring your garden, Father. I'm a keen gardener.'

'I see. Actually, I'm glad you're here. I want to talk to you about Mary.'

'Certainly,' Jim replied. 'How is she?'

'I was hoping that she'd show some signs of improve-

ment after you'd spoken to her,' he sighed. 'Sadly, she seems to be just the same.'

'It's early days,' Jim consoled the man. 'I'll have to talk to her over a period of time before you'll notice any changes.'

'Yes, of course. I suppose I'm rather impatient.'

'Patience is a virtue, Father. By the way, is there a basement beneath your house?'

'A basement?' he echoed, shaking his head. 'No, no, there isn't. Why do you ask?'

'It was just something someone said. I'm interested in old buildings, you see.'

'Jim, I'm not interested in *buildings*. It's my *daughter* I'm worried about.'

'Understandably.'

'The thing is . . . She's been stealing candles from the church.'

'I'm not surprised,' Jim chuckled. 'I mean, I'm not surprised that you're worried about her.'

'She went to the church half an hour ago. I don't know what she gets up to there. But I can tell you that she's been stealing candles. What on earth does she do with them?'

'I'll go there now and have a word with her,' Jim murmured, realizing that the church might have a basement.

'That's most kind of you, Jim. I'll be here if you need me.'

Leaving the garden and heading along the street to the church, Jim reckoned that he was about to solve the mystery of the dungeon. He should have thought of the church earlier, he knew as he walked up the flower-bed-bordered path to the huge oak doors. The building must

have been around a thousand years old. All churches of that era had basements, he was sure. Walking down the aisle towards the altar, he stopped and looked around him. The place was cold, eerie, almost like a haunted castle from an old film. Shuddering, he was at least pleased that the Sunday sermon was over and the church was deserted.

Looking for a door or steps leading to the basement, Jim reckoned that Mary was in the bowels of the church. Who else was down there? he wondered, noticing a small door set in an alcove. Was she enjoying a good anal shagging with a married man? Opening the small door, he made his way gingerly down the stone steps to a dimly lit room. The basement wasn't as large as he'd expected, but that didn't matter. The point was, he'd discovered what he reckoned to be the infamous dungeon of Will-ycombe Village.

'What are *you* doing here?' Mary asked, echoing the vicar's earlier question as she emerged from a shadowy corner.

'Mary,' Jim breathed, gazing in disbelief at the thin pink weals fanning out across the petite mounds of her breasts. 'Are you all right?'

'Of course she's all right,' a naked young lad chuckled, stepping out of the shadows.

'Who . . .'

'This is Davey,' Mary said. 'We . . . we come down here to get away from people.'

'I see,' Jim breathed, eyeing the lad's snakelike penis hanging over the hairy sac of his scrotum. 'Well, I'll leave you to it.'

'You don't have to go,' Mary said, her full lips furling into a salacious grin as she ran her hands down

over her stomach to the swollen lips of her hairless
pussy crack.

'He can't stay,' the lad murmured as Jim scrutinized
the girl's naked body.

'I *want* him to stay,' Mary stated firmly.

'But . . .'

'He stays, Davey.'

'All right,' the youngster finally conceded. 'But not for
long.'

Following the young couple through a heavy velvet
curtain, Jim found himself standing in a large room with
a table set in the centre of the stone floor. This was it, he
thought happily. He was standing in the mysterious
dungeon at long last. Again thinking that he should have
realized that the church would have a basement, he gazed
at the lad. He was in his late teens with unruly blond hair
cascading over his suntanned face. Tall and muscular, he
wasn't bad-looking. But where had he come from? Jim
had never seen him in the village. In fact, he'd never seen
any males under the age of forty in the village. Noticing
several bamboo canes standing in the corner, he turned
and looked at the table. Handcuffs attached to the legs,
two large holes in the wooden top, he now knew exactly
what went on in the bowels of the church.

'You said that I couldn't stay for long,' Jim said,
watching the girl lean over the table, her young breasts
slipping through the holes in the polished top.

'We're preparing for the monks,' the lad murmured,
spreading Mary's feet wide and cuffing her ankles to the
table legs.

'The monks?' Jim echoed, his face grimacing. 'What
monks?'

'There's a sect of devil worshippers,' Mary enligh-

tened Jim as the lad pulled her arms down and cuffed her wrists to the table legs.

'Devil worshippers? Fucking hell. I really don't think—'

'You've been going on about the dungeon ever since you arrived in the village,' Mary cut in. 'You've been asking anyone and everyone. Now you've found it.'

'Yes, but . . .'

'What's the matter?' Davey asked him. 'You've found what you were looking for, so what's the problem?'

'I didn't realize that . . .'

'I'm the sacrifice,' Mary announced. 'They don't kill me, of course. They sacrifice me sexually.'

'Sexually? Christ, I can't believe this.'

'You'll have to get out of here before they arrive or there'll be trouble,' Davey warned him, taking a long bamboo cane from the corner of the basement.

'No, don't go,' Mary breathed. 'There's a habit on that hook over there. Put it on and they'll think that you're one of them.'

'I'd never get away with it,' Jim said.

'This is dangerous,' Davey said, grimacing.

'I want him to stay,' Mary persisted.

'All right. They might ask you for the code word. It's Veneris.'

'Veneris. OK.'

Frowning, Jim gazed in horror as the lad brought the cane down across Mary's naked buttocks with a deafening crack. Where the hell had the teenage boy come from? he wondered. Surely the vicar must have known about the basement beneath his church? If he turned up and discovered his teenage daughter . . . The vicar must have known what the girl got up to, Jim reflected. To

allow the girl to meet devil worshippers and . . . The man obviously had no choice in the matter.

His mind reeling with confusion as he watched the gruelling naked-buttock caning, Jim didn't know what to think. Feeling anxious as he anticipated the arrival of the monks, he knew that he'd stumbled across something extremely sinister. The cracking of the bamboo cane across Mary's tensed buttocks resounding around the bowels of the church, Jim felt his cock stiffen, straining at his zip as the girl whimpered with a mixture of pain and pleasure. Did he really want to stay and witness the sacrifice of Mary's young body? Did he want to join in? There certainly was far more to Willycombe Village than met the eye.

'It might look better if you're fucking her arse when the others arrive,' the lad said, parting the girl's glowing buttocks. 'I usually give her an anal fucking and cream her up ready for the monks, but it might be better if you do it today.'

'Er . . . no, no,' Jim breathed, still unable to comprehend the situation. 'You do it.'

'OK. But you'd better put the habit on before the others arrive.'

Watching as Davey stood behind the girl and pressed his purple plum hard against the delicate brown tissue of her anal iris, Jim felt uneasy. A teenage couple using the basement for bondage and crude fucking was one thing, he mused. But a group of monks sacrificing the young girl's tethered body? Something was wrong, Jim knew as the lad increased his anal fucking rhythm, repeatedly ramming his solid cock deep into Mary's rectal duct.

Mary didn't seem bothered, he mused as she let out gasps of pure sexual pleasure. On the contrary, she was

enjoying every minute of the illicit anal shagging. But something was very wrong. Wondering whether to stop worrying and enjoy the pleasures of the girl's wet mouth, Jim focused on Davey's anal-slimed cock as the lad announced that he was coming.

'Yes,' Davey gasped, the squelching sound of his fresh spunk resounding around the dungeon as he arse-fucked Mary in his crudity. Watching the boy's swinging balls, his purple glans repeatedly emerging from the girl's inflamed anal hole and driving back deep into her bowels, Jim felt his own cock stiffen fully. He was sorely tempted to drive his knob into Mary's wet mouth and fuck her there. But he was hesitant to join in with the sexual debauchery until he'd met the monks. Realizing that he'd left Cleo alone in the pub yet again, he hoped that she wouldn't be mad at him. He sighed as he watched the young lad slide his sperm-dripping cock out of Mary's gaping anus. He couldn't keep disappearing like this, he knew.

Grabbing the brown habit from the hook, Jim decided to stay as he donned the garment. He might learn something, he thought, pulling the hood over his head. Determined to find out what was going on, this was the finest opportunity he'd yet had to discover the truth about the dungeon. Praying that the monks wouldn't question him as he heard movements outside the basement, he moved to a shadowy corner and pulled the hood further over his face.

'I see you've started, my friend,' a man dressed in a brown habit said as he entered the dungeon and dumped a leather bag on the floor.

'I have,' the lad replied. 'I've warmed her up for you. Er . . . you're not the first to arrive.'

'So I see. Good day, brother.'

'Good day,' Jim murmured, unable to see the man's face hidden beneath a brown hood.

'There'll be seven of us today, not counting our young warm-up friend,' he said, turning to Mary as another five monks filed into the room. 'A good turnout. Seven cocks, Mary,' he chuckled. 'You're a lucky girl. We shall each defile your naked body in turn,' he breathed, standing behind Mary's rounded buttocks and lifting his habit.

Jim couldn't see the monks' shrouded faces as they lined up against the wall to witness the anal fucking. This was all rather odd, he thought, watching the first monk press his purple globe into Mary's spunk-slimed anus. More than odd – he reckoned that this was positively dangerous. Was Mary really a willing participant in the crude abuse of her tethered body? She might have been threatened, Jim thought fearfully. If her father knew about this . . . Was *he* in on the scam? Surely the man wouldn't allow his own daughter to be anally fucked by so many men, treated like a common whore.

As one of the monks moved to a corner of the room, Jim watched him. He wasn't as tall as the others and, judging by his posture, might have been older. Still feeling uneasy, Jim wondered whether Cleo knew about the monks. How did they get to the church without being noticed? If Ruby Rottweiler saw the monks, she'd stick her nose in and demand to know what was going on. Was there a rear entrance to the ancient building? There were too many secrets rippling around the village. One mention of the dungeon and people either clammed up or lied. Frowning as one of the monks pulled two chains down from the low ceiling, Jim wondered whether this was part of the so-called sacrifice. What did Mary get out

of it? he mused. Apart from enjoying several arse-fuck-ings, what was her gain? Did the monks pay her?

'I'm a new member,' he whispered, joining the monk standing alone in the corner. 'Does the girl know who you are?'

'No one knows us,' the man replied softly.

'How long has this been going on? Do you meet here regularly?'

'Every Sunday. Surely you know that?'

'Yes, yes, I do,' Jim murmured. 'I meant, do *you* come here every Sunday?'

'I'm able to attend most meetings.'

Looking at Mary as she gasped with the withdrawal of the first monk's spent penis, Jim wondered what the hell they were going to do with her as two men released her ankles. Attaching the ends of the dangling chains to her feet, they pulled on a rope connected to a system of pulleys fixed to the ceiling. The chains raised Mary's legs high in the air, lifting her stomach clear of the table as Jim watched with bated breath. Her chest taking the weight of her young body, the small mounds of her breasts forced through the holes in the table top, Jim couldn't believe that she was a willing participant in the weird sex games. Her spine curved, her feet high in the air, her thighs parted to the extreme, her gaping sex holes were completely bared to the eyes of her audience.

Focusing on the girl's hairless vaginal lips rising either side of her yawning crack of desire, her juices of lust tricking over the intricate folds of her inner lips, Jim raised his eyes and gazed at the inflamed eye of her anus. Sperm oozing from her once-private hole, trickling down between the swollen hillocks of her pussy lips, her sex holes were completely defenceless to the perverted

monks. Jim had never seen such an arousing sight. The girl's vaginal crack gaping open, the gully of her bottom yawning, the most private parts of her teenage body were crudely exposed to her audience. Watching the next monk in line lift his cassock in readiness to fuck her there, Jim knew that this was sexual abuse in the extreme.

'In the name of Satan,' the man gasped, pressing the purple globe of his penis hard against Mary's sperm-oozing anal inlet. 'In the name of Satan, we sacrifice this girl. We strip her of her morals and her femininity. We offer unto you, Satan, her very soul.'

Frowning, Jim bit his lip as he watched the man ram his bulbous knob deep into Mary's sperm-flooded rectal canal and begin his anal fucking motions. Even if this was only some sort of obscene game, the monk shouldn't be uttering such words. Frightening himself as he wondered what diabolical powers of evil the monks might conjure up, Jim was sure that this wasn't just a game. Unable to take his stare off the man's thrusting penis, he focused on Mary's delicate anal tissue dragging back and forth along the man's veined shaft as she whimpered and squirmed on the table. This was *not* a game.

Suddenly having a thought, Jim rubbed his chin. If this was the mysterious dungeon, the place that no one talked about, the very basement that was shrouded in secrecy, then why had Mary insisted that Jim stay? Were there other young teenage girls whom they lured to their den of lust and sexually abused? Or was Mary the only victim? More confused than ever, Jim watched the man's sperm-slimed cock as it repeatedly emerged from the girl's rectal duct and drove back into her tethered body. Staring at the forbidden anal fucking, listening to the

sounds of squelching sperm, Jim was pleased that his disguise had fooled the monks and that they hadn't questioned him.

Jumping as Mary let out a scream, Jim gazed in horror as one of the hooded monks yanked her head up by her blonde hair. Ramming his solid knob into her open mouth, he drove his glans to the back of her throat. Her lips stretched tautly around the thick base of his huge cock, he clutched her head in his hands and began his mouth-fucking. The two monks finding their rhythm, ramming their cocks into the squirming girl's naked body in unison, they let out gasps of sexual gratification.

Wondering what to do, whether to leave the perverted monks to their debauchery and return to the pub, Jim watched as one of the men took something from the leather bag. Holding up two thin chains with heavy weights attached to the ends, he clambered beneath the table and gazed at the girl's small breasts emerging through the holes. Fixing two metal clips to the ripe teats of her young breasts, he attached the chains and chuckled wickedly as her nipples pulled away from her mammary globes. Her mammary hillocks stretched into cones of taut flesh, her feet held high in the air, her thighs parted to the extreme, the men continued their double fucking of the girl's defenceless young body.

This was blatant sexual torture, Jim reflected, squatting and eyeing the elongated teats of the girl's nipples. Painfully pulled away from the small discs of her areolae, her nipples stretched to at least an inch in length, this was blatant violation of her femininity. The weights swinging beneath the table, Jim reckoned that the pain must have been excruciating as he stood up and watched the dou-

ble-ended fucking of her tethered young body. She couldn't be enjoying the crude abuse, he was sure as he noticed her bulging eyes. Her mouth bloated by one monk's cock, her rectal canal forced wide open by another monk's huge organ, Jim wondered whether they were going to fill her tight vagina with their unholy sperm.

The monk shafting Mary's rectal sheath gasped and shuddered as he pumped his sperm deep into her bowels. Mary's naked body rocking back and forth with the double shafting, sperm trickled from her bloated mouth and dribbled down her chin as the other monk reached his climax. *Too many questions?* Jim mused, deciding to prise the truth out of Mary once he got her alone. And Cleo was in line for a session of sexual torture. He'd discover what was going on in the village if it was the last thing he did. Perhaps Davey would reveal . . . Realizing that the lad had gone, Jim looked around the basement. He must have slipped out of the room unnoticed – but why?

The monk pumping sperm down Mary's throat finally withdrawing his spent cock from her abused mouth, two more monks took their position at the head of the table and lifted their habits. Holding the girl's head up by her long blonde hair, they pushed their purple knobs into her sperm-flooded mouth and let out gasps of debauched pleasure. Her lips stretched tautly around the two cock-shafts, her cheeks bloated, she was nothing more than a lump of female meat to be used and abused by the monks.

The other spent cock withdrawing from the girl's inflamed anal hole, Jim watched a monk release one of her feet. Her naked body twisted with one foot high in the air and the other on the floor, both her sex holes were

now accessible. Jim watched in amazement as two monks stood either side of the girl, one pressing his bulbous knob against the sore eye of her anus as the other thrust his swollen glans between the engorged inner lips of her hairless pussy.

The cock-shafts driving deep into her sex sheaths as two more penises fucked her pretty mouth, the girl again writhed and squirmed on the table. She really was a contortionist, Jim mused. Her young body twisted, her legs at ninety degrees to her trunk, the weights pulling on her nipples, four cocks fucking her . . . The girl was far too young to endure such crudities, Jim thought, watching the four penile shafts repeatedly driving into her trembling body. She was either an insatiable nymphomaniac or a helpless victim of the perverted sect.

'Why aren't *you* using the girl?' one of the monks asked Jim.

'I'm waiting my turn,' Jim replied, praying that he wasn't about to be exposed.

'Waiting your turn? It's not usual to . . . Tell me the code word,' he breathed, obviously suspicious.

'Veneris,' Jim replied. 'To be honest, I'm feeling under the weather.'

'I understand, brother. In that case, just enjoy watching the sacrifice.'

'I will.'

Breathing a sigh of relief as the man returned to the table, Jim felt his heart racing, his hands trembling. Thanking God that he'd got away with it, he focused again on the men's penises as they rammed into Mary's sex sheaths. Their spunk spraying from her inflamed holes as they double-fucked her, Jim watched the white liquid hanging in long threads from their swinging balls

and finally dripping onto the stone floor. Reckoning that there were two monks who hadn't yet fucked the girl, Jim wondered how much more abuse her tight holes could take.

Making their last thrusts, the monks finally withdrew their deflating cocks from the girl's trembling body. Drinking from the orgasming knobs still fucking her mouth, she moaned through her nose as the next two men pressed their purple knobs against the spunk-dripping hole of her anus. Jim couldn't believe what they were doing as they forced their bulbous knobs hard against her anal ring. She was too young, too tight, to take a double anal fucking. As one knob slipped past her defeated anal sphincter muscles, Jim was sure that it wasn't possible for the second glans to penetrate her rectal duct.

He'd read about this sort of thing and had seen pictures of two cocks rammed up a girl's arse. But he'd thought that the pictures had been fake. Possibly an older, slacker woman's rectal duct could accommodate two erect penises, but not that of a girl of Mary's tender age. But the second man wasn't going to give up. Yanking the girl's rounded bottom cheeks as far apart as they could go without tearing her open, he again forced his purple knob hard against the stretched brown tissue of her anus.

Finally managing what Jim had thought would be impossible, his knob slipped deep into the girl's arse alongside the other man's huge cock and he let out a gasp. The spent knobs leaving Mary's sperm-flooded mouth, she screamed out as the two solid organs glided along her rectal duct until her anal ring tightly gripped the roots of the invading penises. A third monk moving in with his

erect cock in his hand, Jim's eyes bulged as he realized that this one was going to drive his huge member deep into the restricted sheath of the girl's cunt.

'God, no,' Mary cried as the penis drove into her tight vaginal duct.

'Suck this clean,' another monk chuckled, pressing his anal-slimed knob into her gasping mouth.

'And this,' another said, forcing his sperm-glossed knob into her mouth alongside his friend's cock. 'That'll shut you up.'

Wondering whether to attempt to put a halt to the decadence, Jim knew that he'd never succeed. He was outnumbered. There was no way he'd be able to save Mary from the five-cock fucking. Gazing at the heavy weights hanging from the painfully stretched teats of her small breasts, he knew that she'd take several days to recover from her horrendous ordeal. In time for the following Sunday's bout of sexual abuse? he mused.

The sound of squelching sperm and gasping men filling his ears, Jim wondered how long the session of abuse would last. The men would be exhausted soon, he was sure. They couldn't go on fucking the girl's sex holes indefinitely – could they? Again thinking about Cleo alone in the pub, he knew that he should be getting back. But he couldn't leave Mary in the dungeon with the perverts. She'd obviously need help when they'd finished with her young body. Doubting that she'd even be able to walk, he wondered what her father would say when Jim carried the severely fucked and spunk-dripping girl home.

The five men pumping their spunk simultaneously into the girl's tethered body, Jim hoped that this was the end of the debauchery. He also hoped that he'd find

sexual relief before the day was out. Witnessing the crude
sexual acts had shocked him, but had also sent his libido
through the roof. Cleo wasn't only going to endure a
damned good naked-buttock caning to force her to talk,
but a severe rectal fucking. The men's gasps of satisfaction resounding around the basement as they drained
their swinging balls, Jim knew that Mary would be in no
fit state to take his solid cock up her tight arse. She
wouldn't be in a fit state to do anything, he mused,
gazing at her weal-lined buttocks as the monks made
their last penile thrusts into her abused body.

Remaining in the shadows as the monks finally withdrew their deflating cocks from Mary's inflamed sex
holes, Jim watched them adjust their habits. It was over,
he knew as five of them left the basement. Wondering
again what the girl's father would say when he saw the
state his daughter was in, Jim lowered his head as the last
monk stood in front of him. The man's face shrouded by
his hood, he let out a wicked chuckle and placed his hand
on Jim's shoulder.

'I hope you'll be feeling better by next Sunday,' he
murmured.

'Yes, I will,' Jim breathed softly.

'I'll leave you to release the girl. Take care, brother.'

Waiting until the men had left the basement, Jim
slipped his hood off and stood by the table. Mary was
quivering, her eyes closed, her breathing fast and shallow. A thousand questions battering his mind, he released her ankle from the chain and lowered her leg.
Sperm trickling down her thighs, dribbling from her
partially open mouth, he knew that he had to get her
home as he released her wrists and unclipped the chains
from the elongated teats of her tortured breasts. Helping

her off the table, he steadied Mary's naked body as she swayed on her trembling legs. There was no way she'd be able to walk home, he mused as he looked around the basement for her clothes. Hoping that he wouldn't have to carry her along the street, he asked her whether she was all right.

'I think so,' Mary murmured shakily. 'They really gave it to me, didn't they?'

'Gave it to you? Christ, they fucked you senseless. Who the hell are they?'

'Devil worshippers. They come here every Sunday.'

'Mary, you've got to start telling me the truth,' Jim said, slipping out of his habit. 'What the hell is going on in this village?'

'Sex, that's all,' she replied. 'Fucking – and lots of it. You go now. I'll dress and go home.'

'I'm not leaving you here in that state.'

'I'll be all right. I always end up like this after . . . after the monks have fucked me.'

'I want to talk to you, Mary. Come into the pub this evening and we'll talk, all right?'

'If you say so,' she sighed.

'I do say so. You're going to tell me what the hell is going on around here. Are you sure that you'll be all right?'

'Yes, yes. I'll see you this evening.'

'Promise me that you'll be there'

'I promise.'

Leaving the basement, Jim made his way out through the church. The afternoon sun beating down on his head as he walked back to the pub, he found his experience difficult to comprehend. This was a peaceful and quiet country village, he reflected, noticing several kids play-

ing on the green. But the peace and quiet veiled secrets. Feeling completely alienated, Jim began to wonder whether he'd ever get to the bottom of the mysteries of the village. The convent with its sex-crazed Reverend Mother, the hole in the bar, the glass panels in the floor, the church basement and the monks . . . Was this just the tip of the iceberg?

'How nice of you to pop in,' Cleo snapped as Jim entered the pub and leaned on the bar.

'And how nice of you to want photographs of my ex-wife and brother,' he returned.

'What . . . I don't know what you're talking about,' she stammered, pressing a glass to the vodka optic. 'Photographs?'

'Pour me a pint,' he breathed. 'And stop lying and denying everything, Cleo.'

'Lying?' she echoed, cocking her head to one side as she poured his pint.

'Don't give me that innocent look. So, this dossier you're compiling. How far have you got?'

'Dossier? Jim, I have no idea . . .'

'The photographs in that envelope behind the till, Cleo. I've seen them.'

'Where?' she asked him, fiddling with some papers behind the till. 'There's nothing here.'

'No, I don't suppose there is now that you've moved them.'

'Hang on. There was an envelope for you. A man brought it in earlier. I don't know what was in it. Anyway, I forgot to give it to you.'

'And it's miraculously disappeared, I suppose?'

'Yes, it has. It was here, but . . .'

'We'll discuss this later,' Jim said, looking around the

pub at the pale faces of his customers. 'We can't talk now.'

'As you wish,' she sighed, sipping her vodka. 'So, where have you been?'

'In the dungeon, Cleo. In the dungeon with the monks.'

'Monks? Now you really are talking crap. What monks?'

'As I said, we'll discuss it later. I've been kept in the dark for long enough. You're going to tell me everything, Cleo.'

'I can't tell you what I don't know.'

'I'll fuck the truth out of you if I have to.'

'Will you, now? In that case, you'd better come to my flat after we close this evening. It's about time you gave me a length, Jim. You've shafted just about every other girl in the village and completely ignored my own feminine needs.'

'Er . . . well, I . . . I wasn't sure whether you wanted to.'

'You weren't sure? Are you crazy? I invited you in for coffee the other evening but you chose to sleep with Mary.'

'Yes, well . . . OK, after we close this evening. But I still want the truth, Cleo. You needn't think that you're going to get out of this by opening your legs.'

'I was going to open my buttocks,' she giggled.

'Really? Well, in that case . . .'

'In that case, now that you're here, you can clear the glasses from the tables.'

'Yes, yes, of course.'

Downing his pint, Jim knew that the girl was offering him her young body to appease him and divert his

attention from monks and the like. His thoughts turning to the photographs as he cleared the tables, he wondered whether the envelope really had been for him. If that was the case, who would have sent him pictures of his ex-wife and brother? What would be the point? Unless his ex-wife was up to something, he mused. Knowing the cow well, he wouldn't have put anything past her. At least he'd discovered the dungeon, he thought happily, imagining his ex-wife bound to the table with five cocks fucking her slack holes. Perhaps he'd invite the hag-bag down for a weekend. And her lesbian lover.

9

Fortunately, the pub was deserted when Mary arrived at eight o'clock. Cleo had gone out for a while, probably hoping that Jim would be rushed off his feet and unable to cope. Pouring Mary a large vodka and tonic, Jim leaned on the bar and smiled at her. She was wearing her flimsy summer dress, the elongated teats of her young breasts clearly defined by the tight material. He was going to have to be gentle with her, he mused. She'd simply clam up if he became annoyed and angry.

'Where would you like to start?' he asked her.

'There's nothing to say,' she mumbled.

'One thing that strikes me as odd is your swearing. Or, I should say, lack of it.'

'I don't swear all the fucking time,' she replied.

'I noticed that, in the church basement, you didn't swear once. Why was that?'

'Is that what you wanted to talk about? Swearing?'

'You know what I want to talk about, Mary. What did your father say when you got home?'

'He wasn't around. He never is on Sunday afternoons. Just as well, really.'

'How much do the monks pay you?'

'They don't.'

'So what do you get out of it?'

'Sex. What more could a girl want?'

'That wasn't sex, Mary. It was sexual *torture*, for Christ's sake.'

'Call it what you like, I loved it. I realize that you're not going to give up with your questioning, so I'll tell you all I know. When my mother left, I got really pissed off and started looking for some excitement. I screwed around, fucked anyone and everyone. It was great because I had something to look forward to and men liked me. Well, they liked my cunt. Then I met Davey. We fucked like hell, and I loved it.'

'Does Davey live locally?'

'No, he lives in another village a few miles away. He took me to what I thought was going to be a party. When we got there, to this man's house, the place was full of monks. They all fucked me, and I wanted more and more. Eventually, we went to the church basement to fuck. And that's all there is to it.'

This was pointless, Jim thought as he downed his beer and refilled his glass. The girl had no intention of telling the truth. He had thought about sexually torturing the truth out of her but, after her time in the church with the monks, he doubted that she'd bat an eyelid, let alone talk. Wondering whether to make up some fantastic story, spin an incredible web of lies, he came up with an idea.

'I might as well be honest with you,' he said, doing his best to look serious. 'I've been sent here to find out what's going on.'

'Sent here?' Mary breathed, her sky-blue eyes frowning at him.

'I'm working undercover.'

'You're a copper?'

'No, no. I work for a Sunday tabloid. I've been sent here to expose . . . I can't say too much.'

'Er . . . So, how much do you know?'

'A hell of a lot. But I need to discover more before we run the story and expose . . . I can't say who it is we plan to expose. I'm telling you this because I don't want to see you caught up in the mess when the shit hits the fan.'

'I . . . I don't know anything,' she lied. 'Apart from having some fun in the church with the monks, I don't know anything.'

'The *fun in the church with the monks*, as you put it, is very much a part of what I'm working on. Do you know anything about photographs of my ex-wife?'

'Photographs? No, no, I don't.'

'This is big, Mary. And I don't want to see you get into trouble.'

'Just leave me out of the story, then.'

'It's not as easy as that. I'm not working alone. I don't want to say too much about it. The thing is, since I've now witnessed the sex in the church basement . . .' His words tailing off as Cleo breezed into the pub, Jim donned a huge grin. 'Cleo,' he said. 'How are you?'

'I'm fine,' she replied. 'More to the point, how are *you*?'

'On top of the world, as always. I'm just going up to my flat to change my shirt. I won't be a minute.'

Leaving the girls to chat, Jim slipped into the back room and rubbed his chin. Mary would no doubt tell Cleo about his undercover work, he mused. Wondering how long it would take before word got round the village, he crept up the stairs as he heard Cleo approaching. Watching the girl, he wondered what she was doing as she looked around the room before opening the cellar door and calling out for him. She knew that he'd said he was going up to the flat, he mused. So why check the

cellar? Crouching in the shadows at the top of the stairs, he gazed wide-eyed as the cellar door creaked and opened.

Stunned, he watched Crystal look around the back room before slipping into the bar. What had the girl been doing lurking in the cellar? he wondered, his mind riddled with confusion. Had she been spying up through the glass panels at Mary's knickerless pussy? Perhaps there was a man down there, he mused. Had she been enjoying a quick fuck over the beer barrels? Noisily descending the stairs, he returned to the bar to find the three girls chatting and laughing.

'Hi, Crystal,' he said, smiling at the horny girl.

'Hi, Jim. Sorry about the food cabinet. The caretaker said that he'd drop it off as soon as he can.'

'There's no rush. Although it would be nice to have it here for tomorrow lunchtime. The sandwiches are selling like hot cakes. Perhaps we should sell hot cakes?'

'Maybe. Anyway, I was just passing and thought I'd call in to apologize.'

'You were passing?'

'Yes, I was on my way back to the convent.'

'I thought that you were going to change your shirt?' Cleo murmured to Jim.

'Yes, I . . . I forgot. I'm always doing that. I went up to the flat and then forgot what I went up there for. I'll go and change it now.'

Leaving the bar once more, Jim crept down to the cellar to try to discover what Crystal had been up to. Cleo must have known that she was down there, he thought, looking around him. And she'd obviously checked that Jim wasn't around before . . . But she hadn't called out for Crystal, he reflected. She'd called out for Jim, which

was odd. If she'd thought that he might have been down there, then she'd have known that he'd have seen Crystal and . . . None of this made sense, he mused. What the hell would Crystal have been doing in the cellar? His confusion suddenly clearing as he pondered on the mystery, Jim smiled.

'That's it,' he breathed, tapping on the wooden panelling lining the far wall. Grinning as a panel swung open, he stared in disbelief into a dimly lit tunnel. Slipping into the tunnel and closing the panel behind him, he instinctively knew that this was the dungeon he'd been looking for. At least, this passageway led to the dungeon, he thought, making his way along it. The musk of time filling his nostrils, he reckoned that the tunnel had been there as long as the pub. Possibly one hundred years or so. Probably used by smugglers, it was bound to lead to some sort of chamber.

After walking for what seemed like miles, Jim came to an oak door. This was the dungeon, he reckoned, gingerly opening the door and peering into a large room. Staring incredulously at what could only be described as a sexual torture chamber, he wandered into the centre of the room and looked around him. Chains, whips, handcuffs, shelves lined with vibrators and a host of sex toys . . . This was an amazing discovery. This was the mysterious fucking dungeon.

Wondering what to do as he cast his gaze over an examination couch and a glass-topped trolley laden with vaginal speculums and other medical-type instruments, he stared in awe at several leather whips and gags hanging from the wall. The place was fully equipped for any and every sexual perversion. But why the massive cloak of secrecy? he wondered. Cleo could have told him about

the dungeon. After all, she knew that he wasn't exactly a prude. He was as sexually deviant as any normal man. More so, in fact. Crystal understood his attraction to schoolgirls, so why hadn't *she* let him in on the secret?

Hearing voices in the tunnel, Jim looked around for somewhere to hide. Diving behind a large cupboard in the corner of the room as the door opened, he watched in amazement as Crystal led a middle-aged man into the dungeon and closed the door. Not recognizing the man, Jim kept perfectly still, spying on the unlikely couple as they moved to the examination table. The man mumbled something and laughed as Crystal pointed to the glass-topped trolley. Was he a potential customer? Jim wondered as Crystal picked up a vaginal speculum. Passing the device to the man, she waved her hand at the trolley and proudly announced that the surgery was well equipped with gynaecological instruments.

'Excellent,' the man breathed. 'But are we safe here?'

'Oh, yes,' Crystal reassured him. 'As I said earlier, only a select few know about this place.'

'What about this new landlord? I've heard that—'

'You don't have to worry about him,' Crystal giggled. 'He believes that the church basement is the sex dungeon. A friend of mine has put him way off the scent.'

'I hope so,' the man sighed. 'If it came to light that I've been here . . . In my position as a high-court judge, all hell would be let loose if this came to light.'

'We have police officers, MPs, solicitors . . . I promise you, there's nothing to worry about. The only difficulty is gaining access to the dungeon when the pub's landlord is around. Cleo was saying that he found it odd that some customers disappeared into thin air. He now believes that they left the pub via the toilet.'

'It sounds rather risky to me,' the man said, rubbing his chin. 'What happens when we leave the dungeon and go back through the tunnel to the pub? The landlord might be in the cellar and . . .'

'No, no,' Crystal interrupted him. 'Cleo presses a button beneath the bar when the coast is clear. When we hear the buzzer, we know that it's safe to leave the tunnel.'

'Ingenious. Well, you seem to have catered very well, security-wise. Er . . . the convent schoolgirls you mentioned. It's possible to have three or four at a time?'

'You can have as many as you like.'

'I'm rather keen to play the role of a doctor and examine the girls.'

'No problem. Er . . . is there anything I can do for you now?'

'Yes, I think there is,' the judge chuckled.

'I'd like you to examine me, doctor,' she said, tugging her short skirt down her long legs.

'Of course. As a qualified gynaecologist, I'd be only too happy to examine you.'

Watching from his hiding place as the girl slipped her blouse over her shoulders and unhooked her bra, Jim could hardly believe that this was happening. *A high-court judge?* he mused. Police officers, MPs, solicitors . . . Willycombe Village was one huge brothel. Crystal had the most exquisite breast bumps, Jim thought, his wide-eyed stare locked to the ripe teats of her suckable nipples. But it was pretty obvious that she was nothing more than a common slut-whore.

As she slipped her tight panties down her long legs, exposing the exquisite lips of her hairless pussy, Jim wondered whether the brewery knew about the illicit

business. Was that why they kept the pub on? he wondered. The place ran at a loss, and old man Hops hadn't wanted any changes. If he was pulling in cash from the dungeon brothel and the pub was nothing more than a convenient front . . . That had to be the answer, Jim thought, watching Crystal as she lay back on the examination couch with her legs spread. Focusing on the petite mounds of her teenage breasts, he recalled reading about this sort of thing in the Sunday papers. Schoolgirls entertaining businessmen and MPs, selling their young bodies to doctors and solicitors . . . To discover that the Tartan Vicar was a façade for a schoolgirlie brothel was incredible.

Pondering on the direction of the tunnel, trying to work out roughly where the dungeon was located, Jim realized that it must have been beneath the vicarage. Probably used originally by rogues and smugglers to store their contraband, the place was ideally suited for illicit sex sessions. But who was the boss? Who ran the business? Cleo? Surely not. This was a big operation, he mused, not some sideline run by the convent schoolgirls to earn some extra cash. Again reckoning that the brewery knew about the illicit business, Jim figured that old man Hops was the pimp. He'd taken Cleo outside for a quiet word, Jim recalled. Obviously, he'd wanted to discuss the underground operation with the girl.

Recalling Mary and the monks, he could hardly believe to what lengths they'd gone to put him off the scent. Was the vicar in on the schoolgirl brothel? he wondered. The man had said that Mary was in the church. He'd probably hoped that Jim would go there in search of the girl and stumble across the basement. How on earth

could a vicar allow his teenage daughter to sell her body for sex? Worse than merely condoning her sexual exploits, he probably actually made money from the sale of her young body.

'Your breasts are developing well,' the perverted judge said, squeezing Crystal's mammary spheres. 'Hard, well formed . . . They're fine specimens.'

'It's my clitoris that I'm concerned about,' Crystal breathed huskily. 'I'm not sure that it's as big as it should be. Would you take a look at it, doctor?'

'Certainly,' he chuckled, parting the swollen lips of the girl's teenage pussy. 'Tell me, my dear. Do you masturbate?'

'All the time' Crystal confessed. 'I can't stop masturbating.'

'That's very good,' the man murmured, examining the ripe nub of her clitoris. 'I'd like you to show me how you masturbate. I'd like you to massage your clitoris until you come.'

'I rather like sucking a cock while I frig my clitty,' Crystal breathed.

'That's not a problem,' the judge said, unzipping his trousers.

As the girl began her clitoral masturbation, Jim watched the man slip his purple knob between her succulent lips and drive his solid cock deep into her pretty mouth. His own penis stiffening as he imagined fucking the schoolgirl's mouth, he wondered whether or not to tell Cleo that he'd discovered the mysterious sex dungeon. It might be best not to say anything just yet, he decided. He could have some fun, he thought, imagining pressing the push-button to indicate that the coast was clear. Apart from having fun, he'd make a list of the

brothel punters and create a dossier to use as insurance in case trouble loomed.

'Drink it,' the judge gasped as Crystal gobbled and sucked on his purple knob. The girl's naked body trembling uncontrollably as she massaged her clitoris faster, she reached beneath her thigh and slipped a finger into the tight sheath of her cunt as she reached her self-induced climax. Repeatedly swallowing hard as the man pumped his sperm into her thirsty mouth, she moaned loudly though her nose. The slurping sounds of girl-juice echoing around the dungeon as she finger-fucked her schoolgirl pussy, she shook wildly in her coming as she continued to drink from the man's throbbing knob.

Jim watched the crude mouth-fucking, grinning as the man gasped and drained his balls. Crystal could have been no older than . . . Jim dared not think how old – how young – the girl was. One thing was certain, the convent schoolgirls were insatiable, sex-crazed nymphomaniacs. But how many girls were involved with the dungeon brothel? Did Elizabeth, the impostor Reverend Mother, know what was going on? Although Jim had discovered the sex dungeon, there were still many unanswered questions.

'Very good,' the judge breathed, slipping his sperm-dripping knob out of Crystal's wet mouth. 'You're something of an expert.'

'I do my best,' the girl laughed, licking her spunk-glossed lips as she slipped her finger out of her tight cunt. 'You'll be a regular visitor, then?'

'Indeed I will,' he replied, zipping his trousers. 'If all the girls are like you, I'll be visiting at least once a week.'

'It's best not to phone,' Crystal said, slipping off the

examination couch and grabbing her clothes. 'Come into the pub for a drink and Cleo will sort out a girl for you. If you want several schoolgirls at the same time, then you might have to wait for a while. Cleo will call me at the convent and I'll send as many girls along as you want.'

'This new landlord,' the man murmured as he watched Crystal dressing. 'What if he's around and we don't have an opportunity to slip into the cellar?'

'Cleo will deal with any such event. She's only got to ask him to go out to buy something or to take a look at a dripping tap in her flat. She'll get him out of the way long enough for you and the girls to go down to the cellar. What I have to do now is give a couple of rings on Cleo's mobile phone,' she said, punching the buttons on her mobile. 'That will let Cleo know that we're ready to leave. We'll go and wait by the cellar door for the buzzer.'

'OK, I'm ready when you are.'

Watching the couple leave the dungeon, Jim emerged from his hiding place and looked around the large room. Noticing a desk in the corner, he opened the drawer and rummaged through a pile of papers. There might be some reference to whoever ran the business, he mused, taking a small address book from the drawer. Flicking through the pages and finding nothing, he realized that this was a well-run operation and so there'd be no incriminating evidence left lying around. Closing the drawer, he decided to leave the dungeon in case another punter was due. The last thing he wanted was to be caught.

Following the tunnel to the cellar door, Jim listened before making his escape. Fortunately, no one was around as he climbed the stone steps to the back room of the pub. Feeling pleased with himself, he brushed his

dark hair back with his fingers before making his entrance into the bar. Pleased to see half a dozen customers sitting at the tables, Jim smiled at Cleo as she poured Crystal a large vodka and tonic. Moving behind the bar and helping himself to a pint of bitter, he realized as Cleo stared at him that he still hadn't changed his shirt.

'You were a long time,' she said.

'I couldn't find a clean shirt,' he complained. 'I'll have to get myself organized. I'm surprised to see you're still here, Crystal. I thought you'd just called to tell me about the display cabinet?'

'I decided to stay and chat to Cleo,' the girl replied. 'Mary went home so I thought I'd keep Cleo company. There's no rush to get back to the convent.'

'I'm pleased that you decided to stay. There's nothing like an attractive schoolgirl to brighten the place up. Er . . . I wouldn't mind a cup of coffee,' he said, turning to Cleo.

'You've just poured a pint of beer. You want coffee as well?'

'If you wouldn't mind?'

'That's what I'm here for,' Cleo sighed, leaving the bar. 'General dogsbody, that's me.'

'She doesn't seem too happy,' Jim said, gazing into Crystal's sparking eyes.

'She'll be all right,' the girl said. 'I reckon that she's overworked. It might be an idea to give her a couple of days off.'

'Yes, yes, I'll do that. By the way, I was talking to an old boy earlier. He was telling me about the Willycombe Village smugglers.'

'Oh?'

'Apparently, the smugglers used an old tunnel beneath the vicarage.'

'A tunnel?' Crystal echoed, her blue eyes widening. 'Who was this old man?'

'I don't know his name. We met in the street and got chatting. It was over a hundred years ago when the smugglers used the tunnel for their contraband, he said. I found it most interesting.'

'Did he say where the entrance to the tunnel was?'

'No, he didn't. I've always been interested in old buildings. To discover that there's a tunnel beneath the vicarage is quite exciting.'

'I don't suppose it's there now. It was probably filled in. What did this old man look like? I just wondered whether I might know him.'

'Not very tall, old, bald . . . He said that he's lived here all his life. I thought I might ask the vicar about the tunnel. Seeing as he lives in the vicarage—'

'I wouldn't bother,' Crystal interrupted him.

'Wouldn't bother with what?' Cleo asked, placing a cup of coffee on the bar.

'Jim reckons that there's an old tunnel beneath the vicarage. Some old man told him about it.'

'Oh, er . . . I've heard that story,' Cleo said. 'It's no longer there. Apparently, it caved in years ago. The council decided that it was dangerous and filled the whole tunnel in.'

'Hi,' Carole said, entering the pub with Melanie.

'Hi, girls,' Cleo trilled. 'Two vodkas?'

'Mmm, please.'

'How are you both?' Jim asked the schoolgirls, noticing two well-dressed men sitting at a corner table nudging each other.

'Great,' Melanie replied. 'We're on our way to the convent and thought we'd have a quick drink.'

'Er . . . Jim, would you mind nipping down to the shop and getting some milk?' Cleo asked him.

'It won't be open, will it?'

'Yes, they stay open late. We've run out and I'll need some for the morning.'

'OK, I'll go after I've finished my coffee.'

Glancing at the grinning men, Jim knew that the girls were going to take them to the dungeon. Checking his watch, he wondered what to do. It was nine-thirty. They had plenty of time for a session of crude sex before the pub closed. It might have been an idea to hang around and make things awkward, he mused. There again, he could go down to the shop and give them the opportunity to go to the dungeon, and then hang around so that they had to stay down there.

'Are you going?' Cleo asked him. 'They don't stay open all night.'

'I have some milk in my flat,' Jim replied. 'I'll go and get it.'

'Oh, er . . . OK.'

'I'll put some washing in the machine while I'm up there. If I don't, I'll have nothing to wear in the morning.'

'There's no rush,' Cleo said, obviously relieved. 'You take your time.'

Making his way to his flat, Jim hovered at the top of the stairs and crouched in the shadows. Sure enough, the schoolgirls led the middle-aged men down to the cellar. The sex dungeon was obviously a thriving business, he mused, wondering whether he could get in on the act. But before he made moves to become a partner he had to discover who the boss was. Finally grabbing a bottle of milk from his fridge and returning to the bar, he didn't

comment on the girls' disappearance. Crystal was still there, knocking back vodka as if it was water, and Cleo was looking decidedly guilty as she smiled at Jim.

'I might rearrange the cellar,' Jim said, placing the bottle of milk on the bar.

'Rearrange it?' Cleo and Crystal echoed in unison.

'I might put some shelves up along the wall with the wooden panelling. We could keep the boxes of crisps there and—'

'I don't think that's a good idea,' Cleo broke in.

'Oh? Why not?'

'Well . . . we don't want to have to go down to the cellar every time we need crisps. The back room is fine for that sort of stock.'

'Ah, the back room,' Jim chuckled. 'I have plans for that, too.'

'What sort of plans?' Crystal asked him, her blue eyes frowning.

'Cleo has to make the sandwiches in her flat. If I turned one corner of the back room into a kitchenette, we could prepare all sorts of food there. And we could have a coffee pot permanently on the go.'

'It might be a good idea,' Cleo said softly, winking at Crystal. 'But I think you should leave the cellar as it is.'

'Perhaps you're right. OK, I'll leave the cellar as it is and sort the back room out.'

'The girls didn't stay long,' Crystal said, obviously trying to establish whether Jim was suspicious.

'Girls?' Jim murmured nonchalantly 'Oh, you mean Carole and Melanie? To be honest, I hadn't noticed.'

'Fucking hell,' Cleo breathed as the vicar wandered into the pub. 'What the hell is *he* doing here?'

'Good evening, Father,' Jim greeted the man.

'Good evening, Jim. I'd like a word, if I may?'

'Yes, of course. Shall we sit over there in the corner?'

'Certainly.'

Following the cleric, Jim turned and winked at the stunned girls. This was a first, he knew as Cleo frowned at him and mouthed something. It must have been important, Jim mused as he sat down opposite the vicar. For the anti-drinking, anti-smoking, anti-sex, anti-everything man to walk into what he deemed to be a den of evil, this must have been extremely important. Reckoning that it had something to do with the monks in the church basement, Jim waited for the man to begin the conversation.

'It's about Mary,' the vicar said softly, looking around the pub to make sure that no one else was listening. 'She's been up to something in the church.'

'Oh?' Jim murmured.

'Did you find her there earlier?'

'Er . . . no, no, I didn't,' Jim lied. 'What's happened, Father? What has she been up to?'

'An hour or so after you'd left the garden, I went to look for her. I was just in time to see her leaving the church. She was in a terrible state, Jim. Her face was flushed, her hair all over the place . . . And she was staggering, as if she'd been drinking.'

'Goodness me,' Jim said, wondering again whether the man was in on the scam and if he knew about the monks. 'Did you speak to her?'

'I tried, but she wouldn't tell me anything.'

'I don't know whether this has anything to do with it,' Jim whispered. 'But I saw several monks leaving the church.'

'Monks?'

'I went to look for Mary but couldn't find her. I went for a walk and, on my way back, I saw several monks leaving the church.'

'How odd.'

'I thought that you might know something about it?'

'No, no, I don't. Monks? What on earth were monks doing in the church? They must have been there when Mary was.'

'I overheard one of them saying something about the church basement.'

'The basement isn't used. It's been empty for years. Come to think of it, you mentioned a basement when I met you in the garden.'

'Yes, I . . . As I said, I'm interested in old buildings. Someone said that the vicarage might have a basement.'

'No, it hasn't. And no one uses the church basement. Unless . . . unless Mary's been going down there?'

'Possibly. But who are these monks? And why would Mary meet them in the basement?'

'I honestly have no idea. Will you talk to her again?'

'Yes, of course.'

'She trusts you and . . . so do I. You're a good man, Jim. I'd be most grateful if you'd talk to her again.'

'Certainly, Father. I'll call round in the morning and exercise my oral skills.'

'You're very kind. Well, I'd better be going.'

'I'll see you in the morning, Father.'

Returning to the bar as the vicar left the pub, Jim was reasonably sure that he knew nothing about Mary's sexual exploits. But there was so much sex around that Jim didn't know what to think. Mary had fucked a group of monks in the church basement, Crystal had sucked off a high-court judge, there were two schoolgirls in the

dungeon right now with a couple of middle-aged perverts . . . What the hell was going on in Willycombe
Village?

'What did he want?' Cleo asked Jim as he sat down on a
bar stool. 'He's never been in here in all the years I've
known him. What the hell did he want?'

'Mary's told him something about a tunnel,' Jim
replied, concealing a grin.

'A tunnel?' Crystal echoed.

'It seems that the tunnel used by the smugglers is still
there.'

'No, it's not,' Cleo stated firmly. 'I told you earlier,
Jim. The tunnel was filled in.'

'That's not what Mary's been saying to her father.'

'What the hell has that cow . . .' Crystal began. 'I
mean, she doesn't know what she's talking about.'

'What did the vicar say, exactly?' Cleo asked Jim.

'Apparently, Mary was drunk and was rambling on
about a tunnel leading to a dungeon. Something's going
on, but I don't know what. Anyway, the vicar is going to
investigate. And he wants me to help him.'

'It's ridiculous, Jim,' Cleo sighed. 'All this rubbish
about a tunnel and a dungeon . . . I don't know why
you're wasting your time even thinking about it.'

'He also mentioned a group of monks,' Jim added,
watching the girls for a reaction.

'Fuck,' Crystal gasped. 'Er . . . he must be mad.'

'Apparently, they've been to the church and . . . Oh,
well. Not to worry. As you said, it's a waste of time even
thinking about it.'

'They've been to the church?' Cleo murmured.

'According to Mary, yes. Mind you, she was drunk.'

Jim took a drink to a table and gazed out of the window

as the girls whispered to each other. He'd put the cat among the pigeons, he mused happily. Before long, they were going to have to tell him all they knew about the dungeon brothel. He'd dropped Mary in it, he reflected. The girls would probably give her a good buttock-thrashing for blurting things out to her father. But that was Mary's problem. She'd conned Jim, and she was going to get all she deserved for her lies and deceit. Again wondering who ran the business, Jim realized that the boss would be told of Mary's big mouth. The outcome was going to be most interesting, Jim mused.

Gazing across the village green as darkness finally engulfed the village, Jim decided to hang around until the schoolgirls had satisfied the men and wanted to leave the tunnel. Cleo wouldn't know what to do, he mused. Unable to allow the punters to return to the pub after their perverted sex session, she'd have to wait until Jim had gone to bed. But he wasn't feeling at all tired and might sit in the bar until the early hours. This was also going to be most interesting.

After a couple more pints of beer, Jim realized that what he hadn't allowed for was his full bladder. He held out for as long as he could but was finally forced to slip into the toilets. When he returned to the bar, Cleo announced that Crystal had gone and she was about to close up. The girls and their punters had gone, he knew as he noticed the smirk across Cleo's pretty face. Perhaps it was just as well, he mused, turning the lights out as Cleo bolted the door. He'd dropped more than enough hints about the tunnel and the dungeon for one day.

Suggesting that they have a cup of coffee in Cleo's flat, Jim wasn't surprised when she turned him down. This was her way of paying him back for prying into the

village's secrets, he knew as he climbed the stairs to his
flat. But there was plenty of fresh pussy around. In fact,
the village was positively teeming with fresh schoolgirlie
pussy. Deciding to fuck Carole and Melanie the following day as he slipped beneath his quilt, Jim closed his
eyes and dreamed his dreams of hairless vulval lips,
creamy-wet girlie cracks, suckable milk teats, lickable
bottom-holes . . .

IO

Much to Jim's disappointment, it was raining when he leaped out of bed on Monday morning. He'd hoped to lure one or two schoolgirls to the woods and drain his full balls, but it wasn't to be. He was in dire need of a hairless young pussy, a tight bottom-hole. Some schoolgirl or other was going to take his cock-shaft into her young body, but who? Dressing after taking a shower, he decided that Cleo would be the lucky recipient of his fresh spunk. It was high time she took his cock into her hot pussy, he reflected as he bounded down the stairs. And up her tight arse.

'Ah, the food-display cabinet,' Jim breathed as he joined Cleo behind the bar. 'Excellent stuff.'

'The caretaker dropped it off just now,' Cleo said, sipping coffee from a mug. 'And guess where I got this coffee from?'

'Er . . . you boiled the kettle and . . .'

'Take a look behind you.'

'That's brilliant,' Jim chuckled, gazing at a coffee percolator. 'I owe Crystal one.'

'It's money she wants, not your cock. By the way, I've been counting the cash. That was the best weekend we've had for months. I'll go to the bank later.'

'Great. Things are looking up, Cleo. What with the sandwiches and now the coffee—'

'Jim, we need to talk,' the girl interrupted him.

'Talk?'

'This nonsense about a tunnel and a dungeon. When you arrived, I told you that people don't like strangers asking questions.'

'Yes, but I'm not a stranger now.'

'You are, as far as the locals are concerned. You've spent more time nosing around the village and asking questions than you have in the pub. You've been to the vicarage, the woods, the convent, the church . . .'

'How do you know where I've been?'

'People talk, Jim.'

'Hang on, hang on. What's brought all this on? One minute we're talking about the sandwiches and coffee, and the next minute . . .'

'As it's Monday, the beginning of a new week, I thought we'd make a fresh start. No more talk about tunnels and dungeons.'

'If you say so.'

'I do, Jim. Now that Mary's gone blabbing her mouth off to her father . . .'

'She was drunk, Cleo. She obviously didn't know what she was saying.'

'That's not the point. The point is that she's been listening to you and your questions about tunnels and dungeons. What is this fixation you have about a bloody dungeon? There *are* no dungeons in Willycombe.'

'Who runs the place?' Jim asked, deciding to go for broke. 'Who's the boss, Cleo?'

'My father . . . I mean . . .'

'Your father?'

'God, me and my big mouth,' she sighed.

'I rather like your mouth. OK, it's time you talked to me.'

'All right. My father owns the brewery.'

'*What*?' Jim gasped. 'Your father is—'

'Old man Hops, as you call him.'

'Good grief. Do you mean to say that old man Hops is your mother's husband?'

'Yes.'

'Blimey. Why didn't you tell me?'

'No one knows. It's the way he wants it, Jim. I work here and live in the flat, but no one is to know that Mr Hops is my father.'

'What about . . .'

'No, Jim. I'm not going to say any more. You can ask me a thousand questions. But I'm not saying any more. And, please, don't tell a soul. If you do, my father will have you out of here before you can blink an eyelid.'

This was a revelation that Jim had never expected. Old man Hops was the barmaid's father? Deciding that Cleo had meant it when she'd said that she'd say no more, Jim reckoned that he didn't need to question her further. Hops was obviously the pimp. His daughter ran the pub and the brothel while he raked in the cash. That was why he hadn't wanted any changes. But why put Jim in the pub? Surely, Cleo was more than capable of running the operation without the need for a landlord? Certain that old man Hops kept the pub on not only as a façade for the brothel but probably a tax loss, Jim smelled money.

When Jim had worked at the brewery, Hops had always thought him stupid and incompetent. That was why he'd put him in charge of the Tartan Vicar, Jim was sure. Hops had obviously reckoned that Jim would make a complete hash of running the pub. What with Jim's salary as well as Cleo's money, the place would run at a huge loss. A huge *tax* loss? While Jim was running the

failing pub, Hops would be raking in huge tax-free profits from the dungeon brothel.

Reckoning that a chat with Hops would prove fruitful, Jim decided to get in on the operation. He wasn't going to be kept in the dark and used like this. Mysteries, secrets, cover-ups . . . Although tempted to grab the phone, threaten Hops and demand a share of the dirty money, Jim remained calm. There was no rush. Besides, he wanted to learn more about the brothel and list the names of all the punters before threatening Hops.

'Are you all right?' Cleo asked Jim as she sipped her coffee.

'Yes, yes, I'm fine,' he replied, smiling at the girl.

'I'm sorry,' she breathed. 'I would have told you but . . . My father . . .'

'Say no more, Cleo. I won't reveal your secret, so you have no worries. And I'll stop asking about tunnels and dungeons.'

'Thanks, Jim. You're . . . you're great. I feel really guilty now,' she sighed.

'Well, you shouldn't. What difference does it make if your father owns the brewery and the pub? None at all, as far as I'm concerned. He's brought me in to run the place which, with your help, is what I'm doing.'

'You don't think that my father is using you, then?'

'Using me? No, of course not. How on earth could he be using me?'

'You might have thought that, what with the pub running at a loss and the money he pays you, this might be a tax fiddle or something.'

'A tax fiddle?' Jim echoed, Cleo's comment confirming his suspicions. 'Hardly. Look, let's forget that we had

this chat. We'll carry on as before, as if I'm none the wiser about old man . . . I mean, *Mr* Hops.'

'That's great,' Cleo trilled. 'Right, I'd better go and buy some bread for the sandwiches and do the banking.'

As she left the pub with a briefcase, Jim rubbed his chin and smiled. There was probably a small fortune in her case, he mused as he imagined taking a handsome cut of the sex dungeon profits. Things certainly were looking up, he reflected, pouring himself a cup of coffee. Pondering on the dungeon, he reckoned that the vicar was, after all, part of the illicit business. Doubting that Mary was really the man's daughter, he grinned as everything began to fall into place. Crystal had told the judge that the farce with the monks in the church basement had been designed to put Jim off the scent. The vicar was obviously doing his bit to steer Jim away from the truth by allowing him to go to Mary's bedroom and fuck her.

'Money, money, money,' Jim chuckled, punching the air with his fist as he looked around the pub. Reckoning that he knew just about all there was to know about the illicit business, he wondered when to drop the bombshell on old man Hops. Recalling Cleo saying that Hops came to the pub every Friday, he thought that would be a good time to take the man to one side and have a chat with him. A business proposition? Jim pondered. Blackmail? It was an ugly word. But it just about summed up what Jim had in mind.

Noticing Mary walking across the village green towards the pub, Jim suddenly had a thought. Was the vicar one of the monks? If the man wasn't Mary's father, he might have gone to the church basement to join in with the debauchery. Recalling what he'd thought was an older monk hovering in the shadows, Jim wondered

whether this had been the vicar. He'd have been able to keep an eye on Jim and make sure that the proceedings went to plan. It was an interesting theory, and one that Jim would have to check out.

'Hi,' Mary trilled as she breezed into the pub. 'It's fucking raining.'

'So it fucking is,' Jim chuckled, eyeing her pert nipples pressing through her wet dress. 'What can I do you for?'

'I just thought that I'd come and see how you are.'

'I'm fine. In fact, I've never been better. How's your father?'

'The old git's OK, I suppose. He said that you were coming to see me this morning.'

'Yes, I was going to come over later. By the way, one of the monks came into the pub last night.'

'One of the monks? Was he wearing his habit?'

'No, no. He came in for a chat. I had no idea that he was a monk until he told me.'

'He *told* you? Who was he?'

'He didn't tell me his name. Obviously, it's all very hush-hush.'

'That's strange,' she murmured. 'They're not supposed to . . .'

'What aren't they supposed to do?'

'Come in here and . . . They're not supposed to tell other people about the basement.'

'He recognized me, Mary. He knew that I'd been in the basement, that's why he came in for a chat. I'm rather looking forward to next Sunday's session.'

'Er . . . yes, so am I.'

Leaving the girl to mull over his revelation, Jim poured her a cup of coffee. He was sure now that the monk standing in the corner of the basement had been

her so-called father. The vicar was nothing more than a perverted pimp, he reflected, placing Mary's coffee on the counter as she perched her rounded buttocks on a stool. Making out to the locals that Mary was his daughter, he probably fucked the girl senseless every night. It was quite a scam, Jim mused. In fact, the entire village was heaving with illegal scams.

'This monk who came in to see you,' Mary persisted. 'Was Cleo here at the time?'

'No, she'd gone out for a while. You look worried. What's the problem?'

'Nothing. So, are you coming over to my place later?'

'Your father wanted me to talk to you about your problems. As you're here, there's no point in going to the vicarage. Are you all right, Mary?' Jim asked her as she stared blankly across the bar. 'Only, you seem terribly preoccupied.'

'I'm confused,' she sighed. 'I can't understand why one of the monks came in here.'

'I told you. He came in to have a chat. What's confusing about that?'

'I'd better be going,' Mary said, slipping off the bar stool.

'Oh, er . . . as you wish.'

There was nothing like tossing a little confusion into the cooking pot, Jim reflected as he watched the girl leaving. Deciding to have Mary's coffee as she'd obviously been too worried by his revelation to drink it herself Jim pondered on the secret button Cleo used to give the all-clear. Kneeling on the floor and discovering a bell push hidden beneath the counter, he let out a chuckle. *Perfect*, he thought, deciding to press the button when the coast was far from clear. The girls would glare

at Cleo as they emerged from the back room with their clients, wondering why she'd given the signal when Jim was hovering behind the bar. More confusion, more fun.

'Was that Mary I saw leaving?' Cleo asked Jim as she lugged several carrier bags of bread into the pub and dumped them on the counter.

'Yes, it was. She just called in to say hello. By the way, some man came in.'

'Some man?'

'He asked for you. When I said that you were out, he asked whether I could book him in for this evening.'

'Oh, er . . . that's odd.'

'I said that this wasn't a hotel, but he went on about booking two girls.'

'Christ,' Cleo gasped, her pretty face turning pale. 'What else did he say?'

'Nothing. I told him to sod off. He was obviously mad. Booking two girls? The man's barmy.'

'Yes, he must be,' she said, forcing a laugh. 'Well, I'll get on with the sandwiches.'

The more confusion the better, Jim mused as Cleo lugged the bread through the back room to her flat. The trouble was, he was also confusing himself. Vicars, monks, church basements, tunnels, dungeons . . . At least he knew now where the secret button was, he reflected happily as he sipped the coffee. Mary was obviously worried and Cleo was completely confused. What would Cleo do? he wondered. Would she phone someone for advice? Her father, perhaps?

As the pub wasn't open yet, Jim locked the door and slipped through the back room. Hovering beneath the stairs outside Cleo's door, he was about to knock and suggest that they have a quick fuck when he heard her

talking on the phone. Business before pleasure, he mused, adjusting his yearning cock through his trousers. Pushing the door open, he stepped into the narrow hallway and listened intently.

'It's difficult to determine just how much he knows,' Cleo said. 'He comes out with so much crap, I'm not sure what he knows. He reckoned that a punter came in this morning asking to book two girls for this evening. I can't see anyone asking him about a booking. All the punters know that they have to see *me* about bookings. No, no, he's in the bar at the moment. I'm in my flat, making the fucking sandwiches. He also said that Mary has been blabbing about a tunnel. Yes, I realize that. No, no, I haven't spoken to Mary yet. I've called a couple of the girls and they're going to bring her over later. Don't worry, we'll get the truth out of her. In the dungeon, yes. The girls are going to make out that they have punters waiting in the dungeon. Whip her? The girls will *thrash* the truth out of her. OK, I'll do that. Yes, of course I will.'

Slipping back into the bar as the girl hung up, Jim wondered who the hell she'd been talking to. Reckoning that it was her father, he imagined the gruelling thrashing that Mary was in for. But it was her own fault, he mused. She'd conned him, tried to put him off the scent with her scam in the church . . . And now she'd have to endure the thrashing of her young life. Feeling a little sorry for the girl nonetheless, Jim wondered whether to warn her. Better still, he'd hide in the dungeon and witness the gruelling thrashing of her pert bottom.

'All done,' Cleo said, finally walking into the bar with a tray of sandwiches. 'The display cabinet's pretty good, don't you think?'

'Yes, yes, it is,' Jim murmured pensively.

'A couple of the girls will be in later. If you want to go out when they arrive, they can give me a hand if I get busy.'

'Er . . . OK. When they get here, I'll go up to my flat for a lie-down,' he said. 'I didn't sleep too well last night.'

'That's fine. It doesn't usually get too busy at Monday lunchtimes so we'll be able to cope.'

This was ideal, Jim reflected. If he slipped into the tunnel and got into the dungeon just before the girls arrived with their victim, he'd be able to secure a good hiding place in readiness for the bondage-and-whipping show. And he might learn a little more about the illicit operation. Friday was going to be interesting, he thought, imagining old man Hops having a fit when he discovered that Jim knew about the sex dungeon. Interesting and, hopefully, extremely profitable.

Making out that he was busy cleaning behind the bar, Jim could hardly wait for Mary to arrive with her captors. Perhaps Carole and Melanie had been given the job of torturing the truth out of Mary, he pondered. Or Crystal and another of the convent girls. No doubt they'd trick Mary, he mused. They'd lure her into the dungeon with some lie or other and then thrash the tight little arse off her. Hiding in the dungeon was risky, he knew. The room was large with little or no cover for voyeurs. And the last thing he wanted was to get caught.

Noticing Carole and Melanie leading Mary across the green to the pub, Jim told Cleo that he was going to have a rest on his bed. Smiling as he left the bar, she was obviously eager to get rid of him for a while. Hovering in the back room to make sure that the coast was clear, Jim

crept down the cellar steps. Slipping through the wooden panelling into the tunnel, he sprinted to the dungeon. He was going to have to hide behind the cupboard again, he thought, looking around the large room. Hopefully, he'd be safe enough there. No sooner had he slipped into his hiding place when the door swung open and the girls led Mary into their lair.

'This is fucking short notice,' Mary complained, walking to the examination table.

'Sorry,' Carole said. 'But it's a late booking. The man's coming down from London.'

'He's a new customer,' Melanie added. 'Hurry up and get undressed and we'll cuff you to the table. He likes bums, so lie on your stomach.'

'Does he want all three of us?' Mary asked her friends as she slipped out of her rain-wet summer dress and lay on the couch.

'Yes, he does,' Carole replied, spreading the girl's limbs and cuffing her wrists and ankles to steel rings at each corner of the table. 'There we are. You're all ready for—'

'For a fucking good thrashing,' Melanie hissed.

'What?' Mary gasped. 'But I thought . . .'

'What have you been telling people about the dungeon?'

'I haven't said anything,' Mary breathed, lifting her head and frowning at her captors. 'What's this about?'

'About you blabbing your big mouth off,' Carole said, grabbing a leather whip from the wall. 'What have you been saying?'

'I haven't fucking said anything. For fuck's sake, who's been lying about me?'

'You've been talking about the tunnel, the dungeon, the church and the monks . . .'

'I told Jim what we'd agreed I'd tell him. I didn't say anything about—'

'Gag her,' Carole ordered her accomplice, raising the whip above her head. 'I've heard enough of her lies.'

Grinning as Melanie slipped an elasticated strap around Mary's head and forced a small rubber ball into her mouth, Jim was looking forward to the gruelling thrashing. His cock stiffening as he focused on the firm moons of the girl's naked buttocks, he jumped as the first crack of the whip echoed around the dungeon. Moaning loudly through her nose, Mary tensed her buttocks in readiness for the next lash of the whip as Carole let out a wicked chuckle. Again, the leather tails swished through the air, biting into the quivering flesh of Mary's taut buttocks with a deafening report.

Mary couldn't have talked even if she'd wanted to, Jim thought as the merciless lashing of her naked buttocks continued. Moaning through her nose, struggling to break free from her bonds as the crack of the whip reverberated around the dungeon, there was no way she was going to escape the cruelty of her so-called friends. Wincing with every lash of the whip, Jim looked at the door as it swung open and hit the wall with a dull thud.

'Good morning, vicar,' Carole, said, halting the punishment.

'What's all this about?' the man asked, eyeing the glowing cheeks of Mary's weal-lined bottom.

'She's been blabbing,' Melanie replied. 'She's been talking to Jim about the tunnel.'

'I've just about had enough of this,' the vicar sighed.

'It's all rather confusing,' Carole breathed. 'Jim told Cleo that Mary had been telling you about the tunnel.'

'Telling *me* about it?' the vicar said, frowning at the girl. 'Why would she tell me about the tunnel when I already know?'

'As I said, it's confusing. The point is that Jim has been getting information about the tunnel. Mary has been to the woods with Jim, she stayed at his flat one night . . . They've been getting on rather too well for my liking. Obviously, she's been blabbing her mouth off.'

'Pass me the enema,' the vicar murmured, rolling his shirt sleeves up.

Jim couldn't believe that the vicar was about to sexually abuse Mary. She obviously wasn't his daughter, he knew now as Carole hung a large glass bottle from a hook on the low ceiling. Eyeing the so-called man of God as he grabbed a length of rubber hose attached to the bottle, Jim watched the girls part Mary's rubicund buttocks to the extreme and fully expose the brown eye of her anus. The glass bottle was full of water and Jim stared, holding his breath as the vicar pressed the end of the hose past the girl's anal ring and deep into her rectum. Turning a small tap at the neck of the bottle, he turned to Melanie and asked her to pass him a vaginal speculum.

'I'll teach the little slut,' he breathed, slipping the steel paddles of the speculum between the swollen lips of Mary's hairless pussy. 'I'll tear her dirty little cunt wide open.'

'Go on, do it,' Melanie giggled, watching gleefully as the priest pushed the speculum deep into the tight sheath of Mary's young vagina. 'Rip her cunt open.'

'Shut the fuck up,' Carole hissed. 'It's a figure of speech. He's not really going to tear her cunt open.'

'A figure of speech?' the vicar chuckled, squeezing the speculum levers and opening his victim's vaginal canal.

'I'm fed up with the way she carries on. She's jeopardizing the business and has to be taught a lesson. And the only way she's going to learn is if I really *do* rip her cunt wide open.'

'Do it,' Melanie urged the man again, her sparkling eyes focusing on the taut flesh of Mary's inner lips stretched around the steel paddles as the vicar squeezed the speculum levers.

Frowning, Jim wondered whether to intervene. The priest wasn't going to hurt the girl, was he? Deciding that the man wouldn't go too far with the sexual torture, Jim looked up at the glass bottle hanging from the ceiling. The water level dropping rapidly, he wondered when the girl's bowels would flood and overflow. The bottle must have been able to hold at least two pints, he mused as the vicar again squeezed the speculum leavers, opening the teenager's cunt to capacity. With her vaginal canal opening, restricting her rectal duct, Jim was sure that the water would soon spurt from the abused eye of her anus.

'So, how much do you reckon Jim knows?' the cleric asked the girls.

'He's getting closer to the truth all the time,' Carole sighed. 'I would have thought that the thing in the church basement with the monks would have been enough to satisfy his curiosity, but it seems not. Cleo has talked to him, tried to get him to forget about tunnels and dungeons, but—'

'I don't trust her,' Melanie cut in. 'She seems very protective towards Jim.'

'I don't think so,' Carole said, watching as the vicar opened Mary's vaginal canal a little further. 'She's just trying to play things down. The trouble is, we've made several mistakes. We should never have got Elizabeth to

lure Jim to the convent, we should have kept him away from the church basement . . .'

'That was a ploy,' the priest said. 'We all thought that he'd believe that the church basement was the dungeon he'd been searching for. What worries me is that he's not going to give up.'

'He'll have to go,' Melanie announced firmly. 'Things were fine until he arrived on the scene.'

'It's too late for that,' Carole said. 'He won't give up. Even if he's chucked out of the pub, he'll stay in the village and go on and on until—'

'Let's go back to the bar and talk about this,' the vicar cut in. 'We'll leave Mary here to enjoy the enema and the speculum. A few hours on the table with her holes bloated might teach her to keep her mouth shut.'

Waiting until they'd left, Jim emerged from his hiding place. With Mary's head turned away from him, he was able to creep across the room and make his escape without her noticing. Wishing that the vicar and the girls had discussed more of their plans in the dungeon, Jim crept along the tunnel, hoping to overhear what was being said in the bar from the back room. At least he now knew for certain that the man of God was heavily involved with the dungeon. But he wanted to learn a lot more before attempting to blackmail old man Hops on Friday.

'He's still in his flat,' Cleo said as Jim hovered in the back room. 'Sleeping, more than likely. So, what happened? Did Mary confess?'

'She insists that she didn't tell Jim anything,' Carole replied.

'We've left her on the examination table enjoying an enema and a vaginal speculum,' the cleric breathed. 'We're going to have to do something about Jim.'

'You know what he's up to, don't you?' Cleo murmured. 'He's trying to confuse us. He tells me that you've told him this and that, he tells *you* that *I*'ve said this and that . . . He's playing one against the other.'

'You're right,' Carole said. 'Mary hasn't told him anything. Jim has made out that she's said things, just to confuse and worry us.'

'OK,' the vicar said. 'I reckon that Cleo's right, so this is what we'll do. I doubt that Jim trusts anyone. But he gets on quite well with you, Cleo. If he believes that you're taking his side, trying to help him discover exactly what's going on in Willycombe Village, we might be able to draw him away from the sex dungeon.'

'I don't see how,' Melanie sighed.

'This might work,' Cleo breathed. 'So far, he's been snooping around the church, the convent, the vicarage, the woods . . . He suspects nothing about the pub. I get on well with him, we work well together, we're doing the food and coffees . . . I don't believe that he connects the pub or me to any of this.'

'You're right,' the vicar said. 'He's been on about a basement beneath the vicarage, he's been to the church basement, he's been poking around the convent . . . But he suspects nothing about the pub. Cleo, I want you to get in with him. Become good friends with him and gain his trust and confidence. Screw him, if that's what it takes.'

'I've been waiting for him to make a move on the sexual front,' Cleo sighed. 'But he just doesn't seem interested in me.'

'He's fucked just about everyone else,' Melanie giggled.

'I know he has. The thing is, I really, really like him. Perhaps I'm just not his type.'

Grinning as he rubbed his chin, Jim decided to get inside Cleo's tight panties now that he knew how she felt about him. But that didn't mean that he'd go without the delights of Mary's hairless pussy slit, or the tight cunts and bottom-holes of any other schoolgirls who happened to come his way. The time had come to return to the bar, he thought. He'd make his entrance, say that he'd slept for a while and then play their game by ear.

'Oh, hi,' Cleo said as Jim emerged from the back room. 'Did you have a sleep?'

'Yes, I did. And I feel much better. How are you, vicar? It's nice to see you again.'

'Fine, Jim, just fine. I called in to drum up some business for the church. We're having a flower-arranging competition this Saturday and I was hoping to drag Cleo along.'

'Flower arranging?' Jim chuckled, turning to the barmaid. 'Are you going, Cleo?'

'Er . . . no, no. Saturdays are busy here so I'll be working. Besides, I'm not too good at that sort of thing.'

'Well, I must be getting along,' the vicar said. 'It's nice to see you all. And it would be nice to see you in church on Sunday.'

'We'd better get back to the convent,' Carole said demurely. 'We'll probably see you this evening, Cleo.'

Wondering how long they intended to leave Mary in the dungeon, Jim thought that Cleo would probably release the girl at some stage. Feeling pleased with himself as he pondered on the latest information he'd discovered, he eyed Cleo's short skirt, her naked thighs. She was ripe for a good fucking, he decided, focusing on

her long black hair cascading over the deep cleavage of her mammary spheres. Mary was also ripe for a good fucking. Picturing her naked body bared on the examination table, Jim was tempted to slip into the dungeon and roger her tight pussy. But he was intrigued by Cleo, her young body, her tight sex sheath.

I've been waiting for him to make a move on the sexual front. But he just doesn't seem interested in me. Recalling her words, Jim knew that the time had come to pay the girl some attention. She was very attractive, he mused, standing behind her as she rearranged the sandwiches in the display cabinet. She certainly knew how to use her mouth – but did she know how to use her tight pussy? Realizing that it wasn't only her young body he was interested in, he pondered on her personality.

Apart from lying about the tunnel and the sex dungeon, she was good company, fun to be with. Not only did she have Mary's qualities – a filthy slut, a dirty little tart, a whore-slag, a mouth-fucking slapper – but she had character. And, as an added bonus, her father was a millionaire. Cleo was the sort of girl he could settle down with, Jim decided. Settle down, but still shag convent schoolgirls' hot little pussies and tight bottom-holes. Slipping his hands around Cleo's waist, he kissed her neck.

'I rather like you,' he murmured.

'Jim,' she giggled, pulling away from him. 'Not behind the bar, for goodness' sake.'

'Behind the bar, over the bar, under the bar, on the bar, against the bar . . . What the hell?'

'Well, at least you've stopped harping on about tunnels and dungeons,' she said, smiling at him.

'Have I? Oh, er . . . yes, of course I have.'

'No, Jim,' she breathed as he squeezed the firm mounds of her breasts. 'Wait until later, OK?'

'Later? When later?'

'This evening, when we close.'

'That's a hell of a long time, Cleo. How about the hole in the bar?'

'I'm not to use the hole any more. Your instructions, Jim. And you *are* the boss.'

'Change of plan . . .'

'Later, Jim. Come into my flat after we close this evening, OK?'

'If I can wait that long to . . . to have a cup of coffee with you.'

Pouring himself a pint of best bitter as Cleo carried on with arranging the sandwiches, Jim wondered again how long Mary was to be left in the dungeon enduring the enema and the speculum. He was longing to go and slip his cock into her sweet mouth and spunk down her throat, but he didn't want anyone to know that he'd discovered the sex dungeon. He was just going to have to wait until the evening. Either that, or nip up to the convent and drag a schoolgirl into the laundry room and fuck her over the dirty-knicker basket. The evening seemed such a long way off, he mused, eyeing Cleo's pretty mouth, her succulent lips. There again, everything comes to him that waits.

11

By four o'clock, Jim was beginning to worry about Mary. He'd been keeping an eye on Cleo and she hadn't slipped into the dungeon to release the girl. Wondering whether she'd forgotten about the prisoner, he knew that he couldn't put an end to Mary's plight. Thinking that it might be an idea to bring the subject of the girl up in conversation, he was about to say something to Cleo when she asked whether he'd go down to the local shop and buy some coffee for the percolator.

Reckoning that she wanted a chance to release Mary, Jim took some money from the till and left the pub. The rain had stopped and the sun was beating down as he walked along the street. Willycombe was a beautiful place, he mused. The village green, thatched cottages, the old church . . . But beneath the beauty lay the tunnel and the sex dungeon. Wondering how many people knew of the debauchery, he went into the shop and froze as he noticed Ruby Rottweiler standing behind the counter.

'I didn't realize that you worked here,' he said, grabbing some coffee from a shelf.

'Neither did I until this morning,' the woman mumbled. 'I'm just helping out. I hope you haven't come in to buy condoms. If you have, then I won't serve you.'

'Condoms?' he chuckled. 'I haven't used a condom since I was . . . It's just the coffee I need.'

'It's a bloody filthy habit, if you ask me.'

'I can't agree with you there, Ruby. There's absolutely nothing wrong with coffee. Taken in moderation . . .'

'I'm talking about condoms. Sticking a rubber balloon on your penis and then shoving it up . . . Vulgar, that's what it is.'

'We're all entitled to our opinion, Ruby.'

'If only all men were like the vicar,' she sighed.

'If only,' Jim chortled.

'He's such a kind man. An upright pillar of the community. Keen to help others, anti-smoking, anti-drinking, celibate . . .'

'Celibate?' Jim laughed. 'Er . . . I mean . . . he has a daughter, so he must have done it at least once.'

'Daughter? She's a common whore, a slut.'

'That may be so, but she's still his daughter. Tell me, Ruby, what happened to the girl's mother?'

'She ran off with a choirboy. Dreadful, it was. She accused the vicar of having sex with convent schoolgirls.'

'Really?'

'It was a terrible thing to say about the man. The vicar has bent over backwards to help young girls.'

'I'll bet he has. Going back to his daughter, do you remember when she was born?'

'Of course I remember. Such a bonnie little thing. Although, after her mother left, she changed.'

'In what way?'

'She became a recluse, never leaving the house or meeting people. After a few months, she started to get out a little. She was never the same, though.'

'Does she ever see her mother?'

'I really don't know. The woman has been to the vicarage on a couple of occasions. But whether she saw Mary or not . . . Why all this interest in the girl?'

'I'm curious, that's all. Well, I'd better be getting back.'

'You're not so bad, for a man,' she said as he passed her the money. 'But if I see under-age girls in your pub . . .'

'Don't you worry, Ruby. I would never allow under-age girls into the pub.'

'I'm pleased to hear it. By the way, you want to watch that Cleo girl.'

'Oh?'

'I've seen her sneaking into the convent at night.'

'Sneaking? What do you reckon she gets up to?'

'I don't know. But I've seen her leaving the place with carrier bags full of something or other.'

'Something or other?'

'Clothing of some description. I reckon that she sneaks around at night, stealing.'

'Right, well . . . I'll keep my eye on her. I'll be seeing you, Ruby.'

'You can be sure of that.'

Making his way back to the pub, Jim was certain that Cleo had been collecting bags of soiled schoolgirlie knickers from the convent. She probably sold them to the sex-dungeon clients, adding to her illicit profits. She was quite a character, he reflected as he walked into the pub and placed the coffee on the bar. Wondering whether she'd released Mary as he poured himself a beer, he asked her whether Crystal could supply him with a few pairs of soiled knickers.

'I expect so,' she replied, frowning at him. 'But why do you—'

'They're for a friend of mine,' he interrupted her. 'It's his birthday soon and I know that he has a thing about schoolgirl knickers. I thought a few freshly soiled pairs would make a nice present.'

'Oh, I see. Actually, there might be a few pairs in my flat.'

'In your flat? You mean, you supply your own dirty knickers to—'

'No, no,' she giggled. 'I . . . Crystal sometimes leaves some by mistake.'

'By mistake?'

'When she has things on her mind, she . . . she sort of inadvertently leaves a few pairs from time to time.'

'In that case, my luck's in.'

'I'll get half a dozen pairs for you later. They're sealed in airtight polythene bags to keep them fresh – so to speak.'

'Perfect. Er . . . does Crystal ever inadvertently leave anything else in your flat?'

'Such as?'

'Well, I don't know. Small bras, perhaps? Or possibly . . .'

'Possibly what?'

'Used tampons?'

'Used tampons?' Cleo gasped. 'What sort of man is this friend of yours?'

'Well, sort of normal, I suppose.'

'Normal?'

'OK, abnormal.'

'I'll see what I can do,' she sighed, pouring herself a large vodka and tonic. 'We should have a few customers in before long. I think I'll go and change before we get busy.'

'Change your knickers?' Jim laughed.

'My blouse.'

'Oh, right.'

Sipping his drink as Cleo left the bar, Jim reckoned again that she was not only very attractive but . . . Realizing that he fancied her rotten, he hoped that he wasn't in love. That would be all he needed, he reflected. Love and lust didn't mix. Love was fidelity, lust was fucking anything and everything with a girl-slit. His cock stiffening as he pondered on going to Cleo's flat that evening and shafting her tight rectal duct, he knew that he couldn't wait that long to drain his spunk-brimming balls. Deciding to order the girl to kneel behind the bar and suck his cock through the hole, he wondered where she'd got to. How long did it take to change a blouse?

Walking into the back room, he noticed that Cleo's door was open and ventured into her hallway. Calling for her, he couldn't understand where she'd gone. Suddenly realizing that she must have slipped into the sex dungeon, he grabbed the opportunity to nose around her flat. If she appeared, he'd say that he was looking for her. But he wouldn't add that he was looking for her freshly soiled knickers. Deciding to start his search in her bedroom, he opened her chest of drawers and grinned.

'Bingo,' Jim breathed, eyeing dozens of pairs of navy-blue knickers neatly wrapped in polythene bags. Stuffing a couple of pairs into his pocket, he checked the other drawers. They were all full to the brim with freshly soiled schoolgirl knickers. This was quite a scam, he reflected, closing the drawers and looking around the room. Cleo must have had several secrets, he mused, eyeing her bedside table. Opening the small drawer, he discovered a vibrator. The pink shaft was sticky with her

vaginal juices and he slipped it back into the drawer as he heard the girl calling him.

'Oh, there you are,' he said, leaving Cleo's flat and finding her in the back room.

'What were you doing in there?' she asked him accusingly.

'Looking for you. The door was open so I went into the hall and called out.'

'I . . . I was in the cellar,' she stammered. 'I must have forgotten to close my door after making the sandwiches.'

'Are you all right? You looked worried.'

'I'm fine. It's just that a girl doesn't like people looking at her private things.'

'All I did was step into the hall and shout out for you. Believe me, I'm not in the habit of prying through other people's personal belongings.'

'I know that, Jim. I wasn't accusing you.'

'Say no more. You get back to the bar and I'll go and change.'

Slipping into the cellar the minute Cleo had gone into the bar, Jim opened the wooden panelling and made his way along the tunnel. Wondering whether Cleo had released Mary, he hovered outside the dungeon door and listened for movements. This was a risky business, he knew as he pressed his ear to the door. If Mary was dressing and was about to leave the dungeon, she'd come face to face with Jim. With nowhere to hide, he'd be in real trouble. Hearing nothing, he finally inched the door open and peered into the dungeon.

Breathing a sigh of relief as he stepped into the room and look around, he was thankful that Mary had gone. The poor girl had endured the speculum and the enema for far too long, he reflected, eyeing the empty glass

bottle hanging above the examination table. A trail of
water was splattered across the floor and it was obvious
that the girl's bowels had drained as she'd left the table
and moved to the door. It would have been interesting to
fuck her tight rectum and force the water out of her
bowels, he mused, his cock twitching at the lewd
thought. Deciding to fill the girl's rectal duct with beer
and drink from her bottom-hole when he had the opportunity, he took a look around the dungeon.

Moving to the cupboard he'd hidden behind during
his previous visits, Jim opened the door. His eyes widening as he stared at a row of habits hanging from a rail, he
reckoned that these were the very garments that the
monks had worn in the church basement. Donning
one of them, he decided to keep it. It might come in
handy, he mused. Particularly if he were to make another
visit to the church basement. Closing the cupboard door,
he looked up at the fluorescent lighting. Someone had
put a lot of work into the sex dungeon, he mused. The
floor was covered with plush carpeting, the stone walls
were painted white . . . Yes, a considerable amount of
time and money had gone into the dungeon.

Eyeing a wooden bar running between two pillars, Jim
was sure that this was a new addition to the venue. Tied
with rope to the wooden pillars, the bar was about waist
height. Unable to work out its purpose, he imagined a
naked girl leaning over the bar. Reckoning that it was to
be used for spanking schoolgirls' naked bottoms, he
grinned. This was all clever stuff, he reckoned as he
moved to the door. About to return to the pub, he heard
voices and dived behind the cupboard.

'Get in there,' a man bellowed as the door swung open.

'May I take the blindfold off now?' a girl asked.

'Of course, Maria. Now take a look around.'

'What . . . what is this place?'

'This is where I punish young girls.'

'Punish? But I didn't steal anything,' a girl whimpered.

'That's not what the Reverend Mother said. This isn't the first time you've been caught stealing, is it, Maria? Is that what you did in Spain? Did you steal from your friends and . . .'

'If my father finds out that I've been in trouble, he'll beat me,' she sobbed.

'If your father has to come over from Spain, it'll be to take you back.'

'You mean I'm to be expelled?'

'The Reverend Mother has been good enough to offer you one last chance, Maria. She has suggested that I try to correct your wicked ways. If that doesn't work, then your father will be told of your expulsion and he'll take you back to Spain.'

Peering around the side of the cupboard, Jim gazed at the young Spanish girl as she cowered in front of a middle-aged man. Her complexion was dark, her jet-black hair matching the colour of her wide eyes. Wearing her school uniform, she hung her head as the man eyed the small mounds of her breasts clearly defined by the tight material of her white blouse. Was this a set-up? Jim wondered, focusing on the girl's knee-length white socks. Was the man a punter and the girl playing the role of a naughty schoolgirl or was this for real?

'I want you to take your shoes and socks off,' the man ordered the trembling girl.

'But . . . why?'

'Just do it, Maria.' Grinning as the girl complied, the

man perched on the edge of the examination table. 'And now take your skirt off.'

'My skirt? But—'

'I'm not here to argue with you, girl.'

'What sort of punishment is this? You want me to take my skirt off? If my father finds out that you blindfolded me and brought me here . . .'

'You don't understand, Maria. You have been caught stealing money. You tell your father that you were brought here, and you'll be expelled for stealing money *and* for indulging in lesbian sex with another girl.'

'Lesbian sex? This is a trick, isn't it? You know that I've never stolen money. It's just an excuse to bring me here and—'

'You have two choices. Either you take your skirt off, or I will.'

The Mediterranean girl was extremely attractive, Jim observed as she unzipped her skirt and allowed the garment to crumple around her bare feet. Her white blouse was long enough to conceal her panties, Jim noticed as she stood in front of the man and awaited her next inevitable instruction. Ordering her to remove her blouse, her captor folded his arms and watched as her trembling fingers released each button in turn. Slipping the garment over her shoulders, her small bra coming into view, she folded her arms to conceal the mounds of her petite breasts.

Focusing on the smooth plateau of her stomach, Jim was sure that the girl was acting as he lowered his eyes to the triangular patch of bulging material hugging the swell of her love lips. She was a rare beauty, he thought, sure that he could just make out the crack of her vulva outlined by her school knickers. And a damned good

actress. The flesh of her outer labia would be Mediterranean-dark, firm, hairless, rising alluringly either side of her pinken valley of desire. His cock straining against his zip, his full balls heaving, he wondered how many convent schoolgirls were brought to the dungeon and forced to strip naked. Imagining a young black girl standing naked by the examination table, he adjusted his solid cock through his trousers. Coffee – and a fuck – with Cleo that evening was a million miles away.

'And now your bra,' the man instructed the dark-skinned beauty.

'No,' she said firmly. 'I don't know what sort of punishment—'

'Do it, girl,' he snapped. 'You're here to be punished. Arguing will only make it worse.'

'Are you going to force me to—'

'Unless you want me to tear your bra off . . .'

Reaching behind her back, the girl released the hook and peeled the white silk cups away from her mammary spheres. Her chocolate-brown nipples standing proud of the dark discs of her areolae, rising in the relatively cool air of the dungeon, she again folded her arms across the mounds of her young breasts. Casting his eyes over the unblemished flesh of her near-naked body, Jim watched with bated breath as she followed the man's order and slipped her thumbs between the tight elastic of her navy blue knickers and her shapely hips.

Easing the garment slowly down her firm thighs, the top of her hairless crack of desire coming into view, she finally allowed her knickers to fall down her long legs. Her outer labia were completely devoid of pubic hair, full and alluring in their symmetry. Jim could just make out the brownish petals of her inner lips protruding invit-

ingly from her virginal valley of lust. *Was* she a virgin? he
wondered as she stood naked in front of the grinning
man. Her teenage body trembling, she clasped her hand
over her pubic mound to conceal the crack of her vagina.
If she was playing the part of a young virgin schoolgirl,
then she was indeed an excellent actress.

'Very good,' the man praised her. 'You have a lovely
body, Maria.'

'What are you going to do to me?' she asked shakily.

'As I said, the Reverend Mother is offering you one
last chance to mend your wicked ways. If I can put a stop
to your stealing, there'll be no need to contact your father
and you'll stay on at the convent.'

'I've never stolen anything,' she murmured softly.

'And you're going to have to stop lying, Maria.'

'So, what are you going to do to me?'

'I have to punish you.'

'You're not going to touch me, are you? If my father
finds out that—'

'The only worry you have where your father is concerned is your expulsion. If you tell him that you were
brought here and stripped naked . . . Don't make it worse
for yourself, Maria. You see that wooden bar over there?'

'Yes.'

'I want you to bend over the bar and touch your toes.'

'But . . . You can't do this.'

'Expulsion, or the bar. What's it to be?'

Watching the girl as she leaned over the bar and
touched her toes, Jim focused on the fleshy swell of
her vulval lips nestling between her firm thighs. The
alluring sight sending tremors through his rolling balls,
he wondered again whether she was play-acting as the
man parted her feet to the extreme and cuffed her wrists

to her ankles. Her young body laid bare, her sex holes completely undefended, she looked up between her legs as her captor moved behind her and ran his fingers over the moons of her naked buttocks.

'Now then, my girl,' the man breathed, parting the firm orbs of her bare bottom. 'The time has come to—'

'There's a problem,' Crystal announced as she burst into the sex dungeon.

'A problem?' the man echoed. 'What's happened?'

'Cleo can't find Jim, the landlord.'

'So? Look, I was just about to—'

'He said that he was going up to his flat to change, but he's not there. His door was open and Cleo has searched everywhere for him.'

'Perhaps he went out.'

'Maybe, but I think it best that you leave the dungeon. You can come back later.'

'What about the girl?'

'Leave her there. She's hardly going to escape, is she? This is only a precautionary measure. In your position, the last thing you want is to be caught here with—'

'All right,' the man sighed, moving to the door. 'From what I've heard, this new landlord is causing too many problems for my liking.'

Frowning as Crystal left with the man, Jim wondered what the panic was about. As Crystal had said, he might have gone out. Something had happened, he was sure. Pleased that he was wearing a monk's habit, he decided to emerge from his hiding place and make his escape. The girl would see him, of course. But with his face shrouded by the heavy hood, she wouldn't recognize him.

'Who are you?' she asked as he stepped out from behind the cupboard.

'No one you need worry yourself about,' he whispered as he moved to the door.

'Please, you must help me,' she said. 'Let me go before that man comes back and—'

'It's all right,' Jim chuckled. 'You don't have to act the part of a captured schoolgirl.'

'Act the part? Please, you have to help me. I'm not acting.'

'Save it for your client.'

'Client? What do you mean?'

'This is what I'm talking about,' he breathed, standing behind the girl and running his fingertip up and down her creamy-wet vaginal crack. 'Selling your cunt, Maria. That's what this is all about.'

'Selling my . . . Please, oh please don't touch me,' she gasped as he drove his finger deep into the hugging sheath of her vagina.

'What did you think that man was going to do?' Jim laughed, massaging her hot inner flesh. 'You stripped naked and allowed him to cuff you over the bar. What did you think he was going to do?'

'Punish me, that's what he said. I was caught stealing and—'

'Punish you? Is this how other convent girls are punished?'

'I . . . I don't know. I've never been here before. I was blindfolded and—'

'Yes, yes, I know,' Jim sighed. 'You're an innocent little schoolgirl and you've been dragged here by a pervert.'

'A pervert?'

'Come on, Maria. This is all a game, isn't it?' he asked her, sliding his finger out of her tightening sex sheath.

'It's hardly a game.'

'I'll show you how he was going to punish you,' Jim said, lifting his habit and hauling his erect penis out of his trousers.

Retracting his foreskin, he ran the purple globe of his knob up and down Maria's vaginal crack, creaming his glans in readiness to penetrate her young pussy. The girl protested wildly, her naked body squirming and struggling as he pushed his bulbous glans past the wings of her inner lips and into the wet heat of her young cunt. Holding his habit to his chest, he looked down at the illicit coupling. The Mediterranean girl's dark outer lips stretched tautly around the veined shaft of his cock, her vaginal muscles spasming, she was ripe for a fucking.

Forcing the solid shaft of his cock deep into the tight duct of her teenage cunt, impaling the girl fully on his huge organ, Jim grabbed her hips and let out a gasp as her vaginal muscles tightened and squeezed his yearning penis. She was a fiery little character, he thought as she spat expletives at him and continued her struggle to break free. Fiery, tight, hot, wet . . . This was just what he needed, he reflected, withdrawing his veined shaft and again ramming his swollen knob deep into the heat of her schoolgirl pussy. Coffee with Cleo that evening was light years away. Maria's schoolgirlie pussy was a godsend.

'No,' the girl cried as Jim's bulbous glans battered the doughnut-like ring of her ripe cervix. 'Please . . .'

'Yes,' Jim gasped, repeatedly driving his rock-hard cock deep into her young cunt. 'This is what you're here for.'

'You don't understand. I was supposed to be punished for—'

'I *am* punishing you,' he chuckled. 'God, how I love punishing young girls with my fucking great weapon.'

Eyeing the dark brown ring of her anus, Jim reckoned that the punishment should include a damned good anal shagging. Besides, it would be unfair to leave her tight rectal duct unfucked. That was what schoolgirls' bottom-holes were for, he reflected. The tight brown inlet, the hot rectal sheath, the cavernous bowels . . . Schoolgirlies' bottoms were made for fucking and spunking. And licking and spanking and thrashing and . . . Schoolgirlies were beautiful, Jim decided.

Peeling the firm cheeks of Maria's naked buttocks wide apart, opening her tight anal inlet, Jim slipped his cock out of her hot sex duct and ran his cream-dripping knob over the delicate brown tissue of her anus. He could feel the heat of her young body as she shuddered and writhed. She was ready for an anal fucking, a bowel-sperming, he was sure. Grabbing his penis by the root, he pushed his purple plum hard against her anal iris as she cried out and protested again.

Ignoring Maria's expletives and desperate pleas, he watched his solid glans defeat her anal sphincter muscles and slip into the welcoming heat of her tight rectum. Holding her hips, driving his cock-head along her burning rectal sheath, Jim grinned as his glans absorbed the heat of her bowels and the hairy sac of his scrotum pressed against the fleshy pads of her swollen outer lips. Her tight arse completely impaled on his rod of lust, she writhed and gasped, her screamed protests now reduced to whimpered words of anal defeat.

'God, you're a tight-arsed little beauty,' Jim breathed, withdrawing his penile shaft until Maria's brown ring encompassed just the rim of his helmet.

'You'll pay for this,' she sobbed.

'No, no,' he laughed. 'Your *client* pays for sex, Maria. *I*'m a monk, so I don't have to pay you for illegal sex.'

'When my father hears about this . . .'

'Surely you're not going to tell your father how you earn extra pocket money?'

'Pocket money? You're mad. You're a sad perverted horrible—'

'Deviant monk?'

'Bastard.'

Sliding his veined cock in and out of the trembling girl's anal canal, Jim gripped her hips and increased his fucking rhythm as his sperm pump sprang into action. His orgasmic cream jetting from his throbbing knob, gushing into the teenager's rectal canal and lubricating the illicit union, he threw his head back and wallowed in his much-needed sexual gratification. How many more convent girls would he fuck during his time at the Tartan Vicar? he wondered. How many tight little pussies and bottom-holes would he drive his solid cock into and flood with spunk?

Repeatedly ramming his orgasming knob into the Mediterranean slut's anal canal, Jim wondered, as he drained his swinging balls, why she'd been blindfolded. Perhaps it was all part of the game, he mused. There again, to lead her into the pub already wearing a blindfold would have been somewhat risky. Had Ruby Rottweiler been around . . . But they wouldn't have bothered to blindfold the girl after she'd entered the pub, he reflected. Surely the idea would have been to lead her into the dungeon, supposedly keeping the place secret.

'Why the blindfold?' he asked the girl as he stilled his deflating knob deep within the wet heat of her sperm-flooded bowels.

'They . . . they didn't want me to know where this place was,' she replied shakily, her anal muscles spasming.

'All part of the deception, I presume. So, where were you when they blindfolded you?'

'Behind the church. We met the man behind the church and—'

'We?'

'Crystal. She took me behind the church and . . .'

'And blindfolded you before bringing you here,' Jim murmured, dragging his anal-slimed cock out of the schoolgirl's inflamed rectal duct.

Zipping his trousers and lowering his habit, Jim left the dungeon and looked up and down the tunnel. He knew instinctively that the girl hadn't been brought in through the pub. Blindfolded, the possibility of the Rottweiler passing by, the customers in the bar . . . There was no way Crystal would take such a risk. Perhaps Maria hadn't been a willing participant? The unwelcome thought struck him and he thanked God that he'd worn the habit, the heavy hood concealing his identity.

Hearing voices, he panicked. It was Crystal and the middle-aged man, he knew as he looked along the dimly lit tunnel. 'Shit,' he breathed, realizing that he couldn't return to the dungeon without Maria spotting him. She'd tell the others about the fucking and . . . Noticing a concealed doorway in an alcove, Jim pushed the door open and bounded up the stone steps. Emerging from an opening surrounded by bushes, he knew that he was in the woods behind the church.

This was amazing, Jim thought, slipping the habit off and hiding the garment beneath some bushes. Leaving the woods and making his way back to the pub, he felt

pleased with himself. Not only had he pumped his spunk into a schoolgirl slut's arse, but he'd learned more about the secret tunnel. Now he could slip into the woods and gain access to the dungeon without rousing suspicion: he'd be able to discover exactly what was going on, who was involved in the illicit business.

'Where the hell have you been?' Cleo asked as he walked into the pub.

'I had to go out for a while,' he replied, smiling at the girl. 'I wasn't very long, Cleo.'

'I didn't see you go out,' she breathed, flashing him an accusing glare. 'I thought you'd gone up to your flat to change?'

'Yes, I did. Then I went out for a while. There are no customers so I don't know why you're so angry. Are you all right? You look awfully worried.'

'I . . . I just wondered where you'd got to,' she sighed as one ring emanated from her mobile phone.

'Someone must have changed their mind about ringing you,' Jim laughed, glancing at the phone lying next to the till.

'Yes, I suppose so.'

Moving behind the bar and pouring himself a beer, Jim knew that Crystal and the middle-aged man wanted to leave the tunnel. Waiting for the all-clear signal, they'd be hovering behind the wooden panelling in the cellar. This was his chance to cause some problems, he mused, discreetly reaching beneath the bar and pressing the button. Wondering why they hadn't left the tunnel by the concealed entrance in the woods, Jim waited behind the bar for the shit to hit the fan.

'Christ,' Crystal gasped as she emerged from the back room with the middle-aged punter.

'Er . . . why did you . . . ?' Cleo stammered. 'I didn't . . .'

'Where have you been?' Jim asked Crystal as the girl told the man to leave.

'I was just . . . just showing my friend the cellar,' she replied uneasily. 'Cleo said that it would be all right.'

'Yes, that's right,' Cleo confirmed hastily. 'He's . . . he's interested in old pubs. May I have a word?' she said, leading Crystal into the back room.

'You pressed the fucking button,' Crystal snapped once they thought that they were out of Jim's earshot.

'I fucking didn't. Jim was behind the bar, for fuck's sake. I'd hardly press the button with him there.'

'*Someone* pressed it.'

'Shush, he'll hear us,' Cleo breathed, unaware that Jim was listening to her every word

'Look, forget the button. There's a major problem,' Crystal sighed. 'A monk fucked Maria.'

'A monk? What the hell are you talking about?'

'We left the girl cuffed over the bar, right?'

'Yes.'

'When we went back, she said that a monk had fucked her arse. I saw the spunk, Cleo. It was oozing from her arsehole.'

'But who . . . No one's been down there. Jim was out, so . . .'

'Unless someone went to the dungeon via the woods?'

'That entrance is only used for . . .'

'So *you* explain it!'

'I can't,' Cleo murmured. 'A monk? None of the men would take one of the habits and . . .'

'Someone did. How the hell did they get hold of a habit? They're kept in the dungeon, aren't they?'

'I'd better get back to the bar. Go and take a look in the woods.'

'What for?'

'I don't know. You might spot someone – or something.'

As Cleo returned to the bar and Crystal left the pub, Jim busied himself by polishing the brass pumps. He'd caused a real problem, he knew as Cleo hovered beside him, her mind obviously in turmoil. She looked extremely worried, her expression reflecting anxiety as she mumbled something about the weather. Jim was sure that she didn't suspect him of being the mysterious monk. As far as she was aware, he knew nothing about the tunnel and the sex dungeon, let alone the entrance in the woods.

'Well, we should have a few in at lunchtime,' he said, checking his watch. 'Let's hope the sandwiches sell.'

'I expect they will,' Cleo murmured abstractedly. 'Jim, when you went out . . . where did you go?'

'To the local shop and then . . . Oh, I meant to tell you. I saw a monk lurking by the church.'

'A monk?'

'Yes. He was looking around as if he was waiting for someone. I only took notice of him because he was acting in a suspicious manner.'

'What did he do?'

'He hovered around by the church for a few minutes and then he went into the woods. Most peculiar, don't you think?'

'Yes, very. You didn't recognize him?'

'No, no. He had his hood up so I couldn't see his face. There are some strange goings-on in this village, Cleo.'

'Indeed there are,' she sighed. 'It's a shame you didn't follow him.'

'I did, actually.'

'Oh?'

'I thought I'd see what he was up to so I kept my distance and trailed him. He followed a path around a bend and disappeared into thin air. He might have been a ghost.'

'A ghost? Of course he wasn't.'

'There's no other explanation. He was there one minute and the next he'd vanished.'

'Perhaps you're right,' she laughed. 'There have been so many strange . . . Oh well, not to worry. I'd better get the coffee on ready for the lunchtime rush.'

'Rush? God, I hope so. What are Mondays usually like?'

'Pretty quiet.'

'We might be inundated with ghostly monks,' Jim chuckled.

'Or worse,' Cleo sighed. 'I'm going to my flat to take a rest for ten minutes.'

'Yes, fine. I'll hold the fort.'

Grinning as he sipped his beer, Jim reckoned that he'd caused enough trouble for the time being. He'd learned a lot, he mused. Looking forward to meeting old man Hops on Friday, he was almost ready to blackmail his boss. The man must collect the dirty money on Fridays, he thought, wondering whether Cleo hung on to it in the meantime. A proper search of her flat was in order, he decided. Plus the anal rogering he'd been longing to give the girl. The evening was going to be interesting, and most rewarding.

12

Much to Jim's disappointment, the lunchtime session had been a complete failure. Two punters, no sandwich or coffee sales, and it was raining again. Jim was beginning to feel the way the sky looked. Gloomy, grey, dull, heavy. It was still early days, he thought, wondering what to do with the curling sandwiches. Once word got around that food was available, business would probably pick up. There again, Willycombe was a strange place, he mused. Strange people, strange goings-on . . . It was like a weird dream. Nymphomaniacal schoolgirls running about, the sex dungeon, the perverted vicar and his peculiar daughter . . .

'Afternoon, Foster,' Mr Hops bellowed as he marched into the pub.

'Oh, er . . . Mr Hops. How nice to see you,' Jim said, wondering what his boss wanted.

'What's all this, then?' the man murmured, pointing at the display cabinet. 'Sandwiches?'

'Yes, er . . . they've been selling quite well.'

'Get rid of them,' Hops ordered Jim angrily. 'I told you, Foster, no changes.'

'What's the matter?' Jim asked his boss, anger welling in the pit of his stomach. 'Are you afraid that I'll make a go of the pub and ruin your tax-loss scam?'

'Tax loss? Er . . . I have no idea what you're talking about, man.'

'Haven't you? Apart from a tax loss, the Tartan Vicar is a front for an underground business. This place is a nice little earner, isn't it?'

'Underground business?'

'I want a cut of the profits, Mr Hops. Say twenty per cent?'

'Have you gone mad, Foster?'

'Not at all. I know what's going on here. You use this place as a tax loss. That's why you don't want any changes. If the pub starts making a profit—'

'I don't like your tone,' Hops cut in. 'Twenty per cent of the profits? Are you threatening me?'

'All I'm saying is that I know what's going on here. God only knows how much you're raking in. I know everything, Mr Hops.'

'You know nothing.'

'I could be very useful to you. Working with Cleo and the other girls, I could—'

'You're fired, Foster,' the man yelled. 'I want you out by this evening.'

Watching Hops storm out of the pub, Jim was sure that he'd change his mind once he realized that Jim knew too much. Hops would be far better off bringing Jim in on the illicit business than continually having the girls trying to conceal the truth. Hops had obviously thought that Jim was stupid enough not to realize that the pub was nothing more than a tax fiddle. And he must have thought that he wouldn't discover the sex dungeon in a million years.

Feeling pleased with himself, Jim knew that he wasn't the best of businessmen. But he had a pretty good head for making money. Once Hops had conceded and brought him in on the scam, the brewer would soon

realize that the younger man was a great asset. Pouring himself a beer, Jim pondered on his next move. All he could do was wait, he decided. Wait for Hops to phone and agree to the deal and then Jim would put every effort into building the sex dungeon business.

'My father just called on my mobile,' Cleo said as she emerged from the back room. 'He's fuming. What the hell did you say to him?'

'We had a little chat, Cleo,' Jim replied, smiling at the girl.

'A little chat? He said that he'd fired you.'

'He'll come round to my way of thinking once he calms down.'

'Calms down? You don't know my father. He does *not* calm down. What the hell did you say to him?'

'I put a proposition to him, Cleo. I know why he doesn't want me to make any changes to the pub and—'

'You've done it now,' she sighed. 'My father is a formidable man. He doesn't suffer fools . . .'

'Exactly,' Jim chuckled. 'He thought me a fool, that's why he put me here. More fool him, don't you agree?'

'I couldn't agree less. Look, I'll have a word with him. If I say that—'

'No, no. The ball's in his court, Cleo. Let him steam for a while and then he'll get back to me and we'll be in business.'

'You're mad, Jim.'

'I think not. Right, I have a little business to attend to at the convent.'

'The convent? Jim, don't go poking your nose in at the convent.'

'I'll be doing more than poking my nose in before long, Cleo. I'll be running the show.'

'Running the convent? You're not going for the Reverend Mother's job, are you?' she giggled.

'I'm about to move into the big time,' he said smugly, downing his drink. 'I'll see you later.'

Leaving the pub, Jim walked briskly to the convent. This was a new beginning, he mused, feeling confident as he marched up the stone steps of the Victorian building. What choice did Hops have? he wondered. Jim knew far too much to be discarded, tossed aside. Either the man agreed to the proposition or he'd face huge problems. It wasn't as if Hops was going to lose money, he reflected. Bringing Jim into the illicit business would actually boost the profits.

'May I help you?' a pretty young schoolgirl asked Jim as he entered the building.

'I'm here to see the boss,' Jim quipped, eyeing the girl's long blonde hair cascading over her shoulders, her ripe nipples pressing through the tight material of her white blouse.

'The boss? Oh, you mean the Reverend Mother?'

'Indeed I do.'

'She's in her study. But she's given strict instructions that she's not to be disturbed. If you'd like to come back in an hour or so . . .'

'She loves being disturbed by me,' he chuckled, walking away.

'But . . .'

'Worry not, my child,' Jim called.

Knocking on the Reverend Mother's door, Jim wondered why she wasn't to be disturbed. She was probably spanking a schoolgirl's naked bottom, he thought, his cock twitching as he pictured the lewd scene. She might be having her clitoris licked to orgasm by a naked young

beauty. She had a pretty good job, he pondered as he knocked again. Surrounded by schoolgirlies, administering spankings . . .

'What is it?' an ageing woman asked as she yanked the door open.

'Oh, er . . . My name's Foster, Jim Foster. I'm here to see the Reverend Mother,' Jim stammered. 'I don't have an appointment, but Elizabeth is always pleased to see me.'

'Is she?' the woman asked him, her beady eyes frowning. 'In that case, you'd better come in.'

Following the woman into the study, Jim closed the door. Reckoning that Elizabeth was probably in the side room attending to a young girl's naked bottom, he was sure that he'd be invited to give her a hand. Or a length of rock-hard cock, he thought, rubbing his hands together and remarking on the rain. The ageing woman wasn't at all friendly. Pacing the floor and grunting as Jim mentioned chatting to Elizabeth in the pub, she finally stood with her back to the window and glared at him.

'What business do you have with Elizabeth?' she asked him.

'Just a little chat,' he replied. 'Er . . . private business, if you get my meaning?'

'Yes, I get your meaning. She's with someone at the moment but she won't be long.'

'Good, good.'

'I'm Elizabeth's . . . How can I put it? I'm her right-hand woman. We work together, so to speak. She's quite a character, don't you agree?'

'Yes, indeed. *Quite* a character. I like her rule concerning the girls shaving their pussies. Elizabeth brought

me in to help with those girls who disobey her. I had to deal with one the other day.'

'Really?'

'I'm rather good when it comes to dealing with your teenage girls. Punishing disobedient young girls is my forte.'

'I'm sure it is. I suppose you've heard about the rape?'

'Rape?' Jim echoed.

'Maria, a young Spanish girl.'

'Oh, that,' Jim chuckled. 'She's a dammed good little actress. And a bloody good . . . Wait a minute. It wasn't rape. You know as well as I do that she was play-acting in the dungeon.'

'Where is this dungeon?'

'You don't know?'

'Mr Foster, *I* am the Reverend Mother. From what you've said—'

'Shit.'

'From what you've said . . .'

'Er . . . I was only joking. Who is this Maria girl? I've never heard of her. And what's this dungeon business?'

'We're going to have a long chat, Mr Foster. Please, sit down.'

'Ah, er . . . can't stop. Have to dash, I'm afraid.'

Fleeing the woman's study, Jim sprinted along the corridor and dashed out of the building. This was a fucking nightmare, he thought, realizing that he'd put his foot right in it. He'd had his suspicions about Elizabeth and should have realized who the ageing woman was. To go blabbing his mouth off to the real Reverend Mother was a fatal mistake. He'd deny all knowledge of the meeting in her study, he decided. Mistaken identity, that was what it was. Breathing a sigh of relief as he

walked down the drive to the main gates, he stopped as he heard the bushes rustling.

'Over here,' the young girl he'd met in the hall whispered.

'Oh, it's you,' Jim murmured. 'What are you doing in there?'

'This is one of our hides.'

'One of your hides? Er . . . right,' he chuckled, looking about before diving into the bushes. 'This is rather cosy,' he remarked, sitting on a blanket in a small clearing beneath the bushes. 'Home from home. Well, not quite.'

'This is where we keep an eye on the gates. We can see who's coming and going from here. I'm on watch for the next hour.'

'On watch? Who exactly are you watching for?'

'Anyone and everyone. We like to know who's coming and going.'

'So do I,' Jim chortled, eyeing the tight crotch of the blonde's knickers as she pulled her legs up and rested her chin on her knees. 'You're a pretty little thing. Do you ever visit the dungeon?'

'The dungeon?' she gasped, her blue eyes widening. 'God, I wouldn't go there even if I knew where it was. I've heard the rumours, of course. But I'd never go there.'

'Why not?'

'They have sex there,' she whispered, leaning forward. 'I'm too young to do things like that.'

'Oh, I wouldn't say that,' Jim breathed, focusing on the firm flesh of her inner thighs. 'I'd say that you're ripe enough for—'

'No, no. That's for the older girls,' she giggled. 'Maybe one day I'll—'

'I don't know what I'm missing,' Jim broke in, his eyes bulging as he gazed longingly at the swell of her navy-blue knickers. 'I mean, *you* don't know what *you*'re missing.'

'I don't know anything about sex,' she sighed. 'The older girls won't let me get involved in their games.'

'*I*'ll play games with you,' Jim said eagerly, running his fingertip along the smooth flesh of her thigh to the alluring bulge of her tight knickers. 'I'm good at playing games with young girlies.'

'Ooh, that tickles,' she giggled. 'You *are* naughty.'

'And I get worse.'

'You're the man from the pub, aren't you?'

'Yes, that's right.'

'The older girls won't let me go to the pub. It's not fair because some of my friends go there and—'

'If you want to go to the pub, then you'll come as my guest,' Jim said, his balls rolling as he imagined the purple globe of his solid cock encompassed by the full lips of her pretty mouth. 'I run the pub and, if I say you can come in for a drink, then no one can stop you.'

'Great,' she trilled. 'But I don't have any money.'

'You don't need money, my pretty little thing.' he laughed. 'You have something far better than . . . I'm Jim, by the way.'

'And I'm Angelica.'

'What a sweet name: It reminds me of innocence. A young wood nymph lying beneath the pine trees with shafts of sunlight playing on the mounds and crevices of her curvaceous body and . . .'

'I've never been into a pub before.'

'We'll soon change that, Angelica. In fact, we'll change quite a few things.'

'Will we?'

'Oh, yes. I have great plans for you, my little cherub. I must say, I do like the way you're sitting. Your knickers are absolutely . . .'

'Oh, my knickers,' she sighed despondently.

'What's the matter? Do your knickers trouble you?'

'I have to wear them for four days without taking them off and then give them to Crystal. She's one of the older girls.'

'Yes, I've met her. Why do you give her your knickers? Surely she has her own?'

'I don't know why. She collects dirty knickers from all my friends.'

'Ah, right.'

'She gets really annoyed if I change them before the four days are up.'

'Yes, I can understand . . . So, you have no idea what she does with them?'

'No idea at all. One of my friends reckons that Crystal sells them but I can't see who'd want to buy dirty knickers.'

'Er . . . no, of course not.'

'The idea of people buying dirty knickers is stupid. Anyone who wants to buy a pair of knickers would go to a shop and get a new pair.'

'Why don't you take them off and let me have a look at them?' Jim suggested, desperate to press the warm crotch to his face and breath in the perfume of her teenage cunny.

'But Crystal won't allow me to take them off.'

'Not even when you . . .'

'She seems to think that they're better when they're wet and smelly. It's strange, isn't it?'

'Not at all. Er . . . it's most peculiar. Perhaps I can help to solve the mystery. Slip your knickers off and I'll examine them. There must be a clue . . .'

'You just want to see my pussy, don't you?'

'See your . . . Good grief. Of course not,' Jim laughed. 'I want to see what's so fascinating about your knickers. There must be something about them that is of interest to Crystal.'

'All right, then,' she conceded. 'You can examine my knickers. But you're only allowed to *look* at my pussy. No touching, OK?'

'Fine, fine.'

Lying on the blanket and raising her buttocks clear of the ground, Angelica tugged her navy-blue knickers down her long legs and kicked them off her feet. Her short skirt concealing the crack of her pussy, Jim wondered whether to suggest that she should take all her clothes off so that he could examine them. No, she wouldn't fall for that, he decided, sniffing the girl-stained crotch of her school knickers. Like a breath of fresh air, the heady scent was extremely intoxicating. Heavily soiled with teenage girl-juice, perfumed with an aphrodisiacal blend of . . . There was money to be made here, he knew.

The girl's skirt rising up as Jim continued to examine the wet crotch of her knickers, she was obviously aware that the hairless lips of her naked vulva were on display. Jim gazed out of the corner of his eye at her creamy sex crack as he once more breathed in the heavenly fragrance of her school knickers. She was beautiful, he mused, imagining running his wet tongue up and down her sweet sex-slit and lapping up her teenage juices of lust. Her knickers were heavily scented, and she was heaven-sent.

'It's not my knickers you're interested in,' she said, following his gaze to where it focused on the naked flesh of her young vulva.

'I'm *very* interested in your knickers,' Jim murmured. 'But I'm also very interested in your beautiful pussy.'

'Look, but don't touch,' she reminded him as he leaned over her young body for a better view of her tightly closed crack of desire.

'Of course, Angelica. Look, but don't touch.'

She was having him on, he knew as she lay with her slender legs parted, the gentle rise of her hairless mons only inches from his juice-thirsty mouth. *I don't know anything about sex. The older girls won't let me get involved in their games. I have to wear my knickers for four days without taking them off and then give them to Crystal. One of my friends reckons that Crystal sells them but I can't see who'd want to buy dirty knickers.* Angelica was a lying little slut, Jim mused, pushing his wet tongue out as he moved closer to the creamy valley of her schoolgirl pussy. Which was just as well because he was heavily into lying little sluts.

Recalling Maria's play-acting, he reckoned that the girls had been taught to come across as innocent little virgins by their older peers. They all shaved their pubic mounds, adding to the illusion of young, untouched little girlies. But who was in charge of the convent side of the scam? he wondered, his tongue moving closer to Angelica's vaginal slit. Cleo appeared to be in charge of the sex dungeon, but who ran the illicit business at the convent? Crystal was his best bet, he decided. She was into anything and everything, from selling soiled knickers to raking off a profit from the sanitary-towel machine. The picture was at last forming. Crystal forced the young

girls to give up their dirty knickers, while Cleo packed the goods in polythene bags and kept the stock in her dressing-table drawers where they were then supplied to the sex dungeon clients. One thing was certain, Jim mused. He was going to keep Angelica's beautifully stained knickers. They'd come in handy for sniffing if he was forced to resort to wanking.

The tip of his tongue finally coming into contact with Angelica's vulval flesh, he breathed in the heady aroma of her girl-scent. She writhed and let out a rush of breath as he ran his wet tongue up and down the full length of her love slit. Raising her pert buttocks clear of the ground and parting her firm thighs, she was obviously offering her young pussy to Jim's mouth as he lapped at her cream-wet vaginal crack. She was no more an innocent virgin than he was, he knew as her sex cream bubbled between the succulent cushions of her outer labia.

Daring to part the fleshy swell of her outer sex pads, Jim eyed the intricate pink folds nestling within her creamy valley of girl-pleasure. Her ripe clitoris fully emerging from its protective hood, her sex hole spewing out her creamy lubricant, she let out another rush of breath as he ran his fingertip over the wet flesh surrounding her vaginal inlet. She was more than ready for a damned good fucking, he knew as he licked the sensitive tip of her erect clitoris. Her young body trembling, her breathing fast and shallow, she was more than ready for a meaty length of solid cock and a pussy full of fresh spunk.

Reaching up to the swell of her tight blouse, Jim squeezed and fondled the firm mounds of her young breasts. Before sliding his huge penis deep into her tight pussy and drowning her cervix in sperm, he decided to

heighten her arousal by pulling and twisting the sensitive protrusions of her milk teats. Once she was in an incontrollable state of sexual frenzy, he'd move between her splayed thighs and ram his purple crown deep into the tight shaft of her hot cunt and fuck her senseless.

Slipping his hand into her blouse, Jim managed to lift Angelica's bra clear of her small breasts. Running his fingertip around the warm teats of her nipples, he grinned as she let out a moan of satisfaction. Pushing his tongue into the wet entrance of her hot pussy, he tasted the cream-dripping walls of her young cunt. Angelica squirmed on the blanket as Jim tweaked the teats of her nipples and caressed the inner flesh of her teenage pussy with his wet tongue. Young and gushing with hormones, the girl was obviously close to her orgasm. Gasping, letting out whimpers of sexual frenzy, she arched her back as Jim centred his oral attention on her solid clitoris. Yet another schoolgirl conquest, he reflected, deciding that his time spent in Willycombe Village had been most fruitful.

'No,' Angelica gasped. 'You mustn't make me come. I'm . . . I'm too young to . . . Oh, God.' Her clitoris exploding in orgasm beneath Jim's snaking tongue, she shook uncontrollably and let out screams of sexual gratification. Hoping that no one would hear her cries of female lust, Jim imagined the hag-bag Reverend Mother peering into the bushes and witnessing the lewd act of Angelica's orally induced climax. The girl would face certain expulsion, Jim would face hell . . . Being caught with his tongue up a schoolgirl's teenage cunt didn't bear thinking about.

Sustaining the young beauty's pleasure with his caressing tongue, Jim drove two fingers into the incredibly

tight sheath of her well-juiced vagina and massaged her hot inner flesh. Her creamy juices of lust gushing from her finger-pistoned cunt and splattering the pale skin of her twitching thighs, she writhed like a snake in agony as her orgasm peaked. Jim had never known a girl come so much. Her orgasmic cream jetting from her bloated vaginal cavern, running over his thrusting hand as he sucked her pulsating clitoris into his hot mouth and painfully pinched the ripe teats of her nipples, she was obviously in her sexual heaven. Again and again, tremors of crude sex rocked her teenage body, reaching every nerve ending, tightening every muscle.

'More,' Angelica breathed shakily, flinging her thighs apart as wide as she could. Again lifting her firm buttocks clear of the blanket and grinding the hairless crack of her vulva hard against Jim's slurping mouth, she tore her blouse open and exposed the petite mounds of her breasts. She was lost in her sexual frenzy, Jim knew as she mumbled incoherent words of teenage lust. She was more than ready for a length of meaty cock, he thought, his penis straining to break out of his trousers. More than ready for a cunt full of creamy spunk.

Slipping his fingers out of the spasming sheath of Angelica's sex-drenched vagina as he continued to suck her multiple orgasm from her pulsating clitoris, Jim decided to attempt a crude violation of her teenage bottom-hole with an anal fingering. She'd either protest wildly or give in to her anal desires and allow him to finger-fuck the tight duct of her rectum. Either way, she was going to endure a most severe rectal finger-fucking.

Slipping his finger between Angelica's tensed buttocks, Jim sucked and licked her orgasming clitoris in the hope that she wouldn't realize what he was doing to

her sweet anus before it was too late. Locating the tight portal to her inner core, he pressed his fingertip into her hole of illicit pleasure. She squirmed and writhed, mumbling something incoherent as his finger glided along the tight tube of her rectum. Sinking his finger deep into the fiery heat of her bowels, he massaged her inner flesh, taking her to frightening new heights of sexual pleasure.

'No, no,' the girl breathed as Jim forced a second finger into her anal canal. Ignoring her protests, he swept his wet tongue repeatedly over the pulsating nubble of her pink clitoris to sustain her mind-blowing climax. She was a dirty little slut, he thought, as the sound of her gasps of girl-pleasure disturbed the still summer air. Young, dirty, horny . . . Imagining her masturbating in her bed at night, her whimpers of sex resounding around the dormitory as she candle-fucked the tight sheath of her teenage cunt, he reckoned that she *did* join in with the other girls' sex games. All teenage girls were latent lesbians, he mused. Rampant hormones, gushing girl-juice, solid clitorises, tight little pussy ducts . . . Of course teenage girls tongue-fucked each other's cunts.

Now the time really had come to shaft the sex-frenzied beauty, Jim decided as her orgasm began to recede. Slipping his anal-slimed fingers out of the hot sheath of Angelica's rectum, he positioned himself between her twitching thighs and hauled out his granite-hard penis. Slipping his purple knob between her splayed inner lips, he pressed his weapon-head hard against the tight funnel of flesh surrounding her vaginal entrance. She was extremely tight, he mused, forcing his bulbous glans into the burning duct of her pussy. Driving his veined cock-shaft deep into her quivering body until his purple globe met her creamy cervix, he

looked down at the girl's outer labia stretched tautly around the broad root of his penis.

'God,' Angelica cried, lifting her head and following his gaze to her gaping outer lips. 'You're so big.'

'And you're so tight,' Jim gasped, withdrawing his cock and driving his knob again into her quivering body.

'I've . . . I've never been fucked before.'

'Me neither,' Jim chuckled, resting his weight on his hands as he repeatedly impaled her on his huge organ.

Listening to the squelching sounds of Angelica's vaginal juices as he fucked her, Jim realized that he'd never shafted such a tight little pussy. The other schoolgirls had been tight, but this beauty's vagina was incredible. Watching his juice-glossed shaft sliding in and out of the girl's cunt, he was already nearing his orgasm. His swinging balls battering the firm cheeks of her naked buttocks, he wondered whether to whip his cock out of her pussy and drive his knob-head deep into her bowels. If she really was a virgin, then it was only fair to strip her of her anal virginity as well as her vaginal purity.

'No,' she gasped as he slipped his knob out of her sex sheath and forced it past the tight ring of her anus. 'What are you doing? That's not my fanny.'

'God, your arse is tight,' Jim gasped as his glans journeyed along her tight rectal sheath to the heat of her bowels. 'And now for an anal spunking.'

'No, please . . . Oh, God. My . . . my bottom is going to tear open.'

'Relax and take it, Angelica. After all, this is what your arse is for.'

'My pussy is for . . . Oh, my God.'

His sperm jetting from his throbbing knob, lubricating the illicit union, Jim increased his anal fucking rhythm.

Angelica's young body rocking with the illicit shafting, she let out whimpers of rectal pleasure as her bowels flooded with fresh spunk and her vagina spewed out its sex juices. She really was a horny little beauty, Jim thought as she slipped her fingers between the splayed lips of her vulva and massaged the solid nub of her clitoris. Fervently masturbating in her sexual frenzy, she tossed her head from side to side as she neared her second massive climax. Jim watched her fingertip massaging her solid clitoris, her juices of lust spurting from the gaping entrance to her sex duct as he continued to pump his creamy spunk deep into the fiery heat of her bowels.

Finally reaching her orgasm, Angelica arched her back and let out a scream of pure sexual bliss as Jim's cock glided in and out of the burning sheath of her rectum. Grabbing her legs and forcing her knees up to her chest, he repeatedly rammed his throbbing knob deep into the very core of her trembling body as she rode the crest of her climax. She was the perfect slut, Jim reflected as his swinging balls drained. Young, dirty, horny, tight, wet, hot . . . What more could a man want in a common slag?

'I'm sure I heard a scream,' a woman said.

'I didn't hear anything,' another woman breathed.

'Fucking hell,' Jim whispered, sliding his spent cock out of Angelica's spunked rectum and zipping his trousers. 'Who's that?'

'It sounds like the Reverend Mother,' Angelica replied, fumbling to conceal her small breasts within the cups of her bra. 'I was supposed to be on watch.'

'It's all right. Just keep quiet and she'll go away.'

Peering through the bushes as Angelica dressed, Jim watched the hag-bag hovering a few feet away with a

younger woman. This was all he needed, he thought
fearfully: caught in the bushes with a half-naked schoolgirl whose bum was spewing out fresh sperm! Praying
that the Reverend Mother would walk away, Jim looked
around for an escape route. Surrounded by thick undergrowth, he realized that the only way out of the bushes
was where the bitch-dragon was standing. Gazing at
Angelica as she finished dressing, he settled on the
blanket beside her and decided to wait. The hag wouldn't
stand there all day, he was sure.

'If that man is hanging around, I'll call the police,' the
Reverend Mother said.

'Are you sure that it was the new landlord of the
Tartan Vicar?' the younger woman asked her.

'Positive. He was talking about shaving the girls' pubic
hairs.'

'How terribly exciting. I mean—'

'Exciting? Don't be ridiculous, Sister Libido.'

'The drama, the police, a strange man lurking . . . I
didn't mean that shaving the young girls was exciting.
There again . . .'

'Life isn't supposed to be exciting, Sister. We're here
to do God's work, not to shave the pubic hair of young
girls. We should not even be talking about such things.'

'I rather like talking about . . . Anyway, there are no
strange men out here. Shall we go back to your study?'

'That was close,' Angelica said as the Reverend
Mother finally walked back to the convent building. 'I
thought that she was going to catch me with my knickers
down.'

'And I thought that she was going to catch me with my
cock up,' Jim chuckled with relief. 'Right up your tight
little arse.'

'I'm an anal slut now,' the girl sighed.

'Are you?'

'Crystal says that girls who take it up their bums are anal sluts.'

'She should know.'

'But I didn't *want* to be an anal slut.'

'I wouldn't worry about it,' Jim consoled her. 'Anal slut, vaginal slut, cumslut . . . what the hell?'

'There's a girl in my class who's a total anal slut.'

'Really?'

'Her name's Annie. She's known as Anal Annie.'

'Wonderful.'

'She's always sticking things up her bum.'

'What sort of things?' Jim asked her eagerly.

'Wax crayons, fingers, candles . . . You name it, she sticks it up her bum. She pays girls to finger her bum.'

'I'll have to meet the young beauty.'

'I don't suppose she'd pay you to—'

'I wouldn't want payment,' he laughed. 'I'd do it for—'

'She likes carrots. Fresh carrots. I tried sticking a carrot up my bum once but I couldn't get it in.'

'We're going to have to meet again, Angelica.'

'Yes, I'd like that. We're anal soulmates now, aren't we?'

'Are we?'

'We've bonded anally. Like blood brothers, we're anal kin.'

'Yes, well . . . I suppose I'd better be getting back to the pub.'

'I'll meet you in the woods this evening.'

'Yes, yes,' Jim breathed. 'I'd like it in the woods. Like to meet you, I mean.'

'Shall I bring Anal Annie with me?'

'God, yes.'

'You'll like her. She's good fun.'

'I'm sure that I'll like her.'

'She is rather common, but a very nice girl.'

'Common? Excellent. I love common girls. Right, I'll meet you behind the church at, say, seven o'clock?'

'We'll be there.'

Slipping out of the bushes, Jim walked briskly down the drive to the gates and made his escape. The evening was going to be most interesting, he mused. Meeting Angelica and Anal Annie in the woods . . . But he had Cleo to face before the evening. She'd probably moan, complain because he was always nipping out of the pub. He'd deal with her later that evening, he decided. A damned good anal shafting would keep her quiet for a while. Angelica's mouth, Anal Annie's rectum and then Cleo's tight little bottom-hole. Jim had a busy evening ahead of him.

13

Cleo had been pretty quiet during the rest of the afternoon. Jim had thought that her mood had had something to do with his earlier disappearance, but she seemed to have something else on her mind. Perhaps her father had been on the phone, he thought, checking his watch for the umpteenth time and hoping that the young girls wouldn't let him down. She might have heard about his visit to the convent, he reflected, deciding to try to strike up a conversation with her.

'Does your offer of coffee after we close tonight still stand?' he asked her.

'What? Oh, er . . . yes, yes of course,' she replied abstractedly.

'Are you all right, Cleo?'

'Yes, yes – I'm fine.'

'No, you're not. I can't stand women who say that they're OK when it's obvious that they're not. What is it? What's on your mind?'

'My father rang,' she confessed.

'I might have guessed. So, what did he say?'

'He'll be here in the morning to make sure that you've left. He wants you out today, Jim.'

'Don't worry your pretty little head about that,' he chuckled. 'Once he realizes that . . . I'll just say that

there won't be any problems. I promise you, there's nothing to worry about.'

'Isn't there?'

'No, of course not.'

'In that case, why is he bringing your replacement in the morning?'

'My replacement?'

'He's got some man or other from the brewery to take over from you, Jim. I still don't know what it was that you said to him to upset him like this. We work well together – when you're here, that is. We get on all right and . . . What have you said to my father to ruin everything?'

'I put a proposition to him, Cleo. A business proposition.'

'What did you mean when you said that you were going to move into the big time? And what the hell did you do at the convent?'

'All I did was—'

'You're involving yourself in everything, Jim. You've only been here for five minutes and you've riled my father, poked your nose in at the convent, tried to get in with the vicar, befriended his daughter, asked questions . . .'

'Mary isn't the vicar's daughter, Cleo.'

'Of course she is. What the hell are you suggesting now?'

'You said that I'm involving myself in everything.'

'Well, you are.'

'Wouldn't you? I hear talk about a secret tunnel and a sex dungeon . . .'

'God, not that again,' she sighed, pressing a glass to the vodka optic.

'Listen to me, Cleo. Something's going on in this village and I—'

'No, *you* listen to *me*,' Cleo cut in. 'Nothing is going on, as you put it. People are going about their business, their private business, and you aren't happy with that. You seem to think that you should delve into people's private lives.'

'OK, cards on the table,' Jim said, filling a pint glass with beer. 'I know about the sex dungeon.'

'Jim, please stop talking about a sex dungeon.'

'I know about the secret tunnel, I know about the dungeon, the soiled-knicker trade . . .'

'Soiled-knicker trade?' she giggled.

'In your dressing-table drawer, Cleo.'

'You've been rummaging through my personal belongings?'

'I've been to the sex dungeon, Cleo. The examination table, the whips and handcuffs, the wooden bar used as a tethering post for the whipping of convent schoolgirls like Maria . . . I know everything.'

Her hand visibly trembling as she sipped her vodka, Cleo moved around the bar and sat on a stool. Fortunately, there were no customers in the pub, giving Jim the opportunity to talk openly to the girl. But would *she* talk openly to *him*? he wondered. The time had come to be honest with each other. Lies, deception, games . . . They weren't going to get anywhere unless they were honest.

'So, what are you going to do?' she finally asked him.

'Do?'

'Well, you can't stay here.'

'I can and I will stay here,' he returned. 'I've been making moves to—'

'Jim, my father wants you out. You obviously don't know him. He might have been your boss for God knows how long, but you don't know him. I'll admit that he put you here to run the pub because he thought that you wouldn't make a go of it. He reckoned that you'd make a hash of the business, allowing him to use the place as a tax loss.'

'Why didn't he put *you* in charge?'

'His own daughter? No, the tax man would smell a rat.'

'What about the sex dungeon? Why the hell keep that secret from me?'

'I couldn't tell you about it, Jim. If my father—'

'I'm hoping that your father will bring me in on the business and—'

'It's disgusting,' Ruby Rottweiler complained as she burst into the pub. 'Two half-naked young girls walking into the woods at this time of night? Good God, whatever next?'

'Half-naked girls?' Cleo echoed, frowning at the woman.

'Skirts so short that they're not worth wearing, blouses hanging open . . . They shouldn't be allowed out like that. When I was their age, I was never allowed out at this time of night.'

'It's not quite seven o'clock,' Jim chuckled. 'It doesn't get dark for a couple of hours.'

'That's beside the point. I'll have a pint of bitter, please. The point is that half-naked young girls roaming the woods at night are bound to be pounced upon by some pervert or other.'

'That's true,' Jim laughed. 'I mean—'

'They need a woman's touch.'

'And you're the woman to touch them, I suppose?'

'What do you mean by that?'

'Er . . . nothing.'

'I'm talking about a proper home with a mother and . . . Oh, what's the point?' she sighed. 'There's nothing I can do to change the world.'

'I'm sure they'll be all right, Ruby,' Cleo said, passing the woman her beer. 'As Jim said, it doesn't get dark for a couple of hours.'

'Perverts also strike in daylight, Cleo. Imagine some perverted man roaming the woods and coming across two half-naked teenage girls.'

'Talking of which,' Jim broke in. 'I have to pop out for a while.'

'Again?' Cleo sighed.

'Would you mind going to the woods and checking up on the girls?' Ruby asked him.

'I'd be delighted to . . . I'll go there now, Ruby. The last thing we want is some sad pervert coming all over the girls. Coming *across* the girls, I mean.'

'Can you imagine it? A pervert loose in the woods with two very young girls?'

'Yes, I can,' Jim gasped, adjusting his twitching cock through his trousers. 'Two very young half-naked girlies roaming the woods . . .'

'Anything could happen to them.'

'Oh, it will. I mean . . . I won't be long, Cleo.'

'I've heard that before.'

Leaving the pub, Jim almost ran down the street to the church. Slipping around the side of the building, he followed the narrow path into the woods and looked around him. Ruby had seen the girls entering the woods, but where were they? he wondered. His cock rising as he pondered on Anal Annie's wonderfully peculiar fetish,

he hoped that she'd invite him to tongue-fuck her sweet anus. If he was lucky, he might even get to watch Angelica sticking her tongue into Annie's bottom-hole.

His balls rolling in their hairy sac as he wandered a little further along the path, Jim couldn't stop thinking about Anal Annie. To get herself a name like that, she must have quite a reputation, he reflected. Wax crayons, fingers, candles, carrots . . . Did she take huge cocks up her arse? He wondered. Girls were lucky creatures, he mused. With two fuckable holes between their thighs and spunk-thirsty mouths, not to mention shaggable cleavages, they were fully equipped for all aspects of crude sex. Three men could simultaneously fuck one girl. But one man could only fuck one hole at a time.

Walking further into the woods, Jim was about to give up on the girls and return to the pub when he heard a girlie-giggle coming from a clump of bushes. Creeping up to the shrubs, he moved a branch aside stealthily and found himself gazing at Angelica and her friend sitting on a blanket. This was Anal Annie, he knew as he heard her telling Angelica that she'd been experimenting with cucumbers. Picturing the lewd act as she explained how she cut a cucumber in half and rammed it deep into her bottom-hole, Jim felt his balls heave, his cock swell and stiffen.

Anal Annie was a very attractive young thing. With long black hair framing her pretty face, her succulent lips furling into a salacious grin, she was also eminently fuckable. Eyeing the ripe buds of her young breasts pressing through the flimsy material of her school blouse, Jim prayed for the opportunity to see her in her naked glory. Black shoes, white knee-length socks, a short pleated shirt . . . And she paid girls to pleasure her bottom-hole? This was too much for him to bear.

'Hello,' he said, walking through the bushes into the small clearing.

'Hi,' Angelica trilled. 'Jim, this is Annie. Annie, Jim.'

'Hiya,' Annie said, licking her full red lips. 'Angelica has told me all about you.'

'Oh?' Jim breathed. He could smell sex in the air, could almost taste the girl's anus. 'Nothing bad, I hope?'

'She's told me everything, down to the last detail.'

'She's told me about you, too,' Jim chuckled, eyeing the girl's naked thighs.

'Everything?'

'Well . . .'

'Everything,' Angelica confirmed. 'From your nickname to your little fetish.'

'I have a thing about my bumhole,' the other girl announced proudly. 'I love my bumhole. It's my favourite part of my body.'

'Well, we all have a favourite part,' Jim said. 'Mine is my cock.'

'Cocks and bums go together,' Annie chuckled. 'As Angelica discovered earlier.'

'I only said . . .' Angelica began, obviously embarrassed.

'You only said that Jim shafted your arse and spermed up you.'

'That about sums it up,' Jim laughed. 'So, you're into bum-fucking?'

'They don't call me Anal Annie for nothing.'

'Tell him the truth,' Angelica said, staring hard at Annie.

'All right,' she sighed, hanging her head. 'I've shoved anything and everything I could lay hands on up my bum. But . . .'

'But she's never had a cock up her bum,' Angelica giggled.

'Really?' Jim breathed.

'The school is full of girls,' Annie whined. 'There are hundreds of fingers and tongues, but not one hard cock.'

'Well, I'm sure that I can do something about that,' Jim laughed.

'I was hoping you'd say that. From what Angelica was saying, you're pretty good at bum-fucking.'

'Pretty good? I'm the best.'

'Before you bum-fuck me, would you like to watch Angelica licking my bumhole?'

'I'm not going to do that,' Angelica protested.

'Of course you are. You want to join in with the girls' sex games, right?'

'Well, yes.'

'Then you'll start by getting to know my anus, intimately.'

'Annie, I . . .'

'You can lubricate my anus ready for Jim's cock. A good helping of spit will make it easier for him to slide his cock into my arse.'

Jim could hardly believe what the girl had said as she unbuttoned her blouse and slipped the garment over her shoulders. Tossing her long black hair away from her pretty face, she unhooked her bra and exposed the ripe teats of her nipples adorning the petite mounds of her teenage breasts. Focusing on her elongated nipples, Jim knew from experience that her breasts were newly developed. The dark discs of her areolae were cone-shaped, almost pointed, rather than flat. A sure sign of recent mammary development, he mused. Anal Annie was so young, fresh, slim, curvaceous . . . She was

filthy-minded, sexually deviant, whorish; sluttish, slaggish . . .

Watching with bated breath as Annie slipped her skirt and shoes off, Jim eyed the swell of her navy-blue school knickers. It was a shame that she didn't have some peculiar fetish with her sex crack, Jim thought, imagining her stuffing candles and cucumbers deep into the tight sheath of her creamy-wet cunt. But her bottom-hole would be interesting enough, he decided, his eyes widening as she tugged her knickers down her slender legs. Revealing the tightly closed slit of her teenage vulva, she positioned herself on all fours and projected the rounded cheeks of her firm buttocks.

'Go on, Angelica,' Annie breathed, resting her head on the blanket and stretching the firm orbs of her buttocks wide apart. 'Lick my bottom-hole.'

'Annie,' the other girl sighed. 'Do I have to?'

'Of course you have to. Come on, Jim's waiting to slide his cock into my rectum and turn me into a real anal slut.'

Settling beside Angelica as she knelt behind Annie, Jim watched the girl push her tongue out and tentatively lick the unblemished flesh of her young friend's rounded buttocks. Her pink tongue working in the top of the girl's anal gully, Angelica seemed to be keeping clear of the tight hole of Annie's anus. Annie let out gasps of pleasure as she yanked the cheeks of her bottom further apart. Her anal inlet dilating, the dank tube of her rectum inviting Angelica's tongue, she again ordered the kneeling girl to lick her bottom-hole.

Finally complying with the crude instruction, Angelica licked the delicate brown tissue surrounding her friend's anus. They must have done this before, Jim was sure as Angelica fervently slurped at her young

friend's anal inlet. Locking her full lips to the girl's brown tissue, she sucked hard, obviously delighting in the aphrodisiacal taste of her trembling friend's rectal sheath. Pondering on the oversexed schoolgirls of Willycombe Village, Jim once more thought it odd that there were no young men around. Where were the sex-crazed teenage boys? Led away by the Pied Piper?

'Now your fingers,' Anal Annie breathed, jutting her naked buttocks out further. 'As many fingers as you can.'

'When did you first discover the delights of your bottom-hole?' Jim asked her as Angelica continued her anal licking and slurping.

'Years ago,' the girl breathed. 'I was in my bed, running the end of a candle up and down my cunt crack, and I slipped it into the wrong hole. I knew nothing about sex. All I knew was that I had a hole. I later realized that I had a fanny hole too, but it was too late.'

'Too late?'

'I was heavily into candle-fucking my bottom. I didn't bother with my cunt.'

This was amazing stuff, Jim mused as he watched Angelica slide a finger deep into Annie's rectum. His cock twitching as the girl drove a second finger into her friend's anal duct, crudely penetrating Annie's tight bottom-hole, Jim gaped as Angelica reached behind her back and lifted her skirt up. Was this an invitation? Jim wondered, eyeing the tight material of her navy-blue knickers faithfully following the contours of her young buttocks. Was she offering him her rectal canal? Did she want another bum-shagging?

Moving behind Angelica, Jim yanked her knickers down and exposed the rounded cheeks of her firm bottom. The crotch of her knickers full of girl-cream,

he knew that she was in a severe state of sexual arousal as she managed to drive a third finger into Anal Annie's inflamed bumhole. Parting Angelica's pert buttocks, fully exposing the brown tissue of her anus, Jim pushed his tongue out and licked her there. The taste of her secret hole driving him wild, he fervently licked her tight hole, wetting her there before pushing the tip of his tongue into the bitter-sweet duct of her arse.

Half-naked young girls roaming the woods at night are bound to be pounced upon by some pervert or other. Recalling Ruby Rottweiler's words, Jim hoped that the woman wouldn't take it upon herself to search the woods. She wasn't concerned for the girls' safety, he reflected, driving his tongue deeper into Angelica's rectal sheath. Ruby wanted the half-naked little sluts for herself. She was jealous, he mused. Hairless little pussy-cracks, barely developed breast buds, tight bottom-holes . . . The dirty lesbian wanted the young girls' young bodies for her own sexual pleasure. Wondering whether Ruby had a female lover, Jim decided that the time had come to shaft Angelica's anal duct and flood her hot bowels with his fresh spunk.

'What are you doing?' Anal Annie asked as Jim unzipped his trousers and pressed his purple plum hard against Angelica's anus. 'I heard your zip. You're not going to fuck Angelica's bottom, are you? She's already had your cock up her bum. It's *my* turn for an anal shafting.'

'Whatever you say,' Jim chuckled, his trousers around his knees, his cock waving from side to side. 'I really don't care whose arse I fuck.'

'You'd better do hers,' Angelica sighed, withdrawing her rectal-slimed fingers from her quivering friend's anal

canal and moving aside. 'Go on, then, turn her into a genuine anal slut.'

'Why don't you give me a hand?' Jim asked the solemn girl as he knelt behind Anal Annie's rounded bottom. 'Come on, grab my cock and guide me in.'

Watching Angelica grab his cock by the root, Jim moved his hips forward. Angelica was obviously enjoying this, he thought as she pressed the purple globe of his cock hard against the tight ring of Annie's arse. As Annie yanked her rounded buttocks apart, opening the portal to her rectal duct, Jim watched his bulbous glans slip past her anal ring and sink into the very core of her trembling body. His knob journeying along the dank tube of her rectum, finally reaching the heat of her bowels' he grabbed her hips and fully impaled the whimpering girl as Angelica moved aside.

'God,' Angelica gasped. 'Look at her bumhole. It's opened so wide.'

'She's a tight little slut,' Jim gasped, withdrawing his cock slowly before ramming his purple knob back deep into the heat of her bowels. 'Christ, she's tight.'

'It's heavenly,' Annie breathed, her young body shaking uncontrollably. 'Fuck me, you're as big as my cucumber.'

'I can out-fuck any cucumber,' Jim laughed, increasing his anal shagging rhythm.

'I'm going for marrows next,' the girl breathed. 'Imagine a fucking great marrow fucking my beautiful bum.'

'You are awful,' Angelica rejoined, settling beside her friend and squeezing the cone-shaped mound of her breast before moving down and slipping a finger between the soft love lips of her hairless vulva.

'Yes, yes, finger my cunt,' Annie cried. 'Fist-fuck my hot cunt.'

Jim had never known such dirty teenage girls. Filthy sluts, vulgar whores, disgusting nymphomaniacs . . . There were no words to describe the decadent little tarts. Dreading to think of their parents' reaction if they were to discover their young daughters' lewd behaviour, he couldn't understand why Willycombe Village was home to so many teenage sluts. The village reeked of girl-sex, reverberated with squelching vaginal juices and whimpers of female orgasm. But where were the hormone-stuffed teenage boys?

'At last,' Anal Annie cried. 'I'm a slut. A real anal slut.' Grinning, Jim repeatedly rammed his swollen knob-head deep into the dirty slag's inflamed rectal canal. His swinging balls battering Angelica's hand as she finger-fucked the other girl's hot cunt, he knew that he couldn't hold back his spunk for much longer. The tightness of the girl's rectal duct, the heat of her bowels, the sound of squelching girl-juice and female gasps of pleasure . . . It was all too much for Jim.

'Yes,' he breathed, his sperm jetting from his knob-slit, lubricating and cooling the burning sheath of Anal Annie's rectal tube. In his moment of orgasmic coming, Jim didn't care about Ruby Rottweiler, Mr Hops, the Reverend Mother . . . All that mattered was the crude fucking of a teenage slut's arsehole. This was what real sex was all about, he mused, his lower belly slapping the anal whore's naked bottom cheeks. Again and again, he rammed his throbbing knob deep into the fiery depths of the girl's bowels, flooding her inner core with his gushing sperm until his balls had drained and his penile shaft began to deflate.

'Fucking hell,' Jim gasped, stilling his cock inside Annie's spunked rectum, his knob absorbing the inner heat of her trembling body. 'What a brilliant arse-fuck that was.'

'That was fucking great,' Annie murmured shakily. 'I've never known anything like it.'

'What about me?' Angelica asked, slipping her cunny-dripping fingers out of her young friend's spasming vaginal duct. 'I haven't been arse-fucked yet.'

'You had it earlier,' Annie retorted.

'Yes, but . . .'

'I'll soon be up and ready to arse-fuck you, my sweet little honeypot,' Jim chuckled.

'In the meantime, you can suck his sperm out of my arse,' Annie giggled.

'No, I don't think I—'

'Just fucking do it, Angelica.'

How deep was their decadence? Jim wondered, sliding his anal-slimed cock out of Annie's arsehole and settling back on the blanket. Watching Angelica part her friend's naked buttocks and lock her succulent lips to the delicate ring of tissue surrounding her anal inlet, he couldn't believe that this was happening as he listened to the sucking sounds of the debased sexual act. Drinking his spunk from the other girl's rectal canal, Angelica was obviously in her element as she stretched the other girl's buttocks apart to the extreme, opening her anal hole wide. Ramming half her hand into the slag's tight cunt as she sucked the creamy spunk out of her hot arse, Angelica managed to force her fist deep into the cavernous sheath of Annie's vagina. Annie let out a cry of debased satisfaction as Angelica twisted her fist, massaging the painfully stretched walls of her young friend's pussy

duct. Looking down at his fully erect cock, Jim knew that the time had come to quench Angelica's anal thirst for a rectum full of fresh sperm.

Kneeling behind the girl, he yanked her firm buttocks apart and stabbed at her rectal eye with his bulbous knob. Sucking the spunk out of Annie's bottom-hole, she moaned loudly through her nose as Jim's huge knob began to open her anus, stretching the delicate brown tissue open wide. His swollen glans finally slipping past her defeated anal sphincter muscles, his knob-eye peering into the dank tube of her rectum, Angelica shook uncontrollably as his rigid veined cock sank deep into her quivering body. Fully impaling the spunk-sucking slut on his huge organ, Jim grabbed her shapely hips and revelled in the heat of her bowels.

'I'm getting to like this arse-fucking business,' he breathed as Angelica's anal muscles tightened around his invading shaft. 'I've been missing out for years.'

'You can fuck *my* arse any time you like,' Anal Annie gasped as Angelica sucked the last of Jim's spunk out of her rectal duct. 'I could take your cock up my arse several times every day and I'd still want more.'

'Harder,' Angelica breathed, taking her spermed-tongue out of Annie's rectal canal. 'Fuck my arse like you've never fucked an arse before.'

Increasing his rectal shagging rhythm, Jim knew that he'd found his true niche in life, discovered his domain. Watching his anal-greased shaft emerging from and driving back into Angelica's rectal canal, the brown ring of her anus dragging back and forth along his penile length, he couldn't believe his luck. A village teeming with horny schoolgirlies? This was a dream come true. But all good things came to an end, he reflected. Nothing

lasted. How long would it be before he was not only thrown out of the pub but exiled from the village of Willycombe?

Old man Hops had it in for him, the Reverend Mother wasn't at all happy with him . . . Determined to enjoy the girls of Willycombe while he could, Jim looked up to the trees towering high above him as his glans throbbed and his spunk jetted from his penile eye. Fucking the slut's rectal duct with a cruel vengeance, his swinging balls pummelling the fleshy cushions of her vulval lips, he wallowed in the illicit act of schoolgirlie-arse-fucking.

No matter what happened, no one could take away his memories of young girls' tight bottom-holes, their hairless vulvas, their tight little pussies, their skyward-pointing breasts, their cone-shaped areolae and ripe milk teats. Far removed from life with his lesbian wife in London, Willycombe Village had brought Jim more happiness, fun and excitement that he'd ever dreamed of. But it wasn't over yet, he mused, the squelching of sperm within Angelica's inflamed rectum echoing through the trees. His time in the village was far from over.

'Girls, where are you?' Ruby Rottweiler's voice rang through the woods.

'Fuck me,' Jim gasped, yanking his de-spermed penis out of Angelica's hot rectum. 'It's the bloody Rottweiler.'

'Who's the Rottweiler?' Angelica asked, rolling to one side and shuddering her last orgasmic shudder.

'That lesbian woman,' Anal Annie replied. 'She's always lurking in the woods, hoping to sniff out young girls.'

'Shush,' Jim whispered. 'She's getting closer.'

'Girls, where are you?' the woman again called. 'Come

on, girls. I saw you walking into the woods in your little
skirts. Come to Auntie Ruby.'

'She's a fucking nutcase,' Jim breathed.

'Come on, my little darlings. Come to Auntie Ruby
and I'll keep you away from those nasty men and love
you better.'

'I'll get rid of her,' Jim said, yanking his zip up and
buckling his belt. 'I'll make out that I'm just taking a
walk.'

'Keep in touch,' Annie said. 'Remember, you can shaft
my bum as often as you like.'

'And mine,' Angelica whispered.

'Oh, I will,' Jim chuckled, slipping into the bushes.
'Bye for now.'

Ambling nonchalantly along the narrow path, Jim
licked his anal-slimed lips. Savouring the bitter-sweet
taste of teenage anus, he breathed in the heady scent of
Angelica's bottom-hole as he adjusted his sperm-wet
cock through his trousers. This was heaven, he thought,
listening to the birds singing, the summer breeze rustling
the leaves. Anal sex with two teenage schoolgirlies, the
peace and serenity of the woods. . . . Sheer heavenly
bliss.

'Ah, Ruby,' he said as the woman approached him.

'Have you found the half-naked girls?' she asked,
flashing him an accusing glare.

'There are no girls in the woods, Ruby,' he assured
her. 'I've searched high and low, turned every stone,
climbed every molehill . . .'

'What are you talking about, man? Are you drunk?'

'Only on life, Ruby. Only on life.'

'You're mad, completely insane. Have you come across
the girls or not?'

'God, yes . . . I mean, no. There are no half-naked girls here, Ruby. They're probably at home by now, tucked up in bed.'

'What do you know about young girls tucked up in bed?'

'Mary, my daughter. You told me to get her into bed, if you remember?'

'Yes, so I did. Where is she? I haven't seen her since she was ill in the pub.'

'She's, er . . . tucked up in bed, Ruby. Where all teenage girls should be. Naked in bed.'

'Naked? What are you suggesting?'

'Nothing, nothing.'

'Why are you thinking about naked teenage girls in their beds?'

'All I meant was that it's a very hot summer and it's probably best to sleep naked. What are *you* suggesting, Ruby?'

'I never make suggestions. It's obscene and uncouth to make suggestions to strange men in the woods. I'm putting myself at risk just by standing here with you.'

'At risk?'

'You could try anything. Alone here in the woods, you might attempt to—'

'I can assure you, Ruby. You are *not* at risk,' Jim chuckled. 'Far from it, in fact.'

'Don't be ridiculous. An attractive woman like me? Not at risk from perverted men? Huh. You must be out of your tiny mind.'

'Yes, well . . . I'd better be getting back to the pub.'

'And I have to go to the WVLA meeting.'

'The WVLA? What's that?'

'I told you. I'm the chairperson of the Willycombe Village Lesbian Association.'

'Oh, yes, of course.'

Reckoning that the woman had wanted to capture the half-naked young girls and drag them along to her lesbian meeting, Jim chuckled as she walked away. Ruby was a genuine character, that was for sure, he mused as he called out for the girlies. Realizing that they must have crept out of the woods as he peered into the deserted clearing, he wasn't too bothered. He'd had his fun with them, he reflected. And, from what they'd said about wanting him to shaft their rectums whenever he liked, he knew that he was going to have plenty more fun.

Deciding to take a look at the secret entrance to the tunnel before returning to the pub, Jim slipped into the undergrowth. Searching for the concealed entrance, he was sure that he wasn't far away as he noticed the huge oak tree that, he recalled, was only yards from the spot. Pushing several branches aside, he grinned as he gazed at the entrance to the tunnel that led to the sex dungeon. It was rather tempting to slip into the underground passageway and take a peek at the dungeon, he mused. Besides, it was a quick way back to the pub.

Entering the tunnel and moving swiftly and silently along it, Jim listened at the dungeon door for signs of movement. Hearing nothing, he inched the door open and peered into the well-lit room. Noticing what looked like an electric chair by the examination table, he frowned. A new addition, he mused, wondering when and by who the chair had been delivered. Focusing on a huge pink dildo emerging from a hole in the leather seat of the chair, he grinned. The dildo was motorized, he observed, noticing several controls and wires beneath the chair. Picturing a young schoolgirl with the dildo embedded deep within her tight cunt, he could hardly wait

to see the chair in action. Hearing voices outside the door, he leaped behind the cupboard and prayed that he wouldn't be discovered. He should have gone straight back to the pub, he knew as the door opened. If it was Cleo, he'd be safe enough.

Peering around the cupboard, Jim frowned as he gazed at the vicar and Crystal. What the hell were they up to? he wondered as another man entered the sex dungeon. If they were going to stay for an hour or two, Jim would be late back to the pub and Cleo would go mad. Wishing again that he hadn't ventured into the dungeon, Jim sat on the floor with his back to the wall and waited.

14

'Where's Jim?' Mary asked Cleo, perching herself on a bar stool.

'God only knows,' Cleo sighed, pouring the girl a vodka and tonic. 'I've never known anyone disappear as often as he does.'

'Perhaps he's got some girl or other in his flat.'

'He went out. Probably looking for young girls, if I know him – you're right as far as that goes. Actually, I beginning to worry. He said that he wouldn't be long. That was at seven o'clock, and it's now ten.'

'I wouldn't worry,' Mary said, smiling at Cleo. 'He's probably searching for secret tunnels and dungeons.'

'That's why I *am* worried. He's discovered . . .'

'Discovered what?'

'Nothing. He'll probably come marching in before long.'

'And if he doesn't?'

'I don't know, Mary. I have a feeling that . . . Call it a woman's intuition. I think he's in trouble.'

'What sort of trouble? He can hardly get into trouble in Willycombe.'

'Can't he? Look at the way he's been asking questions. People don't like the way he's been snooping about and . . .'

'So, what are you saying?'

'I don't know. The brewery want him out of the pub.'

'Why? What has he done?'

'Again, I don't know. He spoke to my . . . my boss. Mr Hops wants Jim out of the pub this evening.'

'God, he must have said something awful. Perhaps he told him to fuck off. Whatever he said, that explains where he is, doesn't it?'

'If he's moved out, then why leave his things in the flat? And his car's still outside. I don't think he's moved out, Mary. Have you heard anything?'

'Such as?'

'Are there any rumours going around the convent?'

'Only that Jim met the Reverend Mother. Elizabeth made out that *she* was the Reverend Mother when the old bag went away for a couple of days. Jim fell for it and . . . Cleo, I don't think that has anything to do with it.'

'Maybe not. But I reckon that something's going on. Ruby was in earlier. She was going on about two half-naked girls in the woods.'

'That doesn't surprise me,' Mary laughed. 'There are more half-naked girls in Willycombe Woods than—'

'I have an idea that Jim went to look for the girls.'

'That doesn't surprise me, either. He's shagging some girl, Cleo. I'll bet anything that he's got his cock up some girl's pussy and he's shagging her senseless.'

Pouring herself a large vodka, Cleo wasn't so sure that Jim was enjoying the delights of a young girl's naked body. Besides, it was getting dark. The dark always made her a bit nervous. Wondering whether her father had made moves to evict Jim from the pub, she reckoned that he'd have phoned her and said something about it. He wouldn't leave her wondering what had happened. Not

wanting to tell Mary that Jim had discovered the tunnel and the sex dungeon, she thought that perhaps she was overreacting. Jim was all right, she was sure.

'I'm in need of a pint of bitter,' the vicar said as he entered the pub.

'We're seeing rather a lot of you in here,' Cleo remarked, pouring the man his beer. 'I thought that you were supposed to be playing the God-fearing cleric who was anti-drink and—'

'I am,' he chuckled. 'But, seeing as there's no one in here apart from you and Mary, what the hell?'

'Have you seen Jim?' Cleo asked him, placing his drink on the bar.

'He's left the village. I'd have thought that you'd have known that.'

'Left?' Cleo breathed. 'I know that the brewery wanted him out of the pub, but . . . Did you see him?'

'About two hours ago. He was on his way to the railway station.'

'His things are still in the flat. And his car's outside.'

'He said that he'd be back to pick up his things. Why he didn't take his car, I have no idea. Perhaps he'd had a couple of beers and didn't want to risk driving.'

'That's odd,' Cleo murmured. 'Why not wait until the morning?'

'I don't know and I don't care,' the vicar replied, sipping his beer. 'He asked too many questions for my liking. He was a nice enough chap, but I'm pleased that he's gone.'

'I wonder what the next man will be like?' Mary said.

'Next man?' Cleo echoed. 'Oh, you mean the next landlord?'

'Things would be a damned sight easier if *you* ran the

place, Cleo,' the cleric said. 'There's a lot at stake here. Can't you talk to the brewery about it?'

'Yes, yes, I might do that,' she murmured as the man finished his pint.

'Right, I'm going home. Are you coming, Mary?'

'Yes. I'll see you tomorrow, Cleo.'

'Er . . . yes, tomorrow.'

Locking up as the vicar and Mary left the pub, Cleo couldn't understand why Jim had left the village without saying a word to her. They'd got on pretty well together, she reflected. Why leave without so much as a goodbye? They were supposed to be having a coffee together after closing the pub, and she knew how much Jim had been looking forward to spending the night with her. Her mind spinning with a thousand thoughts as she turned the main lights off, she refilled her glass with vodka and sat at the dimly lit bar.

Her father was a hard man, Cleo mused. But he was fair. Jim must have said something terrible to him. To throw him out of the pub at a moment's notice . . . Wishing that she'd taken Jim into her confidence, Cleo realized as she sipped her vodka that she'd have been far better off telling him about the sex dungeon. Had she told him, he wouldn't have roused suspicion around the village with his continual questioning and prying. Things were a mess, she thought, wondering what to do. Worrying about Jim, there was no way she'd be able to sleep.

The whole thing had been handled badly, Cleo decided. From her initial mistake of sucking Jim's prick through the hole in the bar to introducing him to the young schoolgirls, everything had been a massive cock-up. The vicar hadn't helped by confiding in Jim about his supposed concern for Mary. Melanie and Carole had

obviously roused Jim's suspicion with their short skirts and talk of candles. And as for the scam in the church basement with the monks . . . One massive cock-up.

'What is it?' Cleo called as someone hammered on the door. 'Jim, is that you?'

'It's me, Crystal.'

'I've closed up,' Cleo sighed, opening the door and letting the girl in.

'Sorry, but I saw you through the window and thought that you looked lonely.'

'Have you seen Jim?' Cleo asked the other girl, locking the door and pouring her a vodka and tonic.

'Jim? No, no, I haven't. Has he gone missing again?'

'Apparently, he's left the village. The vicar saw him going to the station.'

'Left? Well, I can't say that I'm surprised.'

'Why's that?'

'He was trouble, Cleo,' Crystal replied, gulping down her drink. 'I think I'll have another vodka.'

'Why do you say that he was trouble?' Cleo asked the other girl, refilling the glass.

'All his bloody questions, poking his nose in around the village . . . I thought, as you did, that he was going to concentrate on running the pub.'

'But we all roused his suspicions, didn't we?'

'You're right. We should never have . . . oh, well. What's done is done.'

'Crystal, I don't think that he's left the village.'

'You said that the vicar . . .'

'I know. But I can't think why Jim would leave without saying anything to me.'

'Does he know about the sex dungeon?' Crystal asked her, almost accusingly.

'The . . . No, no, of course he doesn't. Why do you ask?'

'As you said, we all roused his suspicions. He's been poking his nose in, asking questions . . . He might have discovered more than we realize.'

'I don't think so. He'd have said something to me if he'd discovered the tunnel and the dungeon. We'd planned to have coffee and a chat after we'd closed this evening.' For some reason, Cleo felt it best not to tell Crystal about her most recent conversation with Jim.

'And sex?'

'Well, yes.'

'You need relaxing,' Crystal breathed huskily. 'Why don't you allow me to relax you?'

'Oh, I don't know. I'm not really in the mood for . . .'

'Of course you are. Get the footstools and I'll lie on the floor.'

Taking two footstools from an alcove as Crystal lay on the floor, Cleo placed them either side of the other girl's head. Lifting her skirt, she lowered her young body, placing one buttock on each of the low stools with the gaping crack of her vagina pressed against Crystal's open mouth. She'd enjoyed this many times in the past, she reflected, sitting with her knees up and her feet parted wide. The feel of Crystal's hot breath between the swell of her outer lips sending ripples of sex throughout her young body, Cleo quivered uncontrollably. Crystal had been right, she mused, closing her eyes as the other girl's tongue delved between the petals of her distended inner lips. She *did* need relaxing.

As Crystal's tongue entered the moistening sheath of her hot pussy, Cleo let out a rush of breath. She'd hoped to enjoy sex with Jim, but it wasn't to be. Again wonder-

ing why he'd deserted her without so much as a word, she felt her young womb contracting, her juices of desire flowing from her yawning vaginal entrance. As Crystal moved away from her sex hole and licked the delicate brown tissue of her anus, Cleo whimpered in her soaring arousal. The tip of the other girl's tongue slipping into her rectal tight duct, Cleo shuddered as her clitoris swelled and pulsated.

She'd wanted Jim's tongue there, she mused, the heavenly sensations emanating from her salivated anus driving her wild. Jim's tongue, his fingers, his solid penis . . . Massaging Crystal's firm breasts through her tight blouse, she tweaked the other girl's nipples. Crystal would appreciate a reciprocal licking, Cleo knew. In the past, they'd swapped places, taking turns to lick and suck each other's clitorises to orgasm and drink the lubricious cream of desire from each other's vaginal ducts. The footstools were ideal for licking and sucking, Cleo reflected, leaning forward and pulling Crystal's skirt up over her stomach. Massaging the fleshy swell of the other girl's knickerless vaginal lips, Cleo slipped her fingertip into Crystal's moist sex valley and caressed the solid tip of her expectant clitoris.

Carried away on a cloud of lesbian lust, Crystal mouthed fervently at Cleo's anus, sucking and tonguing her there. Finally moving to the solid nub of Cleo's clitoris, Crystal sucked on the pink protrusion of pleasure, sending tremors of sex throughout her friend's quivering body. Gasping as she neared her orgasm, her young womb rhythmically contracting, Cleo thought how much Jim would have enjoyed the sex games in the bar. Imagining sucking on his purple knob as Crystal had

tongued her clitoris, she felt a gush of juices leaving her gaping vaginal entrance.

'God,' Cleo breathed, her clitoris erupting in orgasm beneath her lesbian lover's sweeping tongue. Looking between her parted thighs at Crystal's mouth locked within the valley of the splayed lips of her vulva, she massaged the other girl's clitoris faster. Again and again, shock waves of mind-blowing pleasure transmitted throughout her young body as Crystal's clitoris burst into orgasm beneath her vibrating fingertips. The whimpers and gasps of female orgasm resounding around the pub, Cleo let out a cry as her orgasm peaked, rocking her trembling body to the core.

Her juices of lust gushing from the yawning entrance to her vagina and flooding Crystal's flushed face, Cleo leaned forward and buried her face between the other girl's vulval lips. Lapping up each other's orgasmic juices as Crystal pushed the footstools aside, both girls drank from each other's vaginas. Cunt-tonguing, slurping, sucking . . . Again, the sounds of lesbian sex reverberated around the pub as their orgasms peaked and shook their very souls. Their tongues moving between their buttocks, the girls fervently licked each other's bottom-holes, delighting in the bitter-sweet taste as their lust-juices pumped from the burning holes of their tight pussies.

Finally rolling to one side and lying on the floor, Cleo breathed heavily in the aftermath of her lesbian-induced coming. Her young body trembling uncontrollably, the hairless lips of her vulva swollen, she tossed her head from side to side as she recovered from her incredible climax. Her young body sated, she massaged the sensitive tip of her deflating clitoris, bringing out the last ripples of sex as her breathing slowed. Jim would have

enjoyed the games, she reflected again. Lying on the floor with the footstools either side of his head, his tongue entering Crystal's vagina and then Cleo's hot pussy sheath . . .

'That was great,' Crystal breathed shakily. 'You really are a good cunny-licker.'

'I needed that,' Cleo sighed. 'I've been waiting all day to spend some time with Jim. I was looking forward to . . . oh, well. Not to worry.'

'Are you feeling better now? More relaxed?'

'Yes,' Cleo replied, hauling herself up from the floor. 'But I'm still worried about Jim.'

'He'll be back in London by now. Why don't you go to bed and get a good night's sleep? I'm sure he'll ring you in the morning and explain everything.'

'Yes, yes, I think I'll do that. Thanks for . . . well, for relaxing me.'

'Any time, Cleo,' Crystal giggled as she climbed to her feet. 'You know how much I like loving you. I'll call in tomorrow, OK?'

'Yes, thanks.'

Locking the door as the other girl left, Cleo knew instinctively that Jim wasn't going to make contact with her: Something was wrong, she mused, making her way to her bedroom. At least she felt relaxed now, she thought, slipping out of her clothes and burying her naked body beneath her quilt. Jim should never have said anything to her father, she reflected. He should never have asked so many people so many questions. Tunnels, dungeons . . . Things were a mess.

'It's a lovely day outside,' Crystal said, gazing at Jim as she ran her hands over the petite mounds of her young

breasts. 'It's a shame that you're stuck down here in the dungeon.'

'What's this all about?' Jim asked the girl, pulling on his bonds. 'I've been on this bloody examination table all night. What the fucking hell . . .'

'You have a pretty good body,' Crystal chuckled, running her fingertips over the hairy sac of his scrotum.

'Crystal, will you please tell me what's going on? I was dragged onto the table by two monks and—'

'Too many questions, Jim. That's why you're here. Poking your nose in, prying, questioning everyone . . . They had to put a stop to it. You *do* understand, don't you?'

'No, I bloody don't,' Jim retorted. 'I discovered the tunnel and this place. So what?'

'So what? I'll tell you what. You've been poking your nose into something that's . . . This isn't a game, Jim. This place earns a fortune, and you were jeopardizing everything. They had to stop you.'

'*They*? Who the hell are *they*?'

'You're to be dealt with.'

'Dealt with? If I'm to be subjected to rampant sex, then go ahead,' Jim quipped, eyeing the hairless lips of Crystal's teenage vulva. 'Do what you like to me.'

'No, torture wouldn't work.'

'Torture?'

'If they let you go, then you'll only come back and cause trouble. If they allow you to stay on at the pub, you'll be shooting your big mouth off about this place. I don't know what they plan to do with you.'

'Where's Cleo? Does she know that I'm here?'

'Cleo was very upset last night. They've had to lock the tunnel door in the cellar to keep her out.'

'Keep her out? I don't understand any of this,' Jim sighed as Crystal stroked the warm shaft of his penis. 'I thought that Cleo was part of the set-up. Why lock her out?'

'They don't trust her.'

'They? I wish you'd tell me who *they* are.'

'They want to find out exactly how much you know before deciding what to do with you.'

'All I know is that this is bloody ridiculous.'

'You obviously know about the tunnel and this place. But what else have you discovered?'

'Just let me go, Crystal. This is bloody crazy. Handcuffed to an examination table like this—'

'Even Cleo doesn't know the full extent of the operation.'

'The full extent of the operation? Crystal, this is a small village full of nymphomaniacal schoolgirls. This isn't London. This isn't some massive underworld business. I reckon that you're deluding yourself.'

'Thankfully, you don't seem to have discovered a great deal.'

'A few sad perverts and plenty of sex-crazed teenage girls. That's what's going on here. Old men having sex with schoolgirls. There's no "operation", as you put it. Now, for God's sake, let me go.'

'I can't. They'll be here in a minute.'

'And what are *they* going to do to me?'

'I have no idea, Jim. Perhaps they'll torture the truth out of you.'

'What the hell are you talking about? Who are these bloody monks?'

'I'm sorry about this,' Crystal said, running an elastic band around his head and gagging his mouth with a rubber ball. 'It's just that you talk too much.'

Watching Crystal as she dragged the strange-looking chair closer to the examination table, Jim wondered whether this was some kind of joke. He'd thought that the chair with its electric dildo had been brought into the dungeon to satisfy young girls, but now? Was it designed for *torturing* schoolgirls? he wondered. Perhaps he *had* gone too far with his questioning, he reflected as voices echoed along the tunnel. But to strip him naked and tie him to the examination table . . . Reckoning that Hops was behind this, Jim was surprised that the man would allow his daughter to have any part of what could only be termed a brothel. What sort of man was he?

'I dragged this little beauty out of the convent,' the vicar chuckled, frogmarching a young schoolgirl into the dungeon.

'I haven't seen her before,' Crystal said, looking the petite blonde up and down. 'She must be a new girl.'

'What are you going to do to me?' the girl asked, her blue eyes wide as she stared at Jim's naked body.

'I'll tell you,' the vicar began. 'We need to find out how much this man knows about our business exploits in Willycombe Village. The idea is that he'll talk once he sees what we're going to do to you.'

'So, what *are* you going to do?'

'We'll start by taking your clothes off,' Crystal giggled, tearing the girl's blouse from her trembling body.

'No, please . . .'

'Shout and scream as much as you like. No one will hear you down here.'

Jim was sure that this was a set-up as Crystal ripped the girl's skirt off and tore her bra away from the small mounds of her young breasts. The vicar wouldn't risk abducting a young girl from the convent and dragging

her down to the sex dungeon. There again, why would an innocent girl agree to take part in the scam? Why were all the convent girls hell-bent on having sex with anyone and everyone? Eyeing the girl's petite mammary hillocks, the cone-shaped flesh of her areolae, Jim reckoned that the girls were actually paid well for the use of their young bodies.

Forcing his victim to sit in the chair, the vicar clamped her wrists to the arms of the chair and pulled her shoes and socks off. This *was* a set-up – wasn't it? Jim thought about the problem as the man took a pair of scissors and cut through the navy-blue material of the girl's knickers. Tearing the garment away from her vulval mound, he grabbed her kicking feet and cuffed each ankle to steel rings set in the bottom of the chair legs. The girl was a bloody good actress, Jim thought as her screams resounded around the sex dungeon.

'You'll enjoy this,' Crystal said, grabbing the electric dildo and slipping the rounded end between the girl's firm vaginal lips. 'We're going to start by giving you an electric fucking.'

'No, please . . .' the girl whimpered.

'You have a beautiful little cunt. I don't suppose that you've been fucked before?'

'No, no, I haven't. Please . . . why are you doing this to me? No, I don't want—' she sobbed as Crystal flicked a switch, the dildo driving slowly into her tight vaginal sheath. 'God, no. Please, oh please . . .'

'We'll begin with a long, slow fucking,' the vicar laughed, watching the cunny-slimed phallus repeatedly emerging from the girl's cunt and driving back into her quivering body. 'A nice, slow, cunny-stretching dildo-fuck.'

Gagging the girl with her shredded knickers as she began crying out, Crystal flashed Jim a wicked grin. This wasn't a game, Jim was sure as the vicar slipped out of his cassock and stood in front of his victim with his solid cock pointing to the ceiling. Watching the dildo sliding in and out of the girl's tight pussy, her creamy teenage juices dripping from the pink shaft, Jim wondered how far they'd go in their quest to make him talk. He knew nothing other than the whereabouts of the dungeon, he reflected. Apart from the tunnel and the sex dungeon, he'd discovered nothing about the goings-on in Willycombe Village.

'Where did you find her?' Crystal asked the naked vicar. 'She really is a little cutie.'

'She was in one of the dormitories,' he replied. 'Since I was dressed in my cassock, no one thought anything of me wandering around the convent. Finding this little beauty alone in one of the dormitories, I grabbed her.'

'And no one saw you?'

'No, no. They were all in the chapel by the time I marched her out of the back of the convent and through the woods. Isn't it time to increase the dildo speed?'

'Yes, I think it is,' Crystal giggled, turning a control on the side of the chair.

The dildo speeding up, repeatedly ramming deep into the young girl's cunt, the dungeon resounded with the squelching sounds of her teenage sex juices. Grimacing, Jim watched Crystal fix two metals clamps to the sensitive brown teats of her victim's nipples. The girl moaned loudly through her nose as Crystal attached two thin chains to the clamps and Jim felt his cock stiffening. Shocked by the fact that witnessing the torture of a

young schoolgirl was sending his arousal soaring, he tried to drag his gaze away from the lewd scene.

The electric chair humming, the huge dildo ramming repeatedly into the girl's inflamed vagina, Jim wondered what Crystal was going to do as she switched the machine off. Unable to believe his eyes, he watched her attach the ends of the chain to the base of the dildo and switch the machine back on. The girl's firm breasts were repeatedly pulled into taut cones of flesh each time the phallus withdrew from her vaginal sheath. This wasn't a set-up, Jim was sure as the girl shook her head from side to side, her blue eyes wide as she stared in horror at her tortured breasts. Jim could almost feel the pain as her nipples were repeatedly pulled away from the mounds of her young breasts, the sensitive milk teats stretching to at least four times their normal length.

'Are you ready to talk?' the vicar asked Jim. Shaking his head in refusal, Jim glared at the priest. There was nothing to talk about. He knew nothing about the sex dungeon operation, apart from the location of the tunnel and the existence of the evil chamber of sexual torture. 'All right,' the cleric chuckled, switching the electric dildo off. 'We'll just have to use the anal dilator on the girl. I'm sure that you'll be only too willing to tell us exactly what you know once you witness the dilator in action.'

Turning a handle on the side of the chair, the vicar chuckled as it tilted back. Disconnecting the chains and sliding the plastic dildo out of the girl's inflamed vaginal sheath, he pressed the dildo's rounded end against the miniature brown starfish of her tightly closed anus. The girl shuddered, struggling to break free as the man of God forced the huge phallus into her tight rectal canal.

Switching the machine back on, he let out a wicked laugh as the dildo repeatedly impaled the girl and withdrew from her hot rectum. The machine humming, the girl moaning loudly through her nose, Jim could do nothing to save her as the vicar knelt on the floor and ran the bulbous knob of his solid penis up and down her cream-drenched sex crack.

'This is an ingenious device,' the man breathed, ramming the entire length of his veined shaft deep into the girl's violated vagina. 'All I have to do is keep my cock still, and the dildo fucking your arse massages my knob through the walls of your pussy. It's great, fucking and spunking a girl's tight cunt without even having to move.'

'It works the other way round, too,' Crystal enlightened the shaking girl. 'The vicar's cock up your arse, the dildo fucking your cunt . . .'

'We'll try that after I've spunked her dirty little cunt,' the vicar chortled.

Taking the chains clipped to the girl's distended nipples, Crystal ran them down either side of the chair and attached heavy weights to the ends. The girl's inflamed nipples painfully stretched, her rectal canal pistoned by the huge plastic phallus, the vicar's cock bloating her teenage vagina, she tossed her head repeatedly from side to side. Pulling again on his bonds and trying to break free as Crystal stood beside him, Jim noticed a wicked glint in her eyes. She was evil, he thought, eyeing the dark discs of her areolae, the ripe buds of her milk teats. Young, attractive, sensual . . . and yet evil. Wondering what she was going to do as she grabbed his semi-erect cock, his gaze followed her hand to the glass-topped trolley. Grabbing a vibrator and

holding the rounded tip against the purple plum of his knob, she switched the device on.

'You want to come, don't you?' she asked him. 'Watching the girl being tortured has turned you on, hasn't it? You'll enjoy what we're going to do to her after the vicar has spunked up her sweet cunt. We're going to whip her, give her an enema, and then bring in half a dozen men to play with her.'

Ignoring the girl as the vibrations permeated his swollen glans, Jim knew that he wouldn't be able to hold back. Pressing the vibrator harder against his cock-head, kneading his rolling balls with her free hand, Crystal let out a giggle as his solid penis twitched and swelled. The electric dildo humming, the vibrator buzzing, the vicar's gasps growing louder as he neared his orgasm . . . The dungeon was reverberating with the sounds of crude sex. Lifting his head and gazing at Crystal as she switched the vibrator off, Jim wondered what the hell she was doing now.

'Desperate to come, are you?' she giggled, climbing onto the table and placing her knees either side of his head. 'So am I,' she breathed, parting the fleshy swell of her vaginal lips and exposing her dripping inner folds to his wide eyes. 'I'd like you to tongue-fuck my hot cunt but I don't want to remove your gag. I'll use the vibrator,' Crystal chuckled, switching the device on and pressing the buzzing tip against the erect budlette of her exposed clitoris. 'You can watch me come.'

Crystal's rock-hard clitoris only inches above his face, Jim focused on the pink funnel of creamy-wet flesh surrounding the entrance to her tight sex sheath. Stretching the hairless lips of her vulva wider apart, opening the very centre of her naked body, Crystal

tightened her vaginal muscles and squeezed out her
lubricious juices of desire. Dripping onto Jim's face,
her creamy offering ran over his nose, his cheeks, as
she began gasping in her wanton act of masturbation.
Her clitoris swelling to an incredible size, her copious
pre-orgasmic juices flooding Jim's face, she was about to
reach her self-induced climax.

'Can you see it?' she gasped. 'Can you see my clitoris
throbbing? God, that's . . . that's beautiful. Watch my
cum spurt out of my hot cunt. Watch my creamy cum
. . . Yes, yes. God, I'm there.' Her naked body shaking
violently, her vaginal cream gushing from the bared
entrance to her young cunt and splattering Jim's face,
Crystal let out a cry of satisfaction. The vicar's gasps
echoing around the dungeon as he filled the young girl's
vagina with his unholy seed, Jim breathed heavily
through his nose as Crystal lowered her naked body,
massaging the gaping entrance to her cunt hard against
the rubber ball gagging his mouth.

His solid cock in dire need of intimate attention, Jim
gazed in awe at Crystal's orgasming clitoris. The pink
protrusion pulsating wildly against the buzzing tip of the
vibrator, pumping pleasure through the girl's shaking
body, he realized that he'd never witnessed the orgasmic
pulsing of a girl's clitoris in such close-up before and so
he watched the incredible spectacle closely. The pink
nodule swelling and deflating, the sensitive tip glowing
red, he knew that the girl was experiencing a massive
multiple orgasm as she let out a cry of sexual gratification.

The rubber ball slipping out of his mouth as Crystal
ground her hot cuntal flesh hard against his face, Jim
pushed his tongue into the fiery sheath of her sex-

drenched vagina and lapped up her flowing cream of orgasm. She tasted heavenly, he thought, drinking from the duct of her young cunt as she sustained her massive climax with the buzzing vibrator. Creamy, lubricious, warm . . . Her pussy milk filling his mouth, Jim swallowed hard repeatedly as her young body rocked with another massive orgasmic peak.

'God, I'm coming again,' Crystal cried, forcing the burning flesh of her vaginal hole hard against Jim's gobbling mouth and pumping out a second gushing of girl-cream. Swallowing hard again, sucking out her orgasmic milk, Jim had never known a girl come so much. On and on her pleasure rolled, shaking her young body to its core as the vibrator played on her pulsating clitoris and Jim's tongue caressed the fiery walls of her teenage cunt.

Finally coming down from her massive orgasm, Crystal switched the vibrator off and rocked her hips back and forth. Her gaping sex valley sliding over Jim's open mouth, the last of her milky fluid draining from her spasming vaginal duct, she breathed heavily in the aftermath of her coming. Jim licked and nibbled on the engorged wings of her inner lips, his face drenched with cunt-milk as the girl swayed in her sexual delirium. As she moved aside and clambered off the table, Jim was about to tell the vicar to free his young victim but Crystal slipped the cunny-wet rubber gag back into his mouth.

'You talk too much,' she said, running her fingertip up and down the veined shaft of his painfully hard cock.

'God, I needed that,' the vicar gasped, finally withdrawing his deflating penis from the young girl's sperm-flooded cunt.

'Shall we go and have a coffee?' Crystal asked, grab-

bing her clothes and dressing. 'We'll bring the others back with us later and give the girl a fucking good whipping before they take turns to fuck her sweet bottom.'

'Good idea,' the vicar chuckled, donning his cassock.

Trying to push the rubber ball out of his mouth with his tongue as the couple left the dungeon, Jim knew that there was nothing he could do to save the young girl from her fate. She was going to have to endure several cocks, he knew as he gazed at her curvaceous body. Focusing on the sperm oozing between the hairless lips of her vulva, he was thankful that the vicar had at least turned the electric dildo off. The plastic shaft still embedded deep within her rectal canal, her pretty mouth gagged with her own knickers, she was a sorry sight. All Jim could do was hope that Cleo would come to their rescue.

15

'I'm really worried about Jim,' Cleo sighed, gazing at Crystal as the girl sipped her coffee.

'I don't know why you're worried,' the vicar said. 'I told you, he went back to London last night.'

'I'm sure that he'll ring you at some stage,' Crystal said reassuringly.

'I suppose so,' Cleo breathed. 'He'll have to pick his car up sometime or other, so . . .'

'Yes, his car,' the vicar murmured pensively, glancing at Crystal. 'That will have to go. I mean, he'll have to collect it.'

'Why is the door to the tunnel locked?' Cleo asked the vicar.

'Didn't I mention it to you?'

'No, you didn't. I tried to get in earlier but the door's locked from the inside.'

'Sorry, I must have forgotten to tell you. We're making some alterations in the dungeon. We don't want punters slipping into the tunnel while the work is going on. I'm sure I mentioned it to you.'

'He told you yesterday, Cleo,' Crystal said. 'You couldn't have been listening.'

'What sort of alterations?'

'Some new equipment. We'll be taking it in through the entrance in the woods so as not to rouse suspicion. It

would look rather odd if we carried it through the pub. It'll be business as usual by this evening, with any luck.'

Pouring herself a cup of coffee, Cleo was becoming increasingly suspicious. The tunnel door had never been locked before. The electric-dildo chair had been carried in through the pub when no one had been around, she reflected. The entrance in the woods had only been used in emergencies. And punters never went into the tunnel without Cleo giving them the all-clear. Reckoning that the door had been locked to keep her out, she decided not to ask any more questions or mention Jim again. Cleo could understand why the vicar and Crystal didn't trust Jim, but it seemed that now they had their suspicions about her too. But she had no idea why. Nothing like this had ever happened before, she mused. She'd run the pub end of the operation without a hitch for several years. What had changed? Deciding to slip into the sex dungeon via the entrance in the woods when she had the chance, she knew that the vicar and Crystal were hiding something from her.

'I'd better be going,' the vicar said, finishing his coffee.

'And me,' Crystal said. 'I, er . . . I have a new girl to see to.'

'Be seeing you, Cleo.'

'Yes, yes. I'd better make the sandwiches for lunchtime. It looks as though I'm going to have to cope without Jim.'

'Let me know if you hear anything from him,' Crystal said, leaving the pub with the vicar.

Dashing down to the cellar, Cleo tried the tunnel door again. There was no way that she'd be able to break the lock, she knew as she leaned against the door. The only

way in now was through the entrance in the woods. But since she was running the pub single-handed at present, she couldn't see how she'd have an opportunity. There was nothing that she could do for the time being, she decided, mooching up the cellar steps. Pouring herself a vodka, all she had to look forward to was making the sandwiches. And waiting, in the hope that Jim might phone her.

Watching Mary slipping out of her blouse, Jim wondered again what the hell was going on as she unhooked her bra and revealed the ripe teats of her small breasts. At least he was discovering exactly who was involved in the sex dungeon, he mused, gazing at the triangular patch of navy-blue material concealing her vulval flesh as she slipped her skirt down. But how long was he to be kept prisoner? From what Crystal had said, they couldn't allow him his freedom for fear of him shooting his mouth off. So, what was his fate going to be?

'You're a pretty little slut,' Mary said, removing the metal clamps from the young girl's painfully inflated nipples. 'I'm going to enjoy playing with you.'

'Please let me go,' the girl whimpered as Mary slipped the gag out of her pretty mouth.

'Let you go?' Mary giggled. 'A pretty thing like you? No, no, I can't let you go. You see, I have a little fetish. I like young girls because they're tight. I'll bet your pussy is hot and very tight. And your bottom-hole will be even tighter. Shall I tell you what my fetish is?'

'I just want to go back to the convent,' the girl sobbed.

'That's not possible, I'm afraid. I'll get you in the right position and then tell you about my fetish. Better still, I'll *show* you.'

Jim watched as Mary turned the handle, the chair tilting back until her young victim was lying on her back with her feet in the air. Pulling two chains down from the low ceiling, Mary released the girl's feet from the chair and cuffed her ankles to the ends of the chains. Jim knew that Mary had something horrendous in mind as she pulled on another chain and raised the girl's feet high above her naked body. Her legs parted wide, the dildo slipping out of her anal duct, she pleaded again for her freedom.

'You have a beautiful cunt,' Mary commented, kneeling on the floor and gazing at her prisoner's gaping vaginal valley. 'What's this?' she breathed, pushing her finger into her wet sex hole. 'It's sperm,' she giggled. 'You've been fucked, haven't you?'

'What are you going to do to me?' the girl murmured shakily.

'Do to you? I'm going to enjoy your pussy. And your sweet bottom-hole, of course.'

'If you let me go, I won't say anything.'

'Unless you want me to gag you, stop asking me to let you go,' Mary snapped. 'You're here, and you're staying here. Now for my fetish. Have you ever had a fist up your cunt?'

'A fist?' the girl echoed fearfully. 'No, please . . .'

'Obviously not. I'm about to change that. I'm going to push my hand deep into your cunt and fist-fuck you until you come.'

'No, I'll tear open,' the girl gasped as Mary parted the hairless lips of her teenage vulva. 'Please, I . . .'

'I'll gag you unless you shut the fuck up.'

Parting the girl's swollen vaginal lips, Mary leaned forward and ran the tip of her tongue over her sperm-

dripping inner folds. This was the vicar's sperm, Jim thought as Mary lapped at the girl's open sex-hole, drinking the creamy liquid from her vaginal duct. If she knew that she was lapping up her father's spunk . . . There again, Mary was a slut. She probably wouldn't give a damn whose spunk it was. The situation was bizarre, Jim thought. The idea had been to make him talk, to tell all he knew about the illicit operation. And yet Mary seemed to be quite content to enjoy the prisoner's young body without questioning him. Perhaps she was leaving that to her father, he mused as she parted the girl's vaginal lips further and sucked hard on her pinken inner folds.

'You're very wet,' Mary breathed, her cunny-juiced face grinning. 'With a good helping of spunk and girlie-juice lubricating your tight little cunt, I shouldn't have too much trouble forcing my fist up you.'

'Why are you doing this to me?' the girl breathed.

'Why? Because I love fisting young girls' tight cunts, of course. Have you ever licked another girl's cunt out?'

'No, of course not.'

'That's something you can look forward to, then. You're going to tongue-fuck my cunt and—'

'I am *not*.'

'But you are. And it's no good arguing because you have no choice.'

Watching Mary slipping several fingers into her young victim's sex sheath, Jim wondered again whether this was a set-up. The idea was to make him put a stop to the abuse by talking. But he had nothing to say. They knew damned well that he'd only discovered the sex dungeon. What other secrets did the village harbour? he mused. Why go to all this trouble to make him talk when they

could have simply invited him to join them in their illicit business activities? Old man Hops had sacked him and told him to get out, so why had he ordered the monks to capture him?

There were too many unanswered questions, Jim thought, listening to the young girl's gasps as Mary continued to force her fingers into the tight sheath of her teenage cunt. His thoughts turning to Cleo, he reckoned that the girl had dropped him in it. She must have told the vicar that Jim knew about the sex dungeon. That was why he'd been captured and tied to the examination table. But what did they intend to do with him? They couldn't keep him there for long. The punters would hardly be pleased to find a naked man on the examination table when they'd gone to the dungeon to enjoy crude sex with young girls.

'God!' the girl cried as Mary's fist slipped deep into her vaginal cavern. 'Please, take it out!'

'I've done it,' Mary announced triumphantly, gazing at her victim's inner lips stretched tautly around her slender wrist. 'I've got my entire fist right up your dirty little cunt.'

'Take it out,' the girl sobbed again, her pretty face grimacing.

'Can you feel my fingers?' Mary giggled. 'Can you feel them opening and closing?'

'No, no . . . I can't take it. Please, no . . .'

Slipping her fist out of the girl's vaginal cavern with a loud sucking sound, Mary parted the firm orbs of her victim's young buttocks and gazed longingly at the brown tissue of her tightly closed anus. Jim knew what she had in mind as she licked the small hole, lubricating the inlet to her rectal duct. Slurping and sucking, Mary

was obviously delighting in her crude act of lesbian anilingus. Judging by the look on the tethered girl's face, Jim reckoned that, despite her protests, she was enjoying the crude experience. But he was sure that she wouldn't enjoy a fist forced deep into the tight sheath of her rectum.

Wondering again when he'd be given his freedom, Jim looked down at the veined shaft of his solid cock, the swollen globe of his glans. He was desperate to come, but reckoned that his penis would remain neglected all the time Mary had the young girl to play with. Wondering where the vicar and Crystal had got to, he recalled the cleric's words. *We'll bring the others back with us later and give the girl a fucking good whipping before they take turns to fuck her sweet bottom.* Would Mary allow her father to whip the girl? he pondered. Like father, like daughter, he mused. The evil pair would probably delight in thrashing their victim's naked buttocks before watching several men pump her bowels full of spunk.

'Mmm, you taste heavenly,' Mary breathed, her wet tongue darting in and out of the girl's anal entrance. 'Do you like it?'

'I . . . I don't know,' she replied softly. 'I want to go now.'

'Go?' Mary giggled. 'You mean, you want to *come* now?'

'No, I . . .'

'You're not going anywhere. You'll be here for a hell of a long time yet. And so will Jim.'

'But I have to get back to the convent and—'

'You don't have to go anywhere, my little angel. You're here, in the sex dungeon, and that's where you'll

stay. Besides, you have my cunt to look forward to. You *do* want to tongue-fuck my wet cunt, don't you?'

'No, I don't.'

'And my tight arsehole?'

'Please . . .'

'I think the time has come to finger-fuck your bottom. And if you start fucking complaining I'll gag you again.'

Watching the girl's grimacing face as Mary forced her finger into the tight tube of her rectum, Jim felt his cock twitching, his balls heaving. Driving a second finger into the young blonde's arse, Mary let out a wicked chuckle. She probably let her father fuck her, Jim thought, watching her trying to force a third finger into the quivering girl's rectum. Was there nothing she wouldn't do to find sexual gratification? he wondered, imagining her pretty mouth sucking the spunk out of the vicar's orgasming knob. Finally managing to force half her hand past the girl's painfully stretched anal ring, Mary was obviously determined to fist-fuck the tight sheath of her victim's rectum. Crying out, her naked body writhing, the girl grimaced again as Mary's fist slipped past the defeated muscles of her anus and sank deep into the abused duct of her young arse.

'Fuck me, you're tight,' Mary trilled, gazing at the delicate flesh of her victim's anal tissue stretched tautly around her slender wrist. 'Tight and fucking hot.'

'Please . . .' the blonde sobbed. 'Please, take it out.'

'Take it out? But I'm preparing you for the men's huge cocks. You'll need to be well greased and stretched to take half a dozen cocks in succession. They're going to take turns to fuck your tight arse and spunk up you. Then I'll suck their spunk out of your arse and they'll pump you full again.'

Jim had never heard such vulgar words tumbling from anyone's lips, let alone a young teenage girl's pretty mouth. Watching as Mary lapped up the schoolgirl's flowing vaginal cream, drinking from the hot centre of her young body, he looked at the door as it swung open and the vicar led six middle-aged men into the room. This was for real, he thought as the men gathered around the chair and gazed longingly at the blonde's naked body, the blatantly abused ring of her bottom-hole stretched around Mary's wrist.

'Is she ready?' the vicar asked Mary.

'Hot, wet, stretched and as ready as you are,' she giggled, sliding her fist out of the girl's rectum, leaving her anus gaping wide open.

'Help yourselves,' the vicar chortled, looking at the men. 'I want her arse overflowing with spunk, so get to it.'

Unable to say anything with the rubber ball in his mouth, Jim could only watch as the first man knelt on the floor and unzipped his trousers. Fully retracting his foreskin, he pressed the purple globe of his huge cock hard against the blonde's inflamed anal ring and drove his shaft deep into the hot sheath of her rectal canal. The girl let out a cry, her young body squirming and writhing as Mary pulled on the chain and lifted her legs higher into the air. Her vaginal crack gaping wide open, her sex hole crudely bared, she shrieked as the man drove several fingers deep into her teenage cunt and began his anal fucking motions.

'I see that you're in need of some attention,' Mary said, standing by the examination table and gazing at Jim's erect penis. 'I'll give you a little suck to keep you going.' Leaning over, she took his purple plum into her hot

mouth and ran her tongue over its silky-smooth surface.
She was a nymphomaniacal, bisexual slut, Jim thought as
she bobbed her head up and down, mouth-fucking
herself on his solid organ. Every teenage girl in Willycombe was a nymphomaniacal, bisexual slut. Not that he
was complaining.

Leaving his knob and moving down his veined shaft,
Mary licked the hairy sac of his scrotum as Jim listened
to the enforced violation of the young girl's rectal sheath.
Six men, six cocks, six loads of spunk . . . The girl was
going to be an anal wreck by the time the vicar freed her.
Did he intend to free her? Jim wondered as Mary's wet
tongue ran down between his parted thighs and moved
dangerously close to his anal hole. Did the vicar intend to
free Jim? The situation was ridiculous, he mused as
Mary's tongue reached his anus, licking the sensitive
brown tissue there. Cleo locked out of the tunnel, the
vicar sexually abusing a young schoolgirl, the cleric's
daughter licking Jim's anal inlet . . . Was the underground chamber a sex dungeon or a prison or a lunatic
asylum? Jim didn't know what to think.

'I don't think I'll allow you to come just yet,' Mary
giggled, standing upright. 'We'll save your spunk for the
girl's face. You'd like me to wank you off over her face,
wouldn't you? In the meantime, you can enjoy watching
her take six cocks up her dirty little arsehole.'

'How's he doing?' the vicar asked Mary as he stood by
her side.

'He's desperate to come,' she replied. 'But I'm going to
make him wait.'

'I'll tell you what,' the vicar chuckled. 'Climb onto the
table with your pussy above his face.'

'Like this?' Mary laughed, taking up her position.

'That's it. Now lean over so that your face is near his cock. Don't suck it, though.'

'He can't lick my cunt with that rubber ball in his mouth.'

'He's not going to. *I'm* going to fuck your cunt, Mary.'

'I was hoping that you'd say that,' she breathed, jutting her naked buttocks out.

Jim gazed in awe at the girl's yawning vaginal valley hovering inches above his face. The vicar's purple knob moving in, running up and down the creamed crack of her vulva, he couldn't believe that the man was going to fuck his own daughter. Watching the girl-juice dripping from his bulbous glans, Jim reckoned that, even if he didn't push his cock into the tight sheath of her young cunt, this in itself was already an act of incest. If Mary wasn't his daughter, then who the hell was she? Had she been masquerading as his daughter to disguise the fact that she was living with the vicar? If she *was* his daughter, then—

'You're as tight and hot as you were when I first fucked you,' the vicar gasped, ramming his purple knob-head deep into the girl's vaginal canal.

'And you feel as big as you did on that day when you stripped me of my virginity,' Mary giggled. 'Now, fuck me rotten and spunk up my wet cunt.'

'Anything you say, my horny little angel.'

Watching the vicar's pussy-slimed penis withdrawing from the girl's young body, his heavy balls swinging, Jim realized that he had never witnessed a sexual union before, let alone one in close-up. The girl's pinken inner lips dragging back and forth along the man's solid penile shaft, her juices of arousal dripping from the bloated cavern of her teenage cunt, she let out gasps of debased

pleasure as the cleric increased his fucking rhythm. The slurping sounds of sex filling his ears, Jim wondered again when he'd be released.

The schoolgirl's screams resounding around the sex dungeon as the man shafting her anal canal pumped his spunk deep into her bowels, Jim began to fear his destiny. If the girl wasn't play-acting and this was truly anal rape . . . they'd hardly allow the girl her freedom. Or Jim his, come to that. Reckoning that this was far more serious than he'd imagined, he pulled on the handcuffs securing his wrists to the steel rings in the examination table. He was going to have to escape, he knew as the vicar let out gasps of pure sexual bliss and Mary's naked body began shaking uncontrollably.

There was no way to break free of the metal handcuffs, Jim mused, watching the vicar's cock-shaft repeatedly emerging from and driving back into the girl's juice-spewing vaginal opening. His only chance was Cleo, he reflected. There again, he was sure that the girl had dropped him in the shit by telling the vicar that Jim had discovered the tunnel and the sex dungeon. Far from being his only chance of escape, he reckoned that Cleo was actually behind his present imprisonment.

His thoughts turning to the photographs of his ex-wife and his brother, he reckoned that Cleo and her father ran the entire set-up. The pub was a tax loss, the underground brothel brought in a small fortune. They'd both thought that Jim was an idiot and had used him to make a hash of running the pub. They'd obviously thought he was so stupid that he'd never realize what was going on, let alone ask questions about tunnels and dungeons. How very wrong they'd been, he reflected. *They* were the idiots.

But that didn't change the fact that he was their prisoner. Cleo had said that her father was a formidable man. So much so that he'd think nothing of doing away with Jim? Was that the plan? There was a hell of a lot at stake, Jim mused, suddenly realizing that word was going round about him leaving the pub and returning to London. Was that the idea? he wondered. The villagers would believe that Jim had been sacked from the pub and had returned to London. In reality, he was in the dungeon, awaiting his final fate.

Reckoning that by now his car would have disappeared and his belongings cleared from the flat, Jim began to grasp the seriousness of his predicament. Who would miss him? he wondered. His ex-wife certainly wouldn't even know that he'd disappeared. And, if she did, she wouldn't give a damn. His brother spent most of his time travelling abroad. It might be a year or more before he realized that Jim had vanished. The village was full of clammed-up mouths that wouldn't say a word and . . . His mind drifting as he watched the vicar's penile shaft fucking Mary's tight cunt, he wondered whether the secret entrance in the woods was for carrying out the dead. Was that why they'd locked Cleo out of the tunnel? Maybe they planned to carry Jim and the schoolgirl out though the secret entrance and busy them in the woods.

'Coming,' the vicar cried, grabbing Mary's hips and repeatedly driving his cunny-drenched penis deep into the tight shaft of her teenage cunt. 'God, you're a tight-cunted little whore.'

'No, I can't take another one,' the schoolgirl screamed.

'You've only been fucked by two of us,' a man chuckled. 'You have another four cocks waiting to fuck your dirty little arsehole.'

'God, I'm there,' Mary gasped. 'I can feel your holy spunk. Fuck me like you'd fuck the Devil's daughter.'

'You *are* the Devil's daughter,' the cleric chortled, his swinging balls draining as he pumped the girl's cunt full of his unholy seed.

'If I'm the Devil's daughter, then you're the fucking Devil,' Mary giggled.

A warm, creamy blend of girl-juice and sperm splattering Jim's face as the couple fucked in their quest for illicit sexual gratification, Jim was sure now that he was in dire trouble. This was no game, he reflected, recalling Crystal's words. *This isn't a game, Jim. This place earns a fortune, and you were jeopardizing everything. They had to stop you.* The more Jim thought about his predicament, the more frightened he became. As long thin strands of creamy spunk and girl-cum dropped onto his face, he decided that he was going to have to make a real effort to escape once he was alone.

'You really are the best fuck I've ever had,' the vicar laughed, dragging his slimed cock out of Mary's hot vaginal sheath. 'As soon as we get home, I'll fuck you again.'

'I know you will,' she giggled, clambering off the table. 'You'll fuck me again and again until I'm fucked senseless.'

'You'd better suck Jim's spunk out of his cock,' the vicar murmured. 'Suck him off and make his last time in the dungeon happy.'

Bending over and sucking the purple head of Jim's solid cock into her hot mouth, Mary snaked her tongue over his sperm-slit. She was an expert cocksucker, he reflected, hoping that this time she'd allow him to come in her mouth. A teenage beauty, an expert cocksucker, a

nymphomaniacal bisexual slut . . . Would she really allow Jim and the young girl to be done away with? Hoping that he was wrong and that he'd be released eventually Jim shuddered as Mary sucked his swollen knob to the back of her hot throat and sank her teeth gently into the rigid flesh of his veined shaft.

Kneading Jim's full balls, Mary wanked the granite-hard shaft of his cock and took his ballooning knob between her succulent lips and sucked hard. He was going to come, Jim knew as his penis swelled and twitched. Feeling easier as he reckoned again that Mary and Crystal would have nothing to do with carrying bodies out of the tunnel into the woods, he thought that he'd been overreacting. Making money from an underground brothel was one thing. But murder?

His sperm finally jetting from his knob-slit, bathing the girl's snaking tongue and filling her cheeks, Jim closed his eyes and wallowed in the amazing sensations of his orally induced orgasm. Mary was certainly a young beauty, he thought, wondering again whether she was an incestuous slut. Deciding, as she cupped his draining balls in her warm hand and gobbled fervently on his throbbing glans, that the vicar wasn't really her father, he imagined old man Hops fucking *his* daughter's mouth through the hole in the bar. The villagers might have been sex-crazed, he reflected as Mary drank from his orgasming fountainhead. But they weren't incestuous murderers – were they?

'Mmm,' Mary breathed through her nose as she sucked the last of Jim's spunk from his cock before slipping his spent knob out of her hot mouth. 'I just love the taste of fresh spunk.' Jim gazed at her pretty face as she licked her sperm-glossed lips and grinned at him.

'I'm going to drink from the schoolgirl's bottom-hole after all the men have fucked her arse,' she giggled. 'I reckon that she'll be bubbling with hot spunk by the time they've finished.'

As Mary walked over to the electric-dildo chair and watched the next man in line forcing his solid cock deep into the sobbing girl's tight anal canal, Jim felt a last globule of sperm dribble from his knob and run over the smooth flesh of his stomach. He was surrounded by sex, he mused, listening to the protesting schoolgirl as the man began his anal fucking motions. He decided again that the whole thing was a set-up probably designed to frighten him off. The vicar would have heard that Hops had sacked Jim and the purpose of imprisoning him in the dungeon was simply to scare him. At some stage, they'd allow him to escape in the hope that he wouldn't be stupid enough to return to Willycombe Village, let alone the sex dungeon.

As the last man fucked the wailing schoolgirl's inflamed rectal cavern and pumped his spunk into her cream-flooded bowels, Jim wondered whether his chance to escape was nearing. They'd probably loosen the handcuffs and *inadvertently* leave him in a position to free himself before they left the dungeon. This was all a stupid game, he mused as the men dressed. If they didn't want him around, if the villagers really didn't like him, then he'd go back to London, he decided. He wasn't going to hang around the village when everyone had made it blatantly clear that he wasn't wanted.

There were other breweries, Jim mused. Other breweries, other pubs, other villages, even other convents brimming with hot young schoolgirlies dying for a meaty length of solid cock. Feeling a lot happier as the men finished

dressing and filed out of the dungeon, Jim watched Mary lock her lips to the young girl's anal ring and suck out the fresh spunk. She was a right little slag, he thought, listening to the gulping sounds of her crude drinking as she drained the abused girl's hot rectum. Willycombe Village? It should have been named Slutcum Village.

Licking her lips, Mary slipped into her school uniform and finally left the dungeon with the vicar. Jim frowned, wondering why they hadn't given him a chance to escape as the door closed. Had he been wrong? he wondered, gazing at the exhausted schoolgirl, the gaping eye of her abused bottom-hole burning a fire-red. Raising his head and pulling on the handcuffs, he wondered what the hell the vicar had planned for his prisoners. Staring at the low ceiling, he became despondent as he felt hunger pains in his rumbling stomach. He couldn't spend another night on the examination table, he knew as he closed his eyes and thought about his car. Had it been driven away and hidden somewhere? Had his belongings been cleared out of the flat and destroyed?

'You fucking idiot,' Cleo hissed as she burst into the sex dungeon.

'Cleo,' Jim breathed. 'What . . .'

'You wouldn't listen to me, would you? Poking your fucking nose in, asking fucking questions . . .'

'Where's the young girl?' he asked her, staring at the empty chair.

'Young girl? I have no idea what you're talking about.'

'Of course you have, Cleo. This was your father's doing, wasn't it?'

'My *father*? What the fuck are you talking about *now*?'

'Imprisoning me here, pretending to torture a young girl . . .'

'My father knows nothing about this place, you fucking idiot.'

'Oh, come on, Cleo,' he laughed. 'He owns the brewery, he owns the pub . . . and he knows nothing about the tunnel or the sex dungeon? Give me some credit, for fuck's sake. So, what's the plan? Have you been sent here to release me?'

'No one knows that I'm here. You don't seem to understand that . . .'

'Cleo, that's where you're wrong. I understand only too well. I'll tell you how I see it. Your father sacks me. The vicar has me imprisoned here and forces me to witness the cruel torture of a young schoolgirl. The idea behind all this is that I'm scared stiff and, when you come here to free me, I do a runner and never set foot in this strange village again. How am I doing so far?'

'You're talking complete and utter fucking bollocks.'

'Am I? OK, carry out the next part of the plan and release me.'

'I *am* here to release you, Jim. But it's not part of a plan. No one knows that I'm here. My father knows nothing about this place, the vicar and the others don't know that I'm here . . .'

'Look, cut the crap and get me out of here. I need a shower, I'm fucking starving . . . I'll go along with the scam if it gets me out of this fucking dungeon.'

Finally clambering off the examination table as Cleo released the handcuffs, Jim stretched his aching legs. Grabbing his clothes, his body swaying, he finally managed to dress. He'd deal with Cleo once they were clear of the dungeon, he decided, following her into the tunnel and up the steps. Emerging from the secret entrance, he looked around the woods. Freedom, he mused, reckon-

ing that they were being watched as they followed the narrow path deep into the trees.

Not wanting to return to the pub just yet, Jim decided to force Cleo into the bushes once they were well away from the tunnel entrance and give her the anal shagging of her sweet life. Grabbing the girl's arm, he hurried her up, virtually dragging her behind him as he raced along the path. The vicar and his accomplices wouldn't realize where they'd got to, he reckoned as they turned corner after corner and finally came to thick undergrowth. Dragging the girl into the thicket, he threw her to the ground in a small clearing. Now she was going to endure the anal fucking of all motherfucking anal fuckings.

16

'What the hell do you think you're doing?' Cleo asked Jim as he tore her blouse open and gazed at the cups of her bra straining to contain her full breasts. 'We haven't got time to piss about.'

'Piss about?' Jim laughed. '*You*'re the one who's been pissing about, Cleo. All this crap about your father knowing nothing about the dungeon and—'

'Jim, will you please listen to me?'

'Go on, then. But no crap, OK?'

'No crap. *I* own and run the dungeon.'

'*You*? What, you're the *sole* owner?'

'Yes.'

'Then why were you locked out of the tunnel?'

'It's a long story.'

'That's OK. I have a long cock, so—'

'Be serious, for fuck's sake. My mother started the sex dungeon several years ago.'

'Your—'

'Stop interrupting. She ran the pub and, when she was clearing out the cellar, she discovered the tunnel. My mother was . . . How shall I put it? She was heavily into sex.'

'Rather like you, then?'

'Shut up. She transformed the dungeon into a place of relaxation for discerning businessmen. Her words, not

mine. Anyway, the vicar discovered what she was up to. Initially, he threatened to expose her unless she closed the place down. But then he decided that he'd join her. She had no choice but to agree. He gradually took control and, when my mother left the pub, he took over completely. When I started work at the pub, I found out what was going on and tried to get the vicar out. He threatened me, as he did my mother, so he continued to control the business. I was the one who brought in the convent schoolgirls. I was the one who transformed the business into a highly profitable set-up. I was the one who found potential punters with my hole-in-the-bar idea.'

'Where's your mother now?'

'She left my father and moved to Australia. My father knows nothing about the dungeon. You were right about the tax-loss scam. My father thought that you'd make a right cock-up of running the pub, which was exactly what he wanted. You started nosing about, asking questions, interfering . . . When you threatened my father and he sacked you, the vicar saw an opportunity to get rid of you and he decided that you should be dealt with.'

'Dealt with? How?'

'I don't know what he had in mind. The problem is that the vicar is a very influential man in the village. There's nothing I can do to get him out of what is essentially *my* very profitable business. I've tried to get him out on several occasions, but he threatens to expose me.'

'Then why not threaten to expose *him*?'

'No, it wouldn't work. No one would believe that he had any part of what could only be described as a brothel. Once he discovers that I released you—'

'Let's go back to the pub,' Jim interrupted the girl.
'Now that I know what's going on . . .'

'My father has sacked you, Jim. There's no way he'll
take you back, believe me.'

'Isn't there?'

'No way at all.'

Eyeing Cleo's naked thighs as she brought her legs up
and rested her chin on her knees, Jim gazed longingly at
the triangular patch of bulging white silk concealing her
full love lips. He'd shagged many a Willycombe Village
schoolgirl, he reflected. But Cleo's hot pussy and tight
rectal sheath had remained virginal – at least, as far as *his*
cock was concerned. Although he had important things
to think about – such as his future – his mind was locked
on crude sex. There was something particularly alluring
about the triangular patches of moist material covering
young girls' sex lips, he mused. The feminine intimacy
straining the white material, the V-shaped creases between young thighs, the perfume . . .

Running his fingertip over the smooth flesh of Cleo's
inner thigh, Jim smiled as she let out a sigh of pleasure.
The long-awaited fucking of the barmaid's cunt was
imminent, he knew as she lay back on the grass beneath
the trees and parted her slender legs. Pulling her skirt up
over her stomach, offering her young body to Jim, she
stretched her arms out behind her head and closed her
eyes. Her long black hair fanning out across the ground,
she was an extremely attractive teenager. She also had a
millionaire father, Jim mused. Not that he'd be swayed
by such things when contemplating marriage.

Marriage. Wondering why the vulgar word had entered his head, Jim frowned. That would be one way to
get back in with old man Hops, he mused, pressing his

fingertip into the soft swelling of Cleo's warm panties. Marry his daughter, become his son-in-law, and . . . There again, Cleo was right. Hops was a formidable man. Wishing that he'd never threatened his boss, Jim leaned over Cleo's young body and kissed the triangular patch of white silk bulging to contain her sex lips. Breathing in her girl-scent, he felt his cock stiffen, his balls heave.

'If my father could see you now,' Cleo giggled. 'He'd go mad.'

'I thought that he was already mad at me,' Jim sighed.

'He'll be mad at *me* if he finds out that I've closed the pub and disappeared.'

'Cleo . . . Do you want to stay on at the pub?'

'Yes, of course. Why do you ask?'

'No reason.'

'I'd prefer it if you were there with me, but that's not possible.'

'No, I suppose not.'

His cock now straining against his zip, his balls fully laden, Jim tugged Cleo's panties down and revealed the tightly closed crack of her young vulva. Running his fingertip over the gentle rise of her mons, the fleshy swell of her vaginal lips, he was surprised to find a fleece of black pubic hair covering her vulval flesh. He'd begun to think that every girl in the village shaved between her legs. This was a pleasant change, he mused, her dark curls tickling his face as he licked the warm valley of her sex slit.

Cleo sighed, her young body writhing as the tip of Jim's tongue delved between the outer hillocks of her teenage pussy. Tasting her there, breathing in the aphrodisiacal scent of her feminine intimacy, Jim parted the

smooth pads of her vulva and sucked the pink protrusion
of her clitoris into his hot mouth. Her juices of teenage
lust decanting from her hot sex-hole, her clitoris now
solid, she let out a rush of breath. Running his tongue
down her valley of desire and lapping up her lubricious
sex cream, Jim drank from the sexual centre of her young
body.

'Wait,' Cleo breathed, pulling her panties off over her
feet and slipping her skirt down. 'If you're going to have
me, then you'll have all of me.' Slipping her blouse over
her shoulders and unhooking her bra, she smiled as Jim
focused on the ripe teats of her firm breasts. 'Now I'm all
yours,' she sighed, reclining on the soft grass and spreading the limbs of her naked body.

Moving between her parted thighs, Jim repeatedly ran
his tongue up and down the drenched crack of her young
pussy. Pushing her outer labia wide apart with his
thumbs, he snaked his tongue around the base of her
solid clitoris to the accompaniment of her gasps of
pleasure. Thinking again about marriage, he reckoned
that he could still have his fun with the convent schoolgirlies even though Cleo would be his wife. Adultery was
one-sided, of course. It would be all right for him to
screw anything and anything in the convent, but Cleo
would have to remain a faithful and loving wife. That was
fair enough, he thought. Wasn't it?

Sucking Cleo's clitoris into his hot mouth as she
writhed and gasped, Jim knew that she wasn't far from
reaching her orgasm. He was a damned good clit-sucker,
he reflected, the vacuum within his mouth swelling her
pleasure button. Running his tongue over the sensitive
tip of her cumbud, he held her teetering on the brink of
her orgasmic explosion. Girls liked that, he knew as she

begged him to make her come. There was no rush, he mused. After all, he had nowhere to go. No home, no job . . . There again, if old man Hops became his father-in-law, things might be very different.

'Yes,' Cleo cried, her screams sending the birds fluttering from the trees as her clitoris erupted in orgasm. 'God, yes.' Working expertly on her pulsating clitty, Jim sustained her earth-shuddering climax as she writhed and squirmed on the ground like a snake in agony. Her juices of orgasm gushing from the neglected sheath of her teenage cunt, her naked body shaking violently, she screamed out again as her pleasure peaked. Sucking and mouthing on her throbbing budlette, Jim couldn't believe the apparent strength and duration of her orgasm. Again and again, she cried out and squirmed, obviously in the grip of a massive climax. Her copious juices of sex spewing from her hot vaginal entrance and spraying her inner thighs, she was obviously lost in her feminine pleasure, blown away on clouds of lust.

The girl had a beautiful cunt, Jim thought, his chin running with her pussy milk. Beautifully formed outer lips, a good-sized clitoris, inner lips large enough to suck and nibble . . . She also had wonderfully developed breasts topped with wedge-shaped, suckable nipples perched on the dark discs of her areolae. Her long black hair shining in the sunlight streaming down through the trees, her dark eyes sparkling, her succulent red lips and most fuckable mouth . . . Her young body was perfect in every way. But, apart from sex, she was also good company. Fun to be with, charismatic, fairly easygoing . . . A perfect wife?

Finally slowing his clitoral licking and sucking as Cleo began to drift down from her mind-blowing climax, Jim

unzipped his trousers and hauled out his rampant erec-
tion. His balls aching, his cock-shaft twitching, he
pressed his purple plum between the pinken wings of
her inner lips and drove it along the hot, wet sheath of her
cunny. His bulbous glans pressing against the well-
creamed ring of her cervix, her outer labia stretched
tautly around the thick root of his penis, he sucked
the ripe teat of her breast bud into his hot mouth and
ran his tongue over the sensitive tip.

'God, you're so big,' Cleo complimented him, her dark
eyes rolling. 'I've been waiting for this since—'

'Since when?' Jim asked her without releasing the
elongated protrusion of her brown nipple.

'Since the first day . . . I've just been waiting for you to
fuck me, OK?'

'OK.'

Jim wondered whether she felt the same about him as
he did about her as he withdrew his penile length and
rammed his solid knob deep into the hugging tube of her
teenage vagina. *Shit*, he thought. *Is this love?* It was sex,
he tried to convince himself as he increased his fucking
rhythm. As beautiful as Cleo was, as attractive as she may
have been, as horny, as vivacious . . . The squelching
sounds of vaginal juices, the gasps of a teenage girl
fucking . . . No, no, no. This was nothing more than
sex. Wasn't it?

Jim came quickly, too quickly. His sperm jetting from
his throbbing knob, bathing the girl's ripe cervix, lubricating the squelching coupling, he mouthed and
sucked on her milk teat as she reached another mind-
blowing orgasm. Gasping beneath the trees, her eyes
rolling, her long black hair fanning out over the ground,
Cleo drifted away on clouds of lust to her sexual heaven

as Jim fucked her for all he was worth and drained his spunk-brimming balls.

'Are there any half-naked girlies in the woods?' Ruby Rottweiler called.

'Fuck,' Jim gasped, making his last penile thrusts. 'That's all we need.'

'Bloody woman,' Cleo sighed, her naked body shaking uncontrollably in the aftermath of her second coming. 'If she finds us here . . .'

'Come on, girls. Come to Auntie Ruby.'

'Don't worry, she won't find us here.'

'Melanie, are you hiding somewhere? Carole? Mary? Come on, girls. You know how thirsty Auntie Ruby is for your little pussy-cracks. Here puss, here puss. Bring your little pussies to Auntie Ruby.'

'She's a fucking nutcase,' Jim whispered, finally withdrawing his spent cock from Cleo's sperm-flooded vagina and zipping his trousers. 'She's insane.'

'Here puss, puss, puss.'

'We're all mad, to a greater or lesser degree,' Cleo sighed, grabbing her clothes and dressing. 'My father's mad, I can tell you that much. Not mad as in insane, either.'

'We'll have to go away somewhere,' Jim breathed as Ruby walked deeper into the woods in search of fresh pussy milk. 'We'll have to—'

'Go away?' Cleo interrupted him. 'Jim, I . . . I can't leave the pub.'

'Oh. Right. Er . . . no, No, of course you can't. How stupid of me.'

Leaving the clearing, Jim stood beneath the trees and smiled at Cleo. This was it, he thought, a strange feeling welling from the pit of his stomach. Cleo had to return to

her life at the pub, and he had to . . . He wasn't sure what to do. There'd be no job for him at the brewery, he knew. London? There was nothing there for him apart from sad memories of marriage and lesbionic infidelity. This was it. This was goodbye.

'They have to be here somewhere,' the vicar yelled. 'That fucking bitch released him. They can't be far away.'

'God,' Cleo breathed. 'They're coming after us.'

'This way,' Jim said, grabbing her hand and running along the path in the opposite direction.

Coming across an old barn, Jim led the girl inside and closed the door. By the sound of it, the vicar had meant business, Jim reflected. There was no way Cleo could return to the pub now. There again, if she went back and denied all knowledge of Jim . . . No, no. The vicar would never believe her. She'd closed the pub and disappeared at exactly the same time as Jim had escaped. It wouldn't take much to work out that the pair had run off together. Settling in the hay in the corner of the barn, Jim held Cleo close. Now the future looked bleaker than ever.

'Oh, er . . . Mr Hops,' the vicar stammered, walking into the pub the following morning. 'Er . . . where's Cleo?'

'Gone,' the man grunted. 'Run off with Foster, by the look of it.'

'Run off?'

'I sacked him, told him to be out of the pub by last night. It would seem that he's gone. And taken Cleo with him.'

'Oh, well. She was only a barmaid. You can replace her without too much trouble. And as for Foster . . .'

'She was more than a barmaid, vicar,' Hops sighed despondently.

'How do you mean?'

'She was – she *is* – a fine girl, vicar. She worked hard running this pub. I should never have put Foster here.'

'Well, he's gone now so you don't have to worry about him.'

'I'm not worried about *him*. It's Cleo I'm worried about. The funny thing is, I never make mistakes. I thought that Foster would . . . It doesn't matter what I thought. I totally misjudged Foster. To run off with my . . . er, with my barmaid like that . . .'

'Mary,' the vicar said triumphantly. 'Mary is my daughter. She's a fine girl, Mr Hops. Why not employ her?'

'Well, I . . .'

'She's often helped Cleo out behind the bar. She's a hard worker, honest, dependable, reliable . . .'

'I don't want to have to close the pub,' Hops murmured pensively. 'I suppose she could at least fill in until I—'

'I'll go and get her,' the vicar broke in enthusiastically. 'She knows all there is to know about this pub and . . . and everything. The villagers love her. She's the perfect girl for the job in every respect. I'll go and get her.'

Pouring himself a cup of coffee as the vicar dashed out of the pub, Hops leaned on the bar and sighed. Never in a million years would he have dreamed that his daughter would run off and desert the pub. And to run off with a man like Foster . . . Cleo had never wanted for anything, he mused. He'd given her more than enough money, never saw her go without . . . Perhaps he'd been too hard on her, he reflected. Perhaps he should have spent more

time with her, been a proper father . . . Money was no substitute for love. Had her mother not run off . . . Blaming himself, Hops sipped his coffee and thought about closing the pub for good.

The tax-loss fiddle had worked well for years. Perhaps the time had come to sell up and retire? Hops pondered the question. All good things come to an end, he thought. Had his relationship with his daughter come to an end? Would he ever see the girl again? Filling a glass with neat whisky, he placed it on the bar and stared at the brownish liquid. Raising the glass to his lips and breathing in the intoxicating fumes, he sighed. It had been five years since spirits had touched his lips. He could take the odd pint of bitter, but not the Scotch. Owning and running a brewery had had its pitfalls, he reflected. The drink had got him, gripped him with its promises of dreams and a carefree life. It had worked, he mused, again breathing in the scent of the whisky. Problems faded into oblivion, nothing mattered. Looking up as the vicar breezed into the pub with Mary, he placed the glass on the bar.

'Mr Hops, this is Mary,' the vicar announced proudly.

'Good morning, Mr Hops,' the girl said, a huge smile on her pretty face.

'Good morning,' Hops replied, eyeing the girl's long summer dress. 'Well, I have to say that you certainly look the part. Attractive, well dressed . . . Your father said that you've helped Cleo out behind the bar?'

'Oh, yes,' she trilled. 'I know more about this pub than *you* do. About the customers, I mean. Their likes and dislikes and—'

'Who better to run the place than a vicar's daughter?' the cleric chuckled. 'She's well liked in the community, she's honest and—'

'All right,' Hops breathed. 'Whether or not this will be a permanent job, I can't say. However, if you'd like to fill in until I decide what to do, then you can start straight away.'

'You won't regret it,' the vicar said. 'Mary is conscientious, hard-working . . .'

'Yes, yes, all right,' Hops sighed. 'You've sold her to me so you don't have to go on.'

'Sold her,' the vicar laughed. 'Many a true . . . Well, I'll leave you both to chat about the pub. I'll see you later, Mary.'

Waiting until the vicar had gone, Hops poured himself another cup of coffee and told Mary that he was going to take a rest in Cleo's flat. He was in no mood for idle chit-chat. Mary was a lovely girl, he thought. But she trilled and breezed about and bubbled with enthusiasm. She reminded him very much of Cleo the day she'd started work at the pub. He didn't want to be reminded. He didn't want to be with a trilling and bubbling teenage girl. As he walked out into the back room, Mary waited until she heard the flat door close before helping herself to a large vodka. Things couldn't have turned out better, she thought, raising her glass in the air.

'To the sex dungeon,' she breathed, knocking back her drink and refilling her glass.

'Where is he?' the vicar asked her, peering around the pub door.

'It's all right. He's gone to Cleo's flat for a rest.'

'We've done it,' the man chuckled, leaning on the bar opposite the girl. 'This couldn't have turned out better. No Foster, no Cleo . . . Now we can make some real money from the sex dungeon. And fiddle the pub takings and drink for free and—'

'And fuck,' she giggled. 'Drink for free, fuck for free . . .

'Taking of which, how about celebrating?'

'Celebrating?' Mary echoed, cocking her head to one side.

'How about testing out the hole in the bar?'

'Now that *is* a good idea,' she trilled. 'For some reason, I'm feeling really thirsty.'

'I was hoping that you were in need of a drink,' the priest said, standing by the hole in the bar and lifting the front of his cassock. 'Have a nice creamy drink,' he chuckled, slipping his erect penis through the hole as the girl knelt on the floor behind the bar. 'I like to look after my daughter, make sure she's given the things she needs.'

'You're a good father,' Mary giggled, taking his purple plum into her hot mouth.

Taking the man's swollen knob to the back of her throat, Mary sank her teeth gently into his veined shaft as he let out gasps of illicit pleasure. Sucking hard, desperate for his spunk to flood her mouth, she moved her head back until her succulent lips encompassed the purple globe of his rock-hard cock. Savouring the salty taste of his plumlike knob, her tongue snaking over his sperm-slit, working its way around the rim of his helmet, she took his shaft in her warm hand and began her slow wanking motions.

'God, you're good at this,' the vicar breathed, leaning on the bar to steady his trembling body. 'Even though I say it myself, I've taught you well.'

'You like my tongue?' Mary asked him, slipping his knob out of her wet mouth.

'Your mouth, your tongue, your cunt, your bottom-hole . . . I don't know what I'd do without you.'

'You want to come in my mouth, don't you?'

'God, yes. Suck my spunk out and swallow it like a good girl.'

'Anything you say, father.'

Again engulfing his bulbous knob within her sperm-thirsty mouth and moving her head back and forth, mouth-fucking herself on the father's cock, she hoped that he'd pump out his spunk before someone came into the pub. Lifting her dress and slipping her fingers into the moistening valley of her vulva, she massaged the solid nub of her clitoris. If Hops came into the bar now, she thought, fervently masturbating as she mouthed and gobbled on the vicar's knob. If he caught her sucking off . . .

'God, I'm coming,' the cleric announced shakily. 'Suck my spunk out and swallow every last drop.' Her clitoris near to orgasm, Mary ran her tongue around the man's knob and sucked hard as his sperm jetted into her pretty mouth. Massaging her ripe clitoris harder, she shuddered violently as she reached her own mind-blowing climax. Drinking from the orgasming knob, swallowing her prize as she sustained her own climax with her vibrating fingertips, she drifted through the haze of her sexual delirium.

Again and again, tremors of orgasm rolled throughout Mary's shaking body as she drank from the holy man's throbbing glans. His sperm overflowing from her mouth and dribbling down her chin, she repeatedly swallowed hard, doing her best not to waste one drop of the salty liquid. Her own orgasmic juices streaming from the gaping entrance of her spasming vagina and running down the naked flesh of her inner thighs, she moved her head back and forth faster, fucking her pretty mouth

with the priest's granite-hard cock and drinking his gushing spunk.

Her pleasure finally waning, Mary caressed the pulsating tip of her clitoris, bringing out the last ripples of sex from her deflating cumbud as she sucked the remnants of the vicar's sperm from his engorged glans. Moving back, his cock slipping out of her sperm-flooded mouth, she swallowed hard and licked her sex-glossed lips. Dizzy in the aftermath of her self-induced coming, the taste of sperm lingering on her pink tongue, she managed to stagger to her feet and lean on the bar.

'Fucking hell, Mary,' the man of God gasped. 'You're the best cocksucker I've ever known. Did you bring yourself off?'

'Yes, I did,' she replied, her eyes still rolling from her mind-blowing pleasure. 'I frigged my clitty off, just the way you taught me to.'

'You're an angel. You're my little—'

'I need fucking now,' she breathed. 'My cunt's hot and wet and needs fucking hard.'

'Later, my lovely. When you get home, I'll be ready and waiting with a length of hard cock.'

'You'd better be,' Mary giggled.

'And I think I'll give you a good spanking. You like being spanked, don't you?'

'God, you're making me wet,' she sighed. 'I can hardly wait.'

'Now that we're running the pub and the dungeon—'

'You're forgetting something,' Mary interrupted him, sucking the girl-cream from her sticky fingers.

'Oh?'

'Jim and Cleo. Where the fuck are they and what are they planning to do?'

'Yes, you're right. Cleo daren't tell Hops about the sex dungeon, so we've got no worries there. But I'm not so sure about Foster. One phone call to Hops, and we're all in the shit. OK, I'll try to find out where they are. If I threaten Cleo, tell her that, if Foster causes trouble, then I'll talk to Hops about the sex dungeon and say that she's been working as a prostitute—'

'It might work,' Mary said. 'If you can find her, that is.'

'I'll find the bitch,' the vicar chuckled, moving to the door. 'If it's the last thing I do, I'll find the little slut.'

'If it's the last thing you'll do, you'll fuck me senseless when I get home tonight.'

'I'll fuck you every day, Mary. Your sweet cunt, your tight little arsehole, your pretty mouth . . . I'll fuck you rotten. Don't ever doubt that.'

Feeling on top of the world as the man left the pub, Mary downed another large vodka. Thinking again that things couldn't have turned out better, she began to feel a little sorry for Cleo. She'd got on well with the girl, she reflected. But Cleo and the vicar had never really hit it off. He'd taken control of the illicit business and Cleo hadn't liked it. But the girl had gone now, and taken her problems with her. There'd be no more arguing about the sex dungeon, no more fighting over the profits.

Moving to the window, Mary sipped her vodka as she looked out across the village green. It was another hot day, another day of crude sex and . . . But it was also a new beginning, she mused, her juices of desire streaming from her hot vaginal hole and running in rivers of milk down her inner thighs. Hops had no idea that she was naked beneath her dress, she reflected. The man didn't have a clue that she was ready for sex. Once he'd cleared

off back to London, she'd be free to use the hole in the
bar. Free to suck cocks and earn herself a small fortune
from her spunk-swallowing.

'What are you doing here?' Cleo asked her, emerging
from the back room and standing behind the bar.

'Oh, er . . .' Mary gasped, spinning round on her
heels. 'What—'

'Looking after the place for me?'

'No, I . . . I work here, Cleo. Mr Hops has given me
your job.'

'Don't be silly,' Cleo giggled.

'You don't work here any more,' Mary stated firmly,
walking to the bar and staring hard at Cleo. 'I suggest
you get out before—'

'Get out?' Cleo snapped. 'I think *you*'d better get out,
Mary.'

'Jim was sacked, and you no longer work here. *I* run
this pub now. Mr Hops is in your flat. If you don't
believe me, then go and ask him.'

'Mary, I forgot to mention—' the vicar said as he
walked into the pub. 'Oh. If it isn't young Cleo,' he
chuckled. 'I've been looking for you.'

'Have you, vicar?' the girl asked him, grinning widely.
'Well, here I am.'

'Indeed you are. You'd better leave before—'

'Leave, vicar? I'm not with you.'

'Mary runs this pub now. I think it best that you're
barred. What do you think, Mary?'

'Barred for life, I'd say,' the other girl sniggered.

'You can't bar me from my own pub,' Cleo laughed,
smiling maliciously at the vicar.

'If you know what's good for you, you'll leave now,'
the man hissed. 'Leave Willycombe Village now, and

we'll have your things sent on. If you don't, then you'll be taken down to the sex dungeon and—'

'And what?' Jim asked, emerging from the back room. 'Sexually tortured?'

'Foster,' the vicar gasped. 'What the fucking hell are *you* doing here?'

'Running the pub. Or had you forgotten that I'm the landlord of the Tartan Vicar?'

'Landlord? Have *you* forgotten that Mr Hops sacked you? Unless you both leave this pub now, I'll not only tell Hops about the sex dungeon and his barmaid working as a prostitute, but I'll tell the world. It'll ruin Hops once the newspapers get hold of the story. Not that you're bothered about your boss, of course. But think of the damage it'll do to you, Cleo. A prostitute . . .'

'May I interrupt?' Jim asked, pouring himself a pint of bitter. 'You're threatening to drop Cleo in the shit, tell the world that she's been working as a prostitute.'

'That's right. And I'll do it, believe me.'

'Oh, I have no doubt about that, vicar. The thing is, what will the villagers say when they discover that you have been living in sin with a *very* young teenage girl?'

'You mean, Mary?' he laughed. 'Don't be ridiculous, man. Mary is my daughter.'

'Is she?'

'Of course she is. Good God, I've never heard such—'

'Crap? I don't believe that the locals will think it's crap once I tell them . . .'

'All right, all right,' the vicar sighed. 'We're quits. I have something on you, and you have something on me. We'll do a deal, talk about this and—'

'Wait a minute,' Cleo broke in. 'You have *nothing* on us.'

'I have nothing on you? God, that's rich. You're a fucking little tart, Cleo. You're a whore, a prostitute and—'

'And I have photographs of you fucking your daughter,' Jim cut in.

'What? You're bluffing.'

'Am I? God, I've had more enough opportunities to take a few snaps of you with your cock up your daughter's hairless little cunt. Shall I tell the villagers that you're living in sin with the girl, or that you're having an incestuous relationship with her? Either way, you're fucked, vicar. Photographs don't lie. Unlike perverted vicars.'

'All right, so what's the deal?'

'Deal? There *is* no deal. You leave this pub with Mary now, and that'll be that. If you don't . . .'

'All right, we're going,' the man finally conceded. 'But I intend to speak to Hops.'

'Goodbye, vicar,' Cleo called as they left the pub. 'Well,' she breathed, turning to Jim. 'All we have to do now is face my father's wrath. As I said before, there's no way he'll allow you to come back. And after I walked out and deserted the pub . . . God only know what he'll say to me. He'll go mad, I know that much.'

Sipping his beer, Jim gazed at Cleo. Reckoning that she was right, he didn't know what to do. Hops wouldn't throw his own daughter out onto the streets, he was sure of that. Cleo didn't want to leave the pub, Jim wouldn't be allowed to stay . . . Was this to be the final parting? he wondered dolefully. No Cleo, no job, no home . . . The future certainly wasn't looking bright. Plonking himself on a stool as Cleo passed him another pint of bitter, he reckoned that the time had come to throw the bar towel in.

'What will you do?' Cleo asked him.

'I don't know,' he sighed. 'By the way, what were those photographs of my ex-wife all about?'

'The envelope was for you, Jim. Some man came in and—'

'For *me*?'

'That's what he said.'

'Probably my ex-wife playing her mind games. Anyway, fuck her.'

'Jim, what are you going to do?'

'He'll get out of my pub,' Hops bellowed, storming out of the back room and glaring at Jim. 'He'll leave my pub this instant.'

'No . . .' Cleo began.

'You stay out of this, Cleo,' Hops snapped. 'I'll deal with you later. Now then, Foster. What do you mean by running off with Cleo like that?'

'I . . .'

'Shut up, man. I sacked you. I sacked you, and yet you're still here. Why?'

'I . . .'

'Not only are you still here, but you ran off with Cleo. I cannot believe your audacity. In spite of what I said, you went off with Cleo and—'

'Married me,' Cleo murmured.

'What?'

'He . . . he went off with me and married me, father.'

'Married you? Don't be ridiculous. He can't marry you.'

'I can and I did,' Jim ventured fearfully.

'My God,' Hops gasped, holding his head. 'My daughter married to a . . .'

'Wonderful man, father.'

'A wonderful man?'

'Mr Hops,' Jim said, smiling at his ex-boss. 'Or perhaps I should call you father-in-law.'

'Father-in- . . . You'll call me no such bloody thing. Cleo, tell me that this isn't true.'

'It *is* true, father. Jim and I are in love.'

'In love? Don't be ridiculous. I'm warning you, Foster. If you lay one finger on my daughter . . .'

'You mean, on my wife?'

'No, I do *not*.'

'Come on, father,' Cleo giggled. 'We should be celebrating, not arguing.'

Frowning at Jim, Hops shook his head resignedly. 'I suppose what's done is done,' he finally conceded. 'My God. Mr and Mrs bloody Foster. We'd better have a drink. I think we all need one. Cleo, I'll have a Scotch.'

'No, father. You'll have half a pint of bitter.'

'Damn you, girl. All right, bitter it is. You see what I have to put up with, Foster? Damned women. I suppose you'll both be wanting a bloody wedding present next?'

'Of course we do,' Cleo giggled. 'And, father, I think "Jim" sounds better than "Foster", don't you?'

'Jim. Yes, right.'

'Shall I call you Cyril, Mr Hops?' Jim asked the man.

'You'll do no such bloody thing.'

'Of course he will, father. You can't have your son-in-law calling you Mr Hops.'

'She's right, Cyril,' Jim laughed.

'Damn it. Damn both of you. All right, Cyril it is. Er . . . This bloody wedding present. I suppose you'd better have the pub.'

'The pub?' Cleo echoed disbelievingly.

'What's wrong with that? What with Foster here and his bloody sandwiches, you should do pretty well.'

'Thank you, Cyril,' Jim broke in, raising his glass. 'Here's to us. All three of us.'

'Cheers,' Hops mumbled, downing his drink. 'Er . . . I need some fresh air. I think I'll take a walk across the green.'

Laughing as Hops left the pub, Jim shook his head disbelievingly. Cleo downed a large vodka and winked at him as he leaned on the bar, completely speechless. This was incredible, he reflected, still unable to take in the fact that he owned the Tartan Vicar. Mr and Mrs Foster? Cyril? Never in his wildest dreams had he thought that his time in Willycombe Village would bring him love and wealth and . . . Marriage? he mused, coming down from his high and frowning at Cleo. *Fucking hell.*

'Cleo,' he breathed. 'When your father finds out that we're not married . . .'

'He'll go mad and throw you out,' she laughed.

'Fucking hell. What are we going to do? I mean, the pub will be in the name of Mr and Mrs Foster and—'

'So we'd better get married,' she cut in. 'Not in the local church, I hasten to add.'

'Er . . . No, no, of course not.'

'There are no half-naked girls anywhere in the woods,' Ruby Rottweiler complained as she stormed into the pub. 'I don't know what Willycombe is coming to. Er . . . a pint of bitter, please.'

'My wife will get that for you, Ruby,' Jim said, smiling at the woman.

'Your *wife*? Good grief. I thought she was your daughter. You can't marry your own daughter.'

'Mary is my daughter, if you remember?'

'Oh, yes. The vicar's girl. So, you're married, Cleo?'

'Yes, Ruby, I am.'

'Another wasted teenage girl,' the lesbian sighed. 'If only you'd joined the WVLA. Oh well, here's to you both. Cheers.'

'Cheers.'